WHAT I TOLD MY FRIENDS

ALICE LEIGH

CANELO CRIME

First published in the United Kingdom in 2026 by

Canelo Crime, an imprint of
Canelo Digital Publishing Limited,
20 Vauxhall Bridge Road,
London SW1V 2SA
United Kingdom

A Penguin Random House Company
The authorised representative in the EEA is Dorling Kindersley Verlag GmbH.
Arnulfstr. 124, 80636 Munich, Germany

Copyright © Alice Leigh 2026

The moral right of Alice Leigh to be identified as the creator of this work has been asserted in accordance with the Copyright, Designs and Patents Act, 1988.

All rights reserved. No part of this publication may be reproduced or transmitted in any form or by any means, electronic or mechanical, including photocopy, recording, or any information storage and retrieval system, without permission in writing from the publisher.

No part of this book may be used or reproduced in any manner for the purpose of training artificial intelligence technologies or systems. In accordance with Article 4(3) of the DSM Directive 2019/790, Canelo expressly reserves this work from the text and data mining exception.

A CIP catalogue record for this book is available from the British Library.

Print ISBN 978 1 83598 255 6
Ebook ISBN 978 1 83598 256 3

This book is a work of fiction. Names, characters, businesses, organizations, places and events are either the product of the author's imagination or are used fictitiously. Any resemblance to actual persons, living or dead, events or locales is entirely coincidental.

Cover design by Jet Purdie

Cover images © Depositphotos, Shutterstock

Printed and bound in Great Britain by Clays Ltd, Elcograf S.p.A.

Look for more great books at
www.canelo.co | www.dk.com

For those of us who learned our lessons the hard way.

And for the friends who cushioned the blow.

PART ONE

PART ONE

Prologue

The rain had been falling for several hours by the time her body was found. Puddles had formed around her hands and feet, and her soft fleece pyjamas were heavy and wet. Until then nobody was aware of what was hiding in the shadow of the belltower. Not a single light illuminated the courtyard, to chance upon the shape of her death. Six hundred pupils slept in the quiet of the nightly curfew just metres away, until one unlucky girl snuck out for a cigarette. Blood washed across soft-white pebbles towards her feet, and her scream woke us all.

The dead girl's name was Emily, and she was seventeen when she fell from the belltower of High Hill Manor, one short month away from adulthood. Before that she had been on track for five A levels, each predicted to achieve the highest grade. A place at Cambridge simmered in her future, to study medicine at Christ's College just as her father had before her. Her summers passed by in Provence, a crumbling cottage where wisteria grew over pretty archways, and Christmas played out at their chalet in St Moritz. She was head prefect at High Hill Manor, and not one person questioned her position in that role. She belonged in that place, and everyone knew it. Of everything about this story, that's one of the more important things to remember. Emily was undoubtedly one of them.

Still, who she was is less important than you might think in the grand scheme of things. No matter what we recall, or how we paint her memory as perfect as a Botticelli, she exists now only as an idea. We cannot root her in the present or say how her life turned out. Fate rose up to claim her on that wet and windy night. Some people might even struggle to remember her name. *Oh yes, that girl who died*, they'd say. *What was she called again?* Now she can never be anything more than she used to be. The rest of us though? We were the ones left behind. It was us who had to cope with what came next, carrying her death with us into the years and decades of our future. Her murder set a fire through our lives. Because that's what it was. She didn't jump. There was no fall. She was murdered. And afterwards we were all left wondering what part we played. How perhaps it could have been different.

Whether we were to blame.

Before

1

Today the embers of that fire burn brighter. I feel their heat against my skin as I sit in the glare of a pink winter sunset. I pull up on the far side of the carpark, finding a spot between two dirty white lines. Trees shiver all around me, and there are only a few other cars here today. On busier days, whole families, friends and mothers fill these spaces, eager with their crumpled visitation slips clutched tight in their hands. I have been here on those days, watched those people, thought about what it would have been like to walk inside the thick grey walls myself. Twenty feet of solid concrete separates the inmates from the outside world. Once I even wrote a letter, asking if he wanted to see me. *Dear Simon*, I began. Then another, *Dear Mr Aides*. Wasn't quite sure how formal I should be. How should I address my ex-teacher when I haven't seen him for over twenty years? When my testimony was the reason he was jailed. But I never sent those letters. I was always too scared that he wouldn't want to see me.

Or too scared that he would.

I kill the engine, turn off the radio, but I don't get out just yet. Outside I can hear the lull of distant traffic, and crows calling from the damp trees. Rain falls gently against the roof of my car and streaks down the windows in waxy rivulets. My service station coffee has turned cold, but I sip at it now as if it is warm. Check the time. 11:33 a.m. Condensation mists on the inside of the glass, and I watch as the light glimmers in the puddles that form on the ground.

In the time I wait I smoke two cigarettes, lighting the second from the cherry of the first. The crumpled letter rests in my hand, read so many times since I found it there on the post table three weeks ago. *Dear Chloe*, it began. *The time has finally come when I am going to be released and...* When I saw his name scrawled at the bottom, my insides cramped up like a vice. I had expected he might slip from prison without fanfare, away from my life, even though I have been counting the days since he was sentenced. Now I know he has been counting them too. I pull the letter from the envelope, my gaze slipping to the last line.

There are things we need to discuss.

And there are, but I still don't know if that's why I'm here. To talk to him? To see his face after so many years? On the passenger seat my phone rings, another unknown number. I watch it, waiting for the call to end. When it does, I see the notification – the sixth missed call today. Journalists. Like vultures picking at a carcass, everybody wants a scrap of information. A soundbite to put in their article. Well, fuck them all. I pick up the phone, delete the notifications. Then I see another message, this one from Stan. Simple enough, saying he hopes I make a good choice today. He doesn't think I should be here. I delete that one too. He's twenty years too late. That's when my choices were made.

Another fifteen minutes pass before I hear voices behind me. I watch in the rearview mirror, see the bodies moving through the midday mist, a sole figure exiting the confines of His Majesty's Prison Belmarsh. An urgency grips me, and I rush from the car, pulling at my hair to slick it into place. Rainfall intensifies as I lift the black umbrella over my head. His gait is different to what I remember, his shoulders slouched, but I have no doubt that it's him. The way his arms hang at his side, the same soft beard that frames his face. He is still the same man who has haunted the last twenty years of my life.

I have dreamed of this day, the chance to see him again. Feared it in equal measure. Emotions when it comes to Simon Aides have always been confused. I watch, waiting for him to spot me. And when he does, he stands perfectly still, letting the rainfall soak into his clothes. His parka coat is dated, circa 2005. Time bending back on itself. With him there I am seventeen years old again. As if not a single day has passed. And then he is moving, standing before me. Within touching distance. The man whose face has never once left my mind.

'You came?' he says. 'I wasn't sure if you got the letter.'

His gaze falls to the tatty envelope in my hand. A biting cold gnaws at my fingers as I take a step closer. He's paler than I remember, his cheeks hollow. 'I got it,' I say. When he doesn't say anything more, I pull the squashed pack of cigarettes from my pocket and offer them to him.

'It's a bad habit,' he says, not taking one.

'Most habits are.'

Then with a nod he does as I expected, reaching forward to take a smoke. Time hasn't changed his hands, the same elegant look about them, manly but not in some laborious way. His cuticles are soft, the nails well shaped, as if even now he takes care of them. I watch as he rolls the chosen cigarette, straightening out the slim white stick with his nimble, beautiful fingers. I hold the umbrella over his body to shelter him from the rain, and he glides the cigarette between his teeth. I dig in my pocket for the lighter. We are careful not to touch as he takes it.

'Why did you come?' he asks.

'You asked me to,' I say, stating the obvious. 'You wrote me a letter.'

'Yes, I did,' he says, drawing on the cigarette.

'How did you even get my address?'

'Does it matter?' he asks. I say nothing. 'But you wanted to see me?'

A chill passes over my skin as water drips down the back of my neck. And he's right, that part of me, the one stuck in my seventeen-year-old body, wants to see him. Is desperate for him. But another, quieter part of me is telling me to run. Insisting that I shouldn't be here.

Another beat before I speak again. 'I think so.' The quickening of my heart is familiar, reminds me of the first time we met. 'I wrote you letters.'

Mid inhale he stops, turning to look at me for the first time. 'I never received any.'

Quiet then, as I confess. 'I never sent them.'

He nods, sighs, as if it is to be expected. Leans against the edge of my car. 'I should have liked to receive those letters.'

'Maybe you wouldn't have.' I shrug.

'Well, I suppose it depends on what you wrote.' Disappointed, he goes back to the cigarette, and I watch as he smokes, too fast, so much life to recoup. Before he speaks again, he drops the butt to the ground and stamps it out with his toe.

'You haven't changed much,' he says, grey smoke drifting from his lips. I find myself pulling at the length of hair that no longer exists. Tucking the blunt edge of the sharp new bob behind my ear, cut only yesterday, anything to be different from then. 'I, on the other hand, have changed quite a lot. Time inside those walls passes quite differently to time on the outside.'

'You said there were things we needed to discuss.'

'There are.'

He takes a step closer, his face no more than a movement away from mine. Still taller than me, but less than before. If anybody is watching, they will question who I am. We are already breaking the terms of his release. We are not supposed to be together, and yet he is close enough that he could kiss me. My lips tingle with the thought of it. But I step back, open the door and climb inside the car. Push the key in the ignition and wait. My muscles feel weak; the things I have kept to myself are heavier today. Lies grow over time. Demand more space. It gets harder instead of easier to carry them. I listen to the scuff of his shoes, the mechanism as he opens the passenger door. Just us then, inside the car. Still, the crows call from the trees. Rain still drums the roof.

'The girl who died,' he says, thoughtful, concerned, as if he has no right to mention it. He stares dead ahead, stoic and cold. 'No matter what she did, or what she saw, she didn't deserve to die like that.'

'Which girl?' I ask.

'I think you know.' A deep, shaky breath passes his lips. 'She was only seventeen, Chloe. Seventeen years old,' he stresses.

'We were all seventeen years old then, Simon.' His eyes drift closed. 'Only you were older than that.'

Silence falls between us. He sits motionless, a statue with no hint of life. Brushes a crease from his trousers. Twenty years in prison has granted him patience.

'Is it the truth you want?' I ask finally. 'Is that why you asked me to come here?'

'What I want is no longer important.' He reaches for the seatbelt, clicks it in place. 'I should like to know it, but there are more important things to discuss now.' When I turn to look at him, there is a sadness on his face. A space exists between us that I should have expected yet did not. 'I'm afraid there are things I need to tell you, Chloe. You're not the only one who has been keeping secrets.'

'What secrets?' I ask, but he says nothing more. Only stares straight ahead. I swallow hard, wondering what he is hiding. Then I release the handbrake and drive away, with only one destination in mind.

Before

2

Summer, 2005. So hot the temperatures broke all records, and the evidence of it was freckled over my cheeks and nose. James Blunt had been number one for over a month, playing on the radio as my father drove through the country lanes that wound like capillaries along the south coast of Sussex. Twice during the journey, he had been forced to brake around a tight bend to avoid an oncoming car. But all his cursing and gesturing passed me by like the breeze, and I hung a tanned arm out of the window to ride the current with my fingers. Today I was joining High Hill Manor for my final year of standard education. A fresh start. The end of a miserable chapter. Closing my eyes, I drank in the scent of country air. Dry grass stretched like parched skin over the ground.

'Blimey, is that it?' My mother's words roused me from my daydream, and as I opened my eyes, I saw her leaning forward in her seat. Sweat leached along her back in the shape of Africa. 'It's bigger than I thought it was going to be.'

Before us, set back behind a line of trees, was the building we were aiming for. From our position on the road, we could see only the highest parts, four prominent towers and the outline of a roof that resembled the battlements of a medieval castle. In the centre I could see the highest tower. It rose higher than any other part of the building, the inside of it cast in a deep shadow. On one side of the tower I could see a clock, the face so bright in the morning light that it looked to me like an eye, gazing at me across the land, watching as I arrived. And although we couldn't see the school in its entirety, the quickening of my heart suggested she was right. I removed my knockoff Ray-Bans to see bricks the colour of wet sand, crisp against a pale sky. A flag of unknown denomination flickered on a pole rising from the highest of the towers.

'Bloody hell, Sandra.' A driveway to our right appeared before us as we rounded a bend. We slowed, pulling up a short distance before it. Mum checked the map, as if that would help. 'Are we really in the right place?' Dad asked.

'We are,' I said as I leaned through to the front, pointing to a block of rough-hewn stone that rose from the ground at the entrance of the driveway. Mountainous and craggy from behind, the front surface had been smoothed like a tombstone, with elegant words engraved into the centre. The same as we had seen in the brochure.

High Hill Manor School for Girls

My father sighed, his fingers fiddling at the rip in the knee of his jeans. Mum tutted, shook her head.

'I told you to wear something different.'

My parents' worries about whether this place was too good for the likes of us, or whether my dad's jeans were too casual, had little effect on me. I tuned them out, as if already I was no longer part of the life we shared. As if I didn't belong to them anymore and hadn't lived in their home for the last seventeen years. Relief came as my father pulled into the grounds, and we followed the driveway across a large expanse of lawn the colour of fresh hay. Oak trees lined the road, their twisted branches rising over us as if we were driving underneath a giant spider's legs. Cooler now, the grass around the trees was greener, and ivy clung to the trunks. From the backseat I pressed up against the glass, eager and ready to shed the skin of the life I was set to leave behind.

As the trees peeled back and we made our way to the entrance, we came upon a long perimeter wall. Crenelated as a castle might be, with archways and alcoves into which half-moon shelves were built. It was an impressive first glimpse at the place that was to become my home. Wrought-iron gates led the only way through, and they were open in anticipation of our arrival. Other parents were driving out, more girls arriving at the school. Gravel crunched beneath our tyres as we slowed, pulling into a space, and I listened to the gentle movement of the trees as the engine quietened. I opened the door, the taste of salt thick in the coastal air.

The manor house stretched both left and right, with a grand set of double doors in the centre. Steps ran to the main entrance, set between heavy stone balustrades. The whole place looked as impenetrable as a fortress. Details had been carved into the bricks around the windows, multiple crosses and leaves, creatures that looked a bit like a dragon's head. The place was so large, so sprawling, it was as if the ground itself had risen up into the shape of it. Ivy trailed from the lowest bricks across the six floors, as if the land was trying to claim it back. And the four towers we had seen from the road seemed even larger now, with their high arched windows covering most of the floors.

Silence took over as my father switched off the engine, and the radio cut out before James Blunt had a chance to finish his song.

Several girls were walking around the grounds. Others were unloading trunks packed full of clothes and memories of home. I watched as two left the manor, dressed in the neat sky-blue blazers I recognised from the brochure, laughing as they passed the fountain on the lawn. Long grey skirts billowed out behind them, skimming the ground as they walked. Books clutched against their chests. I wondered where they were going. What they would be doing. Whether I would soon look as fitting and effortless as they did. Both wore their hair in braids, and I felt conscious of my long black hair, hanging loose and wavy down the length of my back. Too free. Too individual. I couldn't wait to dress like them, style my hair in the same official way.

To finally fit in.

I stepped out of the car, leaned back to take in the building where the flag was flying, atop the highest of all the towers that rose up through the manor house. Yellow material, a red cross. Saints in each of the corners. Columns encircled the highest level to suggest a walkway inside. Sunlight glinted against an internal bell, and a light breeze drifted through, the soft note of a woman's song. I brought my hand up to shield my eyes, could see carved letters running as a balustrade around the edge, when I heard a voice.

'Ah, there you are. A good morning to you all. You must be Mr and Mrs Carter.' I heard the car doors closing behind me and turned to see a woman crossing the driveway to meet us. She held out her hand, first for my father, and then my mother. A neat watch pinched at her soft wrist. 'Very nice to meet you. And as for you,' she said, turning to me, smiling as if she was bursting with barely contained enthusiasm. 'I certainly recognise you from your wonderful audition. Welcome to High Hill Manor, Chloe.'

The woman's voice was like nothing I had ever heard before. Silken somehow, smooth, yet held together by the tightest of stitches. Heat rose in my cheeks and for the first time in my life I felt conscious of my clunky Estuary accent. I looked to my parents, who were watching our interaction, waiting for my response.

'Thank you,' I said, and my voice didn't quite sound like my own.

Following my parents' lead, I raised my hand, and the teacher took it in a strong shake. I recognised her as well; she had played a prominent role in the brochure they had sent to us when my audition had been accepted. Smiling with other girls, teaching them in a class. I knew her name was Miss McCabe, and that she was a classics teacher. Her long summer dress was buttoned high up to the collar. Earrings hung from her stretched lobes, jewellery that she might have made at home with multicoloured wooden beads and chunks of hazy sea glass.

'I trust you found us with ease?'

'Not exactly.' My father's discomfort made him stiffer and more uncertain than he normally was. He fiddled at the paint stains on his fingers. 'Had a couple of near misses on the way here. The roads are not like they are in our town.'

Our Town, he said, as if we had some thread of ownership of that bland yet inoffensive place. A settlement of nowhere and nobody, purpose-built for those people who had been pushed out of the East End by the Blitz after the war. Generations of factory workers in the 1950s had taken their skills and applied them to fridge manufacturing, to building cars and to whatever else they could find in their new purpose-built home that would only appear on the newest of maps. And as much as I had hated it, I saw now that it was a privilege to have come from such a place. Generic in every way, there was nothing that held me there so strongly that made it in any way difficult to leave.

'I should imagine so,' Miss McCabe said with a laugh. 'Your part of Essex is a little different to the area surrounding High Hill.' Holding out her hands, Miss McCabe guided us towards the entrance. 'Now, Chloe, I'd like to introduce you to somebody.'

As I looked up, I saw a girl arriving at the top of the steps. Dressed in the High Hill uniform, she appeared so at ease as she stood there, her hands clasped together before her. Almost serene. Sleek blonde plaits shot down her back as if she were armed with spears.

'This remarkable young lady is Emily Ashbourne.' The girl descended the steps, her smile wide and welcoming. 'Emily has been honoured with the position of head prefect this year, and as the leader of your house, she has volunteered to take good care of you.'

'It's a pleasure, Miss McCabe.' Emily held out her hand and I reached to take it. Her skin was soft and warm to the touch. 'Welcome to High Hill Manor.'

'Thanks.'

'Now, Mr and Mrs Carter, if you'd please follow me. We have some administration to see to. Emily here will show Chloe around. And don't worry about that,' she said to my father, who was trying to lift my trunk from the boot of the car. 'Somebody will ensure that it arrives in her room. We have much more important business to cover inside.'

Miss McCabe set off ahead, with my parents picking up the pace behind. I did as I was told, following up the stone steps that led to the front door. But as we reached the top, I noticed the way Emily regarded my parents, my father's clothes, my mother's anxious demeanour. Her open smile in front of Miss McCabe had been replaced by something that looked more like a sneer. Whatever she saw when she looked at them, it wasn't enough. And in that moment, I wanted to hang back, leave them behind. I didn't want Emily to see the same thing in me that she saw in them.

'Don't you think it would be better if maybe we did the tour together?' my mother asked then as she reached the top of the steps. I wanted to die, could see the derision stirring on Emily's face. My dad saw it too, and so he rested a gentle hand on my mum's arm.

'Maybe it's best we let Chloe find her own way from here, right? She doesn't need us hanging around, cramping her style.'

'That's the spirit, Mr Carter,' Miss McCabe said. 'Emily will make sure she settles in, won't you, Emily?'

'Absolutely.'

And with that, knowing that she had lost, Mum stepped forward to take me into a hurried embrace. There was such love in that touch, and I could feel it in the pressure of her fingertips, the way she pulled our bodies close. And I thought then how things could have been different. How if they were I could have stayed at home, could have been returning to Clifton, my old school instead of this unknown place. Could have been back with Laura and Kate, gossiping about people we hadn't seen in weeks. But things weren't different, and I couldn't go back. So instead, I pushed the memories aside; I wanted nothing more than for Mum to just let me go.

'Bye then,' she said, as Miss McCabe nodded for me to follow Emily inside.

Turning, I gave her a last half-hearted smile, my father too, before taking my first steps into the school.

Away from the life I had been given no other choice but to escape.

3

Inside, the early September light leached into the thick stone walls, and the warmth of the late summer sun disappeared. Ceilings rose high and grand above me, and from the main hallway the corridor bore left, and beyond I saw the sweep of a stone staircase twisting helically into the upper floors. Even though the arched windows of the nearest tower ran from the floor to ceiling height, it didn't seem to make any difference to the light, and it was as if a soft shadow fell throughout the whole place. And then, through a door to the left I got my first glimpse of life at High Hill, with several students working at wooden desks in what might have once been a drawing room. Little green lamps cast cones of gold across their books.

'This way,' Emily said.

Several doors gave rise to other parts of the manor, and in the background I could hear the voices of teachers giving lectures as we moved through the corridors. History if I guessed correctly, something about the great battle of 1066, and a queen who lost her head.

'The school is split into four wings. Currently we are in the north wing, and there is also the south, east and west.' I hurried to catch up, Emily's pace fast, as if we had lots of ground to cover and little time to do it. 'Each wing consists of the main corridor, the classrooms, the dormitories for the younger students and of course the bedrooms for those of us in sixth form.'

We moved fast, into the corridor of what I thought was the east wing, with girls moving in both directions beside us. Wooden panelling lined the lower half of the walls, but there were windows on the upper half of the internal side, which gave me a view into the courtyard. Cloisters ran along the perimeter of it, and beyond I could see grass upon which groups of girls were sitting, surrounded by multiple fountains, neat hedges and gravel pathways. The other wings formed a perimeter around it. It felt like a castle, like something I had seen on film. Creeping ivy surrounded lichen-covered statues of partially clothed goddesses cast in stone.

'That's Aphrodite,' she said, pointing to one of the statues. 'And Hestia. Those houses are located in this wing.'

'Houses?' I asked.

With a sigh and a lingering look, she said, 'We are all divided into houses. You're going to be in Athena.' And then with a smile, she added, 'With me.'

Sunlight glinted from the statues' hollow eyes, almost as if they were watching me as I passed. From where I was standing I could barely see the sky as the highest floors rose above us.

'What's that one?' I asked, pointing to the last statue. The gaze of the figure was low, her head bowed as if she didn't want to be seen. Hair twisted across her shoulder in thick serpentine braids.

'Medusa,' she said, turning away from it. I couldn't take my eyes off it. All the other statues had their heads raised to the sky, a look of pride and authority. Strength. But this one, relegated to a dark corner of the courtyard, was almost facing the ground.

I had slowed, and when I looked up to see her getting ahead of me I caught up.

'I think it'll be hard to know which wing I'm in to start with.'

Emily stopped, turned to look at me.

'It's not complicated. At least, most people don't seem to think so.' Turning away, she was soon off again, moving at pace towards the stairs I could see ahead. I had taken her initial smile for a tentative friendship, but after the way she looked at my parents, and her apparent disinterest in me, I understood that her kindness had been for Miss McCabe's benefit. I looked back to the entrance then, and for the first time I questioned my decision to attend High Hill. But I took a breath and caught up, not wanting to miss the information that Emily was telling me. 'MDI is held every Wednesday afternoon, and formal supper each Friday night in the Great Hall. Chapel is on a Sunday morning. You are expected to attend.'

'Okay. And where is that held?'

Pausing, her brow creased. She took a moment to digest my question. 'Chapel is held in the chapel, Chloe. Should I assume you brought the recommended formals for these occasions?'

'A black dress for the dinners, right? Not too short, no thin straps.'

'Correct.'

'My mum got me something from Marks.' Her lips twisted and it looked as if she was stifling a smile. I tried to ignore it. I knew it had been a stretch for my mother to afford it, and I really liked the dress when I had tried it on. Felt good in it. Pretty, even, which I hadn't in a long while. 'But what's the MDI?'

A sigh. 'Did you not read the induction material at all? I was told it was sent to you.'

'I did, but… I don't know. I didn't see anything about an MDI.'

She was about to answer, but before she could we arrived at the end of the corridor into a throng of girls, moving at pace as they hurried to their next lesson. Some of them were laughing, and others seemed nervous, with one small girl holding up the rest as she stopped to read a sign on the wall, looking for where to go. Her skirt was so long that the bottom of it was dragging on the floor.

'Christ, what's wrong with the new intake this year?' Emily said to herself when she saw the chaos. Then, with a raised voice, she called across to the lost little girl. 'This is the south wing.' The girl was short, thin-framed. Bags hung dark under her eyes. She couldn't have been any more than eleven years old, but to me she looked like she'd already had the fun of life sucked right out of her. 'Where are you supposed to be?'

'I'm looking for the gym, but I can't find it.' Her lips quivered, and she was close to tears as she spoke. Glassy eyes stared hopefully at Emily. 'I'm supposed to be at games.'

'Why aren't you with the rest of your class?' The girl offered no answer more than a shrug of her shoulders. 'This is not good enough now that you're at High Hill.' Another sigh. 'West wing, left at staircase four. Take the cloisters to West Gate, and the path will lead to the games house.' When the girl still seemed confused, Emily raised her hand, pointed right and spoke with a raised voice. 'That way.' Rolling her eyes, she offered me a tight, wearied smile. 'They get worse every year, but her father heads up wealth management at J.P. Morgan. What are they going to do, say no?' Another moment passed and the peace returned as the last of the girls made their way to their next lessons. 'So, tell me. What is it that your father does?'

'He's an artist,' I said, remembering our trip to London last year, when his latest collection was unveiled at the sweet little gallery in Mayfair. The excitement of the crowd, the thrill of watching the owner stick the little ticket on the first painting that read *sold*. The look on his face, knowing what that meant for our family. 'He paints landscapes.'

'Oh. That explains a lot.'

'How so?'

She took her time, chewed on her lip. 'The ripped jeans. The paint on his skin. In all honesty, it's not very High Hill.'

I felt the heat rise in my cheeks, the intensity of the silence that had fallen over the corridor. Remembered the way she had looked at my parents. Was there something wrong with a career like that at High Hill? Was everybody supposed to have a father who headed up a department in a place I had never heard of before?

'Well, he's really good,' I said then, trying to defend him, but aware of the need to swallow the rising guilt for the brief wish that I could have said he was something else. 'He has a painting exhibited in the National Gallery,' I added after a moment, a truth that I hoped might carry some weight.

'Ooh, incredible,' she said, not trying to hide her lack of enthusiasm. 'At least I know now why you needed the scholarship. Artists only make money once they're dead.'

After that, Emily showed me the Great Hall where the formal suppers would be held. A grand place covered in dark wood and heavy portraits of the family who used to live there. Four fireplaces, one for each wall. On our way through the school we visited each department, and every time she introduced me as the scholarship student, I heard the sniggers of the other girls as they looked me up and down. Was there some reason for shame? A scholarship and a father who painted pictures for a living? I had thought both were a reason for pride.

By the time she led us outside to show me the chapel I was glad of the fresh air. The soft-grey building was more like a cathedral it was so grand. Beautiful stained glass caught the light, flooding rainbows across the stone floor. We crossed the landscaped gardens then, weaving between statues of mythological characters, to where the spray of an angry tide carried forth on the breeze. Towering cliffs marked the southern perimeter of High Hill Manor, and I spotted some little steps traversing the sloping rock down one side.

'Is there a beach down there?'

'A small one,' she said, gazing out to sea.

'And do people go down there?'

'Sometimes,' she said, disinterested as if she had seen all this before and found it terribly boring. 'Occasionally we have beach parties.'

'Cool.'

'Yes,' she said, not looking at me. 'I assumed you might think so. But you should know that the cliffs are quite dangerous. Especially those in the forest past the chapel.' Was that a moment of care? I was grateful for it. There was something different about her then, as she gazed out to sea. Quieter, softer. Almost fragile. But only moments later she turned away from the edge of the cliff and that sharp edge was back. 'Come on. I still need to show you to your bedroom, and I haven't got all day.'

Once we were back inside, we followed what I thought was the south wing, past staircase four, until we reached staircase five. Beyond I could see a sign which read *Staff Only*, and the corridor and cloisters turned into the centre of the courtyard. Another door then, another sign. *North Wing Dormitories*. But sitting on the bottom step was a rakish man, young, not much older than us. Spots puckered the skin around his nose, and his hair was gelled into curtains like a member of a boyband I liked. A box filled with toilet paper sat at his side. Without hesitation, she kicked his heavy black boot. It was as if he barely felt her.

'What the fuck are you doing?' she asked as he looked up, first to her then to me.

'Not seen her before,' he said. His accent was different, more like mine than hers. London, or somewhere just north. 'She a friend of yours?'

Without turning, she looked to me from the corner of her eye. 'No. And I asked you a question.'

'And I didn't answer.'

I saw the blush of her cheeks, the tension solidifying her limbs. 'Come on,' she spat to me, again kicking his foot as she stepped over him. And so I went to follow, only for him to shift his legs at the last minute so that I couldn't pass, resting his feet high on the balustrade.

'She's waiting for you,' he said. 'Over you go.'

I had no choice but to step over him at the level of his waist. I held my breath, hating the proximity to his middle. But just as I passed, I felt sure he muttered something under his breath, and it stopped me in my tracks.

'What did you say?' I asked.

Slowly he got to his feet, a smirk on his face. 'I said that it's rude not to say hello.'

But as he picked up his box of toilet rolls and continued on, I felt sure that what he'd said was something quite different.

'Who was that?' I asked as I arrived at her side, but she didn't bother to answer.

After taking six staircases to reach my allocated floor of the north wing, we arrived at a narrow corridor with open cloisters on one side that looked down into the courtyard gardens below. On the other side were a series of wooden doors. I wasn't the tallest of girls, but my head easily skimmed the lowest part of the frame. Roman numerals marked the uneven wooden surface of each. Slowing when we reached the last door, I saw it was marked with the numerals VI-XIV. Somewhere in the distance I could hear the beat of *Gold Digger*, the new Kanye track.

'This is yours,' she said, lifting an old iron key from her pocket to unlock the door. 'Six Fourteen, in case you can't read it.'

'I can.'

She pushed open the door, and I got the first glimpse of my new home as I ducked inside. Nothing more than a couple of metres in any direction, with a simple wooden frame bed, topped by a thin mattress. Nothing like my room at home with its floral wallpaper and shelves filled with dusty teddy bears. The only other furniture consisted of a small desk with a flip-top surface that had been pushed into one corner, and a single oak cupboard that provided space for my things. The plastic trunk that my mum helped pack was standing in the middle of the floor, with one of my rangy old teddy bears tucked into the handle on top. Fraser, picked up in Scotland when I was four years old, his tartan scarf worn from love. I hadn't intended to bring it.

'Cute,' Emily said, with no hint of a smile.

But I was glad my mum had left it there, and in seeing it I was hit by nostalgia, wishing I could go back home. I walked across to the small window and glanced northeast towards the town I had thought so easy to leave behind. And through the narrow pane of dimpled glass, the top of it shaped like an arch, all I could see for miles around were trees. No city. No other houses. There might as well have been an entire world between me and my old home.

And that was when I saw my parents crossing the gravel driveway. My father's arm draped around my mother's shoulders. They stopped, and my mother looked back to the building. Was she crying? I wanted to rush down, reach them. Say it had all been a big mistake. But then I saw Miss McCabe closing in, offering what looked like reassurance. Urging them away. Snatching at the mechanism, I tried to open the window, wanted to call to them, at least to say goodbye, but the latch for the window was rusted shut.

'Hey,' I said, knocking on the glass. The distance was already too great, and they couldn't hear me. Knocking again, harder that time, I pleaded with them to turn around. 'Mum,' I shouted. 'Hey, Dad.'

'What a shame.' Only then did I remember she was there. I felt the weight of her body leaning against mine to glance over my shoulder. 'It looks as if they didn't even want to say goodbye.'

'Of course they wanted to,' I snapped, sharper than intended. But my voice didn't sound like my own. Pressure was building in my throat, and my words sounded strained, as if I'd swallowed something too big, and couldn't quite set it free. Tears pricked at my eyes. 'Miss McCabe told them to leave. I saw her.'

'Or,' Emily said then, her voice quiet, drawing out the possibilities contained within that word, 'maybe they just couldn't wait to get rid of you.'

'What?' Turning too fast in the tight space, I bumped into her shoulder, and she stumbled backwards. Feigning shock, she straightened her blazer, stood upright, before she spoke again.

'Be careful, Chloe. I'd hate for you to get a reputation as a bully when you've only just arrived. Rumours can travel here just like they do in a state comprehensive, you know.'

'You're the one who got in my way.'

'I'm just trying to help you settle in.'

'You've done nothing but make me feel unwelcome.'

'By showing you around? By trying to teach you the ways of High Hill?' She stepped back as if offended, pulled the door to my room open. Half stepped through before she spoke again. 'If I were you, Chloe, I'd be very careful about making accusations like that. People are already talking about what happened at Clifton.'

'What?' My mouth ran dry at the mention of my old school. I watched as Emily began to smile, and the lie came easy to me. 'I don't know what you're talking about.'

'Of course you do,' she said, a little laugh. 'As the head prefect I'll do what I can to help, but...' she said, pausing, nodding as if her next thought was inevitable. 'It'll be difficult for you. People are already questioning whether you deserve to be here.'

My heart sped up, and my lips pulled tight. 'Maybe that's because you told everybody about my scholarship today, like it was something I should be ashamed of.'

'If there's nothing to be ashamed of, Chloe, why does it matter who I tell?' Leaning back into my room, she set the door key down on the desk. 'But it's got nothing to do with the scholarship. Still, I'm afraid it won't be long before everybody is talking about what happened at Clifton. It's hard to keep secrets from each other when we all live together.'

My skin tightened, and I couldn't find anything to say. How could she know what happened at my old school? This place was supposed to be a fresh start, but less than two hours here, and it was already falling apart.

'And as you obviously weren't able to understand the induction material, MDI is the Mandatory Dormitory Inspection. Like I said before, it happens every Wednesday, and as the head prefect, I'll be conducting it this year. Try to ensure you have everything in place, otherwise I'll have no choice but to give you a demerit. Three of those and you'll receive a suspension.'

'What's a demerit?' I stuttered.

Another smile, before she shrugged her shoulders. 'I guess you'll find out on Wednesday.' Then, before she slipped out, she said, 'Welcome to High Hill, Chloe. I hope you enjoy it here.' A step closer, a tight little snake-smile. 'But perhaps try not to enjoy it quite as much as you enjoyed it at Clifton.'

And with a wink she slammed the door, leaving me alone. I picked up Fraser and held him against my chest. Could smell my old home. My old life. I turned back to the window hoping to see my parents still there. But instead, all I saw was a plume of dust rising into the air as their car pulled through the gate. According to the induction material that I had read more than once, it was going to be four weeks before I was allowed to talk to them again. I watched the wrought-iron gates close, and I pulled the bear up to my face, drank in the smell. Washing powder and home cooking. My room. My bed. A life I was leaving behind. A life I thought I had wanted to forget, only now I wasn't so sure. But no matter how I felt, there was no going back now.

My time at High Hill Manor had begun.

4

Five laundered uniforms were hanging in the wardrobe. Long skirts and blue blazers for the weekdays, a long blue cape for formal events and Sunday Chapel. The inside of the cupboard smelled of the earth. Damp like the forest at the perimeter of the school. Coat hangers hung empty inside, so I opened my trunk and pulled out my clothes, held the grey skirt of the uniform up to my body. Too long, I was sure, like the little girl who was lost. Each item seemed heavy with a question mark. Was everything about me wrong for this place? I was one arm in, one arm out of the blue jacket when I heard a knock on the door.

'Hi,' the girl said when she opened it. I felt stupid, dressed half in my jeans, half in the uniform. She looked so neat in hers, so well put together. Her hair in the regulatory plaits. I was like a child playing dress-up. Wished I had locked the door. But she was smiling, and that came as a relief. It stretched all the way up to her wide, dark eyes, and her skin was the colour of bronze. 'You're the new girl, right?'

After my conversation with Emily, I was hesitant to reveal the truth of it.

'I just arrived,' I said instead, as if that made some difference.

'I'm Iris.'

'Chloe.'

'Nice to meet you. I bet this is all a bit of a shock, right?' she asked, stepping into my room. Hesitating, she looked to me, then the window, before stepping in and closing the door. She was dressed in the school uniform, and her hair was braided like the other girls. But there was something different about her to Emily, a softness that none of the others I had met so far had shown. Flopping down onto my bed, she straightened out the edge of the blue blanket that was draped across it. 'It must be so different to your old school.'

Emily's teasing lingered in the air, stung like a slap across a cheek. 'What do you know about my old school?'

Taking her time, she stroked the blanket into position and then looked at me again, her smile gone. 'There's no need to be like that,' she said. 'We're not all like Emily.'

It was a lifeline, a rope tossed to desperate hands in the sea. And yet it came with danger. Was it a trap? A ploy to get me to bad-mouth the only girl I had met, so that they could label me a bitch as well as a bully? As well as... No, I told myself. Don't think about Clifton, or the things that happened there. But it was true that school was school, no matter how much you paid. I knew well enough the way the game worked. Had hoped it would be different, but already understood that it wasn't.

'I don't know what you mean,' I said.

'Sure you know,' she laughed, sitting up, setting my teddy bear back against the pillow. Central and carefully, as if it mattered to her how I perceived her presence. 'But it's okay. I get it. Anyway, I'm Iris,' she repeated. 'We'll be in history together. And literature.'

'How do you know what subjects I'm doing?'

'My father is Professor Fairhurst. The head,' she said, in case I didn't know the name. 'He told me you were starting today. We can study together if you like. I need all the help I can get with the cold war, and my bedroom is right next to yours. I can help you with ancient Greece and Rome if you need it.' So bright, eager. Completely different to anything until that moment. 'I'm next to you in Six Thirteen.'

'Okay.'

Crossing her legs, then her arms, she looked up at me where I stood. 'You didn't get to say goodbye, did you?' I glanced over to the window, as if my parents might still be there. 'It's not easy moving away for the first time. I mean, it's different for me, because I see my father every day,' she said, rolling her eyes as if there was nobody with worse luck. 'But it's weird, living away from home. I miss my mum. And my dogs.'

'I'll miss my dad,' I said, relenting as I sat next to her.

'Mine told me that he has a painting in the National Gallery.'

I wasn't quite sure how to answer that. It was the truth but admitting that to Emily had brought nothing but derision.

'He said it was really good,' she encouraged. 'That it reminded him of some guy called Turner.'

One hot tear streaked across my cheek. 'That's my dad's favourite artist.' She pulled a crumpled tissue from her pocket, gave it to me. I used it to wipe my eyes. 'Miss McCabe sent them away.'

'Yeah, she thinks the goodbye is too traumatic, or whatever. Imagine how the first years feel.' I remembered the little girl from earlier, lost in every sense. The way Emily shouted at her. 'But you'll get used to it. And it was true what I said earlier; we're not all like Emily Ashbourne.'

'I don't think she was very impressed that my dad's an artist.'

'Who gives a shit what she thinks. Everybody hates her.'

'Really?'

'Yeah. You know, a couple of years ago she made a website about me. A porn site.'

'What?' It seemed so unlikely. 'Why?' I asked. And then, 'How?'

'She's like a genius or something. Nobody could prove she did it, but we all knew it was her. It was just a landing page of me giving somebody a blow job. Fake, I mean. She did it in Photoshop.' Two cheery circles appeared on her cheeks, and I could see the anger over what Emily had done hadn't faded at all. 'And besides, at least your father is not on sick leave,' she said, using her fingers to make speech marks, 'after killing a few too many of his patients.'

'Are you serious?'

'Yeah. It was in the newspaper and everything. He's a surgeon, just not a particularly good one. But ignore her. She's full of herself because her mum's like the eighth cousin of the queen or whatever. And on Friday we're going to have a party. After Formal. You can't tell anybody about it, but if you want to come, you could.'

'Really?' Again, my voice didn't sound like my own.

'God, don't cry about it,' she said, smiling as she nudged her elbow into my ribs. 'It's just a few people down at the beach. You'll have to sneak out, but I'll show you how and where. Anyway, I have to go,' she said, getting up from the bed. 'I have French. But if you need anything, I'll be next door. You better get going too,' she said, standing up. 'Otherwise you'll be late.'

'For what?'

Confused, she opened the door to my room and peered at something on the other side.

'You're supposed to be at music,' she said, reappearing. 'It's on your timetable.'

'What timetable?'

'Here on the wall.' I stood up and joined her at the door, looked at the small piece of paper tucked into a glass holder. And just like she said, there was the instruction for me to be at the music department, an induction session with a teacher called Mr Aides.

'This wasn't there earlier.'

'I told you that Emily's a bitch. She should have shown it to you.' Rage stirred within me, a twist in my gut, as tight as a screw. 'Just tell him you were held up in the library or something. It was nice to meet you though, Chloe. Catch you later at supper?'

'Okay.' And with that Iris headed up the corridor, turning to flash a smile, just before she disappeared down what I thought was staircase five.

5

After hurrying into the uniform, I ran along the corridor and down the staircase. The uneven floor of the cloisters outside my room was wet, even though it hadn't been raining. It was as if the water was seeping from the stone walls. The hem of my long skirt skimmed the puddles, and it hung heavy and wet like a weight I had to drag around. But I was glad to see that there was nobody lingering on the stairs like there had been on my way up. I hated the idea that the man might know which my room was, and I held onto the key, tight in my pocket like some kind of lucky charm. The uniform felt alien as I negotiated the stairs, too tight while also being too big. More than once I almost tripped up on the soggy hem of my skirt. Still, despite my hair, I looked the part. Catching my reflection in the glass, I could almost convince myself that I had always been there.

I followed the corridor, out into the cloisters, where the floor was uneven and polished by centuries of harried feet. Everywhere I went the air was cool, despite the heat of the day. Footsteps echoed behind me, and more than once I stopped, sure that somebody was following me, turning only to find I was alone. My only company were the statues of goddesses, who marked my route. There was Athena with her shield and spear, another who was sitting, a book held in her hand. Another held a creature by its antlers as she reached for an arrow from a quiver on her back. I knew from the brochure they were the female goddesses. But I didn't know whether they were there to watch over me, or there to judge.

Unlike before, the lawns of the courtyard were as empty as the corridors. I had the whole place to myself. Crossing the courtyard, past the statues and central fountain with marble nymphs dancing around the bowl, it felt as if I had slipped into a parallel world. What was this place? The goddesses watched me as I passed, questions in their proud stance, of who I thought I was to walk through their hallowed halls. But I had no answers. It was a question I had asked myself already. Who was I, there in that place? How the hell had I got there? They were questions I didn't want to answer.

After arriving in the east wing, I found a small staircase that wound helically underground into a room with a nondescript sign that read *MUSIC DEPARTMENT*. And despite the plain entrance, seeing that sign gave me a thrill. At Clifton there was no such thing as a department. Music was an activity conducted in the assembly hall, and the equipment was stored under the stage. As I stepped forward and held onto the handle to pull it open, my mouth ran dry with anticipation; I wanted to believe that this was the reason I was there.

On the other side, the room was brighter than I had expected for a space in the basement of a Victorian mansion. And it was different to any other room I had seen that morning. Posters adorned the walls, of composers and concerts held years before at Teatro alla Scala in Milan. Persian rugs bled like watercolours over the floor. It could have been a recording studio, with the vibe more of what I might expect from the student areas rather than an academic department led by a decorated musician. It was unexpectedly circular, with chairs spread out as if an orchestra was ready to play. Amps had been stacked in one corner, and sheet music rested on stands. A few instruments lay across the red plastic chairs. The air was warmer, the room bright. It smelt as if somebody had baked a fresh cake. A refuge from the cold empty halls of High Hill Manor.

'Good morning.'

Shocked by the voice, I turned to see a man, coming from a room behind me. The first thing I noticed was his beard, neat and soft, like some kindly father with time on his hands. But he was too young for that. Blond streaked through the ends of his hair, evidence of the bad summer highlights that hadn't quite grown out. It was obvious from his clothes, the tight jeans, the T-shirt under a jacket, that he was closer to my age than he was Miss McCabe's. I could imagine him in the bar I had worked that summer, pint in one hand, fag in the other. He could have been fresh from the set of a Busted video.

'Hi,' I said, watching as he moved instruments and collected music. 'Are you Mr Aides?'

'I most certainly am.' He was smiling but he didn't stop what he was doing or slow down. 'And you are?'

'Late. But I have a lesson with you. I'm Chloe Carter.'

With a smile he set the flute he was carrying down on a chair. Stood back to take a look.

'The prodigious pianist has arrived at last,' he said, and I wasn't sure whether he was offering me a compliment or taking the piss. 'I've heard a lot about you.' That idea made me nervous. But he said, 'No need to look so worried. It's all good.' Smiling, he looked away then, as if abashed by my presence. 'To be honest though, I recognised you from your audition, and I must say, I was quite blown away by what I saw. In fact, it was me who made the decision to bring you here.'

Heat flared in my cheeks, the thought of him watching my video. That he was responsible for awarding me the scholarship. I watched as he sat down into the nearest chair, picking up a clarinet to place it on a stand. He crossed his legs. Waiting.

'Thanks,' I said.

'No, no. It should be me thanking you. Having a student of such talent, somebody who actually deserves a place here rather than who has paid for it, is, to be quite honest, a dream come true. So,' he said, standing up, looking almost embarrassed. 'Can I show you around?'

Over the next ten minutes he guided me through the practice rooms, each of which came off the central space. Posters of composers hung in each of them, and music covered every surface. Being there made my shaky start with Emily seem like a distant dream. Some nightmare remembered on waking but which, with time, was becoming ever less tangible. Yes, there were people who thought I didn't belong in a place like High Hill, but that didn't mean they were right.

'This is the room I have earmarked for you.'

With a wink of his left eye, he opened the final practice studio. It was the largest room I had seen that morning. A poster of Rachmaninoff was taped to one wall, Satie on another. And in the centre of the room stood a black grand piano, shining and elegant. Little golden letters gleamed in the black paint of the instrument. I wanted to reach out, touch them. Magic might not exist in the bricks of that school, but I felt pretty sure it existed in those letters.

'It's a Steinway,' I said.

'Indeed. Have you ever played one before?'

I shook my head. At my school all we had was an electric keyboard, and at home while I had an old piano, the whites of the keys were all chipped, and it was never really in tune. My dad had found it in the classified ads almost ten years before, free to whomever wanted it.

'It has a beautiful sound,' he added, sitting to run through several broken chords, spanning the octaves. 'Don't you think?' It sounded like nothing I had ever heard before, at least not in real life. I gave him a nod. 'Will you play it for me now?'

'Okay,' I said, stepping forward. I could hardly wait, let my fingers brush against the white of the keys. All intact. I could hear my own heart beating with excitement, could feel the muscles of my cheeks twitching as I tried to stem a smile. 'What should I play?' I asked.

Closing the door behind us, the distant noise of other students on the floors above was softened. A moment of apprehension gripped me then, to be alone with him in this basement room behind closed doors. But I reminded myself that he had been nice and had given me no reason to feel uncomfortable at all. Not everywhere was like Clifton.

Mr Aides leaned against the side of the piano, like a gentleman of a time gone by.

'What about your audition piece? *Clair de Lune*, wasn't it?' I nodded. 'I should love to hear it live.'

It was one of my favourites. 'Okay.'

He nodded to the keys, and so I sat. And as I struck the first notes of the piece my heart raced. I could feel him close to me, hear his breaths in the silences between notes. The intensity of the music grew, and as I played my way into the piece I soon forgot where I was. Lost somewhere in the music. It took me to some other place. My favourite in the entire world. And by the time I'd finished the piece, my hands were slick with sweat, my body shaking from adrenaline.

'Chloe,' he said, quiet, almost breathless. He had moved closer, was crouching at my side. His coffee breath warmed the air. 'If ever I needed justification for choosing you for the scholarship, that was it. What an exceptional talent you possess. Utterly captivating.' Neither of us moved. I counted the seconds until he spoke again. One. Two. Ten. 'If I'm honest, which I must be, you made one or two mistakes. Most people wouldn't notice, but they were there nevertheless.'

The heat of his correction struck me. I had played that piece so many times I could, quite literally, play it with my eyes closed.

'Which part?'

'Chloe, please,' he said with a laugh that made me feel about five years old. 'You should not take it as a criticism.' I stilled as the weight of his hand rested upon my shoulder. 'Mistakes are there to guide our course, not thwart it. They give us room within which to work. And besides, it is our school motto after all.'

'What is?' I asked.

'Didn't you see it on the way in? *Nemo sine vitio est*,' he said with the flourish of a drama student, and I remembered the letters carved into the belltower. 'It's Latin,' he added. 'It means that no one is without fault. So don't be too hard on yourself.' And with a wink, he added, 'Leave that up to me.' Then he withdrew his hand and pushed up his sleeve, checked his watch. 'Ah, I have a class in the next few minutes. I must dash. But it was a delight to meet you. I believe that we will spend a great deal of time together this year. I hope we will become good friends.' He reached down to the other side of the piano where a black duffle bag was resting on the floor behind me. Pushed himself upright with a little gasp, before patting his hand against my shoulder again. 'Would you like that?'

'Um, yes,' I said. 'Of course.'

'Excellent. Then I shall look forward to it.'

After he left the room, I could feel the void of his absence. His praise still reverberating around me. His critique, too. My hands trembled with the weight of it. I watched as he crossed the department, listened to the swing of the main doors opening and closing with his exit. And even then, after just one meeting, I was desperate to check my timetable, work out when I could come back and play for him again.

I didn't ever want to leave.

6

If anybody else was nervous about the first MDI of the academic year, it didn't show. Even as I was tidying my room, trying to get things in order, I could hear the other girls' laughter echoing through the corridors. But I had spent the entire day wondering if I had done it all correctly, and whether I would even make it there on time, because Mr Aides wanted me to hang back and run through some of his ideas for my first performance pieces. And on top of that, finding my way around was proving to be as difficult as I suspected it would. Emily had insisted that it was an easy place to navigate, with its four wings and central courtyard. Its orientation to the sea. But to me everywhere looked the same, and I was only finding my way around by way of the goddesses: four doors past Hestia for nineteenth-century history; second floor and level with Demeter for Monday's English lit. The stairs to my room those closest to Athena with her spear and shield.

And when the knock on my door came, it was five minutes before the designated start time of 6:30 p.m., and I still hadn't put my books away on the shelf. Emily was early, and I knew therefore I had been chosen as the first. I had wasted too much time, trying to get the radiator to work. Goosepimples covered my skin, even with three blankets and a nightly hot water bottle that Miss McCabe had organised for me when I told her I was cold. And now the MDI was starting, and I wasn't ready. Francesca – a girl who I sat with in history, and who was friends with my neighbour, Iris – had been telling a younger girl in the Great Hall that morning while we ate breakfast, that the MDI was nothing more than a quick poke around the door to make sure there weren't clothes on the floor, that the sheets were fresh and pulled up. A demerit, she said – the threat tossed to me by Emily on the day she showed me to my room – was almost impossible to receive unless they found a boy or drugs hidden away, and there was some comfort in knowing I had neither of those.

'Come in,' I said from behind the wardrobe door. But when I turned around, it wasn't Emily I saw. Dressed in overalls, like some malnourished version of Michael Myers, the young man from the stairs took a step into my room. 'What do you want?'

'Just wondered how you're settling in,' he said as he gazed about the room. 'Whether the other girls are being nice to you?' His words were friendly enough, but there was a look in his eyes that I didn't like. Almost wolfish, like he had me in his sights. A weird, cold feeling travelled up my back as he took a step closer. 'Whether there was anything you needed.'

'No,' I said, stepping away. I tried to busy myself, could hear my mum's voice in my head, telling me to be polite. I tried to smile but could feel the nervous shake of my cheeks. 'Thank you.'

'Oh, that's all right. No need for formalities. Because, you know, if there was anything you needed, you would only have to tell me.' He felt closer. The weight of him right behind me in my tiny room. Turning, I almost knocked into him. I looked to the door, was relieved to see it open. 'You know, I could get you—'

'What the fuck are you doing here?' Never did I think I'd be relieved to see Emily, but there she was, standing in the doorway like a saviour. Glancing up, I saw his eyes roll, and it was only now that she was there that I realised just how close he was, how I was leaning back to get out of his way.

'I was just leaving,' he said, but he didn't take his eyes off me. Seconds stretched out dangerously between us. And then, as he went to turn away, he whispered at the last minute, 'You look cute while you're asleep.'

All I could do was watch as he paced out of the room. Emily watched him from the corner of her eye, until he passed, and then for a few moments longer as he whistled his way down the corridor. I was still thinking about the last thing he said to me when she spoke.

'Are you ready?'

'Who is he?' I asked.

'Jimmy Baxter,' she said. 'The caretaker. Do yourself a favour and steer clear. Now,' she said, stepping into my room. 'I asked if you were ready for MDI.'

'I hope so,' I said, stepping back from my desk and trying to sound light. I hadn't seen her to speak to since the first day, but my books were aligned, my clothes were neat and tidy. I tried to push Baxter from my mind, the way he looked at me, the thing he said. Surely I was wrong. He couldn't mean that he had seen me asleep, could he? I convinced myself I must have misheard.

'Looks like you have made quite an effort.' It was true; my bed looked as if it could have been made by an experienced soldier in the army. You could have dropped a penny on the corner, and it would have bounced right back up into your hand. 'But let's make sure there's nothing that you've missed.'

I watched as she opened drawers, inspecting my toiletries, flicking the lids open and smelling some of the bottles. Her presence forced me to look at my room with fresh, judgemental eyes. I saw the height of the ceilings, the damp patch in one corner where the wall was turning dark. The sparse, monastic furnishing. I wasn't sure what level of personalisation I was allowed to make, so I had stuck to the basics. Just one photograph on my bedside table, and a painting of the coast at sunset, completed by my father in secret in the weeks before I left. I had found it packed in brown paper at the bottom of my trunk when I arrived. On the back he had written a message, advice that I wasn't sure would help all that much at High Hill.

'What are these?'

Her words roused me from my daydream, and when she turned, I saw that she had a photograph album in her hands. It was small, had been made by my old friends at Clifton. Inside were images of us hanging out at the local shopping centre, chilling in the park. Badly lined eyes and questionable foundation. At night in the hours when I struggled to sleep, I would look at their faces, wondering how they were doing, whether they missed me at all. How it felt like a lifetime ago since I was there.

'Just some old pictures,' I said. I didn't want to impart any importance, sure that if I did they could be used as a weapon. If my father being an artist could be used against me, I was certain by then that anything could.

'Your old friends?' she asked. I nodded. 'What are their names?'

'Why do you want to know?'

'Jesus,' she said, tossing the album back in the drawer. 'I was just trying to be friendly. I don't really care about Kayleigh and Chantal.'

I didn't correct her, just wanted the whole experience to be over. But she was moving towards the desk, reaching for the painting.

'Did your father paint this?'

She picked it up, taking in the details, not that there was ever much in the way of them in my father's work. When I asked him why, he said it was to show the light in the composition; said it was the only thing he was ever searching for.

'Yes,' I said, wishing she would put it back down. But then I saw her turn it over, find the message written on the back.

'Oh, that's sweet. "Be yourself, Munchkin",' she said, reading aloud. 'Unhelpful,' she concluded with a nod of her head. 'But sweet.'

I set the painting back on the desk from where she'd tossed it to the bed, while she opened the cupboard and continued her search. I glanced again to the clock. She had been with me now for over five minutes. Danger clawed at me with every tick of the clock. I knew that nothing about this inspection was going according to expectation.

'You know, Chloe, I'll go easy on you this time, but really, this isn't good enough.' Hangers clattered as she pulled out my clothes. 'Uniform goes on the right of the cupboard, and your own terrible choices go on the left. These,' she said, fingering my winter jumpers, 'should still be in your trunk, but whatever. I can let that go. You've never had to operate at this level before.' I couldn't see anything particularly highbrow about knowing the rules of what I should and shouldn't do with my clothes, but

I said nothing, just waited instead for her to finish. 'This top drawer,' she said, moving to the drawers below, 'is for your games kit, and the *second* drawer is for underwear.' One by one, I saw her lifting out my knickers, and I had to fight the urge to snatch them from her hands. And I managed it for the first two, until it looked as if she was going to lift the third pair to her nose. Rushing forward, I snatched them away.

'I'll rearrange them.' I threw the knickers in the drawer and slammed it shut, aware of her sniggering behind me. 'Is there anything else?'

'Well, your tuck box is supposed to be on the little shelf under the desk, not by your bed. And personal items like the painting are not really allowed. I could give you a demerit for all of this,' she said, stepping back, glancing around the room, 'but it would be unfair of me considering that this is your first week. The only reason to demerit you now would be if I found something really bad,' she said, kneeling down to search under the bed. Her body half-disappeared under the frame. 'Hiding something under here that indicated an intent at breaking the rules would not be something I could ignore. Something, for example, like this.'

At first, I wasn't sure what it was she was holding in her hand when she knelt up and held it up for me to see. It was only when I heard the crimple of the wrapper as she twisted it in her fingers that it started to make sense.

'That isn't mine.'

'Well, it's in your bedroom,' she said with a shrug and an eyeroll. 'Have you let anybody else in here? One of the Ridgely boys for example?'

'The what?'

'The Ridgely boys. From our neighbouring school.'

'Of course I haven't. I've never even heard of the place.'

'Then how else would you explain it?' And then her mouth dropped open, curling into a smile. She was enjoying this a bit too much. 'Don't tell me it was from Jimmy Baxter... Is that what he was doing here?'

'Who?'

'The caretaker. You know you are not supposed to have anybody in your room.'

The question wormed its way into my brain. How could I explain it? Not just the presence of a condom in my room, but the fact that she had reached under the bed and produced it when I had only cleaned the space myself to store my tuck box the day before. But the explanation hit me with the same force as the shock had moments before.

'You just put it there,' I said.

She took her time answering, seemed to be trying not to smile. 'Blaming another person for such a serious indiscretion is pretty rich when all I'm trying to do is help. But,' she said, placing the little silver packet on my desk, alongside the neatly arranged books and notebooks. 'Perhaps I should have expected nothing less. Letting other people take the blame for your mistakes is how you ended up here in the first place, right?'

Heat rose up my neck, and my pulse skipped a beat in my chest. My throat became so tight it was like her hands were gripped around it. 'I don't know what you're talking about.'

Disinterested in my denial, she looked around the rest of the room as if it bored her. 'I'm sure you do, but I'll let it go for now. But that,' she said, pointing to the condom on the desk, 'is something that I cannot ignore. I'll be informing Professor Fairhurst about what I found this evening. He'll talk to you about your demerit in due course.'

'But it's not mine,' I protested. 'I don't know where it came from.'

'A moment ago you said I was responsible.'

'I don't... I'm not...'

I couldn't get my words out. They were stuck behind the injustice of it. The certainty that I didn't deserve what was happening to me. I wanted to protest but couldn't find the right thing to say. And I was only pulled from my spiralling sense of despair when I heard Iris's voice at my door.

'MDI isn't supposed to take this long, Emily. Stop fucking around.'

I turned to see her with her hand on her hip, dressed in nothing more than a pair of shorts and a lace bra. Gaze fixed on Emily.

'You should be in your room waiting for inspection,' Emily said. 'In your uniform.'

'And you should be on a demerit, not waltzing around as the head prefect. Don't even pretend that you don't know why.'

I sensed the shift, the air changing. White bone gleamed at Emily's jaw as she tilted her nose in the air. But she turned back to me, snatching up the condom.

'Next time, it'd better be exactly as it's supposed to be.'

Emily stormed from the room, brushing past Iris. I was stuck to the spot, could barely move.

'Are you coming, Fairhurst?' I heard Emily call from outside Iris's room.

With a wink, Iris gave me one last smile and swept from the room, and I flopped down on the bed, utterly spent. My mouth was dry, my heart racing. But despite the lie about the condom, all I could think of was how Iris had come to my aid. Rescued me from Emily's grip. How she was starting to feel like a friend.

And how when she had stood there in her bra, I could see her pink nipples, visible through the cloth.

7

Somewhere along the corridor a girl screamed, and I awoke panting and slick with dream-sweat. Outside the last of the summer was a distant memory, and the first rains of the season pattered lightly at the window. Lightning framed the charcoal clouds. I still wasn't used to it, never could quite work out where I was in the moments after waking. There in that room, it was as if the oxygen levels were short, and I could never quite catch my breath. Since the moment I had arrived at High Hill Manor, a pain sat in the middle of my chest like a solid lump. I couldn't seem to swallow it, or bring it up... I had tried on numerous occasions, retching into the toilet bowls that smelt like bleach and piss. Nothing ever came out.

Nothing was right inside those walls. Even my room felt weird, strangely cold, dark even when the sun was out. The ceiling was too far away, the window too small. I pushed it open as far as it would go, desperate for air, but even though I had thought it was rusted shut the first day, I had since discovered that it had been bolted so that I couldn't open it more than a couple of centimetres. I peered into the darkness of the early morning, towards the trees at the far end of the hockey field, twisting and tilting in the coastal wind. I reached across to the clock, turned it so I could see the screen. 4:35 a.m.

Every day since I arrived at High Hill Manor, I had been awake before Miss McCabe called us. She lived in one of the houses at the rear of the school, and would let herself in at six thirty sharp to wake us with a call from the hunting horn. Even when I tried to go back to sleep, it wouldn't come. All I could think about was how it was that I had ended up there, in that tiny room at the end of a cold wet corridor, where the rain snuck underneath my door from the cloisters outside. The hem of my skirt was perpetually wet. I'd remember the look on my parents' faces when I told them that I wanted to move two hundred miles away from home to the south coast. To a school they'd never heard of, on a scholarship worth money they could barely conceive. Their desperate faces, wondering what they had done wrong. What fault permeated our home so that I would take such drastic measures to leave.

Sometimes in those early mornings before the pastel light of morning tore a rip in the horizon, I would close my eyes and imagine my old bed, the posters above my desk of Madonna and Nick Carter. The picture I tore from a *Hello!* magazine of Tom Cruise dressed in a tux at the Oscars. How I'd used a Greenpeace picture of a whaling ship to cover up Nicole Kidman in that stunning chartreuse gown, even though I knew she was more beautiful than he could have ever been. But whenever I did, I'd always remember how my mother thrust the scholarship acceptance letter at my father's chest like an insult, and how he went on for an hour or so about the merit of hard work, the value of an apprenticeship and what it was like to feel the weight of money in your pocket. Somehow in those words of that scholarship offer to a private school, they saw written the inadequacies of their own life. Questions about their own choices.

I said nothing. Gave no answers. Bided my time until they caved.

I reached to the envelope of photographs I had stored underneath the bed. A collection my mother had created before I left, that I found tucked in my trunk when I unpacked. Images of me at various stages of life. A trip around Weymouth Harbour. A sandcastle built with pride and foraged sea glass. Birthdays and parties. A cousin's wedding, a working men's club. Smoke haze that stung my eyes. Others of my friends at Clifton. Our block-heel Pods and ripped tights. Badges sewn into our blazers for rounders and netball. Rolled-up skirts that skimmed our thighs. Foo Fighters playing into shared earphones. All of it gone. Now there was a blue velvet cape hanging on the back of my door, and a pair of regulation Dr Martens which sat neatly to the side.

I reached to the end of the bed for the music score I was halfway through composing, something to distract me, and started to hum through the notes when my door creaked open.

'I thought I heard you awake.' I pulled the sheet up, felt naked despite my M and S pyjamas. It was the girl from next door. Iris. But I remembered how she had supported me, how she was the only person who felt like a friend. 'Want one?'

Holding up a box of Marlboro Red, she shook them before me. A lighter rattled around inside. Since our first interaction, I had seen her a couple of times. Perhaps her father, Mr Fairhurst, had sent her like a temptress to see if I'd break after Emily had reported me for the condom. I wondered what conversations around their dinner table she might have been privy to. What she knew about how I had come to be at High Hill Manor.

'It's really early,' I said. 'Curfew isn't over.'

It was a clear nod to the rules, and she crossed her eyes and stuck out her tongue like I made her sick. And I thought of the pictures I had just been looking at, the girls who I missed. Remembered what friendship felt like, and a desire to rediscover it fought its way free inside me. A sudden and crippling realisation that I had spoken to almost nobody since I had arrived.

'So?' she asked.

'It's chucking it down too.'

As if I was in collaboration with the weather, a clap of thunder rumbled through the sky, a flickering of distant lightning lit up outside my curtainless window.

'I wasn't suggesting we go outside.'

And with that, she gave a quick nod of her head as a suggestion to follow, before she disappeared from my room and back out into the cloisters. Sitting there with the sheets pulled up around me, I somehow knew that the offer was a one-time thing. If I didn't take it there would be no second chance. Whether life played out at a state comprehensive or a twenty-three thousand pounds a year private boarding school, there was always somebody, somewhere, who wanted to break the rules. Still, it was different for her. She had the protection of being the headmaster's daughter. If they caught me sneaking around at night I'd be thrown out. But when I heard another crack of thunder I jumped from bed, wrapped my robe around me and hurried along the dark corridor.

Low light flickered in ancient lamps as I hurried along, the driving rain coming straight for me. Below I could see the goddesses, irreverent to the rain. Lightning flickered from their forms, and shadows crept up the wall, looming over me as if they were watching my transgression. The cold air simmered up and over the cloisters from the courtyard below.

A moment later I was at the end of the corridor, pushing open the door that led to the staircase of the belltower, winding up through the centre of the building like a spine. Each step was built of solid stone, twisting from the main entrance hall right up to the seventh floor. I couldn't see Iris, but I could hear her footsteps on the stairs above.

'Iris?' I whispered. Regret was building, the thought of my mother's inevitable ambivalence if I was sent back home. The idea that I would have to return to Clifton. How I wasn't sure that was even possible. 'Iris, are you there?'

Then I heard another door opening above me, so I hurried on up. The sound of the wind was violent with rage as I made my way up the stairs. I could hear that voice again, the woman's song as the currents brushed against the metal of the bell. And as I reached the door still swinging on its hinges, I pushed it open, saw Iris already sitting by the protection of the wall.

Wind whipped through the open belfry, the spray of rain. I could hear the rush of sea, smell the salinity on the air. In the centre of the space the old mechanism remained in place, the bell and the wheels that would have once been used to make it ring. Miss McCabe had told us on my first day that High Hill Manor had once been the grand home of a local landowner, and after that it had been used as a convent. A home for orphans in the late 1800s, with little children living amongst the sisters of the convent. Those children were the founding pupils of what went on to become High Hill Manor. But for close to two centuries the bells had not been rung. Only that soft whisper of the wind that I could hear today. A cry that carried across centuries.

'Wow, this place.'

'It's something, right?' she said, opening the box of cigarettes for me to take one as I settled in at her side. She drew her fingers over the lighter, holding her hand around the flame to shield it from the wind. 'If you go out through there, you can get onto the balcony.'

I glanced out through the window, beyond the balustrade of Latin letters. 'Have you been out?'

'No,' she said. 'Freaks me out to be so high. But on a clear day they say you can see parts of France.'

I stared through the dark for a bit, wondering whether I was looking out to sea or north towards home. Up there in the dark, I was even more confused than I was in the tight corridors of the lower floors. There was no statue of a goddess to orientate me. I drew on the cigarette, watched the grey smoke drift into the wind. It was months since I'd smoked, and the hit of it went to my head. I pressed myself against the wall, my shoulder soft against hers.

'Do you come up here a lot?' I asked.

'Yeah, I guess so. I like it up here. It's quiet.' The whole school felt quiet to me. 'Was it you that screamed?' she asked. I wondered what she was talking about until I remembered that I too had heard it. That was what had woken me. I remembered the dream I was having, of the maths corridor, of Edward Lyons, my old teacher at Clifton.

'I don't think so,' I said, even though I suspected it was. 'I was already awake. I heard somebody scream too.'

'Must have been somebody else then,' she said. 'Maybe it's Eloise Cunningham.'

'Who?'

She smiled. 'Nobody told you about her? She was a few years ahead of us, but she died, like, two years ago now.'

'Oh, my God.'

'I know. She threw herself from her bedroom window. People say she had manic depression. For weeks she kept saying that somebody was following her, that she could hear voices in the night. It was all bullshit. She was mental.' I thought of the first nights at High Hill, when I thought I could hear voices, the restlessness I felt as I lay in bed. How often I had turned around, certain that somebody was behind me, only to find I was alone. 'That's why all our windows have been bolted shut. Some people say they've seen her stalking the corridors at night, or that they've seen her in the old library.'

'Shit,' I said, drawing again on my cigarette. 'That's the worst fucking story I've ever heard.' But even as I said it, I could see from her grimace that there was more to come. And that's when I realised. When I understood what she was about to say. 'Oh my God. You can't be serious?'

'Afraid so. She was the last person to sleep in your room. They haven't used it since.' I imagined her in there, sleeping on my pillow, sitting at my desk. Standing on the bed to climb up to the window. 'Last year, I often thought I could hear somebody in there. Could hear somebody crying.' I felt my skin tighten, my eyes widen, until her face cracked and she began to laugh. 'I totally got you, didn't I?'

'Oh, my God. Was it all a lie?'

'No. Eloise did jump from your room, but I never heard anything. Anyway, how is your first week going?'

What was I supposed to say after that? That I hated it? That I felt lonely? I knew that the opportunity to be at High Hill Manor was not something to be taken for granted, even after the story about the girl who killed herself. And yet hearing her ask me that question was too real. It was like she took my darkest moments and put them up on a screen for me to relive over and over again.

'Wait, shit. Are you crying?'

'It's just the wind,' I said, bringing a knuckle up to my eye to blot a tear away.

'Oh shit. I'm such a dickhead. I didn't mean to scare you. It's just a stupid story. I thought it would be funny.'

'It is, I mean, it's not, but...' I took a moment to catch my breath. 'It's just really weird to know that I'm in her room.'

It was easier to focus on that. To let that be the hardest thing about the week so far.

'I know,' she said. 'And it's not like your first week has been easy.' The truth of the sentence struck me as odd, unexpected in every way. I watched the cigarette in my fingers, the smoke drifting in tendrils that disappeared on the currents of cold air. 'What Emily said was out of order. And the stupid fucking demerit.' She drew hard on her cigarette and shook her head. 'I told you she's always been a cunt.'

And I wasn't sure what to say then. The choice of word hit me like a punch. On the one hand I was desperate to agree, but I was still aware of the undeniable fact that I was the outsider there. I didn't want to reveal my own feelings about Emily too soon, even though I could sense them, building beneath the surface. I worried that they were obvious in the red flush of my cheeks, that I knew were growing hotter by the second.

'Everybody knows it,' she said then, as if I had disagreed with her. 'She wears that fucking crucifix like she's holier than thou. As if it absolves her from all the awful things she does. But believe me, there is nothing Christian about her. Chapel is certainly not the only place you'll find her on her knees.' The words came with a taste, something I was hungry for. I wanted to gobble them up, digest all the terrible things that she might say about Emily. 'And you know that not everyone believes what she said in English, right?'

It was the literature class. Miss McCabe posed the topic of controversial texts, and somebody brought up *Lolita*. It wasn't a text I had read, but I had heard about it, knew the theme and what it was about. Emily was the one to raise her hand, offer insight into the mystery of why *Lolita* was so often confused as a love story.

'It's Nabokov's language, Miss,' Emily had begun. 'It helps him hide the truth of what he really is. Makes you believe he is something that he is not.'

Miss McCabe had beamed, an obvious pride for what Emily had deduced. 'Emily, that's a wonderful insight.'

'Not really, Miss. People are doing that all the time.' And then she looked across the classroom and smiled at me. 'Like her,' she said, nodding in my direction. The eyes of the whole class turned to me. 'We all know Chloe doesn't belong here. None of us are convinced otherwise, just because she's trying to speak posh,' she said, mocking my London accent. I heard a few girls snigger. 'Just because she's dressed in our uniform doesn't mean that she's one of us.'

'Emily Ashbourne,' Miss McCabe said. The reprimand was sharp, but it didn't deter her.

'What?' she said, pretending to be horrified. 'Everybody knows it's true.'

Already people were turning away. I realised not everybody wanted to be part of her game.

'I will not tolerate that sort of—'

'What are you going to do? Take me into your office and punish me? I bet you'd like that, wouldn't you, Miss?'

'I beg your pardon? I don't know what you are trying to insinuate, but—'

'Insinuate? It's okay, Miss. You don't have to use fancy words with us. We all know already that you're a cunning linguist.'

I looked up, glad that the heat had been redirected from me, but at the same time felt desperately sorry for Miss McCabe, who had been so nice to me since the moment I arrived. Her body seemed limp in the aftermath of the joke, her face growing hotter and redder. I had heard the rumour about Miss McCabe because somebody had written about it on the bathroom wall. *Free dyke sex in room XIX*. I found myself assessing her clothes, her short hairstyle. Felt ashamed that I had looked for a wedding ring that wasn't there and made my own assumptions.

'It doesn't matter,' I said. 'She was way harsher to Miss McCabe than me.'

'Oh, my God, I swear she hasn't let up about that since Miss McCabe brought a friend to the summer fair.' She drew on her cigarette and I watched as she let the smoke drift through her lips. 'But she'll get bored of messing with you. Last year I was the one who took the brunt of it.'

'Really?' I just couldn't see it, the idea of Iris being the subject of Emily's cruel jibes. Iris was such a cool person, so disinterested in it all. 'Why was she mean to you?'

'It was all stupid, and a total misunderstanding. But anyway, I thought...' She stopped, and as she looked to the door, I realised I could hear it too. Footsteps approaching. Her eyes widened, and we tossed our cigarettes over the wall at her instruction, and she started wafting her hands to get rid of any lingering smell. Thundering along in my chest, my heart followed the rhythm of my rapid thoughts. Of how I could get out of the predicament. Of how I would explain it to my mother. But just a second later the door creaked open, and a girl who I recognised from English, and knew to be Iris's friend, stepped into view.

'What the fuck, Iris?' the girl said as I heard Iris breathe a sigh of relief.

'Jesus, Fran. What the hell are you doing, creeping around like that?' Francesca. I remembered her as a girl who had continued to smile when Emily was making her jokes about Miss McCabe. 'You scared the shit out of us.'

'I wouldn't have had to if you'd come to get me as planned.'

'How did you even know I was here?'

'Does it matter?' she said, sitting down. Not a word or a glance in my direction. She held out her hand for a cigarette, but Iris kept the pack back. 'I knocked on your door. We agreed to meet at five.'

'Oh shit. Sorry,' she said, and I watched as Iris relented and Fran took a cigarette. 'I heard Chloe awake, and thought she might like to know about this place.'

'You're neighbours?' she asked me. I smiled and nodded to show she was correct, but she didn't say anything after that.

'We come up here a lot at this time,' Iris said then. 'It's the best time to come, because you can have a shower as soon as you go back down, and nobody will be able to smell the smoke on your clothes.'

'Thanks,' I said. 'If they smelled it, I'd lose my scholarship.'

'For smoking?' She seemed doubtful.

'I think so.'

'Maybe you shouldn't come then,' Fran said. 'That is, if you want to stay.'

'Of course she wants to stay,' Iris said then. 'My father told me that she is a musical genius.'

'Is that the reason you're here?' Fran asked. 'Because it's, like, really weird to be given a scholarship for just your final year of education.'

I drew hard on my cigarette, played at the edge of the broken bits of the bell that littered the floor with my other hand. Cold air screeched over the top of us. And I remembered Clifton then, the weeks before I left. The way nobody would talk to me. How even Laura and Kate, my best friends since we were five years old, had severed the connection that bound us. The heat of the day that the headteacher called me into her office and told me that she thought there was a good solution to the problem we were faced with. That she knew of a scholarship suitable for somebody with my talents. *It would be a privilege, really*, she said. *A clean slate. For all of us.* She even made sure I knew that she would have no need to tell my parents about the nature of what had happened the week before, as long as I took the offer and left Clifton in silence, made no formal complaint. She even guaranteed that nobody at the new school would ever have to know.

'So?' Iris asked. 'Is that the reason? You're like Mozart, or something?'

I tried to smile, pushing the memories of why I really left Clifton aside. 'I guess so,' I said.

'Well, we're glad you're here, right, Fran?'

'Sure,' Fran said, although when I looked up to see her watching me, I wasn't sure I believed her.

But I couldn't help but wonder then if the reason they were asking me was because they already knew the truth. If their questions implied knowledge of what had happened before I left Clifton. But I didn't push it or ask anything more. Instead, I listened as they bitched about Emily while we all smoked another cigarette, before I headed back down the stairs with a headrush, to a bedroom where some other girl had chosen to kill herself.

8

The first week was over. Five dinners and five breakfasts eaten in the Great Hall. Besides the inspection and subsequent meeting with Professor Fairhurst, the week had been okay. People seemed to have forgotten that I was new, no longer cared who was paying for my place. Even after what Emily had said in English, a few other girls started to talk to me, and more than a few had asked whether I was settling in, and whether I needed any help. My weird encounter with the caretaker was yet to be repeated, and although I'd seen him about the school – often, I thought, standing around watching the younger girls – I'd managed to avoid coming into any contact with him myself.

And while I enjoyed the formality of the first Friday night supper, dressed in my black dress that wasn't fancy enough for the occasion but which still made me feel nice, sitting in rows amidst the roaring fires, listening to Professor Fairhurst's welcome address for the start of term, my head was abuzz with the idea of the party that was happening that night.

I hurried back to my room as fast as I could to change my clothes. Just before nine I heard the knock on my door. I was still half-dressed, my black formals tossed on the edge of my bed.

'Come on,' she said, hurrying me along as soon as she opened the door.

'I wasn't sure what to wear,' I said. I was dressed in my jeans, my bra and little else.

'Well, you can't go like that,' she said, laughing. Still smiling, she reached in, pulled out a jumper from my trunk which I had repacked as per Emily's orders. 'Just put this on, and let's go, before the teachers get back from their end of week debrief.'

While I was still pulling my jumper over my head, she grabbed my hand and led me to the stairs, where we ignored the no entrance signs that were on the door of the belltower.

'I thought this was usually locked,' I said.

'It is, but Jimmy unlocks it when we have a party.' Cool air rushed up, ruffled our loose hair. She smiled when she realised my distaste at hearing his name. 'Not a fan?'

'He's a bit...'

'Yeah, he is,' she said, stepping into the tower. 'I wouldn't like to be alone with him.'

The words I thought I'd heard him say on my first day hadn't left me. I'd played them out over and over in my mind in the quiet hours of night. Getting up to check my door was locked when I couldn't quite convince myself he hadn't said something about me looking cute while I was asleep.

'He said something to me on my first day that... I don't know. It was weird.'

'What was it?'

Cool air drifted up the staircase and I felt goosebumps travel across my arms. 'He put his legs up so I couldn't get past him on the stairs, and then when I stepped over him, I was sure he said... like...'

'What?' she said, smiling now at the idea of it.

'That I was a pretty little pussy.' After a second, she scoffed, trying to stifle her laughter. 'It didn't feel funny. More like he was threatening me.'

'While you were with Emily?' I nodded. 'He was probably just talking about her. He's had a thing about her for the last couple of years. There were rumours about... Ah, forget it. We don't have time,' she said, as we heard a teacher's voice in the background. Reaching for my hand, she slipped her fingers around mine. 'Come on. Let's go before they catch us.'

We hurried down the stairs and arrived at the courtyard at dusk, running through the cloisters and out through the west gate. The light was already fading by the time we crossed the gardens, but I could still see a few of the statues of the mythological creatures, women with wings, tails instead of legs. Medusa with snakes on her head. Running past them all, we made our way to the cliffs and behind us the lights of the school dimmed through the darkness.

The wind had picked up by the time we reached the edge, and Iris pointed out the first step, marked by a small green bush.

'Start there,' she said, pointing me on. 'Test each rock as you go.'

I did as she told me, but it was clear early on that the concept of steps was a loose application, each one little more than a rock carved by the elements. The surface was damp with spray from the sea, and it was almost impossible to see where I was going in the dark. The only light came from a low crescent moon, and it was barely enough to see the surface of the water below. All I had to guide me was the experience of a few girls ahead, and Iris's guidance from behind.

'Not much further now,' she said, just a step above me as we picked our way down the cliff. I held onto the rocks to my left, listening as the waves broke at the shore into ribbons of light below. 'But careful on the next bit. It's the hardest part.'

Until then I had been unafraid; the route was slippery, but the rocks were solid, my footing strong. But as I navigated the path, I felt my foot sliding, followed by a sprinkle of rocks disappearing into the laughter whistling up from below.

'Shit,' I screamed, my foot mid-air, remembering what Emily had told me about the erosion. Iris grabbed my sleeve as the soil continued to spill out from beneath my foot.

'Stick to the path,' she said, her body brushing against mine to put herself in the lead. Her breath was warm against my cheek as she spoke. 'And follow me. Otherwise you'll get us both killed.'

By the time we neared the bottom of the cliff, all that stood between us and the beach was a large boulder, the surface of it smoothed by the waves. We jumped over it, landing on the soft wet sand below. My whole body ached with the tension of the descent, and as I looked up, I realised that we must have been over twenty metres below the school. Rocks that had fallen from the cliff face pockmarked the beach.

'Right,' she said, flashing me a smile. 'We need something to drink.'

Ahead, some sort of order had taken shape. Cool boxes filled with sea water, beer bottles floating within. Lanterns, the kind you keep in the drawer for when the electricity fails, hung from rocky outcrops along the line of the cliff. *Galvanize* by The Chemical Brothers hummed from a speaker.

'Won't they hear us down here?' I asked.

Iris linked her arm through mine, and led us towards the cool boxes, where we picked up a couple of beers.

'No chance. And even if they do, they usually turn a blind eye.'

'If they check our rooms?' I asked. 'I'm already on a demerit.'

'The only person who would check whether you're in your bed is Emily. And if you look that way,' she said, pointing across the crowded beach, 'you'll see that she's far too wasted to care.' Near the shore, just as Iris had said, I saw Emily looking out to sea. A little unsteady on her feet. Several girls were watching her, laughing as she stumbled along. 'How the mighty fall, right?'

'What's she doing?'

'Probably waiting for Ridgely.'

'She mentioned something about that the other day.'

'The school just up the coast. Look,' she said, swigging on her beer. 'I can see their lights now.' Glancing out to sea I saw several golden cones picking a route through the waves. There one minute, gone the next as their boats dipped and crested. Three lights at first, and then a fourth. A moment later, I thought I could hear the faint buzz of their engines. 'Let's go and see if we can find Stan before she does.'

Adjusting to the light, I saw at least thirty girls hurrying towards the incoming boats. Some boys were already ashore, kissing High Hill girls. Others were laden with bags of clinking glass bottles. Waves lapped against three beached skiffs, with more still coming in.

'Where is he?' Iris said then. 'Do you think he didn't come?'

Another skiff landed on the beach, and I watched as more boys hopped over the side as proficient as seasoned pirates. Cherries of cigarettes drifted through the air as if the night was alive with fireflies. Following Iris's gaze, I scanned the clusters of boys as they disembarked their boats, not sure what I was looking for. It was almost surreal to see so many of them after a summer spent avoiding everybody I used to know. Then I saw Iris raise her hand, and a boy began his approach.

'I thought you said this was only for losers?' he said, laughing.

'I did,' she said as he draped an arm around her neck and pulled her head to his lips. Planted a delicate kiss against her hair. 'But I'm only here for her.' She turned to me, pointing. He was taller than Iris, but something about the way he moved seemed familiar. At first I couldn't quite work out what it was, but then I saw it as they walked side by side. It was their gait. The confidence of it, as if they had people following them. 'Stan, Chloe. Chloe, Stan. My twin brother.'

And I understood then, started to notice the other familiarities. They had the same large eyes, and long lashes. The same caramel skin and dark hair. It made me feel as if I already knew him, as if we shared something between us, even though we had never met before. But while their features were almost identical, he looked older than Iris, his jaw and cheeks already shaped by the chisel of adulthood.

'I don't think I've seen you before.'

'She's new,' Francesca said, joining us. 'Started this year on a scholarship.'

'It's a music scholarship,' Iris told him then. 'She's really good.'

Hearing the word that had been tossed around like an insult so often during my first days at High Hill used so casually came as a relief, and I drank in the simplicity like a shot. Nothing negative attached to its usage, no distaste in his reaction.

'Nice to meet you,' he said as he held out his hand, and I slipped mine into his. 'But these won't do,' he said then, taking the beers we'd picked up. He dropped the bottles to the sand, the liquid pooling from the neck. Then he reached into the plastic bag to retrieve a bottle of vodka. 'Let's celebrate another year of total parental abandonment properly.'

Laughter and excitement took over as Iris grabbed his hand, and they started towards the other side of the beach. Others followed, mainly boys, but Francesca lingered by me.

'Chloe, hang on a moment.'

The last few days I had spent more and more time with Iris, but only occasionally with Francesca, and never alone. Something about her made me less certain about her friendship. I wasn't sure whether it was her occasional judgemental looks, her probing questions or the fact I knew that somewhere in history her family was related to royalty.

'What is it?' I asked, keeping my eye on where Iris was going.

'About the other day, in the belltower.' She sighed, and I wondered if this all seemed a little beneath her. 'Iris mentioned to me that I wasn't very friendly with you, and I just wanted to say that I'm sorry, or whatever.'

'Oh,' I said, surprised at her apology. 'It's okay.'

'Well, Iris told me that it's not, so...' She ran her tongue over her teeth, smiled and waved at a girl behind us that I didn't recognise. 'It's just, Iris is my best friend. Has been since we were ten years old. It's always just been the two of us and...'

Briefly I saw the façade crack, and realised there was a whole other side of Francesca. I already knew that the whole school looked at her with a wariness in their gaze. Jess, a girl I met in the study hall, had asked me only the day before what it was like hanging out with Cruella, and there was no confusion as to who she meant. But beneath that untouchable exterior, there was just a girl who needed her friend. Who needed me not to take her away. And I could remember what it was like to feel excluded.

'Iris has the room next to me, she is just being friendly and...'

'We learned to ride together, okay?' she said then, and I could hear the desperation cutting through her voice. It almost broke before she caught it. 'Every year our families stay at our place in Courchevel at Christmas. I would do anything for her.'

'Fran,' I said, almost sorry for her by then. 'You're still Iris's best friend. I barely know her. But I'm sure we could all be friends if you like.'

And she smiled, closed her eyes. There was something else she intended to say, but didn't. I wondered what it was. 'It's just a bit weird to think I might have to share her, especially with somebody who...'

She pulled herself up before she could finish the sentence. 'Who what?' I asked.

Another sigh, the façade coming down. 'Iris is trusting, lets people in quickly. I don't know you at all as of yet, and as it stands I am undecided as to whether I want to.'

I remembered the way Francesca sniggered then, when Emily was rude to me in English, when she mocked Miss McCabe and made her embarrassed. Any sympathy I felt for her moments ago was gone, and I was no longer under any illusion that I was welcome as far as Francesca was concerned.

'It's fine,' I said, ignoring what I was sure was the truth. 'No hard feelings.'

I went to walk away, thought I might even head back up the cliff and go to bed, when she reached out to touch my arm. 'Where are you going?'

'You just said…'

'That I was uncertain. That doesn't mean I have written you off just yet.' She held out her hand, and with some confusion, I took it. 'And besides, Iris thinks you're just about perfect, so why don't we go and drink ourselves into an oblivion and forget our differences. I assume it is something at which we both excel.'

We found the others behind the sea caves, and took turns in sipping from the bottle of vodka. I felt my head grow lighter each time it went past. I listened to Stan's anecdotes of a life spent by the river, about how he missed his two dogs called Paris and Hector, and I remembered how Iris had said the same. Other stories about life at Ridgely. The initiation ceremonies, the crude things they did together. How only last week they'd had a new boy cross a lintel on the roof in the dark, and I was glad that I had experienced nothing like that. It made the stress of the MDI seem tame. But I drank it all in, this totally different life. The freedom of it, nobody watching over my shoulder. No checking the clock to make sure I was in by curfew. Maybe at High Hill I could do and be anything I chose to be after all. At one point Stan slipped away, came back with a joint which we passed around. But it didn't take long before I started to feel green, the drugs and alcohol swimming around in my system. I stood up, needing somewhere to go, desperate for air.

'Where are you off to?' I heard Iris say, felt her hands slip around my body. 'Come on,' she said, leading me away. 'I'll look after you.' And then we sat down onto the cool sand, away from the rest of the crowd. At some point the memories blur, and I have no idea what happened for a time after that. But I woke a short while later with Iris stroking my hair, a puddle of the food from our formal supper still warm on the sand by my side.

'I'm going to go and find you some water,' she said, and slipped out from underneath me. And while my head was woozy and thick, I realised that while I had been asleep, things had changed. Less people then, the weather turning. The light breeze had strengthened, and the waves had grown louder, their spray wetting us like rain. The lights picked out a few girls already making their way back up the cliff.

'Hello.' Looking up, I saw Stan looming above me. 'Recovered yet?'

'I don't know,' I said. He settled down alongside me, and I thought how he was attractive, that maybe I might fancy him. Or at least that it would be reasonable to have fancied him in another place, another time. Under different circumstances. He had the same scent as his sister, sweet, almost floral. In the dark I would be able to find either of them from that scent alone, pick them out from a crowd. 'I might have drunk a bit too much,' I said.

'You see what happens when we let in the state school scum?' For a second I thought he was serious, until I saw the smirk, the raised eyebrow.

'I seem to remember that it was your sister who gave me the beer, and you who gave me the vodka.'

'And the joint,' he said with a shake of his head. Dark hair flopped before his eyes, twisted into curls from the damp salt air. 'What a terrible cliché we are. Do you know that you are seventy per cent more likely to be offered drugs at a private school than you are at a state school?'

'Is that true?' I asked, knowing that if my parents had heard those statistics, I would never have made it here in the first place.

'It sounds about right. Too much money and no moral guidance. But we need something to help us cope with the terrible conditions we are forced to live in, don't we? And believe me, here is like a bloody hotel in comparison to Ridgely. My window doesn't even close.'

'That's crap.'

'Oh no. That won't do. You mean "dreadful", Chloe. You really must start speaking like the rest of us if you're going to fit in.' I made a mental note, again unsure how serious he was. 'Anyway, my father says it's character building.'

'I met him this week.'

'Oh,' he said with a wince. 'That doesn't sound too good. Was he *dreadful* to you?'

Professor Fairhurst seemed to move through the school in total silence, gliding along as smooth as mist across a calm sea. His suits were double breasted and stiff. Glasses on the brow of his nose, the lenses set in half-moons of thick wire. How he saw through them I wasn't sure.

'He gave me a demerit.'

'Haven't you been here for like a week?'
'Five days.'
'Shit. What did you do?'

Even to think about how it happened made me furious. Scanning the beach, I looked for Emily, found her dancing with her arms slung around some boy's neck. His hands were pushed down the back of her jeans, the button open at the front. All around us there were people behaving as if there was nobody else there. A girl I recognised from Hestia with her top off, another straddled over a boy with her hands pushed inside his trousers. Her arms were moving in an undeniable rhythm. Some of them were dipping in and out of the water wearing only their underwear. Boundaries were blurred here. Parts of us exposed to the others, even those we didn't like. My proximity to Stan vibrated with possibility.

'Emily told him that she found a condom under my bed.'

'Oh dear,' he said with a sigh. 'Did she?'

'It wasn't mine.'

Overhead a gull cawed, and I watched as it circled before coming to rest on a rocky outcrop near the breaking waves. Something glossy wriggled in its beak. Tossing it down, the bird pecked at the prey, tearing off chunks before swallowing them whole.

'She's always been a liar. But if it wasn't yours, does that mean you're a virgin, Miss Carter?'

'What?' I asked, my voice high pitched as I swung to face him. 'Why do you ask?'

'Curiosity,' he said with a shrug. Again I caught the scent of his skin on the air. He gave me a half smile, just one eye creasing up. Just like his sister. 'You see, if you've arrived here without experiencing it, you'd only end up getting swept away into acts of degradation, like the rest of them. I mean, just look,' he said, pointing to a couple having sex just a few metres away. 'When something is unavailable, it's all you can think about.'

I was about to reply, but as I looked up, I could see one of Stan's friends with his hands on Iris's hips. She was laughing, but at the same time I could see that she was trying to wriggle away.

'All of us at some point...' Stan began to say, but I couldn't concentrate. The more Iris fought, the harder the boy tried to hold on. Tension simmered in my gut, my fingers stiffening. I wanted to run over there, pull the boy from my friend. I went to move but found my head was still dizzy, swimming like the surface of the sea. Every fibre in my body loose, frayed. 'Don't worry about her,' he said, following my gaze across the beach. 'Iris can handle herself.'

And as if he had predicted the future, I saw her twist her body and force her elbow back, catching the boy in the jaw. Seconds later she was free, heading over to us with the bottle of water that she had gone to find for me. By the time she crossed the beach I was breathless with what I had seen.

'Shit company you're keeping this year, Stan.'

'Yes, Jack. Total shit to be honest,' he said, frowning. 'Shall I push him overboard for you?'

'Be my guest.' I laughed, more out of nerves than anything, but neither of them did. 'Anyway, did you get it?'

'Not yet.'

'Well, you better be quick. He's over there,' she said, directing her brother to the rear of the beach before taking my hand. A flicker of golden light weaved cloud to cloud, followed by a clap of thunder that shook my insides. 'We need to get back up,' she said to me. 'The tide is already changing, and that storm is coming right for us.' And without so much as a goodbye to her brother, Iris began to pull me towards the steps.

Near the encroaching shore I saw boys scrambling for boats as the rain began to fall, and girls squealed as they ran ahead of us towards the cliff. By the time we reached the steps, the beach was all but clear. We were the last ones.

'Here,' Iris said, holding her hands together like a step. 'You won't reach otherwise.'

Rain blurred my view, my hair sticking to my face as I pushed one foot into her hands. The surface was wetter than earlier, a little slippery, and I had to scuff my way up it. I felt her hands on my backside, pushing me up and over.

'Let me help you,' I said, reaching out a hand, and with a tight grip and a bit of a tug we were both soon on the big boulder at the bottom of the cliff-side path. Glancing back across the beach, I saw Stan lingering by the sea caves. I wondered what he was doing until I saw Jimmy, the caretaker. An exchange of something in a small plastic packet. Then, stuffing whatever it was into his pocket, Stan turned around and ran to the last boat, jumping over the side just as it began to pull away. I saw another boy trying to catch him, waving his hands for them to stop with his trousers still halfway down his legs. His backside was naked and pale as a moon. It was the boy who'd had his hands on Emily earlier.

'Hey,' I heard a voice say then. 'A bit of help here.' I looked down to see Emily standing on the beach below us, reaching up to the boulder. I had thought we were the last. Drunk didn't cut it; her eyes were wide as desert skies and out of focus, her top half-unbuttoned. Schadenfreude welled inside me, and it was hard to fight the smile forming on my lips. 'Reach down to pull me up,' she said. I held out my hand until I felt Iris block me with her own.

'You've managed it before, haven't you?' Iris said, peering over at her. 'Get up here yourself.'

'I've lost my shoes,' she said then. Looked close to tears. I suspected it was the drink more than anything else, although my eyes still drifted towards the boy she had been with, now hauling himself back over the side of a skiff. 'Help me,' she said, more desperately then. 'Please.'

Mascara smudged in dirty tracks across Emily's cheeks, and there was a look of abject desperation on her face. Had she been crying already? Waves crept steadily closer, inching their way up what was becoming a thin stretch of beach. The place we had been sitting earlier was already under water. And with the music and light all gone, an inauspicious gloom seemed to hang over the shore. The mist was thickening, the waves growing louder.

'Iris, come on,' Emily shouted. 'You can't leave me here. I'll drown.'

'That would be terrible, wouldn't it?'

'Yes, it would.' And then stunned when Iris still didn't offer to help, Emily turned to me. 'I could get you in *so* much trouble for this.'

And she was right. Already on a demerit, I could lose the scholarship if I was repeatedly reprimanded. I didn't need Emily as an enemy. Sea spray stung at my eyes.

'We should help her,' I whispered, but Iris wasn't listening.

'You can't demerit somebody for being at a party that's not supposed to be happening, you idiot,' she said, and I could see from the look on Emily's face that Iris was correct. 'Bet that fucking website doesn't seem so funny now, right?' Iris said.

'What?' Emily said, until her thoughts caught up with her. 'Fuck, Iris. Is that what this is about? It was a fucking joke. And besides, it was like two years ago.'

'The same as when you put that condom under Chloe's bed?'

Emily said nothing then, only turned to look at the shore, watching the creep of the tide. Iris was enjoying her fear, I realised, although I was starting to feel anxious about what came next. Then, from the corner of my eye, I saw Jimmy Baxter crossing the beach, coming closer to us.

'Okay,' Emily said. 'It was shit of me. I'm sorry, okay. But you can't leave me here,' she said, looking at Jimmy as he approached. She lowered her voice as the rain grew heavier. 'Not with him.'

Iris looked up then, saw Jimmy for herself.

'Well, well, well,' she said, laughing now. 'Nothing less than what you deserve.'

And then I felt Iris take my hand and pull me towards the steps. Emily was still screaming for help as we climbed, her voice only fading as we reached the middle of the cliffs. But despite what we'd done, as we topped out, the rain falling fast and strong, the thunder roaring overhead, we couldn't stop laughing. Because she did deserve it, didn't she? For what she had done to me, and to Iris. It was justice. It felt incredible to think we had left her there. Audacious as it was stupid. But more than anything, it felt right because we had done it together. It united us. And with our bodies knocking into each other, our clothes wet and slick to our skin, we ran across the manicured gardens, past the goddesses. I felt their judgement as we passed, could almost feel them casting a sentence as we ran. Asking what we had done. Disapproving of our decision. How we had passed a sentence that wasn't ours to pass. But I didn't care. Not then, as I ran towards the school. Because I was with Iris, my hand held tightly in hers. Nothing could touch me if we were together. So I leaned in close, and she wrapped an arm around me, laughing as we ran. And as she pulled me against her wet skin, I could smell the scent of her body, thick and sweet and free.

9

Wet clothes dropped to the floor, and we were still giggling and shivering as we peeled them off. High on it all. Drunk on what we'd done. It was so stupid, so unexpected, so... deliciously deserved. Hurrying under the sheets for warmth, we couldn't stop laughing as we talked it over, looking at it this way and that. Her screams, her wide eyes. She knew she'd be fine, Iris said. She knew Jimmy would help. I wanted so much to believe it.

That night Iris slept in my room, pressed up against the wall, both of us squashed in my single bed. Not that we slept. Instead, I listened as she described her home, the sprawling old estate with its creaky floorboards and wonky walls. Land that stretched for miles into a forest and a river that sometimes broke its banks across the vast garden. Until then I had kept the details of my life to myself, certain that whatever I had experienced to date was no help at a place like High Hill. But that night, while telling her about my modest home, she listened as if it was a story of which I should be proud, asking questions about our life, and what my room was like.

'I'd love to see it,' she said, and under the sheets my fingers found hers. 'Wait,' she said then, leaning up to look over my shoulder. I stopped, and realised what she had heard, footsteps on the other side of the door. Iris brought her finger to her lips. Shadows moved about beneath it. The handle for my door began to turn with a slow precision, as if somebody wanted to catch me unawares. The key rattled in the lock.

'Emily?' I mouthed.

'Jimmy,' she whispered. 'Last term a few girls said they'd seen him in the corridors at night.'

'So it's true?' I said too loudly, causing her to bring her hand up, place it against my mouth. 'He said something the other day about seeing me while I was asleep. I thought it was just bullshit.'

'He's such a fucking creep. Tries the door handles for girls who forgot to lock themselves in. I heard he was caught staring at one of the year twelves while she slept. She doesn't come here anymore.'

'God, that's so gross. I told you he was a weirdo.'

She shrugged. 'I didn't disagree. Emily also found him in her room once.'

'Really?'

She nodded. 'He was wanking while she slept.'

'Are you kidding me?' She shook her head. 'I feel shit about leaving her with him now.'

More footsteps then, as whoever it was hurried away. By the time we convinced ourselves to open the door to check he was gone, my whole body was trembling with the thought he was telling the truth about staring at me while I slept.

'Just keep your door locked at night,' she said. 'If you like, we can sleep together. It's definitely safer.'

After that, Iris asked about my parents, how we celebrated Christmas, holidays and weekends. She said that she had seen my father's painting in the National Gallery last summer, even described it, the colours, the way the ship acquiesced to the wind. It was the first night when I didn't feel like I was two separate people, or an imposter living a lie.

'And your old school?' she said then. The faces of my old friends in the little frame by my bed caught my eye. 'What was it like?'

'Shit, mainly,' I said. Didn't want to add anything more.

'I heard something,' she said then when sleep was already settling in. 'A rumour about it.'

'What rumour?' I asked, aware of my heart pounding, the flush of fear spreading over my chest and face. 'What did you hear?'

The moonlight picked out the whites of her eyes, the rain still drumming against the window. It seemed like a lifetime before she spoke again. 'Just that it was a shit place to be.' And then she turned over, tucked herself under the covers. 'Let's get some sleep. I have an essay about the crisis of monarchy in Stewart Britain I have to finish tomorrow.'

Weeks passed like that, of broken curfews and sleepless nights. Without any further incidents with Emily. There had been only a few times we had come into contact, a few MDIs, and during each she had behaved as if I didn't exist. Behind her cold face I could tell she was fuming about what happened, but I was grateful she didn't mention it and did nothing more to upset the status quo we had tentatively forged. Routines at the school became second nature, and I began to find my way around without navigating by way of the goddesses. I made friends, learned their names. Coursework was tough, and the teachers expected much more of me than they had at Clifton. I spent hours at my little desk, or in the study halls under the glow of golden lights. But of all my teachers, nobody expected more than Mr Aides. At every practice session he insisted that I could be better, the best. And three weeks into life at High Hill, he told me I was ready for my first performance. Hours had gone into it, early mornings and late nights. Sunday morning Chapel was to be my moment. And although I was tired from the hours of effort, life at High Hill had begun to feel like my own, and when I spoke to my parents for the first time after week four drew to a close, I realised that it felt as if life with them no longer quite fitted.

'Did you manage them?' Iris asked as she turned up at the door on the fourth Sunday at High Hill. It was the first time I had tried to braid my own hair. Until then Iris had been doing it for me, executing the style in less than a minute for each braid. I turned to show her, securing the last elastic band.

'What do you think?'

'Not terrible,' she said, reaching up to poke in a few bumps that had escaped. 'Are you ready for your performance?'

'Chop chop, Fourteen.' Francesca arrived in the doorway, flushed cheeks, a blunt fringe which she had cut in herself only the week before. 'Your best friend is on the prowl.' I looked around at the mess on the bed, pyjamas cast to the floor. A pot of hair gel that Iris had left there, leaking onto my desk. She was always leaving a mess behind her, things pulled out of drawers, clothes left out on the floor. Always denied it too. 'If Emily sees this mess, you're fucked.'

'She won't do anything,' Iris said. 'Not since the beach. She admitted that she was behind the website and the condom.'

'You think she's forgotten what you did?' Francesca asked, stepping into my room, and reaching into my tuck box to take a cookie. She picked up the gel, replaced the lid, before grabbing my pyjamas from the floor to stuff them in my trunk. 'She's just biding her time. And the beach is the reason why.'

'She wouldn't dare,' Iris insisted. 'Especially not after what happened last term.'

It was the second time something had been mentioned that made me question Emily's past. The first time Iris challenged Emily in my room she had suggested she should be on a demerit. Even on the stairs on the way down to the party I had thought she was about to tell me something. Since then Iris had told me about Jimmy being in her room, but this sounded more like a mistake Emily had made herself. And now there it was again.

'What happened last term?' I asked.

Francesca looked at Iris, who said nothing. Didn't even move.

'There was a rumour,' Francesca said, reaching into my cupboard to pull my blue velvet cape from the hanger. Since our talk at the beach we seemed to have formed a sort of truce. She had accepted I was around, and as the days together passed, she had started to include me in things she would normally do with Iris alone. Twice she had knocked on my door on a Sunday to see if I wanted to go for a walk, even though Iris had already refused. Last week she had mentioned the annual trip to Courchevel, which bars they would be drinking in for après-ski, and how she was going to tick off Le Grand Couloir. I had no idea what that was.

'There's no way,' Iris had responded, before turning to me to add, 'it's an eighty per cent gradient, and the first traverse is an absolute mentality killer.' Back to Francesca. 'We both panicked last year, and you know it.'

'You can thank my father for that,' she said with some resentment. 'But I did some off-piste in Espace Killy in March, and those black runs were way harder.' Francesca smiled when Iris seemed to concede, before turning to me. 'Do you ski?' I shook my head, didn't have the words for any further explanation. I knew I was in the kind of environment where to ski was second nature. Just one of the many things that marked me as different. Even the question screamed it. Francesca herself was due to represent Great Britain in the Winter Olympics in Turin the following year, and would have already at Salt Lake City but her father had panicked after the September 11 terrorist attacks, and forced her to pull out. 'It doesn't matter,' she reasoned, shrugging her shoulders. 'There are some green runs, and the family snow park.' Iris slapped her on the leg. 'What? I was being nice,' she said, and they both keeled over laughing. 'Anyway, you should totally come,' Francesca continued, rolling back on the bed as Iris continued the play fight. I had no idea whether the offer was genuine. I already knew I wouldn't go. I watched as Iris tickled Francesca, my jaw tight as their laughter grated, all the while wishing they would stop.

Francesca hoisted the blue cape over my shoulders and turned me around so she could fasten the clip. Everyone protested that they hated the formal cape, reserved for special occasions and Sunday Chapel, but I liked it. It felt different to anything I had known before. Made me feel as if anything was possible.

'Somebody said they saw Emily with Jimmy in the forest,' she said, tapping her fingers against the golden clasp of my cape to show I was ready. 'She was giving him a blow job.'

'Eww,' I said, closing my eyes to drive away the image. 'Was it true?'

'Apparently,' Iris added. 'There were a few people who said they saw them. Gross, right?'

'Whether it was gross or not,' Francesca said, slipping an arm through mine, 'nobody is kicking her out. Not with how much money her parents donate to the school every year. That's why she's the head prefect and you are on a demerit. If we mention it she can fuck up our school record. I won't get into LSE with a suspension on file.' With her connections to royalty I doubted that was true. 'So get a move on. Everybody is already in Chapel, and they are all waiting for the prodigy to play.'

We followed the main staircase down to the west wing, before heading through West Gate to join the path that wove through the gardens to the chapel.

Sundays were supposed to be quiet, so we made no conversation. But in the silence of the misty morning, the incident at the beach resurfaced in my mind. Some nights I'd play it out, thinking about the what ifs. Realising how bad it could have been if Jimmy hadn't been there to help Emily. But also now, if it was true what Francesca told me, that she was left with him after the shame of that gossip… it didn't feel good. I knew what it was to be the butt of the rumours at school. I kept telling myself that it was just a joke, that we meant no harm. But the truth was we hadn't thought it through at the time. It could have ended much worse. And I believed Francesca; any silence on Emily's part was nothing more than a temporary truce while she planned on how best to get her revenge.

Columns rose left and right through the centre of the church, and the ceiling was domed like the chapels of Athens that my father had shown me years before. It was the most beautiful and serene part of the school.

'Good luck,' Iris whispered to me as she and Francesca took their seats near the middle of the church.

'Thank you,' I replied, continuing up the aisle, my cape brushing along the ground. I took my place in the front row as I had been told to. Rows and rows of blue hoods made every one of us look the same. Then her voice whispered over my shoulder.

'I heard they were going to let you sit up here.' With her blue hood still up and covering her head, I hadn't seen Emily was sitting in the seat behind mine. Next to her was Catherine, her skinny friend who could have been a carbon copy of Emily herself. 'You don't belong up here.'

'Aides wants to hear her play,' Catherine said. 'He must be the only one.'

'When I tell Professor Fairhurst what she did, she'll never play here again. She'll be back at Clifton before she can say "please, sir, can I have some more".' Spoken in a breathy whisper, I didn't want to ask what it was she meant. I already knew. 'You left me on the fucking beach.' Her lips were tight, puckered. Little creases wrinkled around her eyes as her gaze locked in on me. 'I could have died.'

'Jimmy was there,' I protested. And the quip came to me. The offer of a win. I was saying it before I even realised. 'We thought you'd like a chance to be alone with him.'

Another girl at my side sniggered, and I saw the recognition on Emily's face. So Francesca had been correct. And as Emily sat back, I realised I'd scored a point.

'Just know...' she said, her voice lowered to a whisper, 'that you'll regret what you did. I'll make sure of it.'

That was when I felt a hand on my shoulder, a gentle touch designed not to startle. Turning, I saw Mr Aides, dressed in a black suit, a crisp, well-pressed shirt. Even his hair was different when he came to Chapel, gelled into place, a side parting with the precision of a blade. Old Hollywood. I could imagine him on a red carpet, gracing the pages of a glossy magazine. The blond highlights of summer were gone.

'Are you ready?' I gave him a nod, still aware of Emily behind me. 'Great. Father John will give his welcome, and when it's time I'll call you over. Okay?'

'All rise.'

Mr Aides returned to his seat as Father John's words hollered out from the back of the church, followed by the three solid strikes of the wooden school staff on the stone ground. With grace the vicar stepped forwards, bringing a large, leather-bound bible to rest on the stone altar before us. Shadows gripped the church that morning. Outside, I could hear the waves breaking against the rocks.

Father John's sermon went on and on, and over time people grew restless. I lost track of what he was reading to us, something from Job about unmerited suffering. While he spoke I ran over my performance in my head, my fingering, the dynamics, where to be careful of a mistake. At one point I caught the gaze of Mr Aides, and when he rolled his eyes I had to stifle a laugh.

'And with that, I invite one of our newest family members to share her gifts with us.'

It took a moment and a nod from Mr Aides to realise that was my cue. So I hurried across, sat at the piano. Mr

Aides drew close to me, his breath hot against my ear as he removed my hood and spoke.

'Give me everything,' he whispered. 'Leave nothing behind. And show them you are more than just a rumour.'

His words froze me. What did he mean, more than just a rumour? Was he talking about what happened at the beach? Or was he talking about something else? Something about my old life at Clifton? I turned, and he was still there, leaning in, his gaze on me. Close enough I could hear his breaths.

'When you're ready,' he said.

With a nod to the crowd, I turned to see the endless number of blue hoods, like an ocean of cresting waves. Everybody waiting on me. A quiet had settled over the chapel. And while his comment had unnerved me, I knew beyond anything that my performance that day was a test, a chance to prove that I was worthy of my place there. But I knew that it could easily become a public execution. So I took a breath, steadied my trembling fingers and began.

And with the first notes out of the way the congregation disappeared into nothing, as if a strong wind had swept them up, carried them all away. I had chosen a difficult piece, one I had often struggled with, but which I knew would leave the right impression even if I missed a few notes. And I did, I knew that. But as I drew to a close on Chopin's *Fantaisie-Impromptu*, not a sound broke the silence of the church. Each and every one of them was lost in the spell I had cast.

I don't know who started the applause, but within moments the whole crowd had joined in. Somehow, I found Emily's miserable face in the crowd before anybody else's. She was, as far as I could see, the only one who was not clapping. Even Catherine looked impressed.

'Chloe.' The voice was low, words whispered into my ear from behind. I didn't turn. His breaths were shallow. His gaze unflinching. I could feel it without even having to look. 'I don't know what to say. You were incredible, and that performance was…'

I turned, and the way he looked at me, his unwavering attention, the graze of his eyes across my body… I had experienced that before. And I knew in that moment he had seen something in me that I had tried to hide, but like a wild creature had broken free, and was now loose. I was not in control of it. Any power my performance had afforded me was lost after that. And I wanted to run. Wanted to get as far away as I could. Because his was a look I knew from my time at Clifton. A look of admiration, of undeniable interest. A look that came with a heavy cost.

It was the price that I had paid for my place at High Hill.

It was a price that I didn't want to have to pay again.

10

Hurrying from Chapel, I exited onto the manicured lawns, desperate for air. But as I tried to get away I was held back by praise and excitement, even from girls who had yet to speak to me before that day. Everybody wanted to congratulate me on my performance. Under normal circumstances it would have felt good, as if I had been accepted, but I wanted only to get to my room. To lock the door and pretend none of it had happened. That look Mr Aides had given me, something dark behind his eyes that I recognised. That I had seen before... I didn't want to go there. Not again. But before I was halfway across the first lawn, I felt somebody who I couldn't ignore touching my arm.

'Chloe.' I looked up to find Miss McCabe glassy-eyed and red-cheeked. 'What I just witnessed was... what I heard you do, I...' She fumbled around for the right words. 'Chloe, what I am trying to say is that you were magnificent.'

'She's right about that.'

His voice settled over me like a heavy fog, and when I looked up I saw Mr Aides heading across the lawn with his hands in his pockets. A half smile, camouflaged by a bright flare of sunlight cast across his face.

Run, a voice implored me. *Get away from him.*

He arrived alongside us, and I felt myself shrink.

'I had thought you might hang around at the end, so that we might talk it over.'

'Oh, you know these young ladies,' Miss McCabe said then. I wasn't sure whether it was my imagination, but I thought for a moment she took a step closer to me, putting herself between us both. 'Little spare time for the likes of us, Mr Aides. Especially on a Sunday.'

A laugh came from his closed lips. 'Well, that is true,' he said, turning to me. 'And I'm sure you have plenty of other things to do with your weekend. But in light of what I've just heard, I've had some preliminary thoughts about the choices for your university auditions. Perhaps you might call by my office this afternoon? Perhaps around four? Five?'

'Mr Aides,' Miss McCabe said, and I felt the reprimand as if it was directed at me. 'As we have just made quite clear, today is Sunday. It's the girls' day off. Surely you must appreciate the sanctity of our routine here.'

I liked Sundays. Homework by the fire, too many snacks and no watching the clock. Doing each other's make-up and playing games like truth or dare behind locked doors. I didn't want to go to his office. I understood the way he looked at me. I didn't want to play his games.

'An imposition on Miss Carter's time, most certainly,' he added, 'but a talent like hers requires very careful management, Miss McCabe. We must make sure we adequately prepare if she is to receive an offer from one of her preferred institutions. You are aware she is hoping to attend Cambridge? An audition there requires careful preparation.'

'Are you, my dear?' I nodded, and Miss McCabe regarded me for a moment, before breaking into a smile. 'Which college?'

'Trinity, I think.'

'An excellent choice,' she said, beaming. 'I myself am an alumni of King's. What a time it was, looking at sculptures all day, discussing their discovery. Translating Ovid's *Metamorphoses*. What a wonderful poem. We might cover that next term, actually.'

'An incredible text,' Mr Aides said.

'Indeed it is, Mr Aides.' Talk of her university days softened her approach, and I sensed her relent. 'Unscheduled meetings are sometimes necessary when such important matters are at stake. Would that be all right with you, dear?'

'Okay,' I said.

'I'll be expecting you then,' Mr Aides said, and I took his nod as my cue to slip away.

On the way back to my room, several other students stopped me, all wanting to congratulate me on my performance. But as I arrived at the foot of the staircase that led to my dorm in the north wing, Emily was waiting for me, as if she knew I was on my way.

'Well, well, well,' she said, her arms crossed, a smirk on her face. 'Turns out that you can play.' I came to a stop before her, and this time held my head up straight, while she picked dirt from the underside of a fingernail. 'But let's not pretend that your skills on the piano are the real reason you are here.' Heat flushed to my cheeks. 'We both know why you were removed from your old school.' Her eyes moved up and down my body. I tried to hold her gaze. 'You were kicked out for fucking a teacher.'

It was strange then, to remember it. So long had passed since that day last April when Mr Lyons, my maths teacher, had unlocked the door to the storeroom and asked me to step inside. By then it was almost routine to follow him at the end of the fifth period, to let him do the things he wanted. Nothing about that day had stood out from the rest, until the door was opened by another member of staff, and whatever had been happening between us, along with my time at Clifton, came to an end.

'Aren't you going to say anything?' Emily pushed. 'Why don't you ask me how I know? Or what I'm going to do?' But I was frozen, couldn't speak. 'Maybe you don't care. Maybe you can't wait to get back there. If that's how you feel, I'll do you a favour, tell everybody about how you let one of the teachers cum all over you.'

'You'll do no such thing, Emily.' Turning, I saw Mr Aides, standing a few steps behind. How had he got there so fast? Was he following me? Surely there was no other reason for him to be in my wing. 'I for one will make sure of it.'

Tears rushed to my eyes, vomit thick in my throat. Despite Mr Aides' threat, her laughter went on as I pushed past them both to run up the stairs. I ran along the corridor, stopping outside Iris's room. I wanted the comfort of her friendship, could hear her moving around inside. But as I reached for the handle, I realised that if I went to her then I'd have to explain what was wrong. I'd have to tell her about what I had done with Mr Lyons. About the way I had unbuttoned my shirt when he asked me to. How I'd pulled my bra aside while he touched himself. That I had told him I liked it, and had begged him not to stop seeing me when he said it was getting too dangerous. I'd have had to tell her about that Saturday when I lied to my parents, telling them I was in town with Laura, when instead I went to his house, where he made us ham sandwiches and strawberry milkshakes, and where, at his request, I had worn yellow cotton shorts and a rainbow T-shirt. Shorts that became dirtied with a patch of his semen. Shorts which were folded into my drawer at home, and which for some inexplicable reason I couldn't bear to throw away.

So I continued up the corridor and locked my door behind me. And that's when I saw the envelope on my bed. The logo of High Hill, the crest from the flag of the belltower in the top left corner. The motto underneath, *Nemo sine vitio est*. Sliding my finger under the flap, I opened the envelope and pulled out the contents inside. Sheet music for *Fantaisie-Impromptu*. The piece I had just performed. It was in a plastic sleeve, the paper brown, the letters calligraphic. A note attached to the top.

> *A small gift to say thank you for the wonderful music. Simon Aides x*

It fell from my hand to the floor, and I threw myself on the bed, closed my eyes. But as I did, all I could see was Mr Lyons' bloated face close to mine, before morphing into the face of Mr Aides, and the way he looked at me when I finished playing. His request to go to his office. Was that why? Did he know what had happened? He had certainly overheard what Emily said on the stairs, so had he invited me because he expected the same? He had even told me to play well, so I could be more than just a rumour. Tears blurred my vision, soaked into the rough cotton of my pillowcase.

What was wrong with me?

I cried for hours, but at some point I must have fallen asleep, because it was the scream that woke me later that night. By then a dark sky filled the small window, and the air was goosebump cold. I turned over, checked the clock. A little before two in the morning. I thought I must have been dreaming at first, but then another scream echoed from the other side of my door. Rain drummed the roof and glass.

'Call for an ambulance,' somebody shouted. A male voice.

'She's dead,' somebody else screamed. 'She's fucking dead.'

Hurrying, I pushed myself from my bed, opened my door to see lights skipping across the courtyard. Rain washed over the stone corridor, but still I stepped out into the wet cloisters and looked over the wall to see a gathering crowd on the grass below. Somebody used a torch to shine a light across the ground, and that was when I saw it. A body. Face up, legs and arms twisted at unnatural angles. White-blonde hair splayed out like the snakes on Medusa's head. Another torch beam settled across her face, and I saw the vacant eyes. The bloody wound. The strange, deformed shape of her skull. But I knew who it was.

It was Emily.

'For God's sake, somebody call the police.'

I gasped for air, my hands pressed to the wall. Driving rain drenched my face. Still I couldn't look away. But it wasn't shock that kept me staring in that dreadful moment. Not the memory of Eloise Cunningham, or the horrible way history was repeating itself. Wasn't even fear or regret or grief. I felt no sadness for the fact that she was gone.

Instead it was a sense of relief; the person who had threatened to expose what I had done at Clifton was dead.

Before

11

It's hard not to picture that night, her body lying on the ground as we drive away from the prison through the wet London streets. I focus dead ahead, but Aides watches the city as if it's magic. Enchanted by laundrettes and pubs, Royal Parks and stucco homes. Life, and everything that I have taken for granted for the last twenty years. His last words to me before we left the prison carpark linger.

You're not the only one with secrets, Chloe.

It is half an hour later when I pull up outside a pub on the outskirts of London. I park up in a small carpark, and we run for the nearest door, avoiding the puddles. My hair hangs in wet clumps by the time we step inside. Even at this time, early afternoon on a wet day, a fledgling crowd has gathered, those clocking off from nearby offices. And inside it's the kind of place that feels as if I've been here before, even though I know I haven't. There's a naval theme, blue panelling and lots of brass. Large Georgian windows overlook the river. Canary Wharf rises into a distant mist, and the O2 arena sits like a giant's crown across the river. London in all its peculiar glory.

We order two glasses of a thick red wine that he chooses, before taking a seat at a small round table. A fireplace crackles and spits by our legs, and a dog unconcerned by the heat stretches out across the flagstone floor. Ordinarily I might reach down to stroke it, but all I can do is watch as Aides removes his coat, settles himself down on the chair. His gaze ravishes the details, as if he can't quite get enough. I listen to every one of his audible breaths.

'To be here, in a place like this…' he eventually says. His hands fold into his body, his head low. 'And with you. I have barely dared imagine such a day.'

To any other person we might be two old friends, or a father and daughter, meeting up for the first time in years. Estranged after some terrible but regrettable disagreement. But that's not what we are. I bite the inside of my cheek until the metallic taste of blood washes down my throat.

'Tell me what you meant,' I say.

He gives a nod, as if only now he has decided to continue.

'I called you here not to wield some sort of power over you, Chloe, but to try to help. If I'm honest, as nice as it is to see you, I'd rather have never had to think about what happened at High Hill ever again.' He sips at the wine, closes his eyes to savour the taste. Heat from the fire bears down on my skin as intense as a lion's bite. 'But I contacted you, Chloe, because I believe you're in danger.'

'What?' Of all the things I expected him to say, this was not it. 'Why?'

Linking his hands together, he leans against the table. After a sharp breath, a lick of his lips, he begins. Behind the bar, a glass smashes against the floor to a mix of laughter and complaint.

'Twenty years inside, Chloe, and I have met a lot of different people. Inmates come and go. Some more than once. But I never expected to meet somebody that I had known on the outside.'

'Who?'

Another sigh. 'Jimmy Baxter, the old caretaker. You must remember him?'

'Of course I do. He testified against you. Said you were in the belltower on the night Emily died.'

Nodding his head, he sips more of his wine. 'Yes. Hard to forget the face of a man who does that. But it seemed that time, or the drugs, had blunted his memory, as he didn't remember me at all. At least not at first. And I was rather glad to be honest. When I realised who he was I expected him to try to use the past against me. Blackmail is rife in prison, Chloe. Rumours spread like plague through a ship, especially those that involve...' Whatever he was going to say slips into the abyss between us. 'Anyway, he had no idea who I was, so I kept a wide berth for a while. Couldn't stand his incessant talking if I'm honest. At least, that was, until I realised what he was talking about.'

Just then the server comes over, carrying two large plates of food that we ordered on our way in. 'Shepherd's pie?' she says, smiling at us both.

'That's for me,' I say, and she sets my plate down. The chicken on Aides' plate is large, the skin golden and crisp. The mound of potatoes piled high.

'Goodness me,' he says with a smile as she places it before him.

'I'll bring some cutlery for you,' the server adds. 'Would you like any sauces?'

'No, thank you,' he says, looking up at her. And I recognise the way she holds his gaze. Twenty years in prison has done nothing to dull his shine. Even now, in the simple grey prison-issue T-shirt, with a lined face and silver hair that mottles his temples, he has cast a spell over her. She must be twenty years younger than him, but one look is all it takes. How easily he could leave here with her today. How simple it would be for him to get what he wants.

'I don't think I'm going to be able to eat all this,' he says after she has left. 'But anyway, we were talking about Baxter. It took a few weeks, but eventually he realised who I was. And it was the first time I witnessed a shred of humility. Until then he had been full of himself, talking about his money and homes on the outside, but when he realised who I was, I saw a bit of that hopeless young man who worked at High Hill. And so I asked him why. Why did he lie at my trial.' Aides leans in, his eyes on me. Voice so low that I get close enough to feel his breath against my face when he talks. 'You know what I'm talking about, don't you?'

I say nothing. Don't even move.

'Anyway, he told me that he was keen to make amends. They thought it was him, you know that, right? Even now there are questions about his behaviour at the time.' Knuckles in his fist burn white hot. 'Anyway, he told me that he had a proposition for me. Told me all about a scheme he had going on the outside. Said that I could get a cut of the proceeds. You know, as payback. What he said he owed me. Because the truth is, nobody wants an enemy in prison, Chloe. Not even idiots like Baxter.' His teeth clamp down, vice-like, turning the bones in his jaw silvery white. 'Until then I had assumed his bravado and talk of money was all a façade, but as it turned out he had developed quite the entrepreneurial mindset. He was running a lucrative extortion racket and was getting paid by those to whom he'd given a false alibi. Others whose secrets he had managed to learn.' His pupils narrow, edged by a ring of fire. 'Including those who he knew had lied in a trial.'

The server returns with our cutlery, sets it down on the table. She catches my eye, and then looks at Simon Aides. It's as if she's wondering how he'd be here with the likes of me. My clothes feel tatty, my hair a mess. After she leaves, I watch as he pulls both knife and fork from the napkin. He sets them down at the side of his plate, his gaze resting on the blade.

'Chloe, Baxter told me that he was extorting Francesca. He had seen her one day, entering the prison to talk to a client. Got her details from his cell mate. He's been taking large sums of money from her for the last five years.'

Heat from my food forms a film of condensation on my face. Either that or I am sweating. I can't tell. I wipe my upper lip and push my plate away.

'That's not true. Francesca would never pay a man like Jimmy. She has no reason to. We didn't lie at your trial.'

'Chloe, I am telling you the truth. He told me, and after I found out I wrote to you to warn you.' I freeze as he rests his large, neat fingers over mine. My eyes burn with the sight of it, blind like I'm staring at the sun. To touch him. To be touched. I have feared this moment. Have waited for it. 'He knows where she works, where she exercises, where she buys her gluten-free bread. Where she lives,' he says, clamping down on me. 'Baxter's not the little shit he used to be, Chloe. He's a dangerous man.'

Brown spots mark the back of his hand, and when he notices me looking at it, he eases off, pats the back of mine as gently as he has in the past.

'I know this is not what you want to hear,' he says. 'But when he told me what he was doing, you were the first person I thought about.'

'Why?'

A sigh, as if he thinks the answer is obvious. 'Because you lied in court, Chloe. All of you lied to send me to prison.'

'No.' I hold the lie up like a shield. No, no, no. I have told myself it's the truth for twenty years. I'm not ready for this. 'I didn't lie.'

'You did. But it doesn't matter. Not anymore. I have completed my sentence, and I am free. But when Baxter told me what he was planning, against my better judgement, I knew I had to protect you. That was when I wrote you that letter.'

The pendulum swings between gratitude and something else. A feeling of old, drilling through me like a nail through wood. Can feel it from my guts to my fingers. Every one of his words coursing through my body like the venom of a well-meaning snake. Wrapping around me, choking me in his hold, just because he wanted to show me how much he cared.

'You're wrong. I told the truth in court. Francesca too.' Anytime I doubted it, all I had to do was think back to that day on the stairs when Emily threatened me, when he told her he would make sure she didn't tell anybody else my secrets. It was a direct threat. She died the same day. 'You went to prison because you took somebody's life.'

'No, Chloe. I did not.' He takes the knife and slices through the meat until he strikes bone. Takes a huge bite, speaks while he chews. 'But that's not what's important now. What matters is Francesca's decision to stop paying him a couple of months ago. Baxter was furious. He said he was going to make her pay for that. And then he told me that once he was out, the next person he would be looking for was you.'

Heat surges through me like a tsunami, smashing every line of defence I have put between me and the past. 'And when is he released?'

Another sigh, another sip of wine. 'He's already out, Chloe. He was released last week. And he's coming for you.'

Before

12

'Get back to your rooms,' the teacher screamed from the end of the corridor. Things were happening quickly, the whole school mobilised in response. 'Nobody is allowed out until we say so.'

Other voices coming from the lower floors were shouting the same thing. Wails of grief and whispers of panic echoed through the cloistered halls. People wanted to know what had happened. Who it had happened to. I stepped back inside my room, knocked the wall to communicate with Iris, but no reply came. The wind whipped through my open door, scattered half-finished essays from the desk to the floor. Within minutes the fire alarm started to ring. A school on high alert.

Unable to keep still, I changed into my jeans and a jumper. Then I saw the flicker of a light against the rain-soaked window, so I pressed myself against it to see a police car tearing up the driveway. I imagined how the pool of blood on the pathway had grown. Closing my eyes, I could see her broken body. The deformed, broken head. Over the next twenty minutes a rolling fog crept in from the sea, slowly enveloped the school.

In the earliest hours after her death, time became fluid. Had the same strange quality of a dream. At some point we were allowed to leave our rooms, although I remember little about it. I recall trying to talk to Iris ahead of me in the line, being shouted at by the teachers to keep quiet. We were marched through the cold cloisters, down the stairs towards the Great Hall, where we were all forced to wait. They filled the time with headcounts, list of names and blankets draped over us against the cold. Teachers stood on guard at each of the doors. They did not want to lose anybody else that night.

'Girls,' came the voice. Looking up, I saw Miss McCabe dressed in her robe, the ends of it swishing about underneath a thick parka coat. Drips of rainwater trickled to the floor at her feet. 'Girls, can I have your attention please.' Murmurings swept through the hall, nobody really listening. Until then we had been threatened into silence. I reached for Iris, who was yet to say a word. 'Please? Can you all face this way?'

'Everybody!' Another voice, deep and loud, it cut through our conversation. 'Come on.'

Looking up I saw that it was Mr Aides, although he seemed unlike any version of him that I recognised. Dressed in a tracksuit, he looked more like a PE teacher than the director of music. His hair was soft and flat to his head, instead of stiff with gel. Like he'd just stepped out of the shower.

'Thank you, Simon,' Miss McCabe said to him once all was silent. 'Girls, I think most of you know by now what has happened, so I am not going to rehash the details of it here. Some of you even had the misfortune to see it for yourselves. But Emily Ashbourne has tragically died.' After pulling a tissue from her coat pocket, she stopped to wipe her eyes. Even from where I was sitting, left of the main fireplace and underneath the wall-mounted statue of

Athena, I could see the tremble of her hands. And yet it surprised me how normal it seemed already, to hear such a thing and not be surprised. I had watched as they strapped her body to the stretcher as if she could still be saved, heavy and unmoving as a wet rag. 'What has happened here tonight is a total... a total...' she tried again, her voice breaking. 'Oh goodness,' she said, her words disintegrating into a snivel as she pulled back. 'Simon, could you please take over.'

Mr Aides, Simon, offered out his arms and held her. We all watched, unable to breathe as she rested against him.

'Imagine if they are shagging.'

Turning, I saw Francesca was just behind me, trying her best not to smile.

'Fran,' I said, remembering the music he had left in my room. The thing he had said to Emily. The thing that had sounded like a... threat. 'He's just a nice man,' I said, as much to reassure myself as anything. He would never have hurt Emily, would he?

'As Miss McCabe was saying, we understand that what has happened tonight is going to be a big shock for all of you.' He stared at us all, uncoordinated, and unsure. I wondered if he'd had a few drinks. That was what it was, I told myself. Nothing more than that. Nothing like... guilt. 'We are going to try and support you in any way we can. Over the course of the next few hours you'll each be given the chance to call home and speak with your parents. Anybody who wants to leave will of course be allowed to. But I'm afraid before all that there are some practical matters that must be addressed.'

As if the whole scene had been choreographed, the doors of the Great Hall opened with a creak and a rush of chilly air, and two plain-clothes police officers approached, followed by several dressed in uniform, who assumed position around the perimeter of the hall. Miss McCabe watched with horror as the suited police officers arrived at her side.

When the officer spoke, his voice echoed around the hall with the force of a thunder crack.

'Thank you, Mr Aides,' the detective who seemed to be in charge said. He was a big man, the kind that would make any woman feel small. 'As of two hours ago when the body of Emily Ashbourne was discovered, you have all become part of an active police investigation.' The thrill of it rippled through the room. 'We are going to have to speak to each of you and establish exactly what you may or may not have seen. Because I'm afraid that based upon our initial findings, what happened here tonight was no accident. Your friend and fellow pupil Emily Ashbourne was murdered.'

13

House by house I watched the other girls go. Artemis was called before us, leaving Athena as the last house to be questioned. Iris and I were some of the few left in the silence of the Great Hall. Even the fire they had lit to keep us warm was going out by then. Dawn was breaking outside. Miss McCabe was sitting on a bench near the hearth.

'I can't believe it,' I said, shuffling over to be closer to Iris. For the first time since we left our rooms, she turned around, looked straight at me. Her eyes were wide as moons. 'I saw her, you know?'

'Emily?' she asked.

'Yes. On the grass of the courtyard. After she fell. Helen's scream woke me.' Those of us in the north wing had all seen Helen leaving the school, taken by the police to meet her parents on the driveway. Iris's breathing became ragged, her lip trembling. 'It's going to be okay, Iris. I know it's awful, but...'

'Don't you get it?' she said then, reaching for me. Her nails dug into my wrist. 'We left her on the fucking beach with no way to get up, Chloe, and now she's fucking dead. That looks really bad. They'll think I wanted to hurt her.'

I knew she was right, evidenced by the fact I had gone over it in my mind a million times since. Regret didn't even cover the choice we made that night. And guilt was rising inside my gut like bile; when I had seen her dead body, it was relief I had felt, not sadness or fear. But despite that, what happened at the beach was the best part of a month ago. Surely it was forgotten by now? Nobody would put that stupid, drunk decision together with what had happened to Emily tonight, would they?

'Nobody would think—'

'Girls! You heard what the police said,' Miss McCabe bellowed as I went to reassure her. 'No talking.'

Turning away from me then, Iris returned to biting her nails. Until that moment I hadn't really thought about the optics of what we'd done in relation to what had transpired that night. But as they called us to take our turn with the police and we wove our way through the cloisters, past the spot where Emily fell, I realised how little we had considered the consequences of our prank. The danger that could have come from a split-second decision. But as we took our seats outside Professor Fairhurst's office, the look on Iris's face made me glad of her continued silence.

'Miss Carter.' Half an hour later, the last to go in. The door opened, and I saw Professor Fairhurst waiting for me, a weariness I had never seen in him before. He stood back, making room for me to pass. 'Please. Come in.'

The office was still dark, only a few of the lamps turned on. Everything was the same as it was the last time I was there. His large oak desk covered by files and books, slightly closer to the window than the door. A threadbare rug at an angle on the wooden floor. Boards creaked underfoot as I crossed.

'Take a seat, Chloe,' Professor Fairhurst said, and I did as I was told. Across the desk, the oversized police detective was sitting with his elbows on the surface, his hands crossed and pressed against his chin.

'Hello,' he said, the same gruff voice, but this time quieter. Another stood at his side, younger, softer, with hair creeping out the neck of his shirt. 'My name is DS Winterburn. I appreciate that this has been a long night, so I'll get to the point.' He straightened a notepad before him on the desk. 'Were you friends with the deceased?'

It sounded so final, so unlike anything I had ever imagined before.

'Not really.'

Professor Fairhurst stepped forward. 'Chloe has only joined us this academic year, Detective Winterburn. She has had little time to make friends as yet.'

'But you knew Emily, right?' I nodded. 'She was the prefect in charge of your house.'

'That's right.'

A beat before he spoke. 'Another girl mentioned that you hadn't got off to the best start. Something about a demerit, and an incident at the beach?'

So, Iris was right. People were putting it together. Professor Fairhurst shifted at my side, and he gave me a nod. 'We are well aware of the party, Chloe. I don't suspect you were responsible for its organisation. Please, just tell us what happened with Emily.'

'It was a misunderstanding,' I said, a little too quickly. 'She was angry at us. She thought we left her on the beach.'

'Others have suggested that was exactly what you did.' Others. More than one girl, then? The walls seemed to shift and give, the faces in the paintings casting down their judgement. 'That you knew she was intoxicated and left her to scale the cliffs on her own.'

'It was just a silly prank. We didn't mean for her to be hurt. We knew she wasn't the last one there.'

'She wasn't?' Detective Winterburn asked.

I could see the information was new. 'No. We knew she had help.'

'From whom?'

'The caretaker. He was there to help her up.'

DS Winterburn turned to the professor. 'She is referring to Mr James Baxter. We call him Jimmy. He's been with us for a couple of academic years.'

'That's the guy we are yet to locate, who was on the return-to-work programme?' Professor Fairhurst gave a nod, and the detective turned back to me, resting his pen on the page, ready to take notes. 'Okay. And when did you last see Emily?'

Our conversation on the stairs, the threats she made. What Mr Aides said. What were his words? That he'd make sure she didn't speak out against me? Being involved in such a conversation would look terrible, especially in light of what they knew happened at the beach.

'In Chapel, yesterday morning,' I lied. It already seemed so long ago. 'Before my performance.'

'You spoke to each other?'

Even there the atmosphere was strained, more than one witness who could attest to it. 'Yeah. She was a bit upset about the thing that happened on the beach. Angry, I guess. She didn't like me.'

'And did you like her?' I shrugged, and everybody understood. 'Okay. And what about you? Where were you today?'

'In my room. I spent the whole afternoon alone.'

He flicked back through the pages of his notebook, tapped an entry when he found whatever answer he was looking for. 'You are the resident in room fourteen on the sixth floor, which means of all the girls here, you are the closest to the location from where we believe she fell. The belltower.' He leaned in. 'Did you hear anything? Hear anybody going up there?'

'No,' I said.

'Not a thing?' I shook my head. 'And under normal circumstances? Do the pupils here access the belltower at all?'

'Maybe,' I said, not sure how to explain.

'Chloe?' Professor Fairhurst pushed. 'If you know something, please tell us.'

'I don't want to get into trouble,' I said.

'And you won't,' DS Winterburn said. 'As long as you don't try and fob us off with some bullshit about looking for the lights on the French coast.' He looked up at the professor and I wondered if that was Iris's suggestion. 'So, out with it,' he said, his tone tight as a knot. I could feel the pressure of it in my throat. 'Why do people go up there?'

My mouth was dry. When I spoke, I barely recognised my own voice. It was a reminder of how much it had changed since I'd arrived at High Hill.

'Sometimes to smoke. Or...' I swallowed, couldn't believe I was going to say it. 'Drugs,' I said, wrapping my hands together to stop them from shaking. 'They go up there to buy drugs.'

'From whom?'

I remembered the party then, the excitement of everybody on the beach. The weed I had smoked, the little metal tubes I had seen several people bringing up to their noses.

'Jimmy Baxter,' I said. The detective leaned in, while Professor Fairhurst brought a hand up to his face to cover his mouth. 'I think some people were buying drugs from Jimmy Baxter.'

'Our caretaker?' Professor Fairhurst asked, and I realised it was the first time he had ever heard the idea.

'Yeah. And he wanders the corridors at night, trying to get in girls' rooms,' I blurted out, some strange sense of relief at saying it aloud. 'He did that twice with me. And with Emily.'

Professor Fairhurst said nothing as the detective stared at him, looking for answers that he found in the silence that followed. 'And did you ever buy drugs from him, Chloe?' he asked then. 'You know this personally?'

'No,' I said. 'If I was caught doing something like that, I'd be expelled. I'm on a scholarship.'

'So who was buying drugs from him?'

I knew of a few girls, Iris being one of them. But in that moment none of that seemed important. But what did seem crucial was the idea of Jimmy selling drugs in the tower. That was the truth. And if Iris was scared that people might associate what happened at the beach to Emily's subsequent death, providing a reason for Emily to be in the tower that had nothing to do with us had to be a good thing. And Jimmy Baxter selling drugs was the most logical choice.

'I'm afraid I only know of one girl who went up there to buy drugs,' I said. 'And that was Emily Ashbourne.'

14

By the time I left Professor Fairhurst's office, all I wanted to do was find Iris, tell her what I'd told the police. I pushed open the door to my room, my fingers tingling from the energy of the evening, and I was relieved to find her lying on my bed.

'What took so long?' I tossed the coat I was carrying on the desk chair and sat down next to her. 'Did they ask about what happened at the beach?'

'Yeah. And about my demerit.'

'A girl from Hestia told them apparently.' Catherine I assumed. Iris slunk back down on the bed, as if any remaining fight had slipped away. 'I can't believe she died.'

And that moment with Iris was the first time it really sank in. The word, died, so final. So past tense. I felt my breathing quicken, the truth of it unavoidable, and then a tremble in my hands when the realisation came to me that I had lied to the police. I had no idea whether Emily had been there to buy drugs. But Iris's warm fingers slipped around mine, her touch reassuring, and I was grateful for it. She moved across in the bed, lying back against the pillow, and I let my head rest only inches from hers. Such a short space of time at High Hill, but something as simple as that, just to lie next to her had become the thing I wanted more than anything else each day. Even, sometimes, more than the piano. And even then, in the face of death, it made everything seem easier.

'The police said that Jimmy wasn't in his room,' I continued, knowing she needed reassurance. 'That even now they can't find him anywhere. He *must* have done something. Maybe she was up there to buy drugs from him.'

Her hand slipped from mine, and I felt her weight shift in the bed. 'I don't think so, Chloe. Everybody knows that Emily doesn't take drugs.'

Lessons over the next two weeks came and went in a blur. Nobody could concentrate on anything but the crime. No matter where I went people were talking about it, how it could have happened, and why Emily was in the belltower in the first place. Jimmy's disappearance went from rumour to confirmed, and we all huddled around the television as they showed a picture of his face on the news. Later, on *Crimewatch*. I handed in essays half completed and received them back with an A grade attached. But my biggest fear was returning to music.

Countless tutorials with Mr Aides had passed by unattended. My lack of attendance was in part due to the look he gave me in the chapel, the feeling I had that he wanted something more from me than my music. But it was also the way he spoke to Emily on the afternoon before she died. He was so short with her, so curt. It seemed absurd to even imagine that he would have hurt her to stop her spreading rumours about me. And yet I couldn't quite shake the idea of it. But it wasn't only that; I also couldn't ignore the possibility that he might have known what she was talking about. To think he knew what had happened with Mr Lyons in Clifton hung over me like a thick coastal mist. I'd think about him knowing and my senses would fade out, until Mr Lyons and that store cupboard were the only things that existed. But even though I was avoiding Mr Aides, I couldn't do that forever. After the second week drew to a close, and I found a prompt in my pigeonhole from him, I had no choice but to return to the music department.

'Chloe,' I heard Mr Aides say as I walked in, and I turned to see him exiting one of the practice rooms. I heard the music coming from inside, a clumsy rendition of *Clair de Lune*. He gave me a nod and a roll of his eyes, as if he understood my assessment. 'Great to see you back.'

With an outstretched hand he suggested we sit, and so I followed him, weaving through the chairs, across the orchestral set-up, towards a couple of sofas that were positioned on the far side of the room. Alongside that was an old chest of drawers, Victorian I suspected, the varnish in places chipped and worn. Picking up two of the mugs stacked on a tray, he boiled a kettle and made two cups of tea, taking the milk from a little fridge at the side. With a smile he handed me a cup and took a seat on the other sofa. Perched on the edge, I didn't know what to say, or how to act. I had missed the department. Missed him.

'Thanks so much for popping in during one of your free periods,' he said, resting back in the chair, balancing his tea on the arm. 'We've all needed a bit of time before we got back into the swing of things after what happened to Emily. It's not the kind of incident that is easily forgotten, is it?' He picked a bit of fluff from his trousers with the utmost concentration before dusting it to the floor. 'But your presence here has been missed, and it's well known that in times of difficulty, many musicians find comfort in their art. I thought that might be the case with you, so I was surprised by your absence. I think we should talk about why you have not been attending.'

A flute trio was playing across the other side of the room, unlikely to hear us, but still he leaned a little closer, lowered his voice.

'The music I left in your room. I suspect that it made you uncomfortable.' I pressed my hands against the mug until it was so hot I could feel nothing but the burning tingle against my palms. 'My intention was to reward you for your incredible performance. However, I suspect I did quite the opposite. Put a certain pressure on you instead.'

'It's not that, it's just...'

A joyless smile, a raised hand, told me that my effort to excuse it was unnecessary.

'I can assure you that I left it there because of your talent, Chloe. Nothing more. Your skill on the piano, it's like...' He closed his eyes, trying to find the right thing to say. I held my breath, waiting for his assessment. 'I have never seen another person of your age play as you do. There is such feeling and emotion to the way you approach the music. You make every piece your own. You almost become the music.' The garish patterns on the rugs blurred before me as my eyes filled with tears. 'I hoped the score I left for you might have been a suitable choice for when we approach Cambridge. I know it's your favoured institution, and Matthew Pemberton, the director of music, is quite the fan of Chopin.'

The things he said seemed to come from deep inside of me. Everything I hoped for somebody to say about the way I played. But in that moment, all I could focus on was the casual way he spoke of the dean. 'You know him personally?'

'Who, Matthew?' I nodded. 'Oh, yes. Pemberton and I studied together at the Royal Academy. Smashing chap, and of course I have already mentioned you to him, after your audition for High Hill.'

'You did?'

'How could I not? He's looking forward to meeting you. But listen,' he said, leaning forward, setting his tea on the table. 'You never came to my office the previous Sunday as you said you would, and have mentioned nothing since of the music I left for you. If you are not interested in a career in music, then it's okay. I can back off. I don't want to push you without reason. Especially after what happened.'

'No,' I said, too quickly. 'I want to be pushed. Cambridge is where I want to study.'

'Really?' There was excitement in his voice. I was glad to please him. 'You're not just saying that?'

His attention and belief were everything I had hoped for when I came here. That I would be judged on my own merit. Seeing the music in my room had taken me back to that store cupboard, made me feel as if Edward Lyons was still right there, like a shadow lingering behind me. But the memory of him risked causing me to blow this chance. I couldn't let that happen. I couldn't let my fear take over.

'Very much so. I was thinking about Trinity College. I know they don't let many people in, but they have so many chances for performance, here and abroad. You know they have a Steinway Model D piano in the chapel?'

'I do,' he said with a smile.

Goodness, I felt like such a child then. 'I'm sorry for not attending my lessons,' I said, wiping away a tear. 'I'll do better.'

'Chloe, it has been a challenging time. For all of us.' His eyes were as grey as the skies outside, the changing colour of the sea. His cheeks flushed pink. 'But you have missed three rehearsals this week. Six in total since... since what happened, happened.' It was neither an accusation, nor a threat. But the flush in his cheeks, the set of his jaw told me he was upset about it. 'You say it's not about the music, but I can't help but think there is something.' He sighed, shrugged as if he could make no sense of it. 'Is it about what happened to Emily?' I shrugged, nodded to agree that it was, and his shoulders relaxed. 'I wonder whether it was our discussion on the staircase?' he asked then, lowering his voice further still. 'I hope the fact that I reprimanded Emily didn't give you any reason to believe that I could have been involved in her death?'

'No,' I said, although even to my ears I didn't sound convinced.

'Well, just in case, let me reassure you that I played no part in the terrible thing that happened to her. I do hope that is clear.'

'It is, I'm sorry. I know I should have been...'

'Ah, a terrible word,' he said, wafting his hands as if trying to shoo away an irritating fly. 'The word "should" must always be replaced by "want". Never attend this department because you *should*. Be here only because you *want* to be.'

What a thing for him to have to reiterate. How had I not made it clear? 'I do want to be here.'

'Truly?' I nodded, feeling silly, small. A child, which since Clifton was something I desperately didn't want to be. Had I really believed he would have hurt her? To protect me? It was so unfair, so unjust to have thought such a thing. 'Excellent. In which case, tomorrow is Friday. Let's start back next week. Okay?'

'Okay.'

He stood up and I joined him. We exchanged a smile. My heart was racing so fast I could feel every pulse strong in my throat. He wanted me to succeed. He was giving me the power. The choice. The chance at Cambridge had never been closer than in that moment.

'Oh, there was one more thing.' I waited behind him, and he turned slowly, as if what he had to say next wasn't easy. 'Your friends, the two girls you hang out with. Remind me of their names.'

'You mean Iris and Francesca?'

'Yes, that's them. You are... close?'

'I guess.' Iris was the glue that held us together. Anytime Iris wasn't there I felt weird and awkward with Fran. Not that she wasn't nice, or that she said anything to exclude me, but there was always some sensation of distance between us. I was aware of just how different our lives really were. Could never imagine her at my parents' home, or me at hers. It was a huge estate, and rumour was that she was the wealthiest of all students. She spoke of their ski chalet like it was a small hut in the middle of a forgotten mountain. But I had seen pictures, the giant glass-walled lodge, knew they kept year-round staff so they could make weekend visits. Christmas there was like a fairytale I could only dream about. 'I'm closer to Iris, I think.'

'Right,' he said, as if my answer troubled him. 'And that's not something that's negotiable for you? You don't have other girls you could spend your time with?'

The truth was I didn't, especially not since Emily died. There had been a few tentative friendships before that, some celebration in the immediate moments after my performance in Chapel, but they had all ended the moment my name became tangled up in Emily's death.

'Should I not be friends with them?'

He nibbled his lip and gave a sharp shake of his head. 'I just want you to have the very best chance at success, Chloe. That's all. Forget I said anything, okay?' And his expression changed. One of worry to desperation. He had spoken out against the head teacher's daughter. Why, I didn't know, but I understood the implications that held for him.

'Sure,' I said. 'Said what?' I joked, and he smiled with relief.

'Good, good. But listen, do me this favour. Focus on your music. On my tutorage. You must allow yourself to be guided by the right influence. I can help you if you will let me.'

'I will.'

'Good,' he said again. And without another word, he offered me a pained smile, before he turned and hurried away.

15

Coastal fog lingered that day, the air crisp with it. Drops of moisture collected on the flyaway strands of hair that escaped our plaits.

'This is so fucked up,' Francesca whispered from behind us as we waited in line. 'She's not even in there.'

'Of course she's in there,' I said, moving through the vestibule of the chapel. 'This is her funeral.'

'Don't be ridiculous,' she added. 'This is a memorial. Don't you know the difference?'

Glancing to the top of the aisle, I stared at the shining black coffin, the ornate golden handles. On top, a framed photograph of Emily, her near-silver hair falling in soft waves about her face. My cape was too heavy, wasn't sitting right on my shoulders. I fiddled at the golden clasp, pulling at my throat, making it difficult to breathe. 'Why would they bring a coffin if she wasn't in it?'

'She died like five weeks ago now,' Francesca said, turning her nose up at the idea. 'She'll be, like, decomposing, or whatever. You can't just move a body around like that. Even when somebody in *my* family died,' she said, with some incredulity, as if she expected her family should be exempt from such things, 'we only allowed eleven days between her death and the funeral. And there was a lot to organise.'

We were all quiet, aware she was talking about the late queen.

'It's because they embalmed her,' said another girl from behind us. 'I saw them opening the lid earlier when they arrived. She looked exactly the same. Only with half a head.'

'Bullshit,' Francesca added. A full stop.

'Francesca's right,' said another girl, turning around as we walked up the aisle. 'They already had the funeral and buried her. This is just a set-up so they have a fancy place to stick that photo with her smug fucking face.'

I slipped my hand into Iris's and held it tight, as we took our position on the left of the chapel, behind Emily's parents. Her mother appeared stoic, but her father sobbed into a tissue. Nobody offered him any comfort. Her brother was in the front row with them, wearing the uniform from Ridgely. I hadn't even known she had a brother. The other side of the chapel was filled with his classmates, and a few rows from the front I saw Stan. I had never seen him in his uniform before, grey trousers and a black tailcoat. White neckties like ours. His hair was neat, and I was struck again by how alike he was to Iris, the darkness of his eyes, the intensity of his gaze. How handsome. He nodded towards his sister.

'Is she all right?' he mouthed. I looked to Iris, noticed that she was picking at a quick of skin around her bitten fingernails. Drops of blood eased from the wound. Because since the night when Emily died, all she could think about was the beach, what happened on that night when we got drunk and high and stupid. At supper we could see people looking at us, whispering behind covered mouths. Even though there was a national search for Jimmy Baxter, the rumours about what Iris had done to

Emily had refused to go away. Turning back to Stan, all I could do was shake my head.

'All rise.'

As we stood, we heard the music of the organ echoing through the cavernous ceiling. The *Funeral March*, grand and solemn, played out as we watched Father John enter the church to begin his slow procession towards the altar. It was then, ahead, that I saw Mr Aides, dressed in the black suit from the day I performed here. The same day as Emily died. He looked different from then, worn out. He was one of the first to sit when we were allowed.

'Today we join together in celebration of a young life,' Father John began, his hands held out in the air. 'We unite our hearts in joyous remembrance of a young woman whose soul was called home to the house of the Lord.' Her father's sobbing echoed through the crowd. I held Iris's shaking hand in mine, pulled it towards my body. She was trembling, every part of her unable to rest. She seemed close to tears. 'We share in the grief of Emily's family, but as faithful servants of our Lord Jesus Christ, we find comfort in the knowledge that Emily Elizabeth Arabella Ashbourne is finally at rest.'

The service was longer and more painful than I expected. Her brother set things off by giving a eulogy, and he returned to his seat a hero. A man. Those closest patted him on the back. It sounded to me to be about a girl I didn't even recognise. Activities like flower arranging with her local church, and the volunteering placement she did in Cambodia. Another in Kenya. We suffered through the fumbled speeches of Emily's father and a cello recital by her younger sister, three years below me and a fellow member of Athena, until it was time to wrap things up. The whole way through, Iris didn't look up once.

'Jesus, that was rough.'

We were outside by then, sipping on hot cups of tea in the garden. I was standing next to a statue of Athena, the plume of a helmet covered in lichen, the top half of her spear eroded by time. No longer ready for battle. Turning, I found Stan, looking ashen-faced and worn out.

'Yeah, I've had easier Sundays,' I said.

He gave me a nod, and then wrapped his arm around Iris. 'You okay, sis?'

Seeing them together took my breath away. The curve of their eyes, the same soft mouth. The ghostly way they both seemed faded in the shadow of the service, a watercolour left out in the sun. And it was confusing too. Looking at them together made it impossible to have the answers. Made me feel like I didn't even know who I was. In their presence I didn't know what to feel.

Iris didn't move for a moment, and then said, 'Excuse me. I need the loo.'

She handed me her tea and then we watched her slip inside. Across the other side of the garden, I could see the crowd of Ridgely boys in their black blazers retreating around the west wing to the front of the school. Their coach pulled up on the driveway.

'I can't believe this has hit her so hard,' Stan said. 'What's wrong with her?'

I hesitated, took a deep breath. 'She's not been right since it happened.'

'Because of the stupid beach thing?'

I felt a heat rush to my cheeks as I nodded. 'People keep talking about it.' Even yesterday, I had gone into the study hall to work, and when I sat down, the girls closest to me got up and moved to another desk. Iris had reported the same sort of treatment. 'If she wasn't dead everybody would've forgotten it by now.'

'She is, though.' The obvious statement silenced us both. 'The police are still looking for Jimmy?'

'Yeah. And they found a footprint in the belltower which they think was his. They even found pictures of students in his quarters, and he's got keys to like every door in the school. Even the bedrooms.'

'That's fucking sick.'

'I know, it's dreadful.'

He looked at me for a moment, then smiled, before staring up at the belltower. I understood. I hadn't been able to take my eyes off it since that night either.

'You know, my sister and I will be going home for the weekend soon. My mother thinks it's necessary. You should come.'

The invitation took me aback. For a second I didn't know what to say. 'Really?'

'I think Iris would like it.' Then he reached out, let his fingers play at mine. He wasn't really holding my hand, but it felt like it. When I looked up, he was staring at me, and it felt like we were the only people alive in the whole world. 'And so would I.'

I pictured their home, the garden with a river running through it, the horses that grazed in their many fields. Could imagine the life there. Wanted, I realised, to be a part of it.

'Anyway, I have to go.' He reached up, let his fingers brush the side of my cheek. 'Look out for Iris, yeah?'

'Of course,' I said, unable to hold his gaze.

Then I watched as he walked away to embark the coach. At the last minute he turned around, waved to say goodbye before he disappeared inside. I turned from the crowd and headed back through West Gate and into the cloisters of the courtyard. Thinking about his touch. Wondering where Iris had gone. With everybody still at the memorial there was not a soul about. As if I was the only person at the whole school. I caught sight of the spot where Emily had died, and I was sure there was still a visible mark on the ground to testify to what had happened.

Hurrying away, I pulled the door to the north-wing corridor open, the hinges creaking as it swung shut behind me. With only the smallest of windows, it was always dark in there. I reached for the light, but when I flicked the switch, they did not come on. I tried a few more times, until I accepted they weren't working.

It wasn't until I reached the second floor that I began to think that I could hear somebody behind me. Not unusual, in a place where six hundred pupils lived together in such close confines. I had felt that way before. But I was disconcerted by the fact that when I stopped, so did they. I started up again, and sure enough, the footsteps resumed. I looked down the central opening of the stairwell, searching for the sight of another pupil. A teacher. Anybody. But I saw nothing.

'Hello?' I asked. No response.

With another two floors to go before I reached my bedroom, I couldn't decide what was safest. Exit onto another floor, or continue to mine, where I could hide in my room? I tried to tell myself there was no reason to be afraid, but my hands reached for the security of the key in my cape pocket. Looking up the dark staircase, I decided to push on.

I started to run, moving as fast as I could. The footsteps picked up their pace too. But I could see the door. I was going to make it. But at the last moment I felt the gush of air as somebody came up before me. And before I could turn, they had flipped the hood of my cape over my head, covering my eyes, pulling it tight against my neck.

They pulled me back, snatching at the material. We fell against the stairs, my body on top of my attacker's. With one hand they held me tight, and with their other, I felt it fumble about across my body. I tried to scream but the material muffled my voice. Flailing arms and legs fought to get free, but still they pawed at me. At first I took it as a sexual attack, trying to feel me up. But the urgency of their touch had nothing sexual about it. They were looking for something. And then all of a sudden, I felt the force behind me and the surge of my body moving forwards as they pushed me down the stairs. Disorientated, I didn't know where I was as I came to land, bumping my way down the stairs until I eventually came to a stop.

My body recoiled and twisted in on itself with pain. A tight stinging ripped against my lip as I opened my mouth, and I reached up to feel the blush of fresh, warm blood trickling across my chin. My wrist was hot as fire, and when I tried to bear my weight, I thought it was broken. But when I looked up and over the stairway, I saw what I thought to be a man, dressed in black. Running along the cloisters of level six.

And it was a man I was sure I recognised.

Before

16

Released last week? I reach for my phone, track back the list of missed calls from Francesca. And that's when they started, almost to the day. Pushing back in the chair, I stand up, looking first to the window, and then the door. All I see is a city shrouded in mist. I need to get out of this pub, away from Aides. Find Francesca. Could Jimmy Baxter really have been extorting her for all these years? I push away from the table, stepping past the dog, until I feel the brush of his hand against my arm.

'Chloe,' Aides says. Not a firm grip, more of a suggestion. When I turn, I see there is desperation in the twisted lines of his face, his crumpled lips. Close to tears, I think. 'I only want what's best for you. To keep you safe. I promise I am telling the truth.'

I go to speak but realise I don't know what to say. Because with him, I have never known what the truth is. No matter what he told me, what thought he presented as fact, there was always an ulterior motive. At High Hill he picked me apart, piece by piece. I have no idea whether he has ever told me the truth at all.

'I have to find Francesca.'

Pulling away from his touch, I push through the busy pub, and hurry into the toilets where I press my back against the door. Sweat spreads across my skin, and I can feel the cool dampness of my T-shirt as it sticks against my body. I move across to the taps and press for water, cupping a shaky hand to bring it to my mouth. It's too cold, gets into my teeth. Fine drops darken my jeans.

'You all right there?' Another lady has come in. I didn't hear her entrance over the sound of the water, but as I turn to her voice, I see that she's older than me, by at least ten years. A smile of concern spreads across her face. 'You look a bit pale, love. Everything okay?'

'I'm fine,' I say, blunt and to the point. Turning, I head to a cubicle and lock myself inside, water still trailing cold down the side of my chin.

Years have passed since I last saw Francesca. She was out for dinner one evening, at the restaurant where I worked. It was the first time I'd had a job like that, taking orders, serving plates. It embarrassed me if I'm honest, the servile nature of the role, dressed in the uniform, the crisp white shirt with my hair twisted into the regulatory bun. I was serving another customer when I saw her, sitting just a few tables away.

'Chloe,' she said, shocked when I approached to take the order. 'Oh, my God. Is it really you?'

After a moment we embraced and she asked polite questions: when my next performance was, whether I liked my job. It was her suggestion that lockdowns had destroyed the performance industry, and I agreed. It was easier for both of us like that. High Hill girls weren't supposed to wait on tables. We exchanged numbers and said we'd see each other again. But she never came back to the restaurant where I worked. Never called. At least, not until last week.

I stare at the list of missed calls, so many of them from her. When I first saw her name I wanted to talk to her. Excited even, at first, her name sending a thrill through my body. But when I went to answer it was as if time folded back on itself, supplanting me back there, to where I was standing in the courtroom during his trial. And I couldn't go back. After that I ignored her calls, until the guilt of my silence forced me to try. I dialled in the deep hours of night, fuelled by wine, but even then I couldn't go through with it. Dropped the call before the first ring. But now I wish I could go back, put my own fears aside and be there for her. Wish I hadn't cut her loose.

Tears threaten as I dial her number, imagining what she has been going through alone. We made a deal. I should have stuck by her. Stan sees her occasionally, I know. I could have tagged along. I could have told her it would be all right. But I was selfish, chose to run away. Now I have no choice. I hold on, waiting for her voice, until the answering machine kicks in.

'Fran.' My voice sounds broken, shattered like sharp fragments of glass. 'I'm with Aides. He's been released, and he told me about...' I pause, wondering how best to say it over the phone. Should have thought about it before. 'I'm so sorry I didn't answer your calls, but please, call me back now, okay? We need to talk about Baxter.'

I leave the cubicle, and I stare at my face in the mirror, take in the tired eyes, my pale skin the colour of the statues at High Hill. It's as if the life has been sucked out of me. But all I can think is that I should have done more. Fran has tried to contact me so many times, and I ignored every call. She used to be my friend. But who is the woman I see in the mirror before me? I don't even know who I am.

On my way out of the bathroom I feel the vibration of my phone, and seeing it's her, I hit the button to answer the call.

'Fran, thank God.' I wait, listen for her voice. 'Fran, are you there?'

The seconds pass, the line connected. Background noises filter through, difficult to place anything at all. Car horns. A radio. Then movement I think, footsteps. I wonder whether she has called by accident. But grandmothers make phone calls from their pocket, not barristers who defend large corporations in lawsuits that total billions.

'Francesca,' I say again, louder this time. 'Francesca, are you there?'

And then I hear it. Movement close to the microphone, the mouthpiece being brought up close to somebody's face. The soft whicker of breath as it filters down the line.

'Fran?' I wait, and still she says nothing. 'Fran, are you there?'

But after another breath, the line goes dead.

For a moment I don't move, just stand in the toilets trying to make sense of it. Staring at my phone. I try calling back, but this time the call doesn't even go through. But why would she pick up my earlier call and then not speak, when she has tried so many times to reach me over the last week? And I wanted to talk to her. I did. I wanted it to be the first weeks of High Hill, watching her across the beach and wishing I was like her, marvelling at that cool fringe she cut for herself. Yet I never had the strength to do what I should have done. So many bad memories wrap like twisted vines around what we once used to be.

But I must put my own fears aside and find her now. She has never needed me more.

I leave the toilets and run from the pub, can hear Aides protesting from the other side of the room, calling my name as I charge through the door. Before he can catch me I'm in the car, already speeding from the carpark. Dodging traffic, I call Francesca again and again as I drive, but she doesn't answer. So eventually I call Stan, the only person who I think might know what to do.

'I'll be there within half an hour,' he says, and so I park up and walk to the place we agree to meet by the river, and then try my best to stay calm while I wait for him to arrive. The Tower of London rises behind me, tourists flooding the pavements. Tours scurry around their leaders, colourful flags held high in the air. It reminds me of High Hill, the belltower, and eventually I turn away, watch the muddy water of the Thames. But all I can think about is how Francesca isn't answering the phone. That maybe I am too late.

'Chloe.' Another twenty minutes have passed by the time I hear his voice. Turning, I see Stan hurrying towards me, a long black coat, his suit underneath. Bright red cheeks attest to what a rush this is. But still he moves with that confidence I remember, the same authority that Iris always had. It could be her coming towards me now. I can almost feel her following him in his shadow. He takes me into an embrace when he can see I'm close to tears. The Shard looms in the distance, its summit lost in cloud. 'What the hell's going on?' Ever since I left Aides I have been unable to stop trembling. And he feels it, firming up his grip, wrapping one hand around the back of my head. His fingers weave through my freshly cut hair. 'I fucking told you not to meet him. You should never have gone to Aides today.'

'I had to,' I say, pulling back. He guides me towards a bench, and we sit down in the shelter of the building. Everywhere I look I see people whose faces morph into that of Jimmy Baxter. 'I needed to know what he had to tell me. And you need to hear it too.'

I tell Stan everything. And once I have finished he guides me into the café on the corner of his building, where we order some drinks, and find a spot in a quiet corner.

'So she answered the call, but didn't say there was something wrong, right?'

'Stan, she didn't say anything. But if Aides is telling the truth and Baxter already found her… What if he hurt her, Stan? What if that's why she didn't speak?'

Pushing his coffee aside, he reaches across the table and rests his hands against mine.

'I think if there was anything wrong with Francesca, she wouldn't have answered the call at all. Maybe she lost signal or something. You know what the reception can be like around her chambers.' I nod, but I don't. Have no clue about signal there at all. His fingers trace the light blue veins that track along the inside of my wrist. 'And more than that, you know very well how Baxter was and always will be a piece of shit. Don't let a few bullshit ideas from Aides drag you back to the worst time of our lives.'

'So we should just pretend that we don't know Baxter's been extorting money from her? That he plans to look for me?'

Stan sighs, sipping again on his coffee. Then he frowns, shrugs his shoulders. 'I mean, I don't want to point out the obvious, Chloe, but Fran is a fucking criminal defence barrister. She helped to free Assange, for crying out loud. You think there is any chance she would be paying extortion money to Baxter?' I sit back in my chair, knowing how unlikely it sounds. 'And listen, I wasn't going to mention it, but Francesca told me weeks ago that she was worried about you. She knew Aides' release was coming up, and she wanted to talk. Make sure you were all right.'

'She said that?'

'Yes. She said too long had passed. No, please, don't cry,' he says, reaching up to wipe my eyes. 'But she anticipated something like this. Knows what he is in ways you can't see; Aides is lying to you, Chloe. And besides that, I spoke to her this morning when she was on her way to the gym. She was fine. But let me try calling her again now, put your mind at ease. Maybe you can talk, yeah?' he says, smiling, as if jollying along a sad little girl. 'We might catch her at lunch.'

He picks up the phone, and I watch as he makes the call. She doesn't answer. But he taps in a new number and puts the call on speaker.

'Good afternoon, Goldsmith's.' Her legal chambers. He has the phone number saved in his phone. 'How can I help?'

'Constantine Fairhurst, here. Is that Elaine?'

'Oh hello, Constantine. How are you?'

Listening to their chat makes me wish I was still in touch with Fran, that we had some shred of commonality in our lives like they do. He asks about Elaine's dog, and whether her husband is better after his recent surgery. He and Fran are much closer than I thought. There is nobody in my life besides my mother who I could ask such things.

'You're so kind to remember,' she says then. I can hear the smile in her voice. 'And of course I will send your regards. But I'm afraid I can't help you with Francesca at the moment. She's in court this afternoon. Won't be out until close to five.'

'Ah, I assumed as much. Not to worry. But just… she was okay earlier, right? No worries lately?'

'I don't think so, Constantine. She seemed her usual untouchable self.'

Stan wraps up the call, fiddling with a box of cigarettes on the table, before knocking his espresso back. Then he sets the phone down, takes my hands in his. 'See?'

'How could she have answered if she was in court?' I see him roll his eyes. 'It's true, right? She wouldn't have had her phone with her. What if somebody else has it, and they answered, and…'

'Chloe, please,' he says. 'She is in court. You just heard it yourself. I don't know, maybe she took a break, maybe court was adjourned. Maybe some dickhead on a bike stole her phone. You know how often that is happening lately.'

And he's right. There are so many reasons.

'It was so believable,' I say. Naïve. Like a child sitting before her father who knew better. I'm running around the city like a fool, when she is fine, working in the Royal Courts of Justice. Living her life. 'He convinced me.'

'Don't feel bad about it. But Aides knows your weakness,' he says, the hairs on my arms standing on end as he brushes his fingers across them. 'That you are kind enough to care about your friends. But Chloe, Aides is a liar, and he's playing you. Just like he was when you were at High Hill. He doesn't care about protecting you. He doesn't care about you at all. If he did, he'd leave you alone.'

'And if he's telling the truth?'

'You just heard what Elaine said, Fran's in court. She's fine. And even if he thinks he's telling the truth, why didn't he tell you in a letter?' Frantic, he taps his finger against the empty cup. He smiles, as if he understands the impossibility of the situation. 'What he did, it was...' His hand runs along my forearm again, fingers tight against it. He shuffles closer. 'I know you suffered, Chloe. I'm not doubting that. But I've known you since you were seventeen years old. Longer than you were alive before you met him. Haven't you given him enough of yourself already?' I had never thought about it that way. 'I never really understood how deep the wounds he inflicted were. At least not until... you know...'

Ten years ago. Still just kids at the time. A birthday, a bar, too many drinks. Negronis and dirty martinis. Stumbling back to Stan's apartment, we shared a foolish kiss, something he tells me I instigated. Too drunk to remember. But I believe it. Because when I'm with him I can feel Iris. I look into his eyes, and I can see her. When he opens his mouth it's her voice I hear. Even now I can remember the discarded clothes that fell to the floor as I kissed Stan, the fumbling hands as we fell back onto his bed. With my eyes closed it was as if I turned back time, could almost convince myself it was her. But I can also still remember the panic attack I suffered, when I felt the weight of his body on mine and opened my eyes to see that she was gone. That she had never been there at all.

'Baxter is the past. Aides is the past. But if you let it, this will become your whole life, Chloe.' His hands on mine again, soft, and warm. 'I'm not asking you to pretend that none of it happened. Neither of us can do that. But neither should we live as if we are still stuck in 2005. We have to give life a chance, don't we?' And then he sits back, a sad little smile I haven't seen since that night we almost had sex. 'Otherwise, we'd all still be seventeen-year-old fools, and I'd be at a shit beach party, hopelessly falling in love with a girl who was already in love with my sister.'

Before

17

I must have passed out, because when I opened my eyes there was a small crowd of worried faces gathered around me. The police were on their way, somebody said. Miss McCabe was there, holding my hand. Iris too. A cloth, red and bloody from where she had used it to dab at the wound on my lip, hung limp and heavy in her hand.

'Did you get a look at who did it?' she asked.

A voice carried up the stairwell, Professor Fairhurst hurrying to get through. His flushed red face appeared just as I was ready to answer.

'Yes,' I said. 'I think it was Jimmy Baxter.'

—

The police questioned me for over half an hour. Where was I going? How did it happen? More questions about my relationship with Emily and Baxter. Whether I thought my attack was related to what happened to her. How did I know it was Baxter when I didn't quite see his face? I didn't even want to think about it. Hordes of them scoured the school for a trace. They found nothing. And why it happened seemed a mystery until I realised the key to my bedroom was missing, taken as part of the attack. A pack of eager teachers, enraged by the violent incursion, hurried up the stairs. Young men looking to become heroes. And they almost found what they were looking for, only a fraction too late. All that remained was a room in chaos, the mattress upturned, the trunk and drawers emptied. Clothes and broken toiletries littered the floor. Even a loose floorboard had been prised from its position. But despite their shouting and desperate efforts, by eight that evening most of the police were leaving the site, and Jimmy Baxter was still nowhere to be found.

News of the incident spread fast, and a band of cleaners visited my room, rectifying the damage and helping return my things to their rightful place. It didn't look like my room when they left, everything a little out of place. But it was good to be in there, the door locked with a spare key, my trunk pushed up against it for good measure.

'What do you think he wanted?' I asked Iris as she sat down next to me. A tightness pinched her face, like a fox on the hunt of prey.

'I don't know,' she said. 'But based on the state of your room, and the fact he didn't really hurt you, I don't think he found it.'

And then as she reached up to stroke my injured face, we heard feet along the corridor, the creak of the door. There were still some police officers searching, on their way up to the belltower. Rumour had it that they were searching for a weapon. When I realised she was shaking I reached for her hand, and it was then, as I looked down, that I saw the marks for the first time.

'Iris.' I fought against her resistance and held her arm before us. She looked away, as if not seeing it made any difference. From wrist to elbow I saw the lines, some pink, fresh. Others the pale silver of the moon. Her skin looked like my grandmother's lace. 'Did you do this to yourself?'

Seconds passed before she spoke, and even then her voice was quiet, almost pathetic. A fact, spoken as a question. 'It helps me cope.'

'No,' I said, my grip harder. One of the marks blushed pink with the pressure, looked as if it had been made only hours before. 'All it does is make things worse.'

The break of my voice stunned us both. I wasn't expecting it, thought I had dealt with any shadows that stretched out from my past to suck the light from the new life I had built. But that day was different. My assault in the corridors of the school had loosened old memories, made me yearn for home. Now, as I looked across the room, I glanced to the oil canvas my father had painted for me, relegated to the space between the wall and the wardrobe. And it all came flooding back.

I felt my body tremble, the tingle of my fingers.

'My father,' I said then. The words felt alien, unlike anything that belonged to me. I had never said them before. 'He tried to end his life about five years ago.'

He had lost his job as a custom framer a few months before, and my mother's salary as a shop assistant hadn't been enough to cover the costs of our life. His artwork was in no great demand, and any paintings he sold offered little more than a financial boost to an otherwise stretched budget. An inch of tape over a gaping wound. After the bailiffs came things got harder still, until one day I found my father lying in the bathroom, his blood soaking into the pink rug I used to step onto after a bath. Later that night I stood in a hospital ward, watching as he cried in my mother's arms, picking the blood that was drying into the knees of my jeans from where I had tried to save him hours before.

'Chloe, I'm sorry, I...'

'It was a long time ago,' I said, knowing it was a lie. It was as good as yesterday. I wished I hadn't hidden his painting. Wished too that he'd never done it. Sometimes it was easier to pretend he was gone, rather than hope he never tried to leave again. 'But if you want to do that to yourself, I'd rather be alone. Go back to your room,' I told her. 'I don't want to come in here and find you hurt like I did him.'

'You found him? Oh, Chloe. I'm so sorry.'

In the silence that followed everything seemed to meld in my mind, inextricably linked in ways I couldn't understand: my father, Edward Lyons, Emily's death. For a moment I couldn't see for the memories I had but didn't want. I closed my eyes but even then they played out as tendrils of light twisting like auroras in my mind until everything was so bright it was almost black. I was caving in, like a void opening up in the earth.

'Chloe, what is it?' Iris's voice, but already my ears were muffled, and I couldn't hear her properly. 'Breathe, Chloe. Please, just breathe. I'm here. It's going to be okay.'

But I couldn't. I gasped for air, but it was as if there was none, that I had been sucked into a vacuum built upon the tragedies of my past. I opened my eyes, tried to focus on Iris. My body felt as cold as ice, my teeth chattering. I looked down and thought for a moment that I saw my father on the floor. Felt sure I could feel the tepid dampness of his blood on my clothes. 'I've got you,' she said, holding me tight. 'You're safe. You're in our room at High Hill. You're having a panic attack, that's all. It's going to be okay. I'm here.'

By the time I became aware of my own body again, gained some semblance of control, I was wrapped tightly in her arms, my head pressed against the softness of her breast. Both of us lying on the bed. She was still talking to me, stroking my hair, but I couldn't focus on what she was saying, couldn't understand the words.

'I feel cold,' I said. I felt the increase in pressure as she pressed her body against mine, the firmness of her hand as she rubbed it up and down my back. The weight of the cover as she pulled it across us both.

'Shhh,' she said. 'I'm here. I'll always be here.'

At some point I must have slept because the light was different when I opened my eyes. The flashing blue lights of the police cars had gone. Birds sang outside in the trees. Awake beside me, she smiled, her breath sweet as she whispered only inches from my mouth.

'Are you feeling better?'

Nodding, I tried to smile, but she didn't offer one back. Instead, our eyes just lingered on each other, staring at something we were seeing only now for the first time. Part of each other that had until then been left unrevealed.

'I'm so sorry, Chloe. I'll never do it again,' she said. 'Not now you've told me about your dad.'

And when she brushed a twist of flyaway hairs from my eyes, her fingertips running across my forehead, my cheek and around the back of my ear, it had felt entirely normal to inch closer to her. When she rested her hand onto my hip I didn't push it away. In fact, I mirrored her action. The softness of her touch, the gentleness with which she treated me – it was a new kind of love. A kind love, even. Something tender. I had never felt anything like it before.

How long passed before my lips were on hers, or who moved to kiss the other first, I don't know. But what I remember was that her eyes never left mine as our lips met, and that as her hands moved across my body, she whispered no apologies as Edward Lyons had. She didn't ask permission, as if I had in some quiet way already given it. At some point she moved her hand between my legs, and as she stroked the folds of my body, I thought of all the times I had tried to do the same thing to myself, only to feel shame and guilt. But with Iris I felt no such thing. She pressed her mouth against the softest parts of me, and I moved against her as if I was trying to fold us together. And when I kissed her lips and she tasted of me, desperation took over. I pulled off the rest of my clothes and watched as she did the same. Our bodies wound together like a spring. It was the first time anybody had wanted all of me. It was the first time I had ever wanted to give it.

'Would you do anything for me?' she whispered afterwards, my body still trembling and unfurled. I kissed her shoulder, then her neck.

'Yes,' I said.

And we both knew it was true.

18

The police discovered it that night, while I lay tangled together with Iris. A small corner of the old disused library, complete with a tatty old mattress and a camp stove. Baxter himself was nowhere to be found, but some of his clothes were draped over a chair, and it looked as if he had been living in there since the night Emily died. Moving around in the dark, sneaking food from the kitchen. Knowing he had attacked me, and most likely killed Emily. Every time I closed my eyes, I thought of him with the keys. What if he still had another set? But the police were often at school after that, packs of their dogs barking through the local fields in search of Baxter. And in making their continued searches, they realised the clapper from the bell in the belltower was missing, and they announced with much certainty that they now knew what had been used as a murder weapon. All they had to do was find it.

Their ongoing presence at the school changed things for us as well. Miss McCabe had started checking on us each night, ensuring that we were in our own rooms, that our doors were locked. Formal suppers were cancelled, curfews extended. Often, she would sit on guard at the end of our wing, sleeping on a chair so that nobody could leave their rooms unseen. The rumours about Jimmy sleeping in the library, trying to get in our bedrooms had shaken her up, and she took a personal responsibility for making sure we were safe. Some sense of regulation and fear descended back over the school after the chaos that had consumed us until then.

But that also meant that Iris couldn't be in my room. I felt her absence like a tangible void, something upon which I could lay my hands and feel the coolness of it. But in the quiet of night, I kept returning to the first morning after Iris and I made love, and how she was gone before I woke up. How in the first days when I tried to sit with her, she would always find a reason to get up, and how she no longer studied in the places I expected to find her. Something had changed between us, and it was no longer easy as it had been before. She was ashamed, I thought, and it was a feeling I recognised. I hated that I had made her feel like that. Disgust twisted in me like a cramp. She couldn't even look at me at breakfast, spent all her time with Fran. After that, life at High Hill felt even lonelier than the first day I arrived.

'So, are we set?'

At the piano I sat staring at the three scores he had positioned before me. Three weeks since my night with Iris. Three weeks since I had felt the warmth of her friendship.

'I think the choices are good, no?'

I needed three pieces. We had been through various ideas, but the way Mr Aides folded his arms made me think that the final decision had been made.

'I think so,' I said.

He had to lean in a little to see the scores, leafed through. 'The Scarlatti will be the most difficult for you. I know you hate Baroque, but the classical schools you are interested in will undoubtedly expect a level of proficiency. The Liszt though is going very well. I am impressed, Chloe. Matthew will want to see a full range, a full appreciation of musical history in the few minutes that you will perform. And I think he's going to get it. You are almost ready.'

'I've been playing every day,' I said.

Most of my evenings passed by in the music department, at least until the eight p.m. curfew came into force. Mornings too. It seemed safer to hide away in the quiet sanctuary of the only place it felt as if I belonged. Francesca and Iris were spending more time together, and on the few occasions I had dared approach them when they were together, the unspoken words between us acted as a barrier that I didn't know how to cross. I suspected that Francesca knew what we had done, and I didn't feel any sense of approval.

'I'm getting better at the Scarlatti,' I suggested.

'Yes, your efforts have not gone unnoticed. Several of the other teachers have commented on your dedication.' His smile was so genuine, so easy. Like I saw the real version of him. 'Honestly, Chloe, it's been such a pleasure to have you here this term.' Heat rose in my cheeks, a tremor in my fingers. Not from embarrassment, but more like the thrill of applause at the end of a performance. His praise felt good. It felt so surreal to imagine that only weeks before I had doubted him. That I thought he could have played a part in what happened to Emily. And I was so grateful for him since Iris had excluded me. His presence at the school was the only thing that made me feel good. 'You're going to have to work at the Debussy though. The timing is a little tricky. You missed some important notes in that last run through.'

'I know.'

'Keep at it,' he said, packing up his things, unperturbed by my mistakes. 'Any time you need help outside of hours, just ask. I'd be happy to spend all the time you need with you to get it right.'

But that innocent offer, at least what I thought was innocent, was enough to bring tears to my eyes.

'Chloe, are you all right? Have I said something to upset you?'

'No,' I said, trying to turn away. 'It's nothing, really.'

'It clearly isn't, Chloe. I can see I have upset you.' Mindless fingers scratched at his head. Sweat collected on his upper lip. 'I certainly didn't want to make you feel uncomfortable, and to think that I did, I...' He shook his head as if he thought himself stupid. 'Goodness me, I'm so sorry.'

'It's not you,' I said, standing up and moving towards him. But what could I say? That Iris was ignoring me after we had sex in my room? That to be alone with him made me afraid, even though he had never really done anything wrong. I had taken his offer of help and in my mind I had made it something sordid. Disgusting. I was the worst person in the world.

But what was it about? I wasn't even really sure that it was about Iris. I was starting to think that it was something more fundamental than that. Something about me. About who and what I was. In my mind there were so many questions I couldn't answer, and I was realising that the biggest and most difficult one was why Edward Lyons had singled me out; why he had done what he did; why I, time and time again, had allowed it. And more than that, why even now I still craved that kind of attention. How I missed him when I was asked to leave the school. What was wrong with me? What void lived in me that on the other side of the whole sorry mess, I wished in some dark, disturbing way that I was still in that maths cupboard with his hands on my body, and had no idea why.

'Hey, hey, hey,' Mr Aides said now, moving closer to me. He reached for me, held me in his arms. Pulled me close. His body felt strong. Warm. 'Whatever's the matter?'

'I don't know,' I sniffled. Wetness leached into his clothes, a mixture of tears and snot as he held me close. 'I just keep making such a mess of everything.'

'Is this about the Debussy?' I shook my head against his shoulder. 'Then what?'

'I'm just...' Too many thoughts: that I was a terrible person, something hateful, tainted and dirty. Something unworthy of any of this, the school, the opportunity, Aides' attention. Most of all, unworthy of Iris, and that she had started to ignore me because she knew it. I said none of that. 'I'm such a mess.'

'You are no such thing.'

'I am.'

A beat. 'Chloe,' he said, holding me tighter still. 'You're one of the most wonderful people I have ever met. I've seen the way you conduct yourself. Hard working and kind. I've seen you helping the younger students find their way around like you have been here for years. And your music. The way you play. Chloe,' he said, lifting my chin with his finger. 'You are magic.'

I shook my head. Heard my old headteacher's words after she hauled me into her office.

There is a scholarship available. We think it would be in your best interests to take it.

'I don't deserve to be here.'

'This school is very lucky to have you,' he insisted, his voice low but firm. 'And when you leave next year, it will be a much poorer institution for your absence.'

Heat flushed to my cheeks. But his kindness, his certainty that I deserved it... it felt so good. He began to move back, but I wasn't ready for it to be over. I didn't want the moment to end. So, I held onto him, and with a sound of surprise, he allowed me to hold him some more. Our faces close, I could smell his skin. Clean, warm. Woody.

'Chloe,' he said, his voice a whisper, a question. Fear. 'Chloe, what are you...'

Our faces came no more than a breath apart. And before I knew what I was doing, I reached up, let my lips rest against his. Just for a moment that was all it was. Not even a kiss. But I felt his body freeze. The power my movement gave me. For the briefest moment, his grip intensified, his warm tongue against mine, before jolting back, pushing me away.

'I'm sorry,' I said. I staggered back, wiping my mouth. Snatching up my music, I rushed for the door.

'Chloe, wait. Please.' He hurried forwards, pressed his hands against the door to stop me from leaving. Trapped. But I wasn't afraid. I knew he wouldn't try to hurt me or force me to stay. So I let go of the door handle, and he took a step back. 'Did I do something here that I... did I make you...' His words were soft, uncertain. A few steps further and I wouldn't have been able to hear him speak.

'You didn't,' I said.

'Good,' he said, nodding his head, straightening his shirt. 'Good. That's good, Chloe.' He stumbled then, moved as if he was uncomfortable in his skin. 'Of all the people here, you are the last one I'd want to hurt.'

'I know,' I said, although I didn't really know it. But his will to make it all right, to not linger over what happened made it possible to stay.

'So, we're okay?'

'Yes. Everything is fine. I shouldn't have... you know... done that.'

'Oh please, no apologies. Nothing happened, right?' We shared a smile, and then standing up straighter, he pulled at his belt, adjusted his trousers. 'But there was something I was going to tell you about your Cambridge audition.' He seemed distracted. Tidying up the edges of sheet music that didn't need tidying. Looking at the pictures on the wall as if he was there for the first time. 'Matthew has a bit of a thing about antique sheet music. Loves it in fact. That was why I bought the Chopin score for you. The one that you threw away.' I went to apologise but he held up his hand. 'No, please. There is no need.' His words shook with harried breaths. 'But it really would be ideal to have one for your audition when the time comes. They'll be announcing them soon. And I was thinking that perhaps before you leave on Friday for your weekend leave, that we might... that you might like me to...' A shake of his head, and he set the music he was holding back down. 'It's just that I'm almost certain that I saw an eighteenth-century copy of the Scarlatti piece in the music shop in the next town. Having it would certainly impress Matthew when you go for your audition.'

'Right,' I said. And it was obvious then, what I had done. Had opened a door. Had given him a view inside, of what could be possible. Of what I would be prepared to do. And I understood then that he had known all along about what happened at Clifton. He was just waiting for the moment when it would be possible for it to happen again. The room shrank away, and all I could see was him. I wasn't there anymore. Couldn't feel the ground. 'If Matthew would like it then...'

'It's a ten-minute drive,' he hurried. 'Fifteen at most. I could have you back here by three, ready to leave for your weekend leave.' I was supposed to be going with Iris, but I didn't even know if I was still welcome. 'Even the smallest details matter, Chloe,' he continued. 'One good choice, and it could all go the right way.'

Picturing their impressed faces as I approached my audition with an eighteenth-century Scarlatti score, I thought of the advantage, the success. The future I wanted. Or, if he chose to, how easy it would be for Mr Aides to tell his friend I wasn't that good after all.

'Sounds like a good idea,' I replied.

'Wonderful. But of course, it might be best...'

'Not to mention it to anybody?'

He gave me a nod. I reciprocated. And that was that. We understood the rules. I remembered the words that Edward Lyons had written in my maths book to direct me to the store cupboard. Asking if it was okay. The way he had erased them after confirming that I understood.

And I understood now, just as I did then. The deal between us was made.

19

I didn't sleep well for the rest of that week. The dawn chorus that had woken me since arriving at High Hill no longer rippled through the lilac skies of morning, the birds all flown south for the winter. Instead, I awoke to the cawing of crows. Sleepless hours rolled by each night, watching the moon track her course across the sky. I wasn't sure whether my insomnia stemmed from the fact the police were still to apprehend Jimmy Baxter, the planned trip with Mr Aides or the absence of Iris from my bed. Even though I was confused by what we had done, I missed her presence, the warmth of her body against mine. With her in my room, High Hill had started to feel like home. And without her, it felt like I was lost.

'Why don't you come here instead?' Mum had asked me when I called her on the Wednesday night before we were due our weekend release. 'We'd love to have you back. The place is so quiet without you.'

It was tempting. 'I'm invited to Iris's house, Mum. I want to go.'

'I know. It's just…' Silences lingered heavily in conversations with my mother. Things we didn't know how to say yet understood all the same. 'It's your dad, he's been…'

I curled the phone cord tight in my fingers. 'Been what?'

'I know he misses you, that's all. We both do.'

Over the years since his attempt to end his life, we had learned to speak in codes like the one she used then. To say that he missed me was enough. Because if that was all it was, he would have been talking to me on the phone. He'd want to hear my news first hand, listen to the cadence of my voice, which he always said reminded him of a lullaby. But we hadn't spoken since the day I started at High Hill.

'Put him on the phone,' I said. 'I'd like to talk to him.'

I listened to the quiver of her breath. 'He's having a bit of a rest. I know he wants to though, and...'

I hung up before letting her finish whatever excuse she was going to offer.

So that lunch time I sat alongside a small bag, packed with two changes of clothes and a few toiletries. Checking the time on my watch, I saw that it was close to half past one, the time I was supposed to meet Mr Aides. After our last theory lesson, he had asked me to meet him near a forest track, away from the school where we wouldn't be seen.

'It's just easier that way,' he'd said. 'You don't want any more rumours flying around about you, do you?'

I didn't dare ask what he meant. I already knew.

Leaving my bag where it was, I took the West Gate exit from the cloisters, followed the path that led towards the chapel. I kept my wits about me for anybody that might see me but was concealed by the fog that lingered on the pathways. Somewhere out to sea, a ferry sounded its horn.

Behind the chapel the path wound south, towards the cliffs, where the solid trunks of the local beech trees twisted into a web of spidery branches. Frost clung to their northern flanks, my breath fogging the air. Beneath the cliffs, the waves fought for their place at the shore.

Following the rough path that Aides had described, I wound through the forest, following the two lines cut in the ground from use by the local farmer. And soon enough I saw a perimeter gate, and behind that his vehicle, a 1999 Volvo estate.

'Goodness me,' he said, opening the door from inside. 'I'm terribly sorry about all this kerfuffle. Making you walk so far. It's much chillier than I expected today.'

Heat from inside the car tingled like needles against my cheeks. Drips eased from my nose. 'Yeah,' I said. 'It's freezing.'

'Where's your coat?'

'I didn't bring it,' I said, and he quickly reached to the back seat, which had been lowered, picking up his to hand to me.

'At least drape it over yourself,' he said, settling it over my knees. 'Strange to see you in your own clothes after so long,' he said, smiling. 'You look nice.'

I listened as he drove, to his stories about growing up on the south coast, his time at the beach with friends. Surfing in Newquay and playing a guitar by sandpit fires. He laughed at my shock when he confessed to smoking pot.

'A bit of rebellion is part of growing up. Sneaking around, getting away with things.' He gave me a wink as he lifted a joint from his pocket, before tucking it back in. 'It's what makes life exciting.'

And then, as we pulled into a village of winding streets and a hodgepodge of buildings, he stiffened up into the Mr Aides I recognised. Parking outside a small shop with a faded wooden frontage, a door that didn't quite seem to fit the space. Sighing as he turned off the engine.

'Here we are. The finest collection you will find of antique music for miles,' he said, holding out his hand as we stepped from the car. 'Even in London I am yet to find a place that stocks more.'

Inside was dark and wooden, racks of books and local maps. Near the back of the shop the music took over, and there were shelves of delicate scores wrapped in plastic files stretching out before me. Leafing through, I saw pieces by Satie, others by Mozart. Even the theme tune for *Titanic*. When I saw it, I let out a gasp.

'You like that?' he asked, and I nodded. 'Far too easy for you. I suspect you could play it on sight. But if I remember correctly, the composer has signed this one.' He turned it over, and there, on the back of the first sheet, I saw the signature. 'Look, it reads "James, I hope this meets your approval", and then here, signed "James" again. James Horner to James Cameron. Lovely, isn't it?' He tucked the file under his arm. 'Now let's see if we can find that piece by Scarlatti.'

Ten minutes later we were leaving the bookstore, both pieces of music in a small canvas tote, together with a copy of *The Da Vinci Code*, which he handed to me.

'Are you sure?' I asked as I took it. 'I feel bad. I don't have enough to pay for it.'

'If I wasn't sure, we wouldn't be here together. I didn't bring you here for you to spend your own money.'

'Yes, but you shouldn't have to buy these things for me,' I said. But all he did was smile, raise his eyebrows. There was no 'should' about it.

I waited in the car while he collected two cups of takeaway coffee, suggesting it wasn't a good idea for us to move about too much together while we were in town. In the bookstore, I had got the impression that the owner was a friend from years before, but anywhere else, he said, would only raise suspicions. Then we drove in silence, until we were halfway back through the forest. A small clearing opened up on our left, trees on all sides. Slowing, he turned into it, and I realised I could no longer see the track.

'Nobody will see us here,' he whispered.

He looked to me then, his mouth gently open, his teeth on show where his lips had pulled back. It almost looked like a snarl. It would have seemed strange if I didn't recognise it from before; it was the same look he gave me in the chapel following my first performance.

'Remember what I told you,' he said then. 'There is no such thing as "should". Only "want". So,' he said, pausing to wet his dry, cracked lips. 'Do you want to be here?'

Three weeks and Iris had barely spoken to me. Twice I had knocked on her door, knowing that she was in there, only to have her leave me on the step. I had nobody here. Wanted desperately not to feel alone. Wanted that moment of power I had felt in the music department when I had placed my lips on his. And so when he reached across, rested his hand against my leg, instead of protesting, I crawled across into the back seats, and undid the buttons on my jumper.

—

'You were supposed to come to my room,' she said. Twenty minutes had passed since I got back. My skin was hot from the water in the shower, pink from where I had scrubbed it. 'I've been waiting for you,' she said, stepping closer. 'My dad is already in the car.'

I glanced through my window, and sure enough I could see Professor Fairhurst standing at the edge of his silver Saab 9-3. But I didn't move. Couldn't, I think.

'Chloe, are you still coming? I left a note in your pigeonhole to tell you to be ready.'

Looking up, I was so grateful for her presence that I could have cried. A burning pain swelled from my core as I looked to the score music on my bedside table, and then back to her.

'I wasn't sure whether I was still welcome,' I said. 'I didn't get your note.'

Without a word she stepped into my room, pushed the door so that it was almost closed. 'Look, I know things have been weird,' she said. 'But it wasn't about you.' The space between us narrowed. I could smell the musk of her body spray. My pillows still smelled of it, of her, because I hadn't changed the sheets in over a month.

'I've hardly seen you since… since we…'

'I know.' Her face softened as she stepped forward. A chink of light through the clouds. 'I'm sorry. Things will be better now, I promise.'

'Are you?'

The floorboards creaked as she crouched before me, taking my hands in hers. Her skin was warm. Always so warm and soft. But then she looked up, and the clouds came back.

'Have you been crying?'

'No,' I said, trying to turn away.

Reaching up, she pressed her fingers to my cheek, bringing our gaze together. The cut on my lip had left a soft pink scar. 'You have. Is it because you thought I wasn't coming?'

I forced my face away to wipe my eyes. I closed them then, but all I could see was him. 'I looked for you,' I said, twisting my hands together to stop them shaking. My voice was breaking, my mouth dry. 'I came to your room so many times, but you never let me in.'

'I'm sorry.'

'And Francesca's. I could hear you inside. Why wouldn't you talk to me? What did I do?'

'Nothing, I'm...' She hesitated, had no answers. 'I'm sorry, Chloe. I thought it was for the best.'

'Why? I know I was a bit quiet afterwards, but it was my first time and I...'

'You don't have to explain. You have nothing to apologise for. It wasn't about you.'

'What was it about?' I gave her time to answer, but she said nothing. 'I haven't seen either of you in three weeks.' So many other things I wanted to say. So many reasons I felt hollow, turned inside out. It was as if I was peering into myself, but there was nothing to see, only a dark, endless void. 'You haven't spoken to me since that night when I told you about my dad, and when we made love,' I said, but coupled in with the words came the tears. 'I needed you.'

'Chloe, I'm sorry, I...'

Saying it aloud made it seem almost ridiculous. I watched as she looked to the painting my father had done, reinstated on the back of my desk. Her gaze ambled about the room as if it was her first time there, before settling on the tote bag I had brought with me from the shop. Lifting the edge, I saw the shadow cross her face as she noticed the plastic-covered sheet music inside.

'Where did you get this?' she asked. 'Who took you to that shop?'

Seconds passed before I could find the answer. 'Mr Aides,' I whispered.

Dropping to her knees, her face was closer to mine than it had been since that night. And before I knew it she was wrapping her arms around me, and my whole body was trembling, tears streaming down my face.

'Oh Chloe, what have you done?'

And then she held me tight, pulled in close to her chest. I let my eyes close, felt safe there in her arms. And even when we heard her father's car horn beeping from below, we didn't move. As if the rest of the world had simply ceased to exist.

20

Being away from the school came as a greater relief than I had anticipated. Professor Fairhurst's car was warm, the seats soft. Oasis played on the stereo as we drove, my hand held in Iris's. We made a pitstop at Ridgely, a school that bore no resemblance to ours. Brutalist concrete gave it the look of a prison, almost no windows at the front. Trees rose up like a perimeter fence, their high salutes offered to the sky.

Under the tyres the gravel of the driveway skidded, and Stan was there waiting, his weekend bag slung over his shoulder.

'You're late,' he said, pulling open the door.

'Are we?' his father asked as Stan slipped into the car and tossed his bag into the back.

'Watch it,' Iris snapped when it landed on her knees, but she shoved it out of the way and Stan said nothing, only looked between her and me, down to our hands linked together, before stifling what I thought was a sneer.

'How was your week?' Professor Fairhurst asked as he pulled back onto the road. Stan said nothing at first, only reached into his pocket, pulled out a packet of Marlboro Red and cracked the window open. 'We've spoken about this, Stan.'

'We can speak about it again if you'd like.'

And with that Stan lit the cigarette, and nobody else spoke for the rest of the journey.

I woke an hour later as the car slowed, my head resting on Iris's shoulder. Turning into the long driveway I saw the house before me rise from behind the neat hedges, a drift of smoke trailing from the chimney. It looked like a smaller version of High Hill, the windows dimpled and reflecting the clouds in the sky. Ivy grew up the walls as it did at the school, and a large oak tree hung like a halo over parts of the roof. Standing in the doorway was a woman dressed in an oversized jumper, with what looked like mud up her arms. Two springer spaniels ran out from behind her, chasing across a wet driveway, from where it looked to have rained only hours before.

'My love,' Mrs Fairhurst said as she wrapped her dirty arms around Iris, who ran from the car, and who in turn eased comfortably into her embrace. 'Goodness me, it's been weeks.'

'And yet you're still working,' Stan said as he strode past without a second glance, snapping his fingers for the dogs to follow. They did.

'You'd think we'd sent him to the gulags,' she said to me, smiling, warm and kindly as Iris stepped back. 'You must be Chloe.'

'Yes,' I said. 'Nice to meet you.' She pulled me close to her, holding her hands away from my clothes so as not to dirty mine.

'You too. I've heard a lot about you.'

'What are you making?' Iris asked, and I wondered if she was trying to change the subject.

'Another beautiful mythological creature,' she said, pulling a cloth from her jeans to wipe her hands. Professor Fairhurst came up to her then, and she placed a soft, tender kiss on his bearded cheek. 'But no more talk of work right now. I want to hear everything about school. It's been a difficult term.' I felt Iris's fingers find mine. 'Come on, let's get you inside. It's freezing out here.'

We stepped through the door, and I could smell spices cooking: cinnamon and apples, something baking in the oven. The heat was almost overbearing after being at High Hill, with a fire spitting and dancing in the grate. Ash spilled across the stone floor. Bookshelves stretched up to a high ceiling the whole wall along the hall, all sorts stacked upon them. Mum's house was always so neat, smelt clean, but this place was brimming with whatever took Mrs Fairhurst's fancy. I followed them up the stairs, where portraits of their family documented the passage of time.

'Here we are.'

Iris dropped her bags by the door and reached for a cat who had stretched out on her bed. White, with a squashed face that seemed disapproving. Its fur marked the coverlet that hung across the bed.

'This is Clio,' Iris said as she scooped it up, to which it meowed as if providing confirmation. She touched its face to hers, and in turn it wrapped its front paws around her neck as if reciprocating the hug. 'She's cute, hey?'

And she was. But although I reached out and stroked the cat, it was Iris who transfixed me. Here in this place, in a room painted orange, with posters of ancient landmarks from what I thought was either Italy or Greece, it was as if I was meeting a different version of the girl I had come to know. A life I had never seen before, a side of her that she had kept hidden.

'She's totally stupid, scared of everything,' she said, dropping the cat gently back to the bed. 'We can share if you like, but if you prefer, you can take one of the bedrooms up the hall.'

I looked over to Mrs Fairhurst, who smiled as she set my bag down on the bed.

'It doesn't matter to me. I had one of the other rooms made up in case, but you're more than welcome to bunk in together.' Her voice was different, an accent which I thought was French. 'Whatever you'd both prefer.'

I wondered if it was an insinuation. What exactly had Iris told her? But no matter what she made of us, no matter what she thought was happening between us, she was already back at the door, reaching for the handle.

'I thought we might grab a takeaway later,' she said. 'Chinese, okay?'

'Pizza,' Iris countered.

'That's a lot of carbs,' Mrs Fairhurst said, patting her tummy, which seemed perfectly toned.

'I know, but the pizza at High Hill is terrible,' Iris said. Entirely correct, the base always soggy and undercooked. 'And anyway, I'm leaving tomorrow.'

Mrs Fairhurst sighed, smiled, although it was tempered in comparison to the one when we arrived. 'Don't remind me. Still pepperoni?' Iris gave her a nod, and her mother winked, before closing the door behind her, leaving us together in the room.

21

She showed me her things and we played with the cat, chasing balls of paper under the bed and over the top. Giggling, we tried on her clothes, with a desperation stirring in my gut to see everything. Afterwards, she gifted me several pieces that she said she no longer wanted. Three crop tops and cargo trousers in army khaki she said her father hated. Uggs, like all the girls were wearing on Sundays at High Hill. A thick grey jumper from Topshop to wear when I said I was cold. Radiohead played on CD as we pored over a magazine with Brangelina inside, wrapped up in domestic bliss. She showed me her books about Rome, and archaeology in Greece. Replicas of beautiful ancient artefacts. Photographs she had taken the year before alongside the Macedonian tombs, and others in a sandstorm, taken before the pyramids of Egypt.

'One day, I'm going to find Alexander the Great's tomb,' she said, and the way she said it, with such certainty, made me believe that she would. 'People will remember me forever.'

That evening we ate the controversial pizza around the kitchen table, drinking red wine that sat heavily on my tongue, listening to mildly sexist jokes told by Professor Fairhurst, whose name I learned also to be Alexander. Iris's mother, Claudette, seemed good at pulling them together in a way her father wasn't. There were no boxes of Marlboro Red hanging around, and nobody swore like they had in the car. That journey seemed like a dream in comparison to the family I sat with now, as if none of it could have actually happened, and I had imagined the whole thing. And by the evening, in front of the fire, even Stan and his father were chatting about which subjects he needed help with, debating whether King Richard III was really the despot he was made out to be in Shakespearean fiction, or whether he died the brave soldier that Alexander resolved to describe.

At some point, Claudette went to bed, and Iris took me to her studio, one of the rooms towards the back of the house that backed onto the garden. Inside the floor was dusty, painted almost pink by the residue of clay. Shelves covered one wall, filled with sculptures of faces and heads.

'Did she do all of these?' I asked, closing in on an alabaster bust of a partially clothed woman.

'Yeah. She has a thing about Greece. That's why I'm called Iris, and the cat is Clio.'

'What about Stan?' I asked.

'Constantine,' she said. 'She wanted to call him Agamemnon, but Dad put a stop to that.' I laughed, tracing my fingers gently over the curves of clay. 'They're beautiful, right?'

'My dad would love them.'

'You see now why I thought it was cool to be an artist?' She lifted the plastic covering of her mother's work in progress and stood back to admire the partially finished bust. 'You should never be ashamed of who you are, Chloe. You are the only person you can ever be.'

But who was I? It was a question I wasn't sure I knew how to answer. So in silence we stood there, staring at the sculpture, dead eyes staring back. 'Who is it?' I eventually asked.

'Medusa.'

'Oh yeah. There's a statue of her in the courtyard, right? The witch?'

She stared at me from the corner of her eye. 'She wasn't a witch, Chloe. Medusa only became what she became because Athena transformed her as a punishment for her rape by Poseidon. Because it happened in her temple.' The word took me back to that afternoon. Soft clay moulded to my fingers as I steadied myself against the edge of the workbench. The car, the cold, the noises he made. The way he thanked me afterwards. I watched as Iris smoothed out a few imperfections on the face, making a stronger pout, pushing the lips into a smile. 'You know, Chloe, what he did to you was…'

'Please don't.' We had talked of it no more, and yet somehow she knew. She had seen me, the music and understood. 'I got into his car. I could have said no.'

Knuckles tapping against the glass startled us both, and we looked up to see Stan's smiling face, peering through the glass with a torch beneath his chin. Laughing over our shock.

'Fuck you, Stan,' she shouted, throwing a lump of soft clay at the glass. It struck at the same level as his forehead and brought a sliver of satisfaction as it slid across the glass. But then he angled the torch beam and we both realised what he was holding in his fingers.

'You want to?' she asked, and I nodded. We grabbed our coats, let the dogs outside as a pretence, before slipping into the dark towards the back of the garden to find Stan.

The flash of his cigarette lighter gave away his position, and so we followed the path down to the line of trees at the bottom of the garden. Nearby I could hear the flow of water, the wind rustling in the trees.

'Not even one night here and I am already going insane.' The orange flame glowed through the dark as he drew on the spliff. His words seemed to whistle as he handed it over. 'It's like time stood fucking still.'

'That's not such a bad thing,' Iris said as she took the joint, then a drag, before handing it across to me. 'I like being here.'

'Well, that's because you don't come home to...' He paused to balance a set of non-existent glasses on the tip of his nose, impersonated his father's crisp voice. 'Best years of my life were spent in the navy, boy. Didn't teach you to sail for nothing. It'll make a man out of you before you venture into the world.' I couldn't stifle the laugh; it was uncanny, the High Hill version of Professor Fairhurst. But when I turned to look at Iris, she wasn't laughing. It was the first time I felt a disconnect between them. The first time I saw them as two people, instead of two halves of a whole. I took another drag and handed the joint to Iris. I felt the hit of it wheedle into my brain.

'He only wants the best for you,' Iris said. Reaching up, that moment of irritation I was sure she had felt dissipated in a flash when she stroked his arm. I wondered whether I had imagined it, but either way, the tenderness with which she touched him then reminded me of how kind she could be to me. How much I had missed her.

'Bullshit. He wants me gone,' Stan said, before taking another long drag on the joint. 'And you know it.'

The dogs barked at our feet, eager for attention. One of them, the bigger of the two, dropped a ball against Iris's foot. 'You wanna play, Hec?' she said, drawing on the spliff. Passing it to me, she picked up the ball, headed off into the dark of the garden. I drew in a lungful of smoke and handed it back to Stan.

'How are you doing since the thing with Baxter?'

Some days I thought of it, others not at all. I used a different stairway now, going the long way around. But I still didn't know how I felt about what happened to me. Was still trying to work out why.

'They changed the lock on my door,' I said. 'There's a security guard outside at night now.'

'Fat lot of good that will do, he was in the school all along.' A truth I had tried hard to avoid. But also, it made no sense to me. Baxter had keys for every room in the school, so why attack me for my room key? 'Sorry,' he said. 'I didn't mean to make things worse.' I took another hit. 'How is Iris now?' Stan asked then. 'She must feel better now everybody is talking about Baxter. It's obvious he did it.'

I remembered her blank expression, the way she barely spoke when I suggested exactly that. I didn't want to admit that we hadn't seen much of each other for the last few weeks. Or anything about the reasons she had been avoiding me.

'Okay, I guess.'

'That's good,' he said, reaching for the joint. The heat from the end of it warmed my fingers. 'And what with everything else being said about Emily.'

Silence for a moment, before I broke it. 'What's being said?'

'You haven't heard?' I shook my head. 'You must be living under a fucking rock, Chloe.' Another drag, his words wheezing out. 'You saw Emily at the beach party. She got off with like four lads from Ridgely. I mean, it's a shame. Adam's a great bloke, and we all feel bad about it. But the truth is, Emily was a slut.' The word took me back to the toilets at Clifton, finding my name and phone number scratched into the wall, the word 'slut' right there with it.

'I don't see how that's relevant,' I said. 'Even if she fucked the whole of Ridgely.'

'Not far off, to be honest. Don't get me wrong; I'm not judging. But it does raise questions about why she was up there in the belltower. I know you told the police it was drugs, but the only thing she was addicted to was dick.'

'What?'

'Couldn't get enough of it. Rumour is that she was seeing somebody, and he found out about her messing about.'

'Seeing somebody at High Hill?'

'Yeah.' And then he leaned in, whispered in my ear as I heard Iris calling to Paris. 'I heard it was Jimmy Baxter she was fucking. But that's not who she was seeing.' He took one last toke on the spliff before stamping it out. 'They think somebody killed her out of jealousy. That she was seeing one of the teachers.'

—

A short while later Iris and I were in her room. I began to peel my clothes off, my guard down on account of the drugs. But I was also aware that things between us weren't simple anymore. Changing as if I wasn't there, she stripped off before pulling on her fluffy thick pyjamas. I stood like some gormless statue, not knowing what to do, dressed only in my Backstreet Boys T-shirt.

'It's all right,' she said, taking a step towards me. Reaching down she took my hand and pulled me in for a hug. Wrapping my arms around her felt right. Her soft body pressed up against mine, under a poster of the Parthenon. 'I'm glad you're here, and that things are okay between us again.'

I clung onto her certainty like a life raft. 'Are they?' I asked.

'Of course they are.'

She pulled away then and jumped into bed, hauling the covers up and over her. I grabbed the pyjamas she had let me borrow, dressed, and got into bed as well. But although the drugs had softened the edge of things, and I was grateful to be there with Iris, my thoughts were stuck on what Stan had said outside.

'You know what you said, about Emily messing about with Baxter,' I said, snuggling down. We both slipped under the sheets and turned to face each other. 'Well, Stan reckons—'

'Reckons what?'

Something about the speed she interrupted me reminded me of the moment in the garden, the way she had become irritated over Stan's response to their father's handling of his behaviour. These were family dynamics, things as an only child I had no idea about.

'That she was killed by somebody she was sleeping with.'

'Oh, yeah,' she said, and she softened then, pulled the quilt under her chin. 'I heard that too. That would make sense. Jimmy was definitely the one who killed her.'

'Maybe,' I said, and she turned sharply to me.

'You don't think so?'

'Stan said that the rumour at Ridgely is that she was cheating on him with a teacher. After what he did with me, I was wondering if...' And remembered Aides' face then, the anger simmering from him as he stood on the stairway on the night Emily died. The way he threatened her. And the way she responded... it was fearless. She practically ignored him. The words piled up in my throat. 'Do you think it could have been Mr Aides?'

Turning, she lay on her back and looked up at the ceiling. Moonlight gilded the room. She took a deep breath, and for a moment everything was still. Outside one of the dogs barked and a security light came on.

'I don't know,' she said. I felt her hand reaching for mine. 'But I've heard rumours about him. Some people believed that he was sleeping with Eloise Cunningham before she killed herself. And another girl from Hestia last year. He took her to a shop to buy music and books.' I felt something rising in my gut in the same way it had in the first days at High Hill. 'That's why when I saw the music in your room, I just...' She edged closer, pulled my hand against her chest. 'If it was Mr Aides, maybe she threatened him. Said she was going to tell. That would be a reason to hurt her, right?'

'You really think he could have hurt her though?'

'I don't see why not. After all, he hurt you.' Was that true? Had he hurt me? That idea implied he did something against my will, and I wasn't sure whether that was true. 'If you tell my dad about what he did to you, he'd have to tell the police.'

'I can't,' I said, sitting up in bed. I could already feel the tingle in my fingers, the onset of panic. I looked to the window, at the trees shifting and bending to the will of the wind. 'If anybody found out what happened he'd just say I agreed to it. And after what happened at Clifton, I can't face the...' She stared at me, waiting for an answer. I had said too much.

'What did happen at Clifton?'

The words were right there. I could almost feel them moving over my tongue. Yes, I thought. Tell her. She cares about me; she would believe me. But I wanted her to care about me as a whole person, not as a victim. I wanted her to look at me like she did now, not with pity and sympathy. The thought of her knowing the worst thing about me, knowing that whenever she saw me from that moment on would be through the lens of what Edward Lyons did, was too much. She already knew about Aides. I couldn't bear her knowing about Edward Lyons as well. And I also knew what it was like to lose her. I couldn't face that again.

'Nothing. But if they heard about Aides they'd blame me.' Her silence suggested her agreement. 'And plus, Aides knows the director of music at Trinity College.'

'Shit, Chloe. Is that why you did it?'

'No.' The answer came quickly, but was she right? Was that why I had slept with him? I thought the truth was harder to pin down. 'I don't know why I did it,' I said.

But we were interrupted then as we heard the door slam open, and turned to see Stan moving across the room. Without invitation he sat down on the edge of the bed.

'What the fuck, Stan?'

But he ignored her, instead, stared only at me. Something was different about him, some keen edge that I had never seen before. 'We're the same, you know?' he said. 'The same person. You wouldn't know the difference if you fucked me tonight instead of her. And you can if you like. I'm totally game. We can both do you if you want. I don't mind.'

'Stan, fuck off,' Iris said. She was already up and out of bed, shoving him from the room. He stumbled as she pushed her shoulder against him, and from the look in his eyes I wondered what drug he had taken. 'Get the fuck out of my room.'

The door slammed and she turned a key in the lock. I could still hear him on the other side of the door, muttering something about how he was the one with the dick. The expression on her face was one more of irritation than anger, as if she had seen it all before, but it changed when she looked back to me.

'Sorry about him,' she said. 'He's been a dickhead since before birth.' She was still for a moment, before she moved back to the bed to pull me close. But with my head against her shoulder, I felt myself begin to cry. 'Chlo,' she said then, surprised at my reaction. I felt her grip tighten. 'He's just being stupid. It's me he's teasing, not you. Shit,' she said, when she realised her words had not made anything better. 'I'm going to kill him for this.'

'No, it's not him,' I said, and I pulled away, wiped my eyes. I hated the fact I was crying. But it was too late. She already thought she understood. She thought she knew what it was about. But she didn't, not really. Because it wasn't just about Stan, or Aides. It was about something deeper than that. Something that came before High Hill.

'What you did with him today...' she began, her breath ragged as she found the right words. 'Did you want it?'

'I don't...' I began, but I didn't know what to say. Because in some sort of way I had wanted it, hadn't I? I knew what would happen and still I went. Surely that meant it was my fault. That it was my choice. And yet at the same time in that car, when I leaned across, clutching the music in my lap, I had felt no alternative but to reciprocate. Some things I realised weren't black or white. Some things didn't always make sense. Sometimes we were driven by forces we couldn't see nor feel, and yet they acted upon us anyway. Like the wind. He was a force so great, I couldn't even see him coming.

'I need to tell you what happened at Clifton,' I said. Words to describe it opened up like cuts. They bled over the sheets, her pyjamas. Wounds infected years and years before.

'Okay,' she said. 'I'm listening.'

And so I told her. About what happened with Edward Lyons. The scholarship a gift for my silence. The fact that my parents didn't know even now why I had been awarded such an honour. How I couldn't even look at them anymore for fear they would see the truth. About it. About me. About how I was it. That I had been reduced to his assault. Nothing more than a lie told. My tears soaked into her pyjamas. She held me tighter. And after that we didn't say any more, went to sleep with our faces aligned. Perhaps she didn't know what to say. Or maybe she knew that there was just nothing to be said that made any difference.

I don't know what time it was when I awoke, sometime after two, maybe three. But outside the wind was screaming, the tree branches scratching at the glass. My mouth was fuzzy, too dry, and I needed water. So, I slipped from bed, creeping through the almost silent house. The tick of a clock counted my steps. Everywhere was quiet, until I arrived at the edge of the kitchen, and saw a light on the other side. Peering through I could see a glass of wine, Claudette's fingers reaching out to it.

'We can't just ignore what he did, Alexander,' she said. 'We can't let that go by unnoticed. We have a responsibility to do something. It was assault. We both know she wasn't the first. He...' The word was too big, she could barely say it. 'Alexander, he raped...'

'Don't, Claudette. Please don't.'

I couldn't breathe, couldn't move. They were talking about me. Professor Fairhurst knew.

'And what am I supposed to do? Tell me that,' he said then, exasperated. On the verge of tears? 'Throw him out? You know how badly that would reflect on the school. On me.'

'Does it even matter?' Claudette asked. 'Seventeen years old, Alex. She was just a girl. We have to do something, no matter the consequences. What about our daughter? We have to do something to protect her from him.'

I ran away, back up the stairs. Burst through the door and slammed it shut. Iris jumped up, flicking on the light.

'What the fuck?'

And I couldn't help it then, couldn't hold it in any longer. Tears came, and she wrapped herself around me as if we were one and the same. Intertwined like the weave of a basket.

'It's going to be okay,' she said. Had she told her parents already? Had we been seen? Had they guessed? I didn't know what was worse.

'You told them?' I said. 'You told them what he did.'

Silent for a moment, she said nothing, as if she was still trying to understand what I just said. 'No. I didn't.'

'But they know. If people find out... God, if they know what I did with him, if they find out then...'

Panic was settling in, the tremble of it coming for me with total inevitability. But she took my hands, held them down at my sides. She kept me still. Then reached up to align my face with hers.

'I'll make this right, Chloe,' she said. 'I won't ever let him hurt you again.' And then, a whisper in my ear. Her eyes on mine. 'I love you.'

Such a simple phrase, and yet in that moment, it made everything better. 'I love you too,' I said.

She held me tighter, pressed her lips against my head. Nausea swirled in my guts.

'I'm going to make him pay for what he did to you,' she whispered. 'That's a promise. Even if it's the last thing I ever do.'

Before

22

I pull over in the carpark of the supermarket where I work, open the door and puke all over the wet tarmac. With a used tissue from the glovebox I wipe my face, take a sip of water from an old bottle I find on the floor, and wash the taste from my mouth. I check for a reply from Francesca but find nothing. Remind myself that she's in court. That Aides could have told me everything in the letter. That he has done exactly what Stan said he would, using any means to get close to me.

I head into the supermarket and use my pass to enter the storeroom. Stan found it easy to dismiss Aides' fears, but they don't leave my mind for a moment. The things he said, and how easily I believed him. Why does he still have such a hold over me? Why after twenty years do I still run when called like a little dog beaten by its owner? I must do what Stan told me to do and find a way to get past what he did. Find a way to heal.

But I can only do that if I face up to it. The things he did.

The things *I* did.

I grab the items from the storeroom that my mother needs, and at the last minute I take a second bag and fill it with things for Aides. I can't keep running. I need to hear him say he is sorry. Without paying I return to my car, begin the drive to my mum's.

—

The traffic to Harlow is easy, the roads quiet and steady. I pull up onto the kerb, in the shade of the conker tree that I used to throw sticks at as a kid. It takes some time before I let go of the wheel, click off my seatbelt. I can feel the tightness in my fingertips creeping in. It's always the same when I come here, like seeing a friend who thinks they know you, when really all they know is an obsolete version, the person you used to be. All around me I can see identikit houses, the plasterwork façade chipped and dirty, the windows too small. I take a couple of breaths, holding and releasing to a count of four. I read somewhere that it's supposed to make me feel relaxed. But I doubt anything could make that happen here.

As I head down the path, I notice the same details that always stand out, every time I come here. Daisies fading around the letterbox which Dad painted for my ninth birthday. A white trellis rotting at the side of the door. Another winter and it will fall apart. A pot in which the last flowers died seasons ago. I knock twice, trying not to think about any of it.

It takes time before Mum opens the door. Her hair is a mess, her body bent over a little. Dressed in a pink housecoat with a quilted section at the chest. Her slippers are tartan. Blue. Mine from High Hill Manor.

'You took your time,' she says before anything else. 'Did you get that body lotion?'

'Of course,' I say as I step inside and close the door. Kids tear up the street on bikes. I used to do the same. My old bike is still in the shed, discarded somewhere around the age of twelve. The same day my father tried to end his life. Nothing was fun like it used to be after that. A red steel frame and white wheels. Glittery streamers that have long since lost their shine.

'Too long on my own, that's the problem,' she says as I follow her into the lounge, my eyes on her stick. A new addition. 'What if I'd had a fall?'

'Then you'd use your lifeline,' I say, noticing the buzzer she wears around her neck. 'That's why I got it for you.'

'Stupid bloody thing,' she says, tossing it aside. 'I'm not an invalid.' She flops into her chair. 'And I wouldn't want any old stranger seeing me at my worst.'

I take the bag of shopping through to the kitchen, put the things away, tidying up the cupboards as I go. Place the shower gel and the body lotion on the stairs. The carpet is a little more worn than it used to be. Dust collects in the corner of each step.

'Did you boil the kettle?' she calls through from the lounge. 'I haven't had a cup since breakfast.'

'I'll make us one now.'

I reach for the cups from the sliding glass cupboard above the drainer and empty the old tea bags from the dish she keeps by the sink. One or two had started to mould. Details like this make everything worse, every time I come here. Like the dust on the stairs, or the drips of tea on the lino that nobody has cleaned. Unthinkable changes. Unavoidable truths. She was always so proud. How did we ever get here?

We drink our tea, watching a rerun of *Escape to the Country*. I make a second cup which I leave in a flask, and prep her a sandwich for that night, another covered by a cloth which I leave in the fridge for tomorrow. I bleach the stains from the floor and try to leave the kitchen as I know she would like it. Fresh sheets for her bed, a nice clean bathroom. I do what I can. Temptation stirs as I pass my bedroom, and I open the door, peek inside. Still a poster of Nick Carter on the wall. CDs stacked on the side. Other things, hidden away, that I don't want to remember. Letters and music and books. The shorts I kept from Lyons. Everything tainted. Time in this house has stood still. I close the door, catch my breath, and head back down the stairs.

'I'd better make a move, Mum,' I say, pulling on my coat. 'I'll see you in a few days.'

'Yes, yes,' she says as I kiss her on the head, not even bothering to look up. 'You've got a life to live. You can't waste all your time here with me.'

'It's not a waste,' I say. 'It's just I have some things I need to do.'

'I'd have things to do if your father was still here.' Tightness whips through my body, like a running stitch pulled tight. 'No man should have ever heard the things he did about his daughter.'

I look to the top of the TV. A picture frame, a small candle next to it, with a little carnation in a jar. I wonder where she got it from, as nothing grows in the garden anymore. And then to the frame, my father's face inside. Smiling, a happy day, although I don't know from when. Remembering how he left us never comes easy. It's like she forgets that when she lost a husband, I also lost a father. That I was there when it happened as well.

'Mum, I have to go.' I am at the door before I notice it. A piece of paper, my name written on the top. A telephone number underneath. I hold it up for her to see. 'What's this?'

She doesn't answer at first, as if she is trying to remember. Then I think, no. It's not trying to remember. It's like she is trying to decide whether to tell me or not.

'Mum?'

'Somebody called here looking for you.'

'Who?'

She shuffles past me towards the telephone table, seems frail, weak. There is a stale smell about her, and I feel helpless when I realise what it is. The alkalinity gets in my eyes. A failure on my part, in every way.

'I don't know.'

Spidery writing takes flight across the page. Not a number I recognise.

'I'll give them a call.'

And then, unlike her, she reaches out to take my hand. Her grip is tight, desperate. I look down at her zigzag fingers, the swollen knuckles and dry skin.

'Mum?' I say, watching as her grip intensifies and her fingers turn white with effort. 'Mum, stop it. That hurts.'

'Don't call them,' she says then, her piercing eyes focused on me in a way they never usually are. Her breaths are hurried, her words desperate. 'No good will come of it. It's not right.'

'What isn't?'

Her grip loosens, her eyes glistening with unshed tears. 'The past is the past, Chloe. You have to leave it there. Please,' she says, reaching for my hand again. 'Do it for me.'

'Did you really just say that?' I ask. All the times we have gone over it, the grief and guilt I have been forced to shoulder. 'You of all people telling me to leave it in the past?' And suddenly I am furious, cannot believe she has the nerve. For so many years she has lingered in the shadow of my father's death, and now she dares to tell me to move on. So, I take the note and storm from the house. Behind me I can hear her pleading, begging me not to leave like that. But by the time I reach the car she has already gone inside and has closed the front door.

And then I sit in my car, my hands trembling. Can't seem to catch my breath. I close my eyes, but when I do I see my father's face instead of the blackness I'm looking for. The last moments before he stepped in front of a tube train on the way to the final day of Aides' trial. I was standing right there, got his blood on my shoes. I listened as they cast Aides' sentence with flecks of it on my dress. Mum changed in an instant, me too I suppose. It's hard to convince myself that I wasn't the one to blame.

Once my breathing settles, I dial the number and wait for somebody to answer the call.

'Hello?'

A woman. At first I think it's Francesca, until I realise the voice is different.

'Yes, hello? Can I help you?' she asks again.

'My name is Chloe Carter. You left a message with my mum.'

'Oh, Miss Carter. Thanks so much for calling back. I've been trying to reach you for weeks. My name is Isobel Watts, and I am calling from the *Evening Herald*. I could really do with talking to you about...'

I should have expected it. Journalists, desperate for a story, any soundbite I can offer. I end the call and slam the phone down on the side. It rings again, so I silence it and toss the device into my bag. I look to the supplies I brought for Aides. Something twists in my gut. Pulls at me. A voice whispering in my ear. To go there. To see him. That Isobel Watts is not the only one with questions.

Stan said it earlier, asked me whether I wanted to be eighty years old and look back at my life, only to realise that Aides is the most significant thing about it. My mum died that day with my father. She gave up. But I don't want to give up. Don't want to live as if it's still 2005. I don't know how I'm supposed to move on, but I do know that I want to. That I have to at least try.

So, I turn the engine on, release the brake, and make my way to his place.

Before

23

Things with Iris were better after that, our connection renewed. Every morning since being at her house I had awoken to find her there. My hand in hers. We established that Miss McCabe checked on the other floors between ten and eleven, the same time as the guard made a round of the other wings, and we used that time for Iris to sneak in. We had made love, and it was even better than the first time. I had almost forgotten what happened with Aides. She made it easier. And every time I looked at Aides now, I thought about Emily, wondering if it was possible that he could have hurt her. If he could have been the one to have been there. Fear grew in my gut like an ulcer, worse every time I saw him.

When it happened, the Great Hall was full. Breakfasts of thick porridge and a shot glass of juice. One of those rare mornings when everything seemed to fit, including me. Light shone in from outside as the doors to the Great Hall opened. Silence washed over the pupils closest to the door, and I understood who it was. Immediate fears came to me: whether I had collected my linen back from the laundry, whether I had forgotten to change my sheets or lock my tuck box when I took a biscuit out the night before. Rules I was supposed to follow, that I often did not. Iris was always leaving stuff out too. Glancing down, I checked my uniform was correct, and that I hadn't forgotten to attach the white double neck band like I had the week before. A girl sitting opposite from me, worried about a drip of milk on her long skirt.

'What the fuck does he want now?' Iris whispered. But before I could answer, she was saying, 'Oh shit, he's coming to our table.'

'Good morning, Professor Fairhurst,' said Miss McCabe, standing up to greet him. Even she checked the lines of her dress, the neat pinning of her hair. 'A pleasure to have you join us for your morning refreshments.'

Somehow, her shock at his arrival only served to increase my anxiety. As if I already knew, could feel the truth of it in my bones. He looked around at the table, his eyes settling on Iris, and then me. No hint of a smile.

'I am not here for breakfast, Miss McCabe. I would like a word with one of your senior girls.'

'Oh,' she said, glancing around at us all. She spent no more time on me than she did any of the others. She had no idea what was coming. 'May I ask what it might be about?'

'You may not.' And then he turned to me. 'Miss Carter, please, follow me.' Nodding, half looking down, half at him, I began to stand, the girl to my right moving out of the way so that I could swing my legs from underneath the table. When I looked down at Iris, she was unmoved, her gaze still on her porridge.

'Miss McCabe,' he said then, any hint of the man whom I met at his home gone. 'You will also join us.'

And then he was away, striding across the Great Hall, all eyes on him. I quickly followed, could hear Miss McCabe

'All right,' I said, spoken as a question. 'I've made friends, I think.'

'Yes, I know Iris is very fond of you, and Claudette too. Which is why I find it terribly uncomfortable on the back of your visit to our home to have this discussion. But an item has come into my possession with your name on it.' My heart kicked against my chest as he set a copy of *The Da Vinci Code* on the desk. 'Might you recognise this?'

'No,' I lied. 'I don't think so.'

'You are, however, the only Chloe at this school. Considering the extensive nature of our grounds, and the fact we have no near neighbours, I can only assume that you were the intended recipient of this, and the dedication that we have found written within it.'

Miss McCabe reached forward, picked it up, opened the front cover. Read the verse inside. Her breathing shifted, and she set it back down, pushed it away. Her gaze fell to me.

'I suspect it is unnecessary to read out what is written,' Professor Fairhurst said then. And it was. Aides' words were forged in my brain ever since I had seen them. *Chloe,* he had written. *You have become the darkest of my secrets, but I will love you in the shadows that fill my tormented soul. I will miss your touch until we can be together again, Simon.*

'Professor Fairhurst,' Miss McCabe asked. 'Where was this found?'

He linked his fingers together, set them down on the desk.

'It is not important,' he said. 'But Chloe, if you have seen this inscription before, you must tell me.'

'I've never seen it before in my life.'

Silence then, as they worked out what to say next.

struggling to keep up behind. Nobody spoke, or moved, just the steady gallop of our footsteps to break the silence. We passed the Christmas tree that had gone up the week before and cut across the courtyard. The goddesses stood with their heads high, unmoved. As if reminding me to be strong. To not cave. But then I saw Medusa, turned into a monster for the things she had suffered. Her head cast to the floor. I was sure I could still see the rough stain of Emily's blood on the path.

I followed him through the cloisters and up the stairs until we reached his office. As he opened the heavy oak door, carved with scenes from the Bible, he stood aside to let me pass. I took a seat in the same chair as before, and Miss McCabe, when she caught up, took the second.

'What's going on?' I asked.

With a sigh, Professor Fairhurst closed the door and crossed the room, pulled out his chair.

'I know it must seem to you that I am a somewhat distant figure at this school, often up here in my office, locked away in my work,' he said as he sat down. 'Especially since we do not share any of the few classes I still teach. But I'd like to reassure you that I care very deeply about the wellbeing of our students here at High Hill. Your welfare, Chloe, as a pupil at this school is of paramount concern.' His skin was pale as winter fog, and he licked urgently at his dry lips. 'I know that it must have been a difficult adaptation for you over these first few months. Miss McCabe has reassured me that you are fitting in well, that you are in fact popular with the other students.' That was news to me. 'But I appreciate that you are in an unfamiliar environment, away from those you love. And the circumstances of this term have been, at best, challenging. How do you think you have coped?'

'It was noticed, by some, that you have become close with Mr Aides.' Words stirred, found a blockage in my throat. 'It would be only natural that you would develop a rapport, considering your talent in music.' Miss McCabe leaned closer. 'But if there was anything about your relationship with him that left you feeling uncomfortable, now would be the time to tell me, Chloe.'

I remained silent, didn't know what to say.

'Chloe?' Miss McCabe ventured, a gentle hand on mine. 'Do you have anything to say?'

And I did. There were questions I had. I hadn't known it until that moment, but it now seemed a priority to ask. 'Is it true that a girl jumped from the window in my room?' My voice was unrecognisable. So faint I could barely hear myself. 'Eloise... something?'

They shared a look, before Miss McCabe turned back to me. 'Chloe, I don't know how you—'

But Mr Fairhurst cut her off. 'Idle gossip is of no concern to you right now, Miss Carter. I want an answer to the question I have posed.'

They had said nothing, given me no direct answer, but I could see the truth of it in Miss McCabe's expression. The desperation as she looked from me to the book, before returning to my face. And so I shook my head, and when neither of them spoke, I said, 'Mr Aides is just a teacher, that's all. That's not even my book.'

'You are telling the truth?' he pushed.

'Yes.'

He took the book from the desk, stared at it for a moment, before placing it in his drawer.

'I suppose if you have nothing to say, you might as well go.' I went to get up, couldn't get out fast enough. 'But there was just one more thing.' He handed over an envelope, plain white and business-like, and franked with the mark of the University of Cambridge. 'I believe you have received an audition. It will take place in the first week of December. Congratulations, Miss Carter.'

I took the envelope, held it close to my chest, and walked towards the door. But the whole way there I could sense them watching me. And it was the sympathy on Miss McCabe's face that hurt more than anything. As if in some way I'd wronged her by not being able to speak. Her look of disappointment was worse than the judgement on his.

24

'It was you.'

Iris was sitting on the bed waiting for me when I got back. Her nails were bitten down, drops of blood seeping into the blue of her shirt.

'What did you tell him?'

Watery eyes stared back at me. Clear that she knew what was coming. But all I could see was the way it had happened. Her snooping through my things, finding the note. Looking for her opportunity since the night at her house.

When I spoke my voice was clear, and cold. 'I told you that if they found out what happened I could lose my scholarship. Do you want them to kick me out?'

'Of course not,' she said.

I tossed the audition letter down on the desk, and her eyes followed it. Picking up the envelope, a smile crossed her face. 'You got the audition? Oh, my God, Chloe. I am so—'

'Stop.' The words were right there. I wanted to celebrate. I wanted her to hug me and tell me she was proud. But I couldn't get past what she had done. 'I want you to leave,' I said instead.

'Chloe,' she said, reaching for me. Still, I remained like one of the statues in the gardens. A head full of snakes. I told myself she wasn't there. That I couldn't feel her touch. 'But I did it for you.'

But when I said nothing, she set the envelope back down on the desk. With a nod, she stepped past me, left the room, barely making a sound.

—

Another week passed like that. The weather set in, frost and mist shrouding our days. I'd listen at night to Iris moving around in her room, wishing that she was really there with me. She had tried numerous times to make amends, to talk to me, to spend the night, but I couldn't get past what she had done. Her betrayal deepened a wound I already carried, one that would need more time to heal.

Instead, I focused on the rehearsals for the Christmas concert in the Great Hall, inaugurated by an early covering of snow that blanketed everything in white. Fires crackled in the hearths, and colourful decorations glittered in the flames. Green garlands dripped from every surface. Days spent listening to the others play, sing and perform. I tried not to be alone with Mr Aides. Rumours had spread, and people were talking about the book that had been found in my room. But it wasn't just that. Since my discussion with Stan, I couldn't get it out of my mind that he could have been the one to hurt Emily. But on that particular day, he had scheduled me as the last person to practise. I had no choice but to stay.

'Fine,' Aides told Francesca as she finished her rendition of *Hark! The Herald Angels Sing*. It was strange to see her there, after weeks of not talking, avoiding her as much as I could. I hung back, almost afraid to get close. 'That's all I need from you.'

I watched as she stood up, collected her things, stopping only briefly when she noticed me waiting there.

'Enjoy rehearsals,' she said as she moved past me with a sneer.

'Ready, Chloe?' Mr Aides broke my daydream, and I turned to see him waiting by the grand piano. He held out a hand to motion to the stool. 'In your own time.'

I played the music we had selected for the Christmas concert, a romantic piece by Debussy. By then I wasn't sleeping well, and dark shadows hung under my eyes. But my insomnia meant that I had hours to practise, and I knew then that it was more than perfect.

'Well,' he said, smiling as he approached. 'You have made wonderful progress. Such movement in the notes, so much emotion in the presentation. If you play like that when you audition next week, they'll have no choice but to let you in. I have told Matthew to get ready.'

Admission into Cambridge felt like a dream. A life raft, the only thing I was holding onto that was getting me through each day. But his connection to the director could swing either in my favour or against me. Since the day in the forest, we had not tried to meet up again, and I was grateful for the fact he said he was too afraid.

'You don't seem all that pleased with it,' he said then. 'Is there something going on that I don't know about?' I hadn't told him that it was Iris who gave her father the book, but to even think about how I had cut her out after only just getting her back brought more tears to my eyes. 'You are upset about something.' He took a step closer. 'Does it have something to do with us?' I shook my head. 'Iris, then?'

I nodded, and a tear streaked across my cheek. He sat at my side and lowered his voice so that I had to lean in to hear the words he spoke.

'I know it was Iris who found the book.' A deep sigh, weary, as if he had expected better from me. 'You should have been more careful with it, should have expected something like that to happen if you left it lying around. She feels betrayed because of what happened between us.' Warmth from his hand brushed my cheek. 'And I know you care for her, Chloe, but you must not trust her. Iris is dangerous.'

'Dangerous?'

His eyes tight shut, he tried to force the words out. 'I have tried to keep it to myself. I shouldn't really tell you anything, but...' Nibbling a nail, he agonised over what to say next. 'I saw her, Chloe,' he whispered. 'On the night that Emily died.' My skin contracted, head to toe. 'I saw her coming down the stairs from the belltower.'

I tried to make sense of what he was saying, but I couldn't. It sounded so ridiculous, so impossible to think that she would be at the scene of a crime. And yet the more I tried to deny it, the more clearly the image of us returning from the beach came to me, the way she told me to ignore Emily's terrified cries. Pulling me away when I said we should go back. Laughing as she told me it was nothing less than what Emily deserved.

'What time did you see her?'

'Late.' The word came tight and strained. 'It wasn't long before the body was discovered. Ten minutes. Fifteen at most.' The implication was obvious, the two events twisting together like the DNA of a crime. But then I remembered what Stan told me, the rumours about Emily and one of the teachers. The fear I had been carrying around with me that he could have been involved.

'What were you doing there?'

With a nod of his head, he sighed. 'I know it doesn't look good. I should have been at home, in my quarters. But Chloe, there has been an increasing issue with drugs in this school. We are trying to prevent that information from leaking to the parents, worse still the press, but it's a problem. We are trying to prove the who and the how and the where. I was on duty. We believed that the transactions were taking place in the belltower. But how could I go to Professor Fairhurst and tell him I saw his daughter at the scene of a crime? I'd have lost my job.' He sighed, and I could see the difficulty he had wrestled with. But my thoughts were racing, desperate for a better explanation as to why Iris was in the belltower that night. Why she would keep it secret. I was about to probe further, wanted to know what else he might have seen, when the doors swung open at the rear of the Great Hall.

'Mr Aides.' The voice snapped like a reprimand, as if we had been caught doing something obscene. Everything becomes obscene when two people have seen each other naked.

'Miss McCabe,' he said, standing quickly from his chair. 'Welcome to the rehearsal. You have just missed Francesca Wright, but would you like to hear our star performer play?'

I smiled at her, one of the few people who had been nice to me since the day in Professor Fairhurst's office. Her care meant a lot, and occasionally she stopped by my room, knocked the door gently, to enquire whether I was doing all right. But my expression quivered, my thoughts still distorted by what Mr Aides had just told me. My lips trembling, my hands shaking.

She rested a hand against mine. 'Not this time, my dear,' she said. 'And in truth, Mr Aides, judging by the way she is shaking, she is in no fit state to perform. I can only assume that you are responsible for that.'

'I beg your pardon?' He was so calm. Such an easy lie. 'What are you trying to imply?'

'Oh, there is nothing left to imply. You are to report to Professor Fairhurst's office immediately. Chloe, I will escort you back to your room, and I will wait with you until Professor Fairhurst is ready for us.'

'Would you care to tell me what this is about?' Aides asked.

She looked at me. Then at him. Her cheeks were shaking as she pointed her finger and locked it like an arrow just an inch away from his face. 'You might be able to pull the wool over her eyes, but don't try the same act with me. I'll be escorting Miss Carter back to her room where her mother is waiting for her, and...'

'My what?' I asked.

'It's okay, dear. Nobody is angry at you. But as for you,' she said, turning again to Mr Aides. 'I look forward to tomorrow morning when it will no longer be necessary for me to pretend in your presence. For two years I have had to look upon your deceitful face and question what I thought I saw.' Her voice rose as a crescendo, her cheeks flushed with rage. 'To think of poor Eloise, the things I thought I knew... Your deceptions have made a mockery of us all.'

'I'm not sure I understand your...'

'Oh, you understand me well enough.' She looked at me, then again back to Aides. 'Whatever game you've been playing, Simon, it's done.'

25

By the time I was sitting in Professor Fairhurst's office a diary had been laid out on the desk, open to what they deemed a pertinent entry. Even though I knew I hadn't written it, I felt as if the words exposed something broken inside me, and that now, like a freak show, I was standing on display. Professor Fairhurst was sitting at his desk, in his Tudor king's chair, his face pale and drawn. My mother was in the seat that I had been sitting in weeks before, her eyes swollen with tears. Wet tissues crumpled in her lap, another on the floor, lost under her seat.

'Come, Chloe,' Professor Fairhurst said. 'Sit alongside your mother.'

I did as he asked, and as I sat my mother looked at me. Any fight she might have had long gone, her muscles barely holding her up. It was as if she could barely recognise my face.

'Now Chloe, I am sure you recognise the diary before you.'

I looked from the pale cream pages to him, and told the truth. 'I've never seen it before in my life.'

My mother let out a sob, her shoulders shaking.

'Chloe, if you speak with us honestly now, I promise you won't be in any trouble. We have already spoken to Mr Aides, who has told us that the contents of the diary are nothing more than a childish infatuation. He claims in fact that you have been pursuing him, trying your very best to...' He paused over the shape of the next word, struggling to say it. 'He suggests that you have been making efforts to seduce him.'

'What?' It was a lie. I hadn't done that, had I? It was less than half an hour since Miss McCabe had walked into the Great Hall, and in that brief time he had already sold me out? 'That's not true,' I said, not sure I sounded totally convinced.

Warm fingers stretched out to meet mine, my mother's hand. Something so familiar, that had touched me thousands of times. And yet between the day I left home to sitting together with her in that office, it felt as if a million things had changed. Her face was different, thinner. Her hair the colour of autumn instead of spring. Time had moved differently for us both, living now on separate timelines. In that moment she was nothing more than a stranger.

'Just tell the truth, love. That's all you've got to do.'

I sniffed back a tear, glanced over my shoulder, checking the rest of the room.

'Why isn't Dad here?' I asked.

She bit her lip, the tightness of her grip increasing around my fingers. 'He had a lot on with his work. He couldn't manage the time away.'

'Now, Chloe, please,' Professor Fairhurst pushed. 'What do you know of this diary?'

'I told you the truth,' I said, tears falling hot across my cheeks. 'I've never seen it before.'

Professor Fairhurst let out a sigh. 'But this is indeed your handwriting, is it not?' I lean forward as he taps the page, take in the letters. The scoop of the G and the long cross of the T. I nod, even though I cannot understand. It is my handwriting, but I did not write it. 'In which case Chloe, it's very difficult to believe you, especially when we have a witness who has seen you together with Mr Aides.' Another sob from my mother, her hand over her mouth as if she could have thrown up all over his green leather desk topper. I wanted to know who his witness was. Felt sure I already knew. Remembered the way Iris couldn't look at me as I was called from the Great Hall when the book was found. 'Of course, it is their word against yours. Almost impossible to decipher the truth. But you are not the first pupil that has caused me to question the conduct of Simon Aides.'

'I beg your pardon?' my mother said then, sitting forward in her seat. 'You mean to tell me that he's done something like this before?'

'I can assure you that a thorough investigation took place at the time, and we found no evidence of inappropriate conduct two years ago. I bring it up now only because…'

His words broke my trance. Two years ago? Was he talking about Eloise, just as Miss McCabe had done so in the Great Hall? When he said he had had the same conversation before, I had assumed he meant with me when they found the book. But now I knew it was not. It was about Eloise. This had all happened before, and Simon Aides had got away with it, while Eloise had taken her life. Professor Fairhurst reached forward, closed the diary. They all felt it, the shift. The truth settling in that I was not the first.

'Perhaps this diary is a work of fiction, as he says it is. But that does not mean he did not act in a way that encouraged it. And I might say to you both that I take the responsibilities of my staff very seriously. If he has done anything to encourage you, Chloe, anything at all,' he added, louder as if to make a point, 'I want to hear it.'

What could I say? The possibility that it had happened before made me feel so fucking stupid. I wanted to jump up from my chair and smash the things from his desk. Rage bubbled in my fingertips like I was on fire.

'From your silence I can only assume you do not wish to cooperate,' he said finally. 'But I might remind you that the very nature of your scholarship, Miss Carter, is based upon the excellence of both your performance and conduct. Without further cooperation on your part, you leave me with no choice but to exclude you from the school. Especially when taking into consideration the events that caused you to leave Clifton. I cannot permit something like that to happen here.'

'What happened at Clifton?' my mother asked. His cheeks flushed. He had said too much. She turned to me. 'She only left Clifton because of this scholarship. Right, Chloe?'

'I do not wish to go into the details, Mrs Carter, but there was an incident involving your daughter with a male teacher. It was most unfortunate, but here we like to believe we set a higher standard of conduct. I do not wish for such rumours to gain ground about High Hill Manor.'

She was shaking with emotion. 'It sounds to me as if something like that is already happening here. Right under your bloody nose.'

'Mrs Carter,' he shouted. 'I will not have you take that tone or use such language with me.'

'Why not? It's true. From what you're telling me it sounds as if my daughter has been taken advantage of. You can't exclude her because of that.'

'I can, and I will. Mr Aides was quite clear that you were the one who wrote the inscription in the book, Chloe. It seems there were no lengths to which you would not go to indulge this disturbing fantasy. Without a better explanation, I can only assume you are trying to cause trouble. Unless...' he said, taking his time. 'If you were encouraged in any way, forced into something against your will, irrespective of the contents of this diary, then I am happy to hear your side of it. Otherwise...'

The threat lingered between us. Until then my silence protected my place at High Hill, but now it was that very silence that would be the reason I lost it.

'And Cambridge?' I asked. 'My audition is in a couple of weeks.'

A brief nod. 'It would be most unfortunate if we were unable to support that.'

More tears were coming, I could feel them. I wanted nothing less than to cry in front of them all. But it wasn't even about the place or the audition; it was the fact Aides had blamed me. Said that I wrote the words in the book, that I was trying to seduce him. And although I knew I wasn't blameless, I didn't believe I should have to burden it alone. I thought of him with other girls. The music he had bought at least one of them. The complaint from two years prior. I was just the last in a long line of idiots who fell for his charade. Encouraged it, even. I felt so stupid. And it was with that realisation that I decided to speak.

'He bought me music,' I said then. 'He made me meet him in the forest and drove me to the shop. On the way back he pulled in. He touched my leg. I didn't have a choice.'

'Oh, Chloe,' my mother sobbed.

'You were forced? Into a sexual encounter?' The words were vomit in the professor's mouth. I nodded. 'Very well,' he said, standing up from the desk. 'Miss Carter, you may head back to your room. When we have further questions, we will come and find you. But my honest hope is that you and I might never have cause to speak of such distasteful matters again.'

I don't know what happened next. How I left, what I did. My mother was there for some time, but at some point I remember she told me that she had to go home. But I later learned through the grapevine of gossip that Aides was removed from the school. That at some point a decision was made not to involve the police. I didn't know whether I was grateful for that or not. How many men would get away with the terrible liberties they'd taken?

At one point that evening Francesca knocked on my door, Iris too. I let neither of them in. Didn't want to see anybody. All I could think about was how that afternoon I had been holding two lives in my hands: his in one, mine in the other. The scales tipped over my decision to speak up. If I hadn't, my life here, my chance for the future, would have been destroyed. If I told them the truth, I destroyed his. But what I couldn't get past was that when pushed, I chose to save myself. I had betrayed him. The most selfish thing I had ever done. And yet the most nefarious thing of all, that would taint every day of my life going forward, was that the act of confessing what he did to me had made me feel as if I had lied, when in fact all I had really done was tell the truth.

Before

26

'I'm not really supposed to let anybody in,' the man who opens the door says. He seems kind, reminds me of a social worker, the genteel way they have about them, even when they are discussing difficult things. I saw one after my father tried to kill himself the first time, and she spoke with a similar soft, breathy voice, which did little to put me at ease.

'I just want to give him this,' I say, holding up the bag. 'He's an old friend. I'll only be five minutes.'

A gentle nod thanks me for my thoughtfulness. 'Of course, but we've given him everything he needs.'

I don't see how that's possible. From outside I thought I had the wrong place, a graffiti-covered red-brick house on a forgotten East End street, green industrial-sized windows and a smell that got into my eyes. Derelict, I thought, until somebody exited, held open the door and asked me if I was going inside.

'Please,' I say, damp air creeping in through my clothes. The inside of the halfway house smells like mould. I can hear music coming from a pub next door, the voices of the bouncers outside. 'At least just ask him if he wants to see me.' He wavers on that, his training telling him that protocol does not always know best. And after another moment he relents, goes to check with Aides that he is awake, and that he's happy to receive a visitor. A few minutes later he is back in reception.

'Take the stairs to the second floor,' he says. 'Flat number six.'

I follow the narrow corridor, past the posters on the wall about searching for a job, and the rules of being on licence. Thin, threadbare carpet lines the stairs, reminds me of a cheap hotel. Fingerprints and grease mark the bannisters. By the time I reach the second floor, my cheeks burn pink, my back damp.

The door for flat six is ajar. When I knock it swings open on a loose hinge, and I see him sitting on the edge of the bed. Hands linked in his lap. When he sees me, he stands, as if he is suddenly uncertain of where he finds himself.

'It really is you,' he says, with a degree of confusion wrinkling up his face. 'How did you find out where I was staying?'

'You told me in your letter,' I say, holding it up. His responsibility for it takes him by surprise, and his eyebrows raise, lids close, like they used to when I'd make a mistake on the piano. 'You still never told me how you found my address.'

'No,' he says. 'I didn't.' Then he moves a jumper that is resting on the bed to clear a space for me to sit. I don't. 'After the way you left earlier, I didn't expect to see you again.'

'Yes, I'm sorry about that.'

Closed eyes, he bats his hand as if I shouldn't give it any more thought. But his gaze settles on the bedsheets, the mirror hanging on the wall. On the old, mismatched furniture. 'I can only apologise for where you find me. It's a little different to anywhere I have lived before.'

I only know one of those places, the small, terraced house at High Hill Manor, and even then I never saw inside. But I remember his stories about central Europe, how he was leading an orchestra in Austria. Can imagine his little flat, overlooking the Danube, with its lofty ceilings and draughty, eastern charm. Here the wallpaper is damp in places, the glue visible at the seams. A single bed covers one wall, and to the left there is what I suppose you could call a kitchenette. I push the door all but closed, and hand over the bag.

'What's this?'

'I thought you might need some things.'

Taking it, he sits back down, opening the carrier to see what's inside. Weird now, to see him without his coat and shoes. Like seeing inside a person's bathroom cabinet. Brown stains mark the toe of his sock, and his shoes stand proudly by the sink. His coat hangs on the back of the door, a creased T-shirt over a chair. Hairs poke out from around the neckline of the vest he was wearing underneath.

'Thank you very much for this,' he says, holding up the bag. 'I appreciate it.' He holds out a hand and suggests that I sit on the edge of the bed. As I do, he shuffles a short distance away.

'It's nothing really. I took the things from work.'

'Work?' he says, standing up, running some water into a kettle. 'What is it that you do?'

'Stack shelves.' If the idea of it surprises him, he doesn't let on. He always said I'd be commanding a stage within three years of leaving High Hill. 'A supermarket, five nights a week.'

'Do you still play at all?'

'I did for a while.' He takes cups from the cupboard and washes them in the sink with what looks like a new sponge. I wonder if he picked these things up himself, or whether they came with the flat. Taking a folded towel from the top drawer, he dries the cups and makes two mugs of tea. Hands one to me.

'I always imagined you performing,' he says, sitting down on the edge of the plastic chair. The T-shirt wrinkles under his weight. 'I thought about searching for you once. I don't mean in real life,' he adds when my face gives away the shock. 'I thought there would be some videos of you playing. I imagined you at the Royal Albert Hall.'

'I did play there once,' I say, uncomfortable at the memory.

And he finds pleasure in that, brighter than I expected. 'Of course you did.' It's almost as if that news comes as a relief. 'But you stopped playing after that?'

'Yeah,' I say, my voice breaking. The rest of the conversation sits on my tongue, but I can't bring myself to say it. Even now I don't want to let him down. 'You must be disappointed to think your efforts to teach me went to waste.'

'Oh, I wouldn't say that.' He presses his lips together into some sort of pitying smile. 'But it is true to say that neither of us followed the course we were supposed to, Chloe.' And the idea of it, the commonality we share, eases the pressure on my shoulders. Being here with him is not as hard as I expected it might be. Together our lives make more sense. And when I still haven't said anything, he speaks again. 'I'm very grateful that you came to me today. Of course I needed to tell you about Baxter, but aside from all that, I appreciate your effort. Seeing a person I know.' His voice softens, almost shy. 'There is nobody else left.'

'Your parents?'

'Both passed while I was inside.'

'I'm sorry.'

'It's okay. I could have attended their funerals if I'd wanted, but...' He shakes his head, his face tormented by memories. 'I didn't want to bring any more shame on them, you know? To turn up in handcuffs.' The pain of it is clear, the unspoken words stuck somewhere in his chest. 'I heard about your father, Chloe. It must have been hard to have witnessed that. I am terribly sorry. I wish I could have said that to you at the time.'

And it is nice to hear the simplicity with which he offers his sympathy. Twenty years and my mother has never once been able to offer me that.

'Thanks,' I say.

'I thought about you a lot after I heard. How hard it must have been.' He screws up his nose, shakes his head. 'Have you thought about me over the years at all?'

How can I tell him he stalks my dreams? There in the quiet moments of the day. How I have seen him sitting in a café, walking down the road and even in my bed when I open my eyes in the dark. That he's in everything I do, a shadow that I can never outrun. How can I tell him that sometimes I look in the mirror and can't believe that twenty years have passed since all of it. That in that time any man I have been with has shared his face. Has tasted and smelt like him. I have lived so much life, and yet, also, have lived not one single day. We are still there, in almost every way, at High Hill.

'Sometimes,' I say, everything from that afternoon swirling around in my head. 'But even now, twenty years on, and you still can't tell me the truth.'

'About what?'

'Jimmy Baxter. About Francesca.'

He shakes his head. 'Perhaps you struggle to believe me, but it's the truth.' Other lies he has told me over the years fight to escape, like when he told me that I was the most beautiful girl he had ever seen, that in his dreams he could see a future for us. That he loved me. I was a fool to believe anything he ever said. 'What reason would I have to lie to you now?'

'You don't need a reason, Simon. Everything you ever told me was one big fucking lie.' His body recedes into itself, his gaze falling. 'I don't think you ever told me the truth once.' Spent, I sit forwards on the edge of the bed, our bodies closer than they have been in years. 'You even lied to Professor Fairhurst about me. You told them it was all me.'

He shrugs as if I should have expected it, rests his head into his hand. 'What was I supposed to say, Chloe? That we had fucked each other in my car?' He gasps for breath. 'We weren't something that was supposed to be discussed.'

'We weren't anything, Simon. I was your student. Just like Eloise was.'

'Who?'

'It doesn't matter.'

With a heavy sigh he reaches into his bag, unzips one of the pockets to pull out a small tin. On the battered front there is a picture of King Edward VII. He flicks open the lid and pulls out a joint.

'You still partake?' he asks, holding it up. I recognise the tin. He's had it since then.

'I never buy it.'

He reaches for the lighter. 'That's not what I asked.'

We find a modicum of relief in the simple act of lighting the joint, even if we both know it is a temporary reprieve. He leans across the bed to open the window. Cool city air sneaks in, a light rain wetting the sheet. The rumble of a train as it passes through Shoreditch High Street. People stumbling out of a bar, having fun, enjoying their lives. They know nothing of us, sitting here together like this. Of what happened. Of what we did. Pinching the spliff between two fingers, the cherry burns bright as he draws in the smoke. The smell, watching him, the way he holds it between his fingers, folds time back upon itself. We could be in his car or walking through the forest before going back to school. *A little walk?* he'd asked after we'd had sex. And so I'd sat alongside him on the clifftop near High Hill, hidden by a wall of winter trees. We'd shared a joint then too, the wind buffeting our feet as they dangled over the edge. And I remember the urge I'd felt in that moment, the thought that I could have jumped. Done what Eloise had done. Wondering what he would have done if I had, flying like a discarded roach clip over the side. And I know he felt it too, because he put his hand on mine, and I saw the panicked look in his eye when he realised what I was contemplating. Seconds later, he suggested we go back.

'I know I lied,' he says then, handing me the joint. 'What I said to them was...' Words wrestle and wrangle to avoid his grip. 'I sold you out. It was unforgivable.' Hearing him say it brings a relief that has long evaded me. I rest against the wall at the other end of the bed, my muscles floppy and spent. 'Is that why you came here tonight? To hear me admit that I lied? To tell you that I'm sorry?'

'Maybe. I think so. I want to hear you be honest about what happened then.'

'Maybe we want the same thing.' Sadness grips him, and he shakes his head. 'I may have lied to the school, but I was honest with the police. Told the truth all the way through the trial, Chloe. I didn't lie as you did. When I say I didn't do the things they accused me of, I meant it.' He draws in another hit of the joint. 'But I don't think that's the reason you came, to hear my confession. Why did you really come here, Chloe?'

And for a while we sit, neither looking at each other. My gaze travels across the details of the carpet, a kaleidoscope of green and beige and blue. Across to his shoes, his jacket. Paperwork stacked in a little pile.

'I don't know what I want from you.'

'I think you do,' he says, little more than a whisper. 'You know what's in that bag, right?' I nod, look up to him. See the same look on his face as when I reached up to kiss him in the music department at High Hill. The thrill of something promised. The expectation taking shape. 'Did you put the condoms there?' Something shifts. Whether it's the drugs or just us, I don't know. Something loosens within me, some catch unhinged. 'Did you come here to fuck me, Chloe? Is that what this is about?'

When I say nothing, he rests his hand on my knee, as he did back then. Questions flood his eyes, rest heavily on his open lips. Questions he has asked before. Like how far I will let this go. How much will I let him do. Over the years I have hated him, regretted him, and yet now that we are together again, I realise I cannot find those same easy emotions. Simple to despise somebody from afar. No effort at all. Like breathing. But how can a person feel two things at once? How can I hate him and need him at the same time? How can I want to run, while needing for some inexplicable reason to stay?

'Would you like it if that's why I was here?' I ask.

He scoffs. 'I think having sex with you again might be enough to ruin me completely.'

'Maybe it would ruin us both.' His words come to mind. 'But that's not what I asked.'

A sigh. We stare at each other, wondering what it is the other one sees. His hand moves further up my thigh.

'It would be a bad idea,' he says.

'Yeah,' I say. 'But it always was.'

And after the briefest hesitation he leans towards me, his hands cold, his skin rough. One of them rests against my cheek, and he brushes the hair from my eye. He will kiss me now, and I want him to. I hate us both for it. Light bends through the open door. I worry somebody will come in. But it was always going to have to be open. I understand now; risk was the only reason it ever worked.

And as his unshaven lips touch mine, I am back there. In that car. It's 2005, and nothing has changed. I am the person I used to be before I lost part of myself. But at the same time, I am sure that I can smell the office in Clifton, feel the cold metal chair of the storeroom. Taste the tea on Edward Lyons' breath. That is where I am really stuck. The place where I was lost. None of this ever started with High Hill. For twenty years I have been trying to get back to the cupboard at the end of the maths corridor, to find the part of myself I left behind. To save myself. I am closer now than I have been in twenty years. Only a fraction away from being whole.

Cloth tears as he pulls at my bra, trapped by the weight of his hungry body. I try to focus on the details of the room, but I can't see properly. I no longer know whether my eyes are open or closed. Everything is dark. And once again I am what he said I am, a dark secret. A thing to be loved in the shadows. But in this dark place I realise that also I am found. With him there are no lies.

I reach down, undo the button on my jeans. With him I don't have to pretend.

Before

27

When I returned from telling Professor Fairhurst the truth, I discovered a vase full of blue iris flowers in my room. The crisp green stems and paper-soft petals were drooping in a rhomboid of light by the window. And I had no question about where they were from; Mrs Fairhurst always kept a vase in her studio to remind her of her daughter. Iris had put them there. But beautiful as they were, I picked up that vase, walked next door to her room and opened the door. She was lying on her bed, earphones in. I waited for her to see me and then launched the vase against the floor. Glass shattered into hundreds of pieces, water and flowers spreading into a puddle. I said nothing, only stared.

'You forged a diary?' I asked, and she gave a nod.

'I did it for you,' she said.

Glass crunched underfoot as I stepped closer, and irregular shards of it cut my skin. My blood leaked to the floor. 'Are you sure you did it for me... and not yourself?'

'What are you talking about?' she said, tossing her earphones to the bed. 'I did it to get rid of him. So that he can't hurt you again. I promised you, didn't I?'

Competing explanations filled my brain. I wanted to believe her. But there was one thing I kept returning to, that I just couldn't shake. 'Are you sure it wasn't something else?'

'Of course I am. Why?'

'Aides told me that he saw you there on the night Emily died.' Her cheeks blushed, and I realised, with disappointment, that it was true. 'Why were you in the belltower, Iris?'

'I don't know what you're talking about,' she said, but I knew she was lying. I could have cried with the truth of it.

'Was it you?' I asked her then. 'Did you kill her?'

'That's ridiculous,' she said, turning away from me. 'Why the hell would I have killed Emily? The whole country is looking for Jimmy Baxter. He is the one who killed her. I had no reason to.'

'But you did. You hated her because of the porn site she created. It was one of the first things you told me when I arrived.'

'So? Lots of people hated her. That doesn't mean I killed her.'

'You had no reason to leave her at the beach, but you still did.'

I turned to leave the room, wanted to get as far away from her as possible. But just as I reached the door, I heard her say, 'I told you that I loved you, Chloe.' Her voice was smaller than ever before. 'Doesn't that mean anything to you?'

I stopped, took two breaths. Said the first thing that came to mind. 'It means nothing.'

'Oh yeah?' Her voice trembled, as slight as a shadow at dawn. I stopped, my hand shaking against the door. 'What about when you said you loved me?'

'I was lying,' I said. 'I never really loved you.' All without turning, couldn't say it to her face. 'And I never want to see you again.'

For the rest of the night I locked myself in. Missed breakfast the next day. I was torn between competing ideas, evidence for more than one theory. I had thought Baxter had killed Emily, then suspected Aides. But Iris? Was I really prepared to entertain that idea? I was still thinking about it after a sleepless night when a heavy fist came hammering on my door. I would have ignored it if it wasn't for their persistence.

'Where is she?' Francesca said as I opened it.

'What?' I asked. 'Who?'

'What do you mean, who? Iris, stupid. Where is she?'

'How the hell should I know?' I asked. 'I haven't seen her.'

'And neither have I. I can't find her anywhere. She's been missing since last night.'

I pushed past and slammed open the door to her room. The flowers were still there, curling into soft twists on the floor. Glass shards untouched from the night before. The bed made. Earphones where she'd left them, as if she had got up the moment our conversation ended. Opening her trunk, I saw that her clothes were all still there. Her cape and uniforms hanging in the wardrobe. I remembered the cuts on her arms.

'We have to find her,' Francesca said.

Together we did another circuit of the school, all the places I could think she might be. We even went into the old library, and after that up into the belltower, past the police tape. Pushing open the door, I could hear the wind howling as it whipped around the bell. I climbed the dogleg stairs and glanced out to the coast. The Latin letters over which Emily tumbled. Nobody without fault. Still a residue of blood on the edge.

'When did you last see her, Fran?'

Breath quivered across her lips. 'We went down to the beach to smoke, and then when we got back up the steps, she said she...' She was close to tears. 'She said that she had somewhere she had to be.'

'Where?' Her hesitance stirred panic in my gut, the concern over what might have happened. Where she might have gone. 'Fran, please. Where did she go?'

'She said she was going to meet Aides in the forest.'

Francesca followed as I ran down the stairs, across the courtyard and lawns. Calling my name, telling me to slow down. But I couldn't. I needed to find her and couldn't waste a second. My chest was tight by the time I reached West Gate, but I didn't stop there. I ran as fast as I could, past the birch trees, the old chapel and the rocks where I had smoked a joint with Aides. Then I turned away from the sound of the sea, until I reached the track, running to the clearing where he had parked that day. It looked different by then, the trees bare, the branches white. And when I looked down, I saw two fresh tracks, little puddles of melted frost in the mud, where a car might have driven overnight.

'Francesca,' I began, and I saw the way she looked at me. Something just out of view in her expression. 'Aides told me about her being in the belltower on the night Emily died. If Iris is missing, you need to be honest with me; does she have something to hide?'

'She never saw Emily.' The response was quick, steady. Formulaic. 'But she knew that if Aides tells the police she was there, and she hasn't admitted to it, it looks...' she said, trying to catch her breath. 'It looks...'

'It looks like she was involved.'

We stood there for a moment then, neither of us sure what to do. It was me who broke the silence.

'Was she?'

'Chloe, how could you really think that?'

'I don't know anymore, Fran.'

But she shook her head. 'Iris was there that night to buy weed from Jimmy. But she never saw Emily. I swear it. But Aides hates her. He told her that he was going to go to the police. He wants revenge, Chloe. She cost him his job. He's going to try to frame her.'

I hung my face in my hands, began to cry. Where was Iris? Had he hurt her? What lengths would he go to to protect himself, if all along he really was the person who killed Emily? But no matter where she was now, hurt or hiding, I knew I couldn't let him get away with framing Iris for a crime she didn't commit. If we got in first, told the police that he was there instead, no matter what he said afterwards they would never really believe him. It would make anything he said look like a lie. And even though what we would have to say would also be a lie, it was nothing less than what he had done to me to save himself.

'We have to tell Professor Fairhurst that she's missing,' I said then.

'But what about Aides?' she asked. 'He will tell everybody that Iris was in the belltower on the night Emily died.'

I held out my hand, and she took it. Trembling, I thought, and I realised she was scared. I was too, but Iris hadn't given up on me when I was hurting. She took matters into her own hands. Now I had to do the same.

'I have an idea,' I told her, and together we made our way back to the school.

It took less than half an hour before the police arrived. They ran up and down corridors, searching the same rooms that I had already covered myself. At one point I lost Francesca, and only found her after they rounded us into the Great Hall for the second time that term. For the duration of the search we kept our silence, the presence of the police stifling any conversation we might have otherwise made. That was, until Francesca whispered to me so that only I could hear.

'What have we done, Chloe?' Her confidence and bravado were gone. When I looked up at her I found her pale, her lips trembling. 'We lied to the police. We've implicated him in Emily's murder. In Iris's disappearance.'

'He was the last person to see Iris before she disappeared,' I said, and she shook her head as if she couldn't quite believe where she found herself. 'If he hurt her, he deserves what's coming to him.'

'And if he didn't? We told the police we saw him in the belltower on the night Emily died,' she said. 'We didn't see what we said we saw.'

I formed the plan in the time it took us to return to the school: to offer the police investigating Emily's murder a vital piece of information that we had withheld. We confessed to having seen Mr Aides leaving the belltower on the night that Emily was murdered. It seemed to me like a perfect answer to his intention to reveal that Iris had been there. Who would believe him if we got in first, especially now that she was missing? The story we decided upon was that the three of us, me, Francesca and Iris, had seen Aides hurrying away from what we had not known at the time was a crime scene. That he had threatened us into silence, until yesterday when Iris had confronted him, told him that we intended to tell the truth. After that she went missing. The rest we would leave up to their imagination.

I took a breath. It was just one lie to protect Iris, but already it felt huge, unmanageable. But the lie had been spoken, brought into existence. We had no choice now but to carry it with us.

'All that matters now is protecting Iris,' I said. 'Until we find her.'

But the search of the school revealed nothing new. Even the next few days slipped by without any progress, the steady presence of the police littering the school grounds without result. Uncertainty garnered a sense of hope that maybe she had just run away. That fear was keeping us apart. It was impossible to concentrate on anything but Iris's disappearance. Everywhere I looked I remembered being with her. In the evenings I would sit at the desk in my window, books spread out before me, trying to find something of value to write. Yet deadlines came and went, and I cared little about whether it brought failure. I even stopped rehearsing for my audition at Cambridge. Nothing else mattered while Iris was missing.

Then one evening, on my way up from the music department, where I had sat at the piano without striking a note for over an hour, I saw Francesca on the stairs. She stopped ahead of me, her white shirt creased, a stain running down the front. A look on her face that sent goosebumps running across my skin.

'What is it?'

She descended the last few steps, her voice so low it was barely a whisper.

'I was just with Stan,' she said then as she sat down. The cold radiated from her clothes as I took a seat alongside her. 'He's pulling out of Ridgely.'

'But it's his final year. What about his exams?'

'Iris is his twin, Chloe.' Her eyes glistened with tears, but I was numb at the idea of it all. 'He misses her more than any of us. Professor Fairhurst's leaving too. They're going to go away for a while. To France.'

'But what if they find Iris? What if she comes back?'

Her body deflated a little, and she shook her head. Tears loosened across her cheeks. 'Chloe, she's not coming back. They found a knife with her blood on it.' My throat tightened. 'Stan just told me. It was discovered in Aides' quarters. A little blade, covered in her blood. You were right, Chloe,' she said then. 'Aides really did hurt her. They've arrested him on suspicion of both Emily and Iris's murders.'

Tears came and I crumpled to the floor. Iris was gone? He had killed her? My scream echoed through the school. I don't think there was another person who didn't hear it.

28

Only a day after the knife was found, Jimmy Baxter was picked up by the police, who, beyond my expectation, confirmed our version of events. That Aides was there in the belltower on the night Emily died. But he took it a step further, saying that he looked harassed, and frightened. With our testimony, and the knife discovered in Aides' home, his arrest came easily. Especially after the blood on the knife was proven to belong to Iris. As for Emily, the evidence was all circumstantial. But with several people all placing him at the scene of the crime, and a rumour that he might also have been sleeping with her, the police saw fit to charge him with her murder too.

I didn't leave my room for days. Francesca brought food that I didn't eat, and teachers pushed assignment notes under my door which I ignored. All I could think about was the empty room on the other side of my wall. The last time I had seen her. The flowers I had thrown back in her face. The last thing she had said. *I told you that I loved you, Chloe. Doesn't that mean anything to you?* And my answer. The awful thing I said. I would have given my own life for a chance to go back and tell her that it meant everything. That I loved her too. Instead I wrapped up in her jumper and tried to find her scent in the weave.

It was a week after Aides was charged when Miss McCabe knocked my door. She had let it go until then, but had decided enough was enough. She marched in and drew my curtains back. Pulled the sheets from over my body, until I was exposed and cold in the chilly room.

'I have had quite enough of this.' I turned, unmoved by her anger. Her face was bright red, her stance one of simmering rage. But it was an effort. I didn't buy it. 'High Hill Manor is not a place where we accept this kind of behaviour.' There was so much I wanted to say to that, and yet all of it went unsaid. 'Your audition is in less than a week, and I have heard on good authority that you are yet to practise once since Iris disappeared.'

'She didn't disappear,' I said. 'She was murdered. By Mr Aides.'

Her hands fussed for something to do, the word so big that it sent her off course. It had hit her like an asteroid from deep space. Murdered. Gone. Utterly unavoidable.

'And you?' she said, a little haughty, her lips pursed, and eyebrows raised. 'Are you dead as well? Because to me you seem very much alive, and yet you are up in this room wasting a scholarship.'

'I'm not wasting it.'

'Oh, then what would you call it? Making the most of the opportunities on offer to you? Because it certainly doesn't look like that to me.' She sat down on the edge of the bed. 'You have no idea how much I have tormented myself with what has happened. I feel responsible, Chloe. I should have acted when I thought something was happening with Eloise. But she was a terribly troubled young girl. I have no idea whether what they said about her and Mr Aides was true. But I am not deaf, nor blind. I heard the rumours just like everybody else did. Saw what I saw.' Part of me wanted to ask what she saw, although I stayed silent. 'I even asked him about it. He denied any wrongdoing, of course. But I know that she took several medicines for her mental wellbeing, and in the months before her death we should have done more. We should have seen it coming.'

'She killed herself because of him, didn't she?'

'I don't know.' Then, stepping back, she reached into my wardrobe, pulled out a uniform and my blue cape. Tossed them onto the bed.

'The state of this room is quite unacceptable, Miss Carter. It smells, it's untidy and you are behind in each of your subjects. I have a good mind to issue you a demerit.'

'I don't care.'

'Then how about I revoke your scholarship? Would you prefer that?' I said nothing, but the tears threatened, and she knew she had my attention. Softening then, she sat on the edge of the bed. A hand rested on my arm. 'Things happen beyond our control, Chloe. Things we don't deserve. Some of them have an explanation, and some of them don't. But regardless, we have no option but to live with them.' And when tears welled in her eyes, when I saw the pain she was trying to hide, my body crumpled. She pulled me close, like I was a little girl, holding me against her body. Breaking all the barriers she had put in place before that. 'She wouldn't have wanted this, Chloe. And you don't deserve to fail. Don't let your talents become poisoned by the things you have experienced here. Cambridge is less than a week away.'

And so that was how, just five days later, I found myself sitting on the blue velvet seats of the audition hall at Trinity College, Cambridge. A few prospective students clutched violins, another a cello. One girl was performing facial exercises, preparing herself to sing. Even with all those people waiting, the room felt huge, the ceiling as high and expansive as the sky. No place had ever made me feel smaller, not even High Hill. The soft wood of the stage was so light it seemed to glow, and on the other side of that was a blue curtain that covered whatever lay beyond like a secret promise. I wanted so much to see what was behind it.

'Miss Chloe Carter?'

I stood from my seat, took a slight glance behind me to see Miss McCabe sitting at the back. I was grateful for her nod of encouragement. I could barely feel my fingers, wondering which of the five professors sitting before the stage was Matthew Pemberton. Wondering what Aides had told him since his arrest. A woman sitting in the front row gave me a smile as I ascended the stage, but it did little to settle my nerves. I took my place at the piano, alone on the incredible stage.

'We have you down for three pieces,' she said, and it appeared to me from her central position that she was in charge. 'Is that right?'

'Yes,' I said. A swallow. 'Scarlatti, Liszt and Debussy.'

I waited as she browsed the list, before looking up with a smile. 'Well, I am looking forward to your choices. Whenever you are ready.'

I looked along the line, two other women, two men. Both men were in their fifties, maybe even their sixties. Where was Matthew Pemberton? Wasn't he supposed to have been at university together with Simon?

'Is the director of music going to be here?' I managed to ask. 'Mr Pemberton?'

The lady in the centre looked left then right at her colleagues, before returning to me. No hint of a smile on her face. 'Miss...' She checked her list. 'Carter. My name is Sophia Volkova. I am the director of music here.'

I looked along the line at their faces. 'What about Matthew Pemberton?' I asked.

The lady sat back in her chair, her arms folded across her chest. 'Miss Carter, I would have rather hoped you might have some prior knowledge of the faculty, if you were serious about attending this institution.'

And the truth was unavoidable. Another lie, then. The friend who worked at my favoured college, the music we just had to have. I felt so foolish, so stupid for having believed him. Believing that he had wanted to help me.

'Miss Carter, are you all right?'

When I looked up, I saw the row of professors waiting for me. Just to their left, Miss McCabe was heading down the aisle, making her way towards the stage. And the look on her face... such sadness, I thought. But not for what had happened, only what I would lose if I messed this up. She pressed her hands together as if in prayer, and gave me a slow, deliberate nod, a little offering of belief. That I could still do this. That I didn't need Matthew Pemberton, or Aides or anybody else.

'I'm fine,' I said, turning to the keys. I closed my eyes for a moment. Took a breath. And then I set the Scarlatti music that Simon Aides had bought for me on the stand of the piano and poised my fingers ready to play.

—

There was no relief as I expected once it was over. I thought there would be, but all I could do afterwards was dissect what I had done, replaying every note, wondering if I struck the right articulation, or whether the dynamics were as they should have been. As Simon had taught me. And when I arrived back at High Hill, I felt no hope for the future. There was a flatness to all things now, the edge of life softened so that every single thing felt the same.

It was late, after curfew, when I decided to cross the school and make my way to Francesca's room. The corridors were empty, the cloisters in darkness. Not a sound from the coast, or the wind. As if everybody else was gone. Arriving at Francesca's door, I pushed it open, and although it was late, I found she was still awake. She was kneeling on the floor with something in her hands.

Startled to see me there, she jumped up, her face red, her eyes swollen with tears. Moving fast, she shoved something from her hands underneath the bed.

'How was the audition?' she asked, brighter than I expected.

I looked from her to the floor, to the small bundle under the bed that I thought I could see. The High Hill-issue gloves she was wearing.

'Why are you wearing those?' I asked, and she quickly pulled them off.

'It's cold,' she said, but as I took a step closer, she took one back. Outside I heard a crow caw. Christmas lights from the trees on the driveway gleamed white and red against the dimpled glass. And when I looked to the space under the bed, she stepped between me and whatever it was she had put there.

'Don't do this, Chloe,' she said, wiping a tear from her cheek as I pushed her aside. 'Pretend you didn't see anything. It would be better for you like that.'

'I didn't see anything,' I said. 'But you're hiding something.' All she could do was shake her head. 'We lied to the police together,' I whispered. 'It's too late to shut me out now.'

Her face crumpled, and she began to cry. 'I'm not trying to shut you out,' she said, sitting down on the edge of the bed. 'I'm trying to protect you.' She took a breath, looked up to meet my gaze. 'Just as Iris wanted us to.' Her breathing quickened, and as I reached under, she caught my hand in hers. 'Once you know, you can't go back. This will change everything.'

There was no point in asking her what she was talking about again. I had seen people in shock before, knew myself what it felt like. Her arms hung pathetically by her sides, but as I crouched down, she didn't try to stop me.

'You weren't supposed to know,' she said as my fingers fumbled under the bed. A short way in, amidst dust and discarded clothes, next to some old paperback books, I found a soft cloth. Heavy as I tried to pull it. And when it came into the light, I realised that it was familiar in some way, as if I had seen it before. I recognised the colour, even in the low light. School grey, the colour of our summer PE uniform.

'What is this, Francesca?'

Her tongue licked at her dry lips. Hands shook as she went to reach for it, hesitating, until they eventually fell back to her sides.

'You'll have to look for yourself,' she said. 'I don't want to see it again.'

The more I looked at the little grey package, the less I wanted to open it up. She was right; once I did this, I could never go back. But I had already gone further than the point of retreat.

Acid rose at the back of my throat as I began to peel the shirt open. I froze for a moment when I saw the dark stains on the underside of it, little splotches that had seeped into the cloth. It could have been anything really. A coffee spill, or some other stain given the time to go brown. But I knew it was neither of those things. I knew without any doubt that it was blood.

My fingers trembled as I pulled open the top part of the cloth, the heavy object swaddled inside like a newborn baby. A blue trim curved around the neckline, and there, on the inside seam, I saw a name.

'This is Iris's shirt,' I said, to which Francesca cried again. Her body slumped in on itself, and she slipped to the floor alongside me. And as I pulled back the rest of the cloth, I saw the object inside: the bloody clapper from the belltower.

'I wanted to tell you,' she said then. 'But Iris made me promise. She didn't want you to know.'

'Know what?'

'Isn't it obvious?' she asked, to which I shook my head. 'Aides didn't kill Emily. Neither did Baxter. It was Iris.'

And with that the last few months came into the sharpest focus. As if time was fluid, and every moment that happened was happening again, all at once. I was standing in the belfry, watching Iris take the clapper. Could picture her hitting Emily over the head when she saw her buying drugs. Saw as she took the weapon and hid it, the bells ringing out upon the discovery of the broken body in the courtyard below. Then after that, sitting in her room, terrified to realise that nothing would ever be the same again, but that she would have to pretend as if they were.

'It was an accident, Chloe. She didn't mean for her to die. But Iris told me that afterwards there was blood, that Emily was confused. Staggering about. She must have fallen after Iris left.'

'That doesn't mean she killed her though.' Desperation had me like a vice. To make it make sense. To absolve her of any guilt. 'Like you say, it was an accident. All she did was injure her.'

'And you think the police would believe that?' And I knew she was right; they wouldn't. From the moment she hit her, she became intrinsically entangled in whatever happened next. Nobody would believe the rest of the story. 'And if you tell anybody, we're all fucked,' Francesca said then. 'They'll know we lied about Aides.'

But I wasn't going to tell anybody. Maybe Aides hadn't killed Emily, but he'd taken Iris from me. The bloody knife was found in his quarters, and there was a rumour there had been blood found on his cuff. I remembered her last promise to me, that she was going to make him pay for what he'd done. And now, with the weapon she used in my hand, I was the one who could help her see that through. He had been arrested on suspicion of two murders, and he would go to jail. All I had to do was lie and it would happen. It came easy. So I closed the cloth, wrapping the bloody clapper back inside, trying to work out how we could dispose of the weapon.

'I will hide it,' I said, uncertain about every option for doing so. But there was one thing I knew beyond any doubt: that I would protect Iris no matter the cost. If she killed Emily, even by accident, I would make sure nobody ever found out. Would make sure that Aides took the blame.

Because maintaining the lie, sending him to jail to protect Iris's memory, was the right thing to do. And it was the only thing I had left.

Before

29

His body stops above me, out of breath and statue-stiff.

'What is it?' I say, my arms wrapped around his shoulders. In his silence I become aware of the nakedness of my breasts. Cool air freezes the places where his saliva still rests. 'Simon, what's wrong?'

'I... I'm sorry, but...' Peeling away, he is panting for breath, moving the blankets to cover my chest. He can't look at me, and I begin to pull back. The truth settles over us. The absurdity of it. 'This is not your fault, Chloe. I'm truly sorry, but I think you should go.'

Only once I'm dressed do I look across to him again, find his eyes closed. His beard is no longer neat, his hair a mess. My head is heavy from the joint we shared. He feels different now, more of a stranger than ever. I glance about the room, the shoddy conditions, the moulding wallpaper and ratty old sheets. I look down at my hands, and barely recognise them. A picture of my own flat comes to me. The nice blanket I keep on the sofa, and the crisp white sheets I always have on my bed. Steamed, clean. Pure. I have to leave. I grab the phone, check the time, then I move towards the door, pull it open. Can't be with him any longer.

'I was going to lose my job,' he says. I stop, wait. The corridor beckons. I could run, but I came here to try to move forward. If I leave now, I might never get the chance to hear his explanation again. 'My fiancée had ended our engagement. My parents were so ashamed they could barely look at me. My whole life had fallen apart when people learned what I had done with you, Chloe.' Turning back, I see him drag a rough hand across his weary face. 'When you told the police that you saw me leaving the belltower, that was it for me. Wasn't my shame enough for you? You needed them to think of me as a murderer too?'

'They found a knife in your quarters, Simon. Iris's blood was on your shirt. I might have told them a lie when I said I saw you leaving the belltower, but I didn't fabricate the evidence. You killed Iris.'

'I did not.'

'I don't believe you. If you were innocent, why didn't you initiate an appeal? Twenty years you have been inside, Simon, and not once did you try to get your sentence repealed.'

'I had my reasons.' He presses the base of his hands against his eyes. 'I never even saw Iris the night she disappeared, Chloe. I was at home, trying to explain to Susan what a massive fucking mistake I'd made, hoping she would stay with me.' It takes a moment to place the name before I remember that was his fiancée. 'She was so angry with me that she refused to give me an alibi.'

'You're telling me she let you go to prison for twenty years when she knew you were innocent? You were supposed to get married.'

'You have to remember just how much I hurt her. How much I humiliated her. She moved away for a while, forgot me I suppose. But a few years later she came to see me. She apologised. She told me that she would confess. Change her statement, and help me launch another appeal. You could ask her yourself if you like.'

'But you never did,' I say. 'Why not?'

He bites his lip. 'It's not always as simple as that, and I didn't want to compromise her integrity. I'd tarnished her life enough. But I promise you I am telling the truth. I was with her the whole night. And yet you *knew* Iris had killed Emily, and still you set me up to protect her.'

'You were going to tell the police that you saw her in the belltower.'

'And would that have been unfair? Would it not have been reasonable to tell them what I thought might help uncover the truth about the death of a pupil? I had stayed quiet for months, trying to protect my job at High Hill. After they fired me, there was no reason to hide what I knew anymore. I was trying to do the right thing.'

'You wanted vengeance,' I say. 'Because she forged the diary that got you fired.'

'Maybe,' he says, sniffling into a tissue. 'I can't deny it felt good. But I saw what I saw. I told the truth. But you lied, Chloe, and because of that I got charged with Emily's murder. Iris's too. But I never killed anybody. And I think, from the very fact you're still here, deep down you know what I'm saying to be true.'

His thumb draws across the lighter as he lifts another spliff to his lips, and I listen to the crackle as he draws life into it. White smoke twists into the room. Three more puffs before he speaks again.

'Everybody involved in the trial, every person who testified against me, was lying. You, Francesca and Jimmy Baxter. I knew it, you knew it, and so did they. Even if you believed that I hurt Iris, which I did not, all along each one of you knew that I didn't hurt Emily, and yet you sold me down the river. But I promise you this: I am no murderer. I didn't kill Emily, and I most certainly didn't kill Iris. I know how much that would have hurt you.'

And the strangest thing, as I close the door to his room and walk down the corridor, is that for the first time since he was charged, I think I might just believe him. Would have to if Susan really could provide an alibi for that night. There were forensics that I thought were foolproof. They had the knife with his fingerprints, her blood. Drops of her blood on his clothes. Another speck by his kitchen sink. Sure, they never found her body, but that didn't mean he hadn't taken her life. But if Aides was an innocent bystander who went to jail for a crime he didn't commit, it means the person who really did hurt Iris is still out there. Who else wanted to hurt her? Who could have murdered her? And the whole way home I remember the marks on her arms. The horrible way I treated her. Just one detail changes, and it creates so many questions for which I have no answers. Other possibilities I don't want to face.

By the time I get home it is almost 1 a.m. I appreciate the kinder atmosphere, the kind of place where people can breathe. I turn into the narrow street, rumbling over the cobblestones, all the way to the end of the road where my apartment awaits. Everything about it is hidden from view. I knew as soon as I saw it that it was perfect for me, and I have that same feeling now. Of returning to a sanctuary. The place I can hide myself from the rest of the world. At a quick glance you'd never even know it was there, yet I can be in Hyde Park in five minutes on foot. Stepping from the car, the rain hammers down as I hurry along the street, eager for the shelter of home. I open the door to my building, passing the table to my right with the flyers and letters that my neighbour no doubt collected earlier on today. When I enter my flat, drop my keys on the table by the door, I'm still thinking about what I just did with Aides. What was I hoping to find with him? The same thing I was always looking for? Some sense of who I really am? Was? Will be in the future? But in the end, I found exactly what being with Aides gave me all along, which was nothing more than a renewed sense of self-loathing.

'You disgust me,' I say at my reflection in the mirror, my hair hanging in thick wet clumps about my face. But then I realise that is not right. 'You are disgusting,' I say as an amendment, realising that is closer to what I believe to be the truth.

I check the notifications on my phone, searching for any sign that Francesca has been in touch. Instead, I find a message from the journalist who I spoke with as I was leaving Mum's place.

> Thanks for calling back earlier. All I want to do is chat with you about the case. I have information you need to know about the disappearance of Iris Fairhurst. Please, give me another call.
>
> Isobel

I realise that I also have another missed call, from an unknown number from that afternoon. I call back despite the time but get the answering machine of a funeral parlour in Sussex. A wrong number, I assume, and so I leave no message. I set the phone down and pace the flat. Make sure the door is locked. The windows too. I picture Aides in that horrible little room, and then picture myself, underneath him, wanting him to fuck me and hating myself for needing it. Even more for his incapability to follow it through. Everything is such a mess. Nothing more than me.

I smoke a cigarette, then step into the shower to let the water fall against my face. The temperature is so high I can barely take it, and yet I force myself underneath until I am numb from the heat of it. I reach for the shower gel, but at the same time I notice the shift in light. The shadow of something moving to my left. I stand dead still. Seconds pass in silence, the fall of water the only sound to break it. But the shadow shifts again and this time it looks like the movement of a person. And just a second later I hear something fall from the shelf where I keep my toothbrush. Glass smashing against the sink. And before I can do anything else, the strike hits me square in the chest.

I am already falling when they reach for me. Hands lock with the force of a vice around my throat. With their weight surging towards me, I crash into the back of the bathtub. The curtain falls as I reach for it, suffocating me like a shroud. Gasping for breath, I try to scream, but nothing more than a choke escapes as my attacker's grip intensifies around my neck. Arms flail and fight against the bulk of their body, but despite how hard I fight to get free, I can already sense my sight is fading. My muscles grow weaker. I try to scream again, but nothing comes out, and I think how if this doesn't end I will die. Can't catch another breath. I am back on the stairs in High Hill, my blue cape pulled over my face as Baxter rifles around for the key. With the shower curtain tight against my face, it is as if I have already been buried.

And then as quick as it all began, I feel the tension around my throat loosen, hear footsteps as the perpetrator chases through my flat. The ringing of a telephone in the background. The slam of a door as they leave. It takes everything I have to pull myself upright, choking for breath as I fight my way out from under the fallen curtain. But as I sit up, the water still running above me, I see that the person who was here has left me a message, one even stronger than the attack on my life. For twenty years I have worked hard to convince myself that I did the right thing, only now, looking at what the attacker left here, I know I was wrong. Eight little letters painted in the steam, drips running from each through the mist. Two words, which leave me in no doubt about the part I played in this mess.

Don't tell.

PART TWO

30

After the attack, I couldn't stay in my apartment. I got out as fast as I could, and came to a café near Liverpool Street, with the kind of busy vibe you'd expect from a place that never closes. Garish rainbow colours cover the walls, adorned with photographs of tired, famous faces. A taxidermy stag's head looms over the front door.

Since three thirty when I arrived, I have seen several crowds come and go. Drunken antics of night replaced by the early morning crew of workers. At least one police car stopped for coffees, which brought me little sense of comfort. Any sane person would have called them after what happened in my bathroom, but what was I going to say? That somebody attacked me upon the release of the man I wrongly sent to prison? The words written in my bathroom mirror were even stronger confirmation that Aides was not to blame for Iris's death; somebody wanted to warn me not to speak out. Calling the police would have raised too many questions, so I left the scene as it was, and ran.

'Chloe?'

I startle at the sound of my name, see a woman approaching from the side. She is older than I thought she would be from her soft voice on the phone, her face lined and sallow. Tired eyes sit in halos of grey, like a war reporter dressed in a bomb vest and protective hat, exhausted, but with a resolve that belies the chaos.

'Isobel?' Holding out her hand, she nods, and we shake, and in her touch I find a degree of reassurance for the first time since the attack. Solid and firm. And just a second later she's in her seat with her arms folded against the table, straight to business. A notebook opened, a pen to hand. 'Thanks for coming,' I say as I sit back down.

'They left their mark all right,' she says, pointing to my throat. I turn to see my reflection in the window and find purple welts forming a broken ring around my neck. I pull my scarf higher, try to cover them. 'I'm going to make some notes if you don't mind.'

As I recap what happened she scribbles down timings, makes a small diagram of my neck, adding crosses in places that indicate the position of my injuries. The waiter interrupts to take her order, and after he brings her coffee to the table, she stirs in some sugar and takes a sip.

'I suppose my first question after hearing all that is why the hell you called me first?'

'Because you said you had information about Iris Fairhurst.'

'Yes, I did.' Another moment passes where she seems to contemplate whether to continue or not. A sigh, wearied by it all, but I see the decision is made. 'And you think this is related to the case?'

A tight knot of pain has wedged itself behind my eyes, and I bring my fingers up, trying to push it away.

'I know it is,' I say. 'I just don't know how or why.'

'You don't remember me, Chloe, but I was also a pupil at High Hill. Unlike you, I loved my time there. Even used to like the uniform.' Her eye roll raises a pathetic smile as it comes to me then, the weight of the cape, the way I used to swing it over my shoulders. How different I felt from anything in my life before that as I made the cold walk across the manicured gardens in the winter. I could be back there now, looking across the chapel pews at Aides. 'And my sister was a High Hill pupil too, three years above me.' A deep breath. 'Her name was Emily Ashbourne.'

Hearing the name stuns me for a moment. I remember the memorial we held when she died, the performance on the cello. And despite the changes to her face, how she has aged, her lack of any effort, I do think I can see the girl I remember from High Hill in Isobel's features.

'You were a cross-country runner. You played the cello.'

A weary nod of her head confirms I am right. 'Until that point, yes. But everything changed for us after Emily was murdered. Nobody in my family was ever the same again. There was always this...' Pausing, she looks for the right word. 'I don't know, this albatross that we dragged around. None of us have ever been able to let it go. None of us more so than me.'

'It was a terrible age to lose a sister the way you did.'

A hardness sets into her jaw, the bones tight and teeth clenched. 'It's got nothing to do with my age, and everything to do with the fact that before she died, I failed her. She died because of me, Chloe. And I need your help to try and put things right.' Another sip of coffee, fiddling with her pen. Her fingers rub at her wedding ring. 'Before you arrived at High Hill, Emily used to be the girl that everybody loved, and until year twelve the only thing she was into was her schoolwork. Her music, the stupid maths competitions she always won. She was a model student. But in the year before she died, she changed. Became moody, stopped working. She didn't want to go to church when we were at home. My parents were clueless. But a few months into this change, I discovered that she had a boyfriend. She never admitted it, but I used to hear her on the phone to him, whispering at night. I used to spy on her, you see, like little sisters do. I was only thirteen, so I'd listen in to her conversations from behind the door. But one night, late in the summer, I heard her crying. She told him that she was pregnant.'

'What?' I can't move for the shock of it. My mouth drops open, loose as a flag when the wind drops.

With her eyes closed, as if she hasn't slept in years, she gives a nod of her head. 'It was a shock to me too. I mean, our parents were strict Catholics, and I thought she cared about that. If I hadn't heard it from her own lips I would never have believed it.' I remember the little cross she always wore, the rumours about her sleeping around. The contradiction of it all. 'I don't know whether she lost the baby after that, had an abortion or what. All she ever wanted to be was a doctor. When the postmortem was conducted they never mentioned anything about a pregnancy, so that information never made the trial. Maybe they never tested her, or maybe my parents knew, and paid for a cover-up. I can totally see them doing that. But whether she was or was not pregnant at the time of her death is not what's relevant here. What matters is that somebody she was sleeping with thought she was pregnant just a few weeks before she died. And based on the conversation I heard, he did not want that baby.'

'Did you find out who it was?'

'My parents tried to protect me from a lot of the details that were read out in court, but when you and Francesca placed Simon Aides in the belltower, I assumed it was him. Especially after you testified that he had abused you too.'

'I never said he had abused me.'

She stares at me for a moment, before giving me a brief nod of her head. 'Either way, that would have certainly explained why she was so secretive about everything. I mean, if she was pregnant by her teacher, that would have been a very good reason for him to want to keep it quiet. And so I spent years hating him, certain that the right man was in jail. I felt so guilty, because I kept thinking if I'd just told my parents what I overheard, she might still have been alive. It ate away at me, to be honest with you. And then a couple of years ago I lost a baby myself, and it nearly broke me when I thought about what my sister must have gone through at the time. When she was so young, and essentially alone. All my guilt for not speaking up came crashing down on me. Strange how one wound opens all the rest.

'A therapist I was seeing said that I should try to forgive Aides as a way to eventually forgive myself. So I managed to arrange a meeting with him. Took me ages; he refused until I told him that I wanted to draft a favourable story, that I believed in his innocence. Wouldn't meet me to say sorry, but he's such a fucking narcissist that he agreed to meet me for a decent headline.' Younger than me and so much braver. How many times did I stand at the gates to that prison, wishing I had the strength to go inside? 'I thought if I could just make him see me, I'd get him to admit what he did. And don't get me wrong,' she says, holding up her hands in protest. 'I know what he is. What he did to you was terrible, and you were not the only one. But what surprised me the most was that when he insisted that he was innocent in terms of my sister's murder, I believed him.'

My hands tremble in my lap, remembering how I felt upon leaving him earlier tonight. 'Why did you believe him?' I ask.

'Because he told me something that wasn't relevant in court. At the time, nobody had known about my sister's pregnancy but me. But Aides had gone through treatment for testicular cancer when he was nineteen years old. He told me to find his medical records, and that it would prove his sperm count was so low that it was almost impossible for him to have been the father. His fertility never became part of the case at the time, but because of what I'd overheard, it became crucial.'

'Could your sister have been lying?'

'It's possible, yes, but I don't believe it. I heard her crying. She was a mess. And even if she wasn't, why would a seventeen-year-old who was going to go to Cambridge to study medicine lie about something like that? So once I knew that he couldn't have been the one to get her pregnant, I started to ask other questions. Like if Simon Aides wasn't sleeping with my sister, what motive did he have to kill her? And Chloe, there was nobody who could testify to him having a relationship with Emily. Nobody had seen them together. There were no notes left in books like the ones he wrote to you. No diaries.' The truth about the diary hits me like a thump in the gut. 'And he took you and at least one other girl to that music shop, couldn't help himself. Wanted the risk. So how does the same man go from being so careful in relation to my sister, to careless with you? They didn't even share classes together. And after just two meetings with Aides I realised that I doubted he killed anybody. Not my sister, not Iris.

Even his ex-fiancée gave him an alibi for the night Iris went missing. Not at the time, but Aides told me to look for her, and when I found her she confirmed they were together.' Again his words come to mind, his statement that Susan refused to provide an alibi during the trial. 'But there was one thing I couldn't resolve.'

'Which was?'

'The fact that he never contested his sentence. No appeal at all. Why wouldn't he try if he was innocent?'

I shrug, feeling my mouth run dry. 'He told me it was to protect Susan's integrity,' I say.

'He told me the same thing, but I wasn't sure I bought it. Nobody would accept two decades in prison just to protect the integrity of somebody on the outside. And let's not forget, it's not like he was averse to causing her pain, right? But I'm an investigative journalist, Chloe. My job is to search for the truth that somebody wants to suppress. So I started looking into everything, his family tree, his employment history, his education. People he'd worked for, people he'd pissed off. Anything that he had hidden. To be honest, it wasn't pretty. He's got some secrets in his past. Do you even know why he left Austria?' I shake my head. 'Probably for the best. But it was only when I searched for his financial records that I found something relevant. An account in his name with regular payments made into it, beginning within a few years of his sentencing. And there were a lot. Nearly two hundred grand in deposits. And when I asked him about it he clammed up, denied any knowledge at first, until I told him that being paid to stay inside would essentially prove his innocence. That it worked in his favour. So the question became not whether he was guilty, but who was paying him to appear guilty on their behalf.'

I reach for my coffee, already going cold. Terrified for what she is about to say next.

'I looked into you, and Jimmy Baxter. It was easy to see that neither of you had the money for something like that. You might have had it early on in your music career, but I tracked it back and saw that you'd put it all into your flat. Francesca I knew could have afforded to pay him, but I didn't think it was her either. Found nothing to support her involvement.' She sits back, folds her arms as if a point has been made. 'But that money was protecting somebody. So I started looking into all the male teachers, asking myself who else could have got her pregnant. But I found nothing. And after a year of work I realised how wrong I was, looking for a man who killed her, assuming that it was the father of her baby. But when I found no answers, I asked myself a new question; if it wasn't the father, was there somebody else at High Hill who had a reason to want her dead?'

I think about all the times I have squashed it down, all the moments when I have thought it would be better to tell the truth, and yet felt unable to do so. And I can sense it again now, the relief like a distant desert mirage. Just tell the truth, and it would all be over. To say it aloud, that Iris killed Emily, that we lied to protect her. No reason for any more lies. But I, too, like Isobel, have carried the weight of my own betrayal. I remember how I hurt Iris with my words on the night she disappeared, and that makes the urge to protect her after her death so strong, even now; defending her memory is all I have left.

'And?' She folds her notepad, and reaches for her bag, indicating this meeting is drawing to a close. 'Who do you think it was?'

She stands up, and I watch as she readies herself to leave. 'You already know, Chloe. And what I have realised lately is that you are not the only one.'

31

I follow as she leaves the café, stepping out into a busy street. Rain clings to the ground in heavy puddles, but dawn is breaking across the grey sky. And there is some relief to see the lilac threads of a new day ushering away the night before.

'My sister was a bitch, no doubt about it. The website she made about Iris was awful. The way the school covered it up worse still. My family were huge benefactors of High Hill, and because of that they protected her. They knew what she had done but they covered it up. But out of everybody, Iris was the one who had the best reason to want to hurt my sister.'

Hearing her say it is overwhelming. But she is moving fast, and so I try to keep up as we weave through the city with purpose.

'But even if she did do it,' I allow, the closest I have ever been to admitting what I know, 'she has been gone for twenty years. What would be the point in paying Aides to stay in prison?'

'There wouldn't be any point, would there?' she says, stopping at the side of the road. Cars whizz past as the city traffic swells. 'Unless she was still alive. Remember, Chloe, they never found her body.'

Still alive? Iris? I stop in the street, can barely breathe for the thought of it. But as much as I wish that were true, it sounds so ridiculous. How could she be alive after all these years, when they found her blood on a knife? On the rocks in the forest. That's what I've always told myself. In all the years she has been gone, I never once doubted she was dead. But for the first time today, I doubted Aides killed her. When he denied it, I believed him. So could Isobel be right? Could Iris really be alive somewhere? A budding excitement builds within me, to think that she could have been the one paying Aides all along.

'Iris's family had money, links to France. They had homes there. They could have easily snuck her away. But to take an idea like that to the police, I'd need proof she was still alive. So, I went back over everything I had collected. But this time, instead of trying to link my sister's death to Aides, I focused on Iris. Anything that might prove somebody knew where she was. Frequent trips to France, say, or money sent to help her survive. I started with you, obviously, but found nothing. But when I started looking into Francesca, it was a different matter. She has been paying massive amounts of money every month to Jimmy Baxter. Since he was released from jail, she's literally been withdrawing it and handing it over. About as untraceable as it gets.' Reaching into her bag, she shows me pictures of Francesca handing over cash in dark corners of London. 'Jimmy Baxter is involved. I don't know how. But I knew the police would have to look into it with evidence like this. It might be enough to get the case of my sister's murder reopened.'

My throat is so tight I can barely breathe. It's just like Aides said. But could Jimmy Baxter have been extorting money for himself? Or could it have been to help Iris? Could they be working together?

'At first, Francesca wouldn't even take my calls. But after I told her I would go to the police with what I found, she agreed to talk to me. She's told me that she's ready to tell the truth.'

Panic surges through me, hot as a poker. What kind of consequences will there be if Francesca tells the police what we did? That I hid the murder weapon? That the initial evidence that placed Aides at the scene of Emily's murder was a lie?

'What truth does she want to tell you?'

'I'm not sure yet,' she says, and relief surges through me. 'But last week somebody broke into her flat. She thinks she is being followed.'

'Oh God.'

'I know. Sounds familiar, doesn't it? I only got back from a trip yesterday, but we agreed to meet before she goes to work today.' And then she stops, turns to me. 'We're going there together now.'

—

Twenty minutes later we are standing on an elegant Georgian street in Holborn, outside a soft sand-brick building with a stucco ground floor. Columns at the door, and a green park across the road.

'Francesca has the first floor,' Isobel says, pressing the bell. 'She said to come before seven, so we should catch her before she leaves.'

We wait on the step, all possibilities running through my mind. Like what she is going to say when we get up there. How I will react if she tells Isobel about Iris killing Emily. Deny it? Confess to everything I have been holding in? Because the truth is that even now I still feel bound to protect Iris. To cover up the truth on her behalf. It has been the only thing I have left of her. But now there is another option, shining like some kind of jewel in the mud of everything we have done; Iris could still be alive, and telling the truth might force her to come forward. Give me the chance to see her again; I can barely even dare imagine it.

'That's weird,' she says, checking her message. A few moments later when Francesca still doesn't answer, she tries again. 'She definitely said to meet today.'

'I tried to speak to her yesterday,' I say then. My feet are unsteady, my breathing too fast. 'She called me but then she didn't speak. I convinced myself that there was an explanation. That it was a mistake, or she was at work or something…' My thoughts tumble around, inadequate, and fragmented. I dare say the thing I really believed. 'What if she had been hurt?'

Isobel is frantic, her eyes wide. And I feel it then. The panic resonates through me, my whole body trembling. I step forward, press the bell over and over, as if that will make her answer the call. And when she doesn't, Isobel bats my hand away and presses for another apartment.

'Yes?' the response comes a moment later.

'Ocado,' Isobel says, without any hint of doubt.

'Must be another flat. I didn't order anything.'

The line goes dead. Without a second to spare, she presses a second button on the panel. We wait in silence for a response.

'Hello?' the voice comes after a moment.

'Ocado delivery.'

'Oh great! You're early.'

And then an electronic buzz comes from the door. We share a glance, scared to imagine what we will find. Isobel reaches forward, pushes it open. Inside the apartment block is exactly what I would expect, warm beige tones and dark wood furniture. Expensive, luxurious. Perfect for somebody who went to High Hill. I follow Isobel up the stairs, the carpet soft and plush. One apartment per floor. I think about how her life has followed the exact path it was set on. This place is everything I imagined, and yet I also know that her life was not what it appeared to be. She too has carried a burden. In different ways, we were both ruined by what we did.

Arriving on the second floor, we turn the corner and approach the front door to her apartment. Walnut wood with a brass number two in the centre. But as we get closer, I see there is something on the floor. From a distance I can't quite make out what it is. But then I realise that the door sits ajar, and that the thing on the floor is shards of wood from where the lock has been damaged. Isobel pushes it open. We look to each other for a sense of reassurance that neither of us find.

'Francesca?' Isobel says, stepping inside. 'Francesca, are you here?'

Low voices echo from within, and I take it for somebody's presence, until I realise it's only the radio. Like I heard on the phone. Her expensive bag is by the door, shoes positioned neatly alongside it. From where I stand, halfway up the hall, I can see a mug of coffee on the dining table, a throw draped over a chair. The rest of the apartment opens out before me like a show home, not a single thing out of place. And although I have never been here before, everything about the scene seems wrong. The dinner in a bag still on the counter, the coffee not yet drunk. It's as if somebody just got home, but yet she is nowhere to be found.

'Francesca,' I say, heading towards the lounge. A few neat chairs, a simple beige sofa. 'Francesca, are you here?'

A neat bookcase on one side of the room is filled with old books. I head across, lean down to look. I should be searching for Francesca, and yet this too calls to me. To see how she lived. Old leather tomes, classics of literature and textbooks about the law. A single photograph on one shelf, of her dressed in her wig and silk, carrying a bunch of flowers. A couple who I assume are her parents stand alongside her, without smiles. Next to the photograph is a small teddy bear dressed as a barrister. One nod to something softer. To a side of her we rarely saw.

'Anything?' Isobel asks as she steps from an internal corridor.

'No,' I say. 'You?'

I checked the bathroom and each of the bedrooms. I can't see her. It doesn't look like she slept here last night. 'I'll check the kitchen. You check in there.'

I watch as Isobel moves away, before moving to the door at the rear of the room. I open it up, and step inside, where I find an office, another bathroom, and a room that looks like she uses it to store luggage and not much else. The only other thing is a riding saddle, and I remember how she told me that she learned with Iris. How she told me that she'd do anything for her.

'Francesca, are you...' I go to say as I open the door of the second bathroom, but I stop, turn back when I hear Isobel cry out.

'Francesca!'

The sound of her voice is as sharp as a blade, cutting through the stagnant air.

'Shit, Francesca!'

I run back to the lounge just in time to see Isobel disappearing onto the floor of the kitchen, and I rush across the room to follow. And as I round the corner, I see it. Francesca's body, supine on the floor. One leg folded under the other, her arms splayed out as if she has been crucified. My gaze scans the scene, and I tell myself I must be wrong. That it doesn't make any sense. I take in the individual details and try to process them.

The blood on her hands.

A wound on her chest.

A red stain beneath her on the floor.

One open eye, winking at me like this is a big fucking game.

But it's not. And no matter how I look at it, the truth is unavoidable; Francesca is dead. She is dead because of what we did. Because she wanted to tell the truth.

Don't tell, the message read.

But Francesca wanted to. And if Isobel is right and Iris is still alive, I have no choice but to wonder whether she was the one who killed her.

32

Within fifteen minutes the police fill Francesca's apartment. Telling the truth now puts a mark on my head. Whatever it was that Francesca intended to tell Isobel, it got her killed. The only question is by whom. But the bruising on my neck is something I can't hide, and the first thing they want to know is how I got it. I have no choice but to tell them the truth.

'And so after they attacked you, they what? Just left you there?'

A detective who introduced herself as DS Lawrence stands across from me in the hallway as forensic teams already search the flat. She's tough, I can tell that straight away. Straight to the point, and everything about her is a little larger than average. For twenty years I have maintained my silence, have not betrayed Iris. I must try to continue to do so now.

'Yes,' I say. 'I was in the shower, and they tried to strangle me.' I say nothing of what was written in the steam on my mirror. 'They ran away before I got a look at them.'

'And can you think of anybody who might have wanted to hurt you? Or Francesca?'

Can I? When I saw Francesca's dead body, after Isobel telling me she might still be alive, I wondered if it was Iris who had done it. If Francesca was going to tell the truth about what we did, Iris would be the only one with a motive to silence her. But even if she was prepared to hurt Francesca, would she also hurt me? Was last night a warning?

'I'm not sure,' I say. 'But I know what this is about.'

I give the abbreviated version: that Emily died at our school, that Francesca and I gave crucial evidence that led to Aides being sentenced for her murder. For Iris's too, after she disappeared as well.

'And this Aides guy, the one who was convicted – you're saying he just got released?'

The connection is obvious. Of course they would think it was him. But I tell the truth, that I collected him from the prison, that I was with him for at least some of the night. The thought that he had time to hurt Francesca crosses my mind, but I know that I don't really believe it was him.

'There is another possibility,' Isobel says when I have finished. She tells them about the fact Francesca was paying Jimmy Baxter money every month. My heart sinks a little when she shows them the photographs, like we are picking over the remains of the life she lost. It sinks further still when she tells them Aides was being paid to remain in jail. 'I don't believe that Aides was guilty of my sister's murder.' Her gaze falls to me, and it doesn't go unnoticed by the police. 'The real killer was Iris Fairhurst. And I believe she is still alive.'

—

They ask more questions, and I tell them everything I can with one exception. When they push me on the idea of Iris being responsible for Emily's death, I hold my nerve, maintain my silence. I tell them she could never have done something like that, and that there is no way she could have hurt Francesca. And after they finish their questioning, and say I am free to go, the first person I contact is Stan. Out of everybody I know, if Iris is alive, he is the most likely to know the truth.

And yet an hour later as I approach the quay to see Stan waiting for me in front of Traitors' Gate, I can't help but wonder if she could be guilty of killing Francesca. Of hurting me. Killing Emily was supposed to have been a spur of the moment thing. An accident. But if Iris disappeared because of what she did, if she set up Aides to take the fall, then I have to consider that she would do everything in her power to both keep him inside and keep Francesca quiet.

And me.

'Chloe,' Stan calls when he spots me. Reaching forward, he takes me into his body, his strong arms weighty and safe. When he pulls back, his gaze slipping to my neck, his fingers brush against the darkening bruise. 'I can't believe you were attacked.' And then, with a sigh as he stuffs his hands into his pocket, 'And Francesca, she's really...' he says, unable to finish the question. I nod. 'God, Chloe. I can't believe it. I only spoke with her yesterday morning. And when we tried to call... You think she was already dead?'

'Maybe.' Her phone call haunts me. To think she was being hurt at the same time as I was trying to reach her is heartbreaking. I was just moments too late. 'I told them what Elaine told us, that Francesca had said she was going to court. They are going to check the records, but it looks like it was a lie. Maybe she was trying to cover up where she was really going, or who she was going to meet.'

'That could be the person who did it,' he says, and I know he is right. We move to stand by the wall of the river. Sweat trickles down my back as the water rushes by, the waves choppy as an ocean tide. Boats rock back and forth, and across the other side of the quay the top of the Shard is covered by a thick layer of cloud. 'And you?' he says, still inspecting my neck. 'You didn't see who attacked you?'

'No. They got away before I saw them. But it has to be the same person.'

'Aides?'

'I don't think so.'

'Jimmy Baxter, then? You said this Isobel woman had proof that he was extorting Francesca just like Aides said. And he was released last week, right?'

'I mean, it's possible.'

'I still don't really get it though. What did he have on Francesca?'

We could play this game for hours, I suppose. Decades really, as we have been for the last twenty years. Each one of us hiding what we know. It's time to stop pretending.

'Listen, Stan. Isobel put forward another theory, and I need to ask you about it.' Concern settles over his face, the tightening of his brow. His eyes narrow as if he has stepped into the path of the sun. 'It's about Iris.'

'What about her?'

'There is something I need to be honest with you about, and it's not going to be easy. But you see, Iris was the one who exposed Aides for what he did to me. She gave your father the note he wrote to me, and she forged the diary that they used as proof to fire him.' His eyes widen. 'And on the night she went missing, she had told

Francesca that she was going to meet him. After she went missing, we assumed it was him who had hurt her.'

'Right. And it was. He's been in jail for twenty years for her murder.'

'I know, but I'm starting to believe that we were wrong. You see, it looks like Aides has an alibi. He was with his fiancée at the time Iris went missing. Iris told Francesca that she was going to meet him, but it couldn't have been true.'

'What difference does that make? They proved that he killed her. Emily too. You saw him coming down from the belltower the night she died.'

'That's what I need to tell you, Stan. We never saw Aides leaving the belltower that night. We lied.'

Still as a statue, his mouth hangs open, as if I have truly lost my mind. Like everything he thought he knew has come into question.

'Why would you lie about that?'

The truth I swore I'd never tell. I can taste it on my tongue. 'We were trying to protect Iris.' I shake my head, trying to hold back the tears. 'We told your father we saw Aides in the belltower that night because Iris was the one who killed Emily, Stan.'

For a moment he just stares, his gaze meeting mine, as if waiting for an answer he might be capable of understanding. In a language he speaks. He looks away, across to the bridge. Goose pimples ripple across my skin as he turns back to me.

'That can't be true.'

'She confessed. To Francesca. Emily saw Iris buying drugs and threatened to tell your father. It was a heat of the moment thing. She hit her with the clapper from the bell.'

A second of silence before a laugh escapes. 'You expect me to believe that?' he says, his voice raised. Then he steps close, his voice lowered to little more than a hiss, the humour all gone. 'That my sister murdered somebody?'

'It's why she was so fucked up after Emily's death. It had nothing to do with what happened at the beach.' He flops down onto a bench, his muscles all limp like the life has been sucked out of him. I sit beside him and reach for his hand. 'We were young, and stupid. We did what we thought was right, thought that we were protecting Iris. I even hid the weapon.'

'You hid the weapon?' His whole body is loose, as if I have pulled the force of gravity out from beneath him. 'This is the truth?' I nod. 'Why tell me now? Iris has been dead for twenty years.'

'That's the thing, Stan,' I say, pulling his hand close, trying to make him see sense. 'I'm no longer sure she is.' I run over the words in my head, can't believe I am about to say it. 'For years somebody has been paying Aides to stay in prison. Iris is the only one with a reason to do that. And besides that, Francesca intended to tell the truth, Stan. She was going to tell people who really killed Emily, and about how we lied. Iris is the only one with a reason to want Francesca to stay silent, and...'

'Hang on,' he says, a finger up now to stop me in my tracks. 'Are you trying to tell me you think *Iris* killed Francesca?'

'She's the only person who has a motive to cover up the truth about Emily's death.'

He stuffs his hands into his pockets, then pulls them out again. He goes to speak twice before he finds the right words. 'And you? You think she did this?' he says, pointing to my neck. 'You think she'd hurt you?' He's right, it's hard to believe. 'She loved you, Chloe. She would never have done that to you.'

'I thought so too, but...'

Unable to focus on anything, his gaze roams left and right. 'We buried her, Chloe. My family said goodbye at her funeral.' Tears glisten in his eyes. 'Her death tore our family apart.'

'But they never found the body, right?'

'True.' But he says it with no surprise. Instead, it's with resignation, bowing to a truth he has suffered a million times already. 'But you were at the trial, Chloe. You know they found her blood on his cuff, remember? In his apartment?' And I remember. I spent months listening to it all. Aides' denials, the forensics that argued against it. But I also remember they were partial samples. That the defence brought in another forensics expert who argued against their validity. That really, when I am honest with myself, there was always room for doubt. 'Are we really here, doubting Aides' guilt again? Doubting now that my sister is even dead? I mean, they found her blood on the rocks.'

'What about your parents?' I ask then. 'Maybe they hid the truth from you. It would be reasonable,' I say, as he is already shaking his head. 'If they knew she killed Emily, faking her death would have been an answer, right? Would have protected her. And not telling you would have made sense.'

'Plausible deniability?' I nod. 'True. Not like we can ask them though, is it?' They have both been dead for years. I attended Claudette's funeral myself. 'But, Chloe, I saw how it ruined them,' he says, wiping his eyes, and standing up from the bench. 'You're wrong. We buried my sister, and then I buried each of my parents,' he says, with a sad little smile. 'There's no way that Iris is alive. And even if she was, she could never hurt you or Francesca. I'm afraid all that's come of this conversation is that I now know my sister was a murderer.'

After he leaves, I watch the river for a while, thinking about everything he said. That Iris loved me. That she could never have hurt me. So much easier to believe than what Isobel told me. And after all, they were her last words to me, weren't they? That she loved me. How could she have tried to hurt me now? Talking to Stan brings a sense of relief, but it poses the question that if it wasn't Aides who killed her, who did? Who had a reason to want Iris dead? The answer I keep returning to is that she ended her own life. That she took that decision for herself. But the hardest thing about that is having to accept that the person who pushed her to do that was most likely me.

I hear my phone ring, reach into my bag to take it out. Looking down at the screen, I see a number I don't know. I have three missed calls this morning, all from the same number.

'Hello?'

'Miss Carter,' comes a woman's voice, and I realise it is the detective who was in charge at the scene of Francesca's murder. 'DS Lawrence here. I was rather hoping you might be able to call by the station. There's a couple of things we need to clarify.'

'Sure. What kind of time do you want me to come down?'

'Now. Is that all right?'

I tell her it is, and then take down the location of the station before hanging up the call. And after that I watch the river flowing for a while longer, wondering what the hell she wants to know. Impressed that she almost made it sound as if attending the meeting is my choice.

33

The station is busy, a number of people crowding in the reception area waiting to be seen. Some push up to the desk, others sit, helpless, already given up on the plastic chairs. The air inside is thick with the smell of bodies and damp, rainwater trodden in from puddles outside. Anger and frustration simmers through the crowd, each of them bartering for attention and help.

'Miss Carter?' I follow the voice through the crowd, and look up to see DC Price, the second detective, leaning out of a door. 'I saw you arrive. Please, come with me.'

Pushing past the few people standing between us, I cross the reception and then follow him into the guts of the station. We move along a tight corridor, the paintwork ageing and peeling. A buzz ripples through the whole place, with officers at their desks, others rushing around, as if the relentless chase of crime is a person on the run. Most of them look exhausted, their eyes bleary. Jaded. The smell of coffee is heavy in the damp atmosphere.

We come to a stop outside a brown door, a small sign to the side. *Interview Suite One*. A musty smell as he opens the door.

'Please,' he says. 'Take a seat.'

The sounds of the station dull as he closes the door behind us. The interview room is small, one old wooden table in the middle, two chairs either side. Machines on the top, like old cassette recorders from when I was a child.

'What is this about?' I ask.

DC Price takes a seat at the table, crosses one thick leg over the other. 'Let's just wait for DS Lawrence, okay?'

It's another minute before she arrives, looking harassed and slightly out of breath. The jacket she was wearing earlier is draped over one arm, and the shirt underneath clings tight against her muscles. Sweat seeps into the material under her armpits. When I spoke to the police as a teenager they were almost sweet, accommodating. But everything about these detectives, from her size to his blank expression, makes me nervous. They have no intention of making me welcome here today.

'Sorry to keep you waiting,' she says, taking a seat at the table alongside her colleague. She sets a plastic cup in front of me, a burning hot coffee. 'So, since we left you earlier, we paid a visit to Aides, and he confirms your version of events. That you were at the prison, that you picked him up and later visited him at the halfway house.'

'Just as I said.'

'Not quite.' Pausing, she searches to find the right words. 'He also told us that you had dinner together, and that later that evening you returned to his accommodation where you engaged in sexual relations. Is that correct?'

To hear it spoken aloud is like having myself exposed. To stand naked on a stage and have a crowd point and stare at my soft thighs, my breasts that have started to sag. And it's hard to believe that this is where I find myself. Like listening to the demise of another person's life, and not being able to believe how it happened where there were so many moments when it could have all been avoided.

Nausea rises in my gut. All I can do is nod my head.

'Don't you think if you were sleeping with Aides it would have been a good idea to let us know?'

'I'm not sleeping with him. We didn't even...' And the shame of the night before rises up like a tidal wave that I have been trying to outrun for twenty years. My need to be near him, to have him in my life. The fact that as absurd as it sounds, it is only with him when I feel anything more than a victim. 'Why does it matter?'

'Oh, come on, Chloe. You're not that stupid. It does add a slightly different weight to the idea that he can support where you were last night, doesn't it? We'd have to wonder whether he was lying on your behalf.'

'He doesn't need to lie for me.' They say nothing. 'And anyway, we kissed but that was it. There's nothing between us. I was with him until I left to go home. Around midnight.'

'Right.' She gives me a nod, unfussed, as if it doesn't really matter to her what I say. That she has already made up her mind. 'Besides that, since we met this morning, I've had a bit of time to go over the old case file for the trial you were involved with, and although you were clear about the role you played in testifying against Aides, you didn't quite tell us everything. For example, you didn't mention anything about you and Aides sleeping together while he was the head of music at High Hill Manor. Why not?'

'I wasn't sure it was relevant,' I say, aware of the tremble in my voice as the focus sharpens on the truth. My whole body feels as if it's shaking. Sometimes I think my secrets might be the only things that hold me together, and that now as they spill out, my insides spill out with them. 'What has that got to do with Francesca being killed?'

'Well, the fact that you testified against a teacher who you had previously accused of sexual abuse is important in this case. He went to jail on the back of your testimony.' Heat rises to my cheeks as if I am back there in Professor Fairhurst's office, confessing for the first time. 'Yet the school never reported it, did they? It wasn't public knowledge until it came out in the trial.'

'That's right.'

Her face wrinkles, her mouth curling down. She finds this whole thing distasteful. 'But a teacher interfering with a pupil is a serious offence.' I can't get past the word. Interfering. It's so, so… seedy. 'The police should have been informed.'

'Why?' I ask. Defiance simmers like a familiar comfort within me. 'It wasn't like I was a child.'

She takes her time, her shoulders softening, her eyes dropping shut for just a moment. Even her voice seems milder when she speaks again.

'I'll give you that, but neither were you a grown woman. You can't tell me now, as a thirty-seven-year-old, that you can't see what he did to you was wrong.'

'He didn't do anything I didn't agree to, though. He never forced me.'

'Maybe not physically, but there's a word for what he did to you, Chloe.' Her face rests on her fist, a deep sigh of regret rushing from her mouth. She's been here before. 'He abused you, Chloe. Simon Aides is a…'

'Please don't say it.'

To hear it spoken aloud takes too much from me. I would have no choice but to accept what really happened when only last night I tried to deny it by going to him again; with Simon, I never have to lie about what we were or question what it meant. Last night when he kissed me, it was possible to pretend. With him, if I go willingly, if I convince myself that I want to be around him, I never have to admit that I was the one who was abused. With him, the truth is whatever we decide it is. Only in his absence does it become something else.

'Nobody would have blamed you, Chloe. You were young. You thought he cared about you.' Wiping a tear, I nod my head. 'Probably you cared about him. Maybe you still do. That's why you went there last night. Or maybe I am way off the mark.'

She reaches to a brown folder that has been sitting on the table all along. She opens the cover with a crisp, sharp movement. Leafing through, I am sure I see a photograph of my face. Another one of High Hill Manor.

'I want to ask you what you know of a man called Gregory Fisk?'

I try to place the name but know I can't. 'Nothing. Why?'

Pulling a picture from the file, she turns it around and pushes it across the table. A man with dark hair and deep-set eyes stares back at me. Something in his features seems familiar, like déjà vu, although I can't quite work out why.

'Ever seen this man before?'

'I don't think so,' I say.

'Well, let me acquaint you. Gregory Fisk is a sixty-year-old man from Morecambe Bay. Works as a labourer on a building site. Did a few years in prison for aggravated assault, and another for GBH about ten years before that. His bank account suggests he's pretty well off for an ex-con who works a job where he gets paid cash in hand.' She pushes another piece of paper across the table. A statement, with numbers that correlate to what she has just told me. Her finger tapping against the balance. Six figures. 'Still insist you don't recognise him?'

I pick up the photograph, study the features. It's his eyes, the way it feels as if he is staring at me across the page. Still, I can't quite bring forth the recognition I need.

'I don't think so,' I say, setting the picture back down.

'Well, this is the man who has been paying tens of thousands of pounds into a bank account in the name of Simon Aides. Payments that started a few years after his conviction for the High Hill murders.' Page after page, she turns papers in her file. How the file has grown so quickly since this morning surprises me. 'What do you know of your mother's family?'

I shrug, not sure what to say. 'Not a lot. We never saw them when I was growing up.'

'Why not?'

I dig around for the vague story my mother told me in the past. 'They didn't like the fact my father was an artist. There was bad blood between them. I never met anyone from my mother's family.'

'So, you're not aware that her maiden name was Fisk?' she asks, producing a birth certificate for my mother.

My heart races as the connection comes. My eyes trawl across the page, looking for the truth. The familiarity in his eyes that I now know comes from my mother. And there before me I see it, printed in black and white. The name. Sandra Fisk.

'She told me that it was Finn.'

'Afraid not. Gregory Fisk is your mother's brother. Your maternal uncle, Chloe.'

That statement settles heavy and immovable before me. For a moment I do not know what to say. My lips move, trying to articulate a thought but with no sounds coming out. An uncle I never knew, paying Aides, who I just said I know nothing of; it makes me look like a liar.

An accomplice.

'I don't know why he would pay money to Aides. I've got nothing to do with it.'

Neither of them speak for a moment. She sighs, sits back in her chair.

'You see, there's something strange about that, Chloe. Because the money being paid to Fisk has been coming from an account in your name.'

Again, she pulls something from the file. Another account, transfers each month into the account used by Fisk. And right there alongside each highlighted transaction is my name. Their gaze rests on me, heavy and expectant.

'You were a performer years ago, right? Even played once at the Royal Albert Hall, didn't you?'

'What's that got to do with it?'

'Must have done all right for yourself. Good payments at that level I suspect. Enough to buy a nice little flat near the Royal Parks, view of the river. Your sort of address doesn't come cheap.'

She's not wrong. 'For a while I made decent money. Only while I was performing. But I used everything I had to buy my flat,' I say, my voice rising at an alarming rate. 'And yes, some of it was money I had earned, but the rest of it was an inheritance after my father died. And I just told you, I haven't performed in years. And besides that, I don't know Gregory Fisk. This account in my name doesn't belong to me. I work in a supermarket stacking shelves. Why would I do that if I had this kind of money?'

'Okay,' she says, her hands in the air as a suggestion I calm down. I look to the door, want nothing more than to run. 'Let's assume you're telling the truth about the payments. That you have no idea about any of it. But is it true what they said about you and...' She consults her file. 'The second victim? Iris Fairhurst? At the trial Simon Aides suggested that you and she were lovers.'

'What if we were?'

'Well, you denied any truth to it in court. You said that Aides had involved you in an abusive relationship, and you were hailed a hero for speaking out against him. But if what he said was true, and you lied about the nature of your relationship with one of the girls he was accused of murdering, it casts some doubt on the accuracy of your statement.' I reach for my coffee, drink it down. It's too hot, bitter. My tongue throbs and swells in my mouth. 'Did Iris get jealous after you slept with Aides? Is that why she died?'

'What? No,' I insist.

'Twenty years he's been inside, and yet last night you were fooling around together as if you've been holding a torch for him the whole time. Was there some sort of plan that you were both involved in?'

'What are you accusing me of?'

'I haven't accused you of anything. But you testified against him, and he went to jail. I have a paper trail to suggest that you have been paying him to stay there.'

'But I haven't. I don't know anything about any of this.'

'And yet these statements suggest otherwise. That the money came from you and went to Aides via your uncle. Let me ask you a straight question, Chloe; was it you who killed Iris?'

'No! I loved Iris,' I say, my voice breaking as I remember the last words I ever said to her.

'And yet you have been paying the man who supposedly killed her.'

'No,' I shout again, wiping a tear. I hear a voice in my head, reminding me that I'm no longer even sure that she's dead. 'I haven't.'

She sits back, crosses her arms in front of her. 'Can I ask you something?' I shrug to show the ridiculousness of her question. 'How do you really feel about Aides now? I know you were with him yesterday, but I mean deeply. There must be a part of you that cares about him, right?'

I wipe my tears. Can feel the truth like vomit rising in my throat. 'There are days when I miss him, I suppose. When I wish he was there.'

That's what it does, a relationship like that. When it happens before your brain is developed enough to understand it. It means that years later you still crave the love and attention of the person who nearly destroyed you. I stood on stage once, the crowd applauding. My biggest ever performance at the Royal Albert Hall. And all I could think as they clapped and cheered was how I wished he could have been there to hear me play. And yet after the success of that event, I couldn't function. Couldn't get out of bed for days. Afterwards I couldn't bring myself to play again, couldn't even sit at the piano. He's like a thread in my life that knits everything together. Everything good, to everything bad.

'Other times I want...' I pull back, can't say it.

'To hurt him?' I nod, even though what I was going to say was much worse. 'Are you sure about that?'

'Yes,' I say.

Sitting back in her chair, she browses through the file, leafing through page after page of information she has collected about me. 'I think it was Aides who you were in love with, and that Iris became an obstacle you needed to get out of the way. Isn't that what this is about?'

'How could I have been in love with Aides when you just said yourself that it was abuse?'

'That's exactly what it was, Chloe, but I'm not sure you know that even now, so I'm sure as hell you didn't know it back then. And if you both thought it was love, it doesn't take a huge stretch to imagine you and Aides working together to rid yourself of people who stood in the way.' She closes the file, and I feel her gaze settle on my neck. 'How did you get those bruises?'

Pain throbs in my neck as I swallow, remembering what happened in my apartment. 'I told you. I was attacked. Probably by the same person who killed Francesca.'

'But you didn't call the police, did you?' Fiddling with a pen, she taps it against the file. 'If somebody tried to strangle me in my bathroom, I wouldn't call a reporter in the middle of the night. I'd call the cops. Unless I had a reason not to.' I can feel the truth, as palpable as a tumour. 'Jealousy can drive people to do all sorts of strange things, Chloe. Things they wouldn't have dreamed of doing before.'

'I didn't kill Iris. I loved her.'

'And what about Francesca?' Reaching back into her file, she pulls out one final sheet of paper. Another finger, pointing at other details I can't see coming. 'You recognise these messages?'

I glance down at the page. I read over them, although it doesn't make any sense. At one point I see Francesca's name, and then a statement that she made as the second person in the text chain.

'Yesterday she told her secretary she was heading to court, but she didn't go there, Chloe. Instead she went home to meet somebody. These messages between you and Francesca were sent yesterday. How about I read this one out. It says, "*We told so many lies, Chloe. I can't live like this anymore. We sent an innocent man to prison. I need to tell the truth.*"' She lets the paper drop. 'What do you make of that?'

'She never sent that message to me. I haven't spoken to Francesca in years. I've tried but…'

'This not your phone number?'

My heart starts to beat faster, blood rushing to the surface of my chewed finger as I realise that, in fact, it is.

'Yes, but I never received them and…'

She doesn't let me finish.

'Twenty years ago, Miss Carter, you lied in court. We spoke to Isobel at length after you left. She was adamant that Francesca was ready to tell the truth about the fact Iris killed Emily. That you both covered that up, pointing the blame at Aides. And it's all here, Chloe. By her own admission you both worked to put an innocent man in prison, perhaps with some agreement in place that he'd be heavily rewarded for paying for your crime.' She sits back, as if the case is closed. 'Isobel thinks Iris is still alive, but there was a full, very thorough investigation. Somebody killed her. And I think it was you.'

'I didn't kill Iris.'

'But it would be understandable, wouldn't it, if Isobel is telling the truth? I'd have been scared too if I knew that Iris killed Emily and that now, because I was sleeping with a teacher, she was angry at me.'

'That's not it.'

'Maybe she threatened you. If Isobel is right and Iris did kill Emily, then I would have been scared in your position. She thought you were lovers, and yet you started sleeping with Aides. You knew about her crime. Was it an accident? Heat of the moment? Is that why Aides covered it up for you?'

'No.'

'I'm sure you thought the payments wouldn't be traceable, executed via your dodgy uncle. That it would be far removed from you, and nobody would ever know you had anything to do with it. All the earnings you made from your performances, gone as a bribe to keep an innocent man in jail who covered up the mistakes of the girl he had abused. And here,' she says, tapping at another message. My eyes scan the text. 'Your last message to Francesca, telling her that you want to meet. Last night.'

My gut twists as I realise what she's saying. 'You're wrong.'

'You went there to tell Francesca to keep quiet, didn't you? Because she knew what you had done. She knew what really happened, didn't she? But you couldn't convince her. Francesca was going to tell the truth. She's been in touch with a lawyer, you know that? We had a call from him earlier when she didn't turn up for an appointment. He claims that she signed a confession, and we are waiting on what that might say. He's bringing it in for us now. But Francesca was going to ruin your life, Chloe. And now it looks as if you've got Aides covering for you again, giving you a false alibi for last night, because you killed her, just like you did Iris.'

'That's not true.'

'Yet my evidence suggests that it is. So, Chloe Carter, I'm arresting you on suspicion of…'

And with that the rest of the world peels away into nothing. Arrest? For murder? Iris and Francesca's murders?

Only an hour ago I was contemplating the possibility that Iris was still alive. Wondering if there was any way she could have tried to hurt me. But the worst thing about it all is that it makes sense. Everything DS Lawrence has just said sounds plausible. But I know that I didn't kill her. I never could have. But I also no longer believe that Aides killed her either. Which means that despite what the police have just said, there is a chance that Isobel is correct; Iris could still be alive. Which means there is a chance that she could have killed Francesca.

For years I have protected her memory, trying to do what I could to keep her safe. Now I must put myself first. But I know that the only way to do that is by telling the truth.

To save myself, I must do the thing I said I'd never do; I must betray Iris.

34

'Anything you do say may be used in evidence against you.'

'Wait,' I say as they both stand up. I take a breath as they pause, prepare to do the thing I promised myself I never would. 'There's something I need to tell you.'

'Okay,' she says. 'We're listening.'

I tell them everything, finally, about what we did. The lie we told, about seeing Aides coming down from the belltower. How after Iris disappeared, we had been so sure that he'd hurt her as vengeance for the diary she forged.

'So, you're telling me that Iris killed Emily.'

The words stick in my throat. 'I think so.'

'And you never saw Aides there at the belltower.'

I shake my head. 'He told me that he saw Iris leaving the belltower. He was going to tell that to the police until she went missing.'

'And so you took the investigation into your own hands.' Her face has turned pink, like she's been out in the cold. I am the opposite of justice. I am what she hates. 'You traded the life of an innocent man for the reputation of your friend. The same friend who you had already learned was responsible for Emily's death. Had killed her.'

'Yes.' Hearing it spoken back to me is like putting it in lights, the injustice I caused. 'He lost his job because of what she did. But you just said yourself that what he did to me was abuse. He deserved to pay for that.'

Bones gleam white in her jaw, her fingers solid at the edge of the file. 'There's no doubt that he deserved to go to jail. But not for murder, Chloe. Not for twenty years. That's not the law. You don't get to decide for yourself what's right and what's wrong. Let me ask you this: today, right now, do you believe he played any part in the deaths of either Emily Ashbourne or Iris Fairhurst?'

I look to DC Price, who has barely taken his eyes off me the whole time I was speaking. The shame of my admission is greater than I expected. Aides undoubtedly wounded me, hurt me and changed the course of my life, but I realise now it is also true that I have done the same to his.

'I don't think so.'

Up on her feet, her hands resting against her back, she paces the room. 'Right, so now we are being straight with each other, Chloe, I need you to tell me the truth. The messages to Francesca: you wrote them, didn't you? You went there to silence her?'

'No. I swear I didn't hurt Francesca. I never hurt anybody.'

'Aides might disagree with that,' she says, her eyebrows raised. 'And the money paid to him?' Before I get the chance to answer, I hear the door to the interview room open, and my gaze is drawn to the young, uniformed officer standing on the other side of it. With some irritation, DS Lawrence paces back to the table and presses her fingers to the buttons. 'Interview suspended at 13:15.' I hear the click from the recorder, and the deep sigh that comes from Price. He sits back in the chair, relaxing as if he is an actor at the end of a scene. 'What is it?' she asks.

'Sorry, ma'am, but I've got something you need to see.'

She nods to Price, who rises to his feet, heading out of the door. With it closed behind her, she uses the moment to adjust her cuffs, sits down on one of the sofas. Not once, not in any dealings I have had with the police over the years, have I ever felt this exposed. But my lies have been chasing me, a shadow on my tail. There's no escaping them now.

'What will happen to me?' I ask.

'Well, you lied under oath and could be charged with perverting the course of justice. We might make that stick,' she adds, although from the weary expression I don't think she is convinced. 'It would be reasonable for the CPS to seek prosecution. You could face a fine, jail time. Aides himself could bring a civil suit against you for damages.'

'He won't do that,' I say, knowing that it is true. 'Will you keep me here?'

'You're forgetting something,' she says, her softer demeanour hardening before my eyes. 'As it stands, Chloe, you are a suspect in a murder investigation. Francesca is dead, and I have messages that link you to the crime.'

'I swear I didn't do it.'

'Without further evidence to support that, I can't let you go.'

I don't even have time to process that before the door is opening again, and I see DC Price stepping into the room. In his hand he is carrying some papers, new things I haven't yet seen. He stops, one hand resting on the cold plastic of the table. Knuckles wrapped up, a solid fist.

'Give me your phone.' I hesitate, suddenly scared for what they might find: the calls to Francesca, the message I sent while trying to find her yesterday. But I have been honest now anyway; what does it even matter anymore when I'm facing charges of murder? 'Believe me,' DC Price says when I still haven't handed it over. 'You want me to check it.'

My gaze still on him, I rummage in my pocket, bring it out and hand it over. I look between him and DS Lawrence, and I don't know whether to be less or more anxious that she is also confused by this turn of events. Both of us are in the dark. He turns the screen, holds it in front of my face, and once the device is unlocked, he navigates the menus. He pulls up an app, and although I strain, I can't quite see what he's doing. He angles it to DS Lawrence, who, upon seeing whatever it is on the screen, sighs, as if all her hard work has come spiralling undone.

'She can't be in two places at once,' he says.

DS Lawrence grabs the phone, checks the screen. I see the realisation dawn on her, before she sets it down on the table, and slides it over to me. On the screen I see two little dots, one flashing in Kensington, in the police station where I sit. Another across the other side of the city.

'Your phone pinged on a mast near Aides' place last night, around midnight. You check it at that time?'

I think back, try to remember the time I left, whether I used my phone.

'Maybe. To check the time, I think.'

'And yet it also pinged at 12:20 a.m. at a location near Francesca's flat. You'd never get there in that time difference. You're lucky that Aides wasn't staying near where Francesca lives, otherwise it might have registered on the same mast.' I reach up to the wounds on my neck. Something sharp in my throat each time I swallow. 'Somebody is using a cloned version of your phone.'

'Which could explain the messages,' DC Price suggests.

'Only the messages?' DS Lawrence says, up on her feet, her eyebrows raised. 'It brings everything into doubt. If somebody has taken the step of cloning your phone, why not also open a bank account in your name?'

'Funny you should say that,' he says, handing her another piece of paper. 'The demographic details for the bank account match for name and date of birth. It was originally opened using an address you stayed at right after you left school.'

'The flat on Old Kent Road?'

'That's the one. But we got the old paperwork from the bank. The National Insurance number used to set up the account doesn't match that of Miss Carter. Belongs to some homeless guy we last picked up for vagrancy about twenty years ago. The account was made using a synthetic identity.'

'A what?'

'Authentic details, just not all from the same person.' He nods, like he's heard the same story before. 'Sometimes that slips through the verification systems, especially twenty years ago.'

'Fucking hell,' DS Lawrence says, pacing the room. It's almost impossible to think that this was all going on, lingering in my future like some potential threat. Some horrible fate to which I might or might not succumb.

'And,' he says, handing her another piece of paper. 'We found this.'

He sets one of the pages down on the table. It looks like a painting, a picture a child might make with their fingers. 'It's a print from Francesca's glasses. I ran it through our database.' His lips twist over his tongue with a look of satisfaction. 'We have a match.'

'Who?' DS Lawrence asks.

With a sigh, he maintains his gaze on me. 'It's the guy you told us about earlier. Jimmy Baxter.'

'What other information do we have on Baxter now?' she asks her partner.

'Been in and out of prison his whole adult life. First offence for supplying Class B drugs was eighteen years ago, not long after the trial ended. Served three years. Did another three for burglary after that. Eighteen months for GBH. Interestingly, he was also arrested twice in connection with an identity theft ring, although he was never charged. Was off our radar for a while, until he was sentenced again for more drug offences. As it happens, he was released last week. But his first sentence, when he was serving time in Wakefield back in 2006...' he says, slow, careful, suggesting there's more to come. 'I ran a check, and it showed that Fisk was also serving a three-year sentence at the same time, in the same wing of the prison.'

'Coincidence?' she asks, turning to her partner.

'Maybe,' he says. 'But I wouldn't like to bet on it.'

'There were rumours at the time that Baxter was sleeping with Emily,' I say. 'That she was pregnant when she died. If he was there that night, and saw what happened with Iris...'

My skin shivers with the truth of it; he knew what had happened all along. I still don't understand why he confirmed our story to put Aides in prison. But now I know it was Baxter who killed Francesca. Could it also be him who tried to kill me? Aides was right all along; I am in danger. He tried to save me. To protect me.

'Where is Baxter now?' DS Lawrence asks.

DC Price picks up the files. We are done here. They will let me go. 'Last address was in Walthamstow. We've got somebody on their way to pick him up now. But there's something else,' the officer says, eyes falling to me. I look to DS Lawrence and realise that neither of us know what's coming next. 'We've had a call from Ipswich Police. There has been an incident involving your mother.'

35

The roads are jammed, and despite DS Lawrence using the blue lights to force our way through traffic, it takes us half an hour longer than it normally would. I open the door as we pull up outside the house I grew up in, the small flat-roofed place I always hated so much. That I couldn't wait to leave. Now I race to reach it. Three houses up from ours, Mr Baggins is out on the lawn, standing with his hands in his dressing-gown pockets, talking to the police. Tape has been drawn around the perimeter of my home. Blue lights flash against the dirty windows, as what began as a run degenerates into small, terrified steps as I reach the door. A uniformed officer stands guard.

'Are you Miss Carter?' the officer asks. I go to speak, my mouth opening, but no words come out. I nod my head instead.

'She is. And I'm DS Lawrence.'

'Okay,' he says, removing his hat. 'Please, come this way.'

Inside nothing is as it should be. The telephone table stands in its usual position, but the telephone itself is on the floor. Notes my mother had taken have been cast about, small white tickets like flakes of snow on the ground. A picture of a dormouse hangs skewed on the wall. Police officers peel away to allow me to pass, and I follow the officer down the hall. One takes photos of marks on the wall. A tray of tea has been dropped, the carpet wet underfoot.

At first the scene in the living room makes no sense. I stare, trying to make the pieces fit, like it's all a jigsaw made up of different images, the pieces not aligned or showing the same thing. There's a chair overturned. A curtain torn. Picture frames smashed across the mantle, and above that, red letters have been painted on the wall.

A cloth covers something on the floor.

'This is Miss Carter, ma'am.'

But I pay no attention to the officer in charge as she begins to talk. Instead, I walk past her to the sheet and fall to my knees. Kneeling in the same spot I used to sit as a child, to let the gas fire dry my hair on a Sunday night. Somebody tries to stop me, but I force their hand away to peel back the cloth. And I see that what they told me at the station is true.

My mother is dead.

They make tea, give me time to settle without telling me anything else. They wait until the person I called arrives, and when he does, he needs no instruction. He sits at my side, his arm around me for comfort, allowing my body to melt into his. But today his face is bruised, his lip fat. It feels like he is the only person I have left.

'How was she found?' Aides asks the officer now. There is strength in his touch, his knowledge of what to say and ask. His steadfastness in my distress.

'The neighbour, Mr Baggins, calls in each morning, brings her a newspaper from the shop. When he rang the bell this time, Mrs Carter failed to respond. He retrieved a spare key that she always kept in the potting shed and let himself in. He found her as we did, on the floor of the living room like this.'

'And do they have any idea how long ago she died?' DS Lawrence presses.

She didn't die, I want to say. She was murdered. The stain of red leaking from the back of her head testifies to that. The words on the wall.

'We believe between six and six thirty. We're canvassing the neighbours for anybody that might have seen a vehicle or unexpected person in the street. Several have Ring cameras fitted, and so we will be looking at that footage, in the hope that somebody might have caught something. Of course, we have to ask what kind of mood she was in the last time you saw her, Miss Carter. What you might have discussed.'

But what can I tell them? We discussed nothing and everything at once. We spent twenty years dancing around a truth that we could never unsay: that she blamed me for my father's death. The fact he was the one who stepped into the path of a train made no difference to her. It made no difference that in the years before he had on three separate occasions tried to end his life. She cared little that my childhood had been built upon that truth, or that any joy we experienced teetered precariously on the blade of his mental health. I wonder now, looking at her dead body, whether it is even possible to blame her for the way she treated me. What chance did we have? How could life have ever been something more than what it became after what he did?

'I saw her yesterday,' I say, pulling back from Aides. I reach without thought, to the tissues on the side table that I knew would be there. 'I brought her some shopping, toiletries and food that she needed.' The lotions were still on the stairs. 'I stayed for a while, we watched TV. I said I'd see her again in a few days.'

'And did she give you any indication that something or somebody might have been upsetting her?' I shake my head. 'And do you have any idea what this means?'

I follow the line of her finger as she points to the message written on the wall. Blood-red letters dribbling towards the mantle. Disappointment crosses Aides' face, as he too understands the writing.

'Chloe, is that really—' Aides begins, but I interrupt him.

'*Nemo sine vitio est.* It's Latin,' I say. 'It was the motto of the school I attended. It means "no one is without fault".'

It's an easy connection; this is about what happened at High Hill. About the lies we told that sent Aides to jail. But the Latin words do much more than connect my mother's death to the historical crime.

'Why do you think somebody would have written it?' the police officer asks.

When the police identified a fingerprint belonging to Baxter on Francesca's glasses, I had wanted to believe it was also him who had assaulted me in my bathroom. I wanted it to make sense. But last night when I was attacked, I think I knew it was her even then. As soon as I saw the words *don't tell* written in the steam. After all, it was my mistake that set this whole thing in motion. DS Lawrence is certain she is dead, but I am now more convinced than ever that Isobel is right. Iris is alive, and she is determined to silence anybody who might know the truth. And she wants to hurt me as much as I hurt her when I told her I didn't love her. When I forced her into faking her death.

And I think the only thing that will satisfy her now is mine.

Twenty minutes later, another cup of tea in hand, made for me by one of the police officers, I am sitting with Aides outside in the back garden. The swing I used to play on as a child tilts in the breeze, one of the ropes broken. The seat twists towards the patchy grass at forty-five degrees. The garden furniture is covered in dirt, moss growing on one of the chair handles. She gave up here. Time in this garden stood still.

'If everything you have told me is true,' Aides says now, 'it would be reasonable to assume that I too am at risk.'

I have spent the last ten minutes telling the police everything I think I know. Aides heard it all. Tightness holds his face together, and I don't know whether it is fear, anger or a mixture of both.

'By the look of your face, I'd say you were more than at risk,' I say. 'When were you hurt?'

'When I went to meet the person who was supposed to give me the account number.' He speaks with his head bowed, as he confesses about the payments to keep him in prison.

'Why didn't you tell me about the money?'

'Shame, I suppose,' he says with a shrug. 'That I didn't deserve it. I thought you would feel aggrieved.'

'Is that why you never tried to appeal?' He nods. It was never about protecting Susan's integrity. It was always about him. 'And the bruising? How did it happen?'

'The man I went to meet to arrange the transfer punched me straight in the face. They had a knife,' he says, lifting his jacket sleeve to show me a deep cut on his forearm, patched up with a dressing I'd guess he did himself. 'He tried to kill me.'

'Did you get a look at them?'

He nods. 'In his sixties. I'd say. Grey hair, a moustache.' Sounds like Fisk, based on the picture I saw. All along, he was part of the plan. The money changing hands. Money from an account in my name, designed to set me up. It's devastating to imagine that Iris has played any part in that. That she could do that to me.

'Was it my uncle who told you where I was living?'

He shakes his head. 'Baxter.'

'Jimmy?'

'Yes. He lied about me as well, remember? I asked him for help to find you, and he agreed. I never told him that I wanted to try to warn you about his plans though.'

'But how did he know where I was?'

He shrugs. 'I'm not sure.' At some point I have to accept that the information stops. That understanding comes up against a dead end. 'Do you really think Iris is alive? That she could have done this to your mother?'

'I think she might be, yes. And the only reason to hurt my mother is to hurt me. And I know she is capable of killing somebody.' I nod, pull a tissue from my sleeve to wipe my tears.

'There's a time you would have thought it was me.'

I stifle the tears and nod my head. 'For what it's worth, when Iris went missing, I really did believe that you had hurt her. I believed I was telling the truth. About that at least.'

And he smiles then, still small, and wary, but genuine. And in that moment, I can see something of the man who shaped me as a musician. The man I liked so much. 'I always had a feeling it was her, you know? The person who killed Emily.'

'And yet you never mentioned your suspicions during the trial.' Again he shakes his head, wipes a tear on his sleeve. 'I kept waiting for you to say something. You had warned me away from her, after all. So why did you stay quiet?'

He brushes a chewed fingernail at the weave of his jeans. In a different light today, I see how time has changed him, the marks on his face. A scar on his cheek that he never used to have. I can't stop wondering how he got it.

'What I did, Chloe...' The words twist from him, his face contorting with the effort to find them. 'How I behaved towards you, it was... was...'

But he has to stop, stands up and moves away. We both need the distance. When he turns again, I see something I have never seen before. Desperation. He looks even more broken than he did at the trial.

'I tried to convince myself I was a decent man back then, but I was not, Chloe,' he says, sinking into a different chair. 'I think there was part of me that was a little relieved at the prospect of some time in prison. I should never have done what I did to you. You weren't even the first.' I think of the rumours, of Eloise, the girl who killed herself, and wonder if he was telling the truth when he said he didn't know who she was. I realise I do not want to know. 'Although I was innocent of the crime to which I was sentenced, it felt a bit like justice. An opportunity even.' Dragging a hand across his face, he wipes the tears from his eyes. When he looks up, his expression has hardened. 'That's not to say I wasn't angry with you. I'll never get those years back.' A shadow crosses his face, his gaze intense. He has hated me too over the years. Hated all of us. 'But at least being inside... it was a chance not to hurt any other girls.' He wipes his eyes, looks around the garden. A smile lights onto his face when he sees the delicate flowers of a winter cherry blossom in the corner of the garden. A bird balancing on a branch. 'What I'm trying to say, Chloe, is that you shouldn't feel guilty about the choices you took. I might find it hard to accept what you did, but I can rationalise it. Understand it, even. And, more than anything, I suppose what I want to say is that I'm sorry.'

An apology from Aides, something I have waited for. I wrap my arms around my body, listening to the sounds of the police who are still working on the inside. Sirens sound at the front of the house, and I turn to see paramedics walking in. Discussions over how best to lift my mother, as if she is still alive, and needs to be transported with care. Gratitude swells within me for that.

'And I'm sorry I lied,' I tell him, and I can see what it means to him. His lips tremble with the truth of it. And while he might never have asked it of me, I see how much he needed me to admit my own failings. That acknowledgement that he too was aggrieved. 'You deserved a fair trial. I took that from you.'

'Thank you,' he says, barely holding it together. His shoulders shake, cheeks too. Both of us broken. 'Perhaps we will both be better off after this discussion.'

I look up to see the police detective who was conducting the investigation into my mother's death sliding the glass door of the conservatory open.

'Sorry to interrupt,' she says, giving me a nod and a smile, casting a strange, questioning look at Aides. He doesn't look up. Used to avoiding judgement, I think. 'You have a phone call.'

'Me?' A phone call here? 'Who from?'

'Somebody called William Payne. He's calling from a local funeral director's office.'

More to organise. Goodbyes to arrange. I stand, head towards the door.

'I can help if you'd like,' Aides says then as he stands. I stop, stare at his frail, withered frame. The man who hurt me is not here anymore. This man holds no power over me as he once did. Like a priest de-robed, naked, and shamed. Paraded through the streets. I see him for what he really is. Fallible. A liar. Nothing more than a man.

'No,' I say. 'I think this might be where we say goodbye.'

A step back, a gentle nod. 'Then I thank you for your apology. It matters to me.'

'Thank you for yours.'

And I turn away, knowing that it's over. Apologies have changed nothing really, but whatever needed to be said has been said. That is the best that any of us could ever hope for now.

'Yes?' I say, picking up the phone.

'Oh, at last. Miss Carter?'

'Yes.'

The man's breath is ragged, as if he has been rushing to find me in a crowd. 'I've been trying to contact you for quite some time. You haven't been answering your phone.' I recall all the missed calls, those I ignored assuming they were journalists looking for a scoop. The answering machine of the funeral parlour the night before. 'I have some information that you might be interested in.'

Police buzz about behind me, and I turn away, lower my voice. 'What information?'

'A small investigation on my part, instigated by Francesca Wright.' Francesca? What would she want with a funeral director? 'She told me if she was uncontactable, that I should get in touch with you. And I cannot reach her at all.'

'What's it about?' I ask, pushing the image of her dead body aside.

'Hum,' he says, hesitant. 'I'd rather discuss it in person. Might you be able to come in?'

I agree a time and place and hang up the phone. And then I stand back, moving out of the way, as the paramedics carry my mother's body from the house.

36

I take my mother's old car, and drive to the location Mr Payne gave me on the phone. The building where is funeral parlour is housed is old and uninspiring. A window spans across the width of it, decorated with pale white stickers, cut into the shape of flowers. Across the middle is a written promise that they can be contacted day and night. *William Payne Funeral Services* stretches in gold letters across a dark background at the top.

Opening the door, I am met by an overwhelming smell of jasmine and calla lilies. A pinboard with various business cards has been mounted to the wall, cars and florists and musicians for hire. Underfoot, the carpet is well trodden to the relentless march of death.

'Hello,' a lady says, looking up from a small table in the corner as I step through the door. 'Can I help you?'

'I have an appointment with Mr Payne,' I say. 'He called earlier and asked me to come in.'

'Is that about the Briarson funeral tomorrow?'

'No,' I say. 'I don't know what it's about. My name is Chloe Carter.'

Two deep wrinkles settle between her eyes. Glancing down, she scans the yellow sticky notes on her desk, running her finger along each, until she finds one with my name.

'Ah, here you are.' She lifts it forth with a neat little tug. 'Take a seat, and I'll let Mr Payne know that you are here.'

I do as she asks, finding a spot on one of the pale cream sofas with a heavy floral pattern. Something my mother would like. Have liked, I correct. And there in that waiting room it begins to sink in; my mother is dead. Killed by blunt force to the back of the head with some object yet to be found. Just like Emily was. Could Iris really be capable of something like that? It's so hard to imagine that young girl who loved me, whom I loved, and realise that this is how it ends.

And now I sit here, looking around the room at the signs for musicians and cars. The brochures with wreaths and crosses made from flowers. A flyer has been left on the table for a therapist. I pick it up and there is a list of her specialities. Grief. PTSD. CBT. And then, seventh one on the list. Trauma. I stare at the word. It makes so much sense. I fold the flyer into my pocket, and I can feel it building, the irrefutable truth of it all. The grief, the loss, the things I have seen. The many things I must do now that my mother has died. The fact that I will have to do them all by myself for her.

'Miss Carter?' I look up with tears in my eyes. 'Would you like to come through?'

I swallow to compose myself, and follow the receptionist down the tight corridor, the light low, the carpet soft underfoot. A wooden door at the end of it beckons, and with a delicate, well-honed smile, she opens it and bids me to enter. Across the other side of an old captain's desk, a small plump man with a kind face sits, his smile wide and easy with relief.

'Miss Carter. Thank you so much for coming down. It has been quite the challenge to get hold of you.' Stepping around the desk with some effort, he holds out a hand which I take, uses his other to brush his hair into place. His skin is rough, his fingers twisted by arthritis. 'In truth, I had all but given up on locating you.'

Holding out a hand, he offers me a seat, and so I sit into the soft brown leather of it. He does the same, linking his fingers across his tummy.

'What is this about?'

Cautious, he takes a moment before he answers. 'Miss Wright never mentioned anything about me?'

'Not at all. I have never heard of you until today.'

Reaching into a drawer, he lifts out a thin manila file, sets it with a thump down on the desk. A few pages inside are filled with his own scribble. Somewhere near the top I think I catch Francesca's name. His breathing is a struggle, his face red and sweaty.

'Miss Wright came to see me a couple of months ago now, and she was quite adamant about your involvement in this… situation, let's call it. Was very insistent that I should contact you should I not be able to contact her. She even paid for the services in advance, just in case, although I might add I was quite clear that it was unnecessary.'

I rub my hand along the leather arm of the chair, imagining that she was here in this very seat, talking about me.

'Francesca was murdered,' I tell him, and I see the shock settle across his face, the colour draining. 'She was found in the early hours of this morning.' My mother too, I want to shout, and when he realises that a tear has escaped across my cheek, he passes me a tissue. His kindness brings forth more uncontrollable tears, and he moves, unperturbed by any of it, to bring me a glass of water.

'What a terrible thing to happen.' He seems genuinely shocked, his shoulders curled in on themselves as if weighed down by the news. 'You have my sincere condolences.'

'Thank you,' I say.

'Do they know who killed her?'

'Not yet,' I say, still wiping my eyes. I pause for a sip of the water, ice cold against my lips. 'But the truth is, I haven't really seen Francesca in close to twenty years. Once or twice, but nothing of any significance. Which is why her giving you my name makes no sense to me. Please, Mr Payne, tell me what this is about.'

He smiles, but with no joy. Closes the file as if he knows what to say by heart.

'She expected you would say that. But she insisted I contacted you and nobody else under any circumstances.' He reaches to a glass of water and takes a sip. His movements are weak, not well coordinated, and a small dribble of it ends up on the desk. 'She came to me about six months ago looking to investigate the death of a friend of yours. Iris Fairhurst.'

My skins shivers as if I have stepped into the cold. Francesca was a step ahead of me.

'If I'm entirely honest, I was not keen. As you might be able to tell, I am not much of a private investigator. And plus, I remembered the case. The terrible deaths at the school. High Hill is not all that far away from this office.' And he is right. I saw the belltower on the way here, rising like a beacon from the past. A message from another time, lost across space. 'Such a tragic course of events that, quite frankly, I did not wish to revisit.'

'But you did.'

'Well, Miss Wright could be quite persuasive.' I notice his watch then as his fingers move to the strap. The oyster cream of the face, the little golden crown in the place of a twelve. Not something that would come cheap, and although it could be a knock-off, I suspect it isn't. 'Anyway, I opened my files and tried to tell her what she wanted to know. About the details of the funeral services provided to the family at the time. The nature of their grief and so forth.'

'And what did you tell her?'

A moment's hesitation takes him then, and he pauses to straighten his tie and to take another drink.

'She wanted to know about the flowers. Which readings they chose. Whether we printed an order of service, and if so, how many. How involved her parents were in the planning of the service. Even which casket they chose. She had a lot of questions.'

'And?'

'Well, I had it all on file. Exactly what was done. It took me some time to locate it to be honest. Can you believe it was twenty years ago? Anyway, here we are,' he says, dipping into the file on his desk. 'This is what I showed her.'

Across the ruby-coloured leather topper on his desk, he slides a ratty old piece of paper. The edges are brown from time. I glance at the list, at a casket on the rider, one car, one spray of flowers. Billing for a cremation.

'What am I supposed to make of this?'

'In simple terms, Miss Carter, the services offered constitute the most basic of funeral packages you could have chosen at the time. But after thirty years in this job, I can tell you that there is nothing as strange as grief. No emotion more likely to change the character of a person who is otherwise perfectly well adjusted. We see people at their absolute worst. So, at the time it didn't strike me as odd, even though the Fairhursts had lost a child and were very well off. I remember putting their streamlined choices down to grief, and an inability to process it. It was only on the day of the funeral itself that I wondered quite what I was supposed to make of it all.'

'How so?'

'Well,' he said, sitting back in his chair, ready to deliver the punchline of a terrible joke. 'They didn't come.'

'What?'

'I took that empty coffin to the church for a closed service. I, and the three other pallbearers, were the only people there. The story at the time was that Mrs Fairhurst was quite delirious with grief. Towards the end of the service Professor Fairhurst did attend, thanked me for my time and efforts, and settled the bill satisfactorily. But I didn't see Mrs Fairhurst at all. Neither the brother.' Francesca, I realise, was a step ahead of me. She was already looking for evidence that Iris was still alive. 'After, we cremated the empty casket and delivered the ashes accordingly to the family home. When I arrived, I saw that the property had already been sold, all the things packed. And after I told Miss Wright such details, she asked me to use my experience to widen the search.'

'For what?'

'You see, she had heard of Professor and Mrs Fairhurst's deaths and wanted to check that indeed they had occurred as she believed. As for the professor, he died of a heart attack under the most unfortunate circumstances, and we buried him accordingly with a distraught Mrs Fairhurst only a year after Iris's death. I saw his body myself. Mrs

Fairhurst, on the other hand, had died several years after her husband in India whilst touring some local caves.' He says it as if the very idea of it is ridiculous in itself. 'The body was repatriated, and she was cremated with only her son present. I took no part in the process, everything done in London. Only, when upon Miss Wright's instruction I came to search for evidence of this, I'm afraid I was unable to produce what she was after.'

'Meaning?'

'Meaning that I could find no record of Claudette Fairhurst's death. I even went to India, tried to find the record of her repatriation, and there was nothing there either. A funeral did take place, and I could find a church record for it, but nothing to officially register her death. And it is this information that I have been trying to get to Miss Wright: that no such record exists.'

I can't breathe. My stomach cramps. 'Then what happened to her?'

'Nothing,' he says, as if he has just announced something as simple as the date. 'Mrs Fairhurst is alive, living as an inpatient at a home for the mentally infirm for the last eighteen years. About fifteen miles away from here.'

37

Before I leave the funeral director's office, he helps me locate the care facility in which Mrs Fairhurst is staying. A place called Monksthorpe Manor. Pictures of it online make it seem like a warm and homely place, an old stately home built in Georgian times, set on a six-acre site with a large fishing lake in the expansive grounds. A central door and four sets of windows on either side. Doric columns hold up a portico. He offers to make a call on my behalf, but something tells me it would be better not to announce my arrival. So, I thank Mr Payne, write down the address, and leave.

It takes no longer than ten minutes, heading into a winter landscape that stretches out as lazy as a cat by the fire, before I see High Hill rising again through the sparse canopy of trees. Winking at me through the bare branches as they shift and move, as if it has been enlivened by my return. The belltower is there, the flagpole. The crenelations along the top of the building. And it's obvious to me now; High Hill has always been here, biding its time until I returned to face it. I pull up to take it in, imagining it as it once was, even though I know the school closed within a few academic years of the trial. Too many students leaving, not enough new registrations, its reputation destroyed. But I can still picture myself there, as if part of me still stalks the corridors like a ghost. Can hear the voices, the call of Father John across the vaulted chapel, Mr Aides' praise for my performance. A whole life hiding in the shadows behind those walls. Only now I realise the memories are quieter than they used to be. Retreating a little, from the prominent position they have always claimed. The panic I used to feel to think of this place does not come as I stand before it today, ready to face up to the truth of what happened to me here.

I get back in my car and wind my way through hair-thin lanes, until I close in on Monksthorpe Manor about ten miles away from the coast. I see a trail of smoke twisting from the chimney breast, but it's different from the pictures online, taken in the summer when the sun was shining, and the light cast everything in gold. There are no ducks on the pond today, still as glass with a fine mist. No happy faces enjoying the terrace or the lawns. The red pillows from the benches and chairs have been put into storage. But the same plush curtains hang at the windows, and the same roses grow in pockets throughout the lawn. From the closest window, I see my arrival has caught the attention of one of the workers. By the time I am at the front door, it is already open.

'Good morning,' the girl says, stepping out onto the gravel. Young, a bright face, a little too much make-up. A nurse's tunic. 'Can I help you?'

'Oh, I do hope so.' I try to remember everything that High Hill taught me. That I am better than this girl. That she is not capable of getting in my way. 'I was hoping to spend some time with Mrs Claudette Fairhurst.'

She smiles, but it does nothing to hide her wariness. 'I don't think we were expecting any visitors today. Might I ask your name?'

'I did call ahead to let them know I was coming.' Just the right amount of dismay. Annoyed, but not so much that I would forget my manners. 'Do you mean to tell me that the record of my visit has not been made?'

I see the discomfort settling in. But she is good at this. Trained to be cautious. 'Perhaps I have made a mistake, but I'm afraid I didn't see it written anywhere. They would usually have let me know at handover if one of my residents was expecting somebody.' So, she is here. 'But I can go back and check. What did you say your name was?'

'I didn't.' What name to give? Mine? There's every chance that Mrs Fairhurst will remember it. She was there for at least some of the trial. She stared at me the whole time. I could never quite make out whether it was with sadness or anger. Or pity. But there is one name she would never refuse. Not if she knows her daughter is still alive as I am sure she is. 'Please tell her that Iris is here to see her.'

She nods, and then I watch as she heads back inside, leaving me out in the cold.

By the time she comes to find me ten minutes later, I can no longer feel my feet, and my face stings from the low temperature. I only realise my nose is running when the nurse hands me a tissue on our way into the hall.

'I'm so sorry to have kept you waiting, but we must be so careful who visits our residents. But when I told Mrs Fairhurst that you were here to see her, she was delighted.'

With a smile I follow her through the hallway, all wooden floors, and grand ceilings. A seating area to my left laid out with a thick Persian rug and plump red chairs, a fire crackling in a classic grate, carved with ornate shells and what I think might be a couple of griffins.

We ascend a wide, central staircase that opens out onto the wraparound balcony of the first floor. Chiaroscuro portraits of the family who once lived here hang on the wall, alongside tapestries that look to have seen better days. Scenes of medieval life. But even here I am reminded of High Hill: nothing too new, too pristine. Without some wear and tear you have no history, and without history at High Hill you were nothing. I have never fitted in better than I do now.

'Here she is,' says the care worker as she opens the door. 'What a lovely surprise, right, Claudette?' And then, with a smile and a wink, her earlier suspicion gone, the nurse turns to me and says, 'I'll leave you to it.'

For a moment, the door closed behind me, I can't move. There she is, Mrs Claudette Fairhurst, sitting like an old lady on the other side of the room. She must be seventy now, her once long black hair all grey, piled up in a twist that somehow seems characteristic of her French roots. A smudge of red lipstick breaches the outline of her lips. But the room itself seems like nothing I can imagine she would choose. I remember her space in the old farmhouse, full of books and nicknacks and ornaments. Here, everything has been well tidied, items put back in their place. But I see on an old table under the window on the far side of the room, something on the surface covered by a small plastic bag. Splatters of clay run up the blue and white striped wallpaper behind. This is the Mrs Fairhurst I met. The astute woman who knew what I was to her daughter. Although her narrowed eyes as she watches me cross the room suggests she does not recognise the woman I have become.

'Hello, Claudette,' I say, taking a seat on the footstool near where she sits. Not too close. Several large magnifying glasses are dotted about the room, and I think if I stay far enough away, she might not immediately work it out. I have no idea what she can and cannot see, so I am careful to hide part of my face with my hair. 'It's been a long time since I have seen you.'

She leans forwards, trying to get a closer look. 'Do I know you?' she asks.

Telltale signs of her condition appear to me then, as if the room has finally come into focus. The word *ART*, printed in big letters and taped above the table where she sculpts. Pictures on the cupboards, one of her clothes, another for mugs in what looks like a kitchenette. By the bed sits a large clock with oversized digital numbers. A jug with the word *WATER* printed on it. A cup that reads *DRINK*.

'We met a long time ago,' I tell her. 'I haven't seen you for twenty years.'

'That is a long time,' she says.

'Yes.' Thoughts battle in my brain, questions I should ask butting up against facts I can't avoid. Like the fact Stan told me she was dead. That her broken body had to be repatriated from India. But why lie to me? Because he was embarrassed about what had become of his mother? Or something much, much worse? 'I used to be friends with Iris,' I say.

It takes a moment, but the name settles over her with the same certainty as night falls.

'They told me that you were Iris.' Edging forward a bit more, she fumbles across the surface of the table in search of a magnifying glass. Even lifting it seems an effort, but she does so, holding it up to my face. I fight the urge to back away. Find the courage to see if she knows who I am. After studying me for a while, she rests back in her chair. 'You are not my daughter.'

'No,' I say, hoping she hears the apology in my voice. 'I am not.'

'But you couldn't be,' she says, setting the magnifying glass back down next to a vase of soft blue flowers. Iris flowers, I realise. 'She isn't here anymore.'

'Isn't she?' I ask, looking again to the flowers.

'No. She hasn't been here for a long time. But I do know who you are.'

'You do?'

'Maybe,' she says. Outside, a crow pecks at the glass. 'It was Medusa, wasn't it?'

'What?' I ask at first, until I realise what she is saying. The night I stayed at her house. A bust of Medusa, the snakes on the head half finished. 'Yes,' I say, smiling now. 'It was Medusa.' She smiles too. 'Do you remember my name?'

'Of course I do,' she says. 'She wanted to say goodbye to you. We told her that she couldn't. You are the girl she loves.'

'Yes, she is.'

The voice cuts through the air behind me. I freeze, knowing that whatever I was doing here is over.

'Stan was always a good boy,' she says again. She squeezes my hand tight. 'Even if he made some mistakes.'

I feel his presence closing in on me, the weight of him behind. She doesn't look up, even though I can feel his hands on the back of my chair. Everything tells me to run, but I cannot move. And then he grabs the chair next to mine, pulls it between me and his mother.

'So,' he says, reaching for my hand. 'You found her.' His grip tightens around my fingers. 'What am I supposed to do now?'

38

His cold blue eyes don't leave me, his hand wrapped tight around mine. The possibilities run through my mind. Refusal, screaming. I could have the nurses at the care home call the police. I could jump up, run as fast as I could to my car, try to get away. If I could make it back to the city I could find DS Lawrence, tell them that Stan has lied. That I know it has something to do with it. But every time I think of a possibility, I can't bring myself to try; I think of Francesca, dead, my mother dead. Aides beaten. I go along with whatever he commands, hoping that will keep me safe.

We leave my mother's car at Monksthorpe Manor, climb into his, and he locks the doors. Across my chest he reaches for the seatbelt, his mouth close to mine. I feel his gaze upon me as he straps me into the soft, plush seats. Then we wind back through the roads I travelled earlier, retracing my steps. I know even then where he is taking me.

'Why are you doing this?' I ask.

At first, it is as if he hasn't heard my question, before his fingers flex against the steering wheel of his luxurious car. The bones of his knuckles turn white. I watch as he decides what to say.

'I could ask you the same question, Chloe. Coming to find my mother like that. Telling her you were Iris...'

he adds, shaking his head as if I have disappointed him. 'Do you know how confusing something like that is for a person who struggles with dementia? When the care home called to tell me that my sister was there, and whether it was okay to let her in, I thought, just for a minute, that they might have been telling the truth. But then your questions from earlier today came to mind, and I knew it was you.'

'You told me she was dead,' I say.

'And by every reasonable assessment she is,' he says, a bite slipping into his voice. 'She's been dead for years. Since we buried my father. Even before that, when we made a show of burning an empty casket for Iris. Gone, in every tangible way.'

'You lied to me. Why?'

He sighs as he grips the wheel. 'There was a good reason for it. She was the last person I wanted you to find. Much easier to cut you off from any link to my family's past than have you talking to her. I mean, don't you remember what they were like? How they suffocated me? She hates me, Chloe. Has done ever since. I didn't want to risk you being near her again.'

'Why not?'

'Don't you get it? I liked you, Chloe, really, I did. I didn't want my fucking mother poisoning you against me like my sister had.'

'Iris never...'

'Jesus,' he says now, red in the face. 'I was so fucking in love with you. Are you really telling me that you never realised?' And of course I did, could see the way he sometimes looked at me, knew there was something more he wanted. It was always just easy enough to pretend I could not. 'I tried to tell you. Tried to show you what it could be like between us. You always fobbed me off. Played the fool. But I give you some leeway out of gratitude, Chloe, for the lies you told. Your decision to tell the authorities that you had seen Aides coming down from that belltower was more than I could have ever hoped for. You protected Iris because you loved her. I respect that. I loved my sister too.' He turns to face me, and I panic as he fails to watch the road. I put one hand up to the dash, bracing myself for the impact of a potential crash. 'I would have done almost anything to protect her.'

'Almost anything?' I ask, as he returns his gaze to the road.

'That's what I said,' he says, clenching his teeth. 'Almost.'

I see the belltower through the trees, can hear the ocean nearby. Smell it in the air. The bushes that surround the perimeter are larger than before, wild, and overgrown. But I can still see the brick peeking through, and the pole where a flag used to fly. The remnants of the weathered cloth are still there, but they hang at a withered half-mast. Weak sunlight reflects from some of the windows, but in others the glass is missing. Ahead, the gate sits ajar, the padlock and chain positioned there years before either rusted, broken, or cut.

He stops the car, taking the keys as he exits to open the gate. I look outside, wonder how far I could run, how easily I could hide. Light creeps through the forest, the bare trees offering no good place. Too great a distance to even reach it before he would be back in the car and coming to get me. All around me the fields stretch into the unknown like a death sentence. There is no escaping whatever he has planned. I was stupid to come here.

'Tell me what you want,' I say as he gets back in the car.

'I think you know,' he says with a smile.

As he continues to drive, I remember the day when I came here with my parents, the excitement I felt, the allure that this place held. They were good, loving people, but I couldn't wait to get rid of them. I thought it was so easy to shun that life, but what I wouldn't give to have it all back now.

He cuts the engine and steps from the car, opening the passenger door to drag me out. My feet slam against the ground as he pulls my sleeve and hoists me to my feet. Windows have been boarded up, and graffiti marks the walls. So different to the grand place I first came to.

'Come on,' he says, reaching in his pocket to pull out a key. 'You should know your way around better than I do.'

He marches me up the front steps, towards the giant double doors that guard what was behind. The Latin script is still there, the same words as were painted in blood above my mother's corpse. And inside, things have changed little, have been strangely preserved. Posters for netball and a field trip to Cumbria remain on the noticeboard, a poster for the end of year show. As if life here simply stopped. Paint peels from the walls, and at least one person seems to have broken in over the years, with more meaningless graffiti. The stairs rise through the building to my left, the carpet as red as it ever was.

'This way.'

He leads me through the north wing, past the windows where the statue of Athena sits. Lichen covers her face, the bushes around her body overgrown and wild. My past is here. Part of me hidden within these walls and cloisters that none of us ever quite left. Ahead I see the door to the old disused library, light coming from inside, pouring in through the broken windows on the first floor. A section of board is missing, light falling like a searchlight on one of the desks. This is the place where Baxter chose to hide. Then Stan raises an arm, offers me to go in. When I don't move, he pushes me inside, and I stumble forward. Dust circulates underfoot. I cough as it settles in my throat.

'Sit,' he says, as he settles down into one of the chairs. I do as he asks, keeping a distance, a table standing between us.

The whole way here I have been trying to make sense of it, so certain as I had become that Iris was behind it all. So convinced that she was still alive. But was that just wishful thinking? Another chance on my part to put things right? No matter what it was, it now seems impossible that Stan didn't play some part in this.

'It was you who killed Francesca, wasn't it?'

'And there was you blaming Iris,' he says, a look of regret on his face. It mirrors my own. Because that was what I did. I started to believe that she could have hurt me. That she could have set me up over twenty years as a back-up plan to cover her own guilt. Could have killed my mother. I should have known she could never have done that. 'Fran left me with little choice unfortunately. One of the best legal minds in the country, and still too stupid to make a decent legal decision for herself. All she had to do was maintain her silence.'

When I offer no response, he gives me a nod, resigned to having to explain himself.

'For twenty years everything has been fine. Aides was in jail, for both Iris and Emily's murders. It made sense, the evidence was strong.'

'The evidence was a lie.'

'Your lie.' He closes his eyes, gives a shake of the head, as if he can't believe his bad luck. 'When Iris disappeared and you and Francesca took matters into your own hands, it was as if it couldn't have gone any better. Paedo teacher knocks off the girls he was fucking. You know how many people now think he pushed Eloise Cunningham out of that window? And they even speculated that he was fucking Iris when everybody knew that she liked girls.' He smiles then, looking at me. 'You remember that headline in *The Sunday Mirror*? *Was She Next*,' he says, referencing a front-page spread with my face on it, some terrible photograph of me looking frightened outside of the court. 'They thought he was a fucking serial killer.'

'Only he wasn't, was he? He never killed anybody.'

'No, I don't think he did,' he says, as if we are debating nothing more concerning than his colour of hair. 'But Iris couldn't live with the thought of what she'd done. When she ended her life...'

I hear nothing else of what he says. I close my eyes, and all I can see is Iris. Her desire to die. To think of her like that is even worse than remembering my father. At least I know how he did it. But with Iris my imagination runs wild. So many awful choices, so many awful conclusions to...

'Hey.' His voice is sharp, snaps me back to the present. 'Listen when I'm talking to you. When they found Iris's blood on Aides' clothes, the bloody knife in his quarters, the police jumped to conclusions. With yours and Francesca's testimony that Iris was going to meet him on the night she died... it all pointed to him. And we needed him in prison. We needed that conviction.'

'We?'

'My family,' he says. 'We took a decision about who was going to pay for Emily's death. Iris, or Aides. We chose Aides.'

'And the money being paid to him? That was coming out of an account in my name?'

He shrugs, as if the answer should be obvious. 'The evidence was strong to start with. They found the knife with his prints and her blood. More of it in his quarters. Francesca was brilliant, doing her bit to help her friend.' Something must change in my face, because he stops talking and smiles. 'Oh yes, you never knew, did you? Francesca was wonderful, setting it all up. She took that knife and a small vial of Iris's blood and staged it perfectly. No wonder she is so fucking good at what she does.' Then he smiles again. 'Or at least, she was. Anyway, after that, for three years everything was fine, until his stupid fiancée came forward and offered him an alibi. He would have taken it to appeal, so we had to give Aides some kind of incentive to keep quiet. If his part in Iris's death could be doubted, the whole trial would have been called into question. It was my idea to pay him, and after we came to that arrangement, he dropped it. Agreed to serve his time. Still, ideally I needed the payments to be untraceable. I discovered that your uncle was in jail, your connection to him frayed. A back-up plan if you like, just in case the intended payments became public knowledge.' He almost smiles, raises his eyebrows with shock. 'If the money came from you, it removed my family from the crime. Wasn't even that hard to be honest. Couple of fraudulent accounts, a bit of help from your bastard of an uncle and...'

Something trips him up. 'And?'

'Nothing,' he says, shaking his head. Something he was going to say, held back at the last minute. There will always be something I don't know. 'There's nothing Fisk won't do for a fee.'

'The police thought that I killed Iris and tried to cover it up by paying Aides to stay in prison. That was your intention?'

'Dreadful of me, I appreciate that. Especially after how much you had done for Iris by lying as you did. But I couldn't have any of it coming back to me. Still, none of us would have needed that back-up plan if Francesca had kept her part of the bargain. And she might have if it wasn't for Jimmy Fucking Baxter and his stupid extortion scheme. Thought he could make a few quid of his own by threatening her. I'd have paid him double to keep out of it. But when she decided to tell the truth, Chloe, my hand was forced. Forensics are better now. We knew the blood on his clothes was questionable, only a partial sample. They'd have thrown it out as evidence, put it down to contamination. If they had started to investigate, they might have acquitted Aides, especially when Susan was willing to change her statement. I couldn't let that happen. They might have reopened the investigation.'

'So what if they did? Iris has been gone for twenty years. What would it have even mattered?'

Again he laughs, stretches back, relaxed with his arm across the back of the chair. 'After everything you have just heard, you still think she did it, don't you?' He stands up, moves closer to me, crouches down at my side as if he wants to comfort me. He takes my hand in his, holds it close, gentle, as if he cares. 'Iris also thought she killed Emily, but it was me, Chloe. I snuck into this school upon her invitation, as I had many times before. It was only supposed to be a bit of fun. And it was, until she got fucking pregnant. I had to come here to sort that out.'

Aides. Baxter. I never thought it could have been Stan. 'You?'

'I appreciate your trust, that's for sure,' he says, the first time he sounds even remotely regretful. 'And I tried to be a gentleman about it. Told her I'd pay for everything. That it would be easy to get rid of it. But she wouldn't go through with it. Wanted to have the fucking child. What is it with fucking Catholics? She was happy enough to betray her faith when it came to screwing around, but not when it came to screwing me over. I don't know what she thought was going to happen. That we'd be some happy little family? I had a place to study at LSE. I wasn't going to fit that around a baby. So, I told her I'd meet her in the belltower that night. Thought I could convince her. But just as I was arriving, I caught sight of my sister crying, running away. She didn't see me, but I found Emily in the belltower with a cut on her head, complaining about how Iris hit her because Emily had seen her cutting a drug deal with Baxter. She was crazed. Screaming that she was going to tell my father that my sister was a druggie and that I was a rapist. A fucking rapist,' he says, on his feet now, his arms animated and wild. 'I picked up the clapper that Iris had used to hit Emily, and I finished the job.'

Tension ripples through him, his knuckles tight and fingers ready. I remember the conversation I overheard at their family home when I crept down the stairs at night. The assault his parents were discussing, the fact they had to do something. I had thought they were talking about me, but they weren't. They had been discussing Stan. They knew that he had assaulted Emily and got her pregnant.

And that's why he was so keen for me never to find his mother.

'I thought it would look like an accident. A fall. Better that than murder, right? Nobody would have to go to jail for that. Imagine what they would have said about us. My parents. What was the point in so many people paying such a heavy price for one life?' How many times have I considered that argument, the value of one life pitted against the other. 'My only mistake was that I ran. Panicked, I guess.'

'Your only mistake?'

Another shrug. 'I should have taken the weapon with me, but I was in shock. Left it on the floor.' He shivers with remembrance. 'But when they found Emily in the courtyard, Iris assumed she was to blame and went back for the fucking weapon. She thought she had killed her.'

'And you let her believe it.'

'The worst of my crimes,' he concedes with a bow.

'The worst? What about Emily? Francesca? My mother?'

'Francesca was going to fuck it up for all of us. Your mother was...' He takes his time, deciding what he wants to say. 'Not a mistake exactly. I thought after that you would drop it.'

'She didn't deserve that.'

'Are you sure about that?'

'Of course I am.'

He nods. 'Just like my sister, then. Totally innocent. And after she set up Aides, she took her own life, threw herself over the cliffs if the blood they found is anything to go by.' Again, there it is. The image I have tormented myself with for years. The thought of her fall, knowing what was to come almost chokes me. I can't breathe for it. To imagine how she must have felt in those moments before she made an impact with the rocks or sea. 'And you cry now, Chloe, but I have to live with that. She was my twin, and I let her believe she killed somebody. She was crying to me, saying she couldn't live with what she had done. She asked me how I managed it? To do awful things and carry on like nothing had happened.'

I imagine the conversation, the way it went. 'She knew what you had done, didn't she? That you raped Emily.'

He pauses, takes a deep breath. Realises he has said more than he wanted to. 'It doesn't matter anymore. But I told her just to get on with it. Told her it would get easier. Don't assume I find that easy. To know she had told me she couldn't live like that, and I did nothing.'

And I don't. I remember my last conversation with Iris too, and know I too will carry the guilt of the last words I said to her for the rest of my life. Telling her I didn't love her. I played my own part in the decision she took.

'But once she was dead there wasn't much point in coming clean about what I had done, was there? Which is why Francesca's decision to confess has brought everything to the fore. I knew I had no choice but to wrap up any loose ends. Baxter, Fisk, the money. Francesca.'

'And me?'

'Yes,' he says, with no sense of satisfaction. 'And you. But of course, before that, you know something that nobody else does: the location of the one thing that could still tie me to the crime. That only you can locate.'

'The weapon.'

'Exactly.' With a sigh, he sits next to me. 'So,' he says, motioning to the shelves. 'Somewhere in here, Francesca said, although I am yet to find it. Tell me, where did you put it?'

'And after that you'll let me go?'

With a smile he starts to laugh. 'There are a lot of books here, Chloe, and I have a boat to catch.'

'It's over there,' I say, pointing to the back of the library. 'Behind Jean-Paul Sartre.'

I watch as he crosses the old library, passing a broken table. He ascends a ladder and then pulls tens of books from the shelf, sending them cascading to the ground in a plume of dust. Stopping, he reaches into the shelf, and I see the cloth of Iris's PE shirt as he pulls the clapper from the same place I hid it twenty years before.

'All this time,' he says, holding the cloth like it is some sort of holy grail. 'All this time and it was right here behind *La Nausée*.'

Back on the floor, ready to crack on now, he whips the clapper up and under his arm, and strides towards me. A renewed spring in his step.

'I appreciate your help,' he says, motioning for me to stand up. 'Now, we have one more thing to do before I'm on my way.'

I hold back, remembering everything I have learned about him in the last twenty-four hours. The fact that he killed both Francesca and my mother. Emily. That he paid Aides to stay in prison, with money from an account he set up in my name. That he is a rapist. Nothing has slipped through his hands. No loose ends left untied. And I know that he intends for me to die. But he is right. I know this school better than he does. There are places I could hide. Looking to the door, I know I must try to get away.

But before I see it coming, he takes a wide swing with the stained clapper, bringing it down on my head. The impact sings out, the shock of it rolling deep into my brain. The ground rises up to meet me, the wood striking hard against my face. My cheek splits as I roll onto my back. And the last thing I see before I pass out is his face peering over mine.

39

Stars twinkle overhead, the ground cold beneath my body as I twist in and out of consciousness. Soft damp grass gives beneath me, followed by the sharp edges of the gravel pathways I used to walk with Iris as Stan drags me across them. And as I drift, no longer sure where I am, I think she's there with me, whispering. I can hear her voice, telling me not to give up. That I'm the only one who knows the truth. That if I survive, I could clear her name. I fight to stay conscious, desperate to put things right. At some point I see the grey spire of the chapel where we said goodbye to Emily, and I realise where he is taking me. To die the same way Iris did. Moonlight reflects in the stained-glass windows. But somewhere around the edge of the forest, despite my effort to stay present, I slip into sleep.

When I come to, I have no idea how much time has passed, but the ground is softer, the light changed. Thick plants surround me but offer no protection from the elements, the wind twisting and whistling over the edge of the cliffs. The waves as loud as the ringing in my head. Bringing my fingers up to the back of it I feel the warm, wet cut where he struck me. My sight blurs, confusion setting in. Where am I? Where is he? I try to push myself up, but my arms are weak, and the ground is slippery with melting frost, as the dawn light rises on the horizon. How long have I been unconscious? My hands slip and slide through the dirt. Grasping forwards, I snatch at the ferns that grow along the edge, but it's only then I realise just how close I am to the cliffs.

'Oh,' he says, brightened by my movement. 'You're awake. But look where I left you. It's not safe for you there.' My body flinches as I feel his grip against my clothes. 'You're not going to die just yet.'

The ground slips out from under me as he drags me along, and although I fight, my movements aren't coordinated or strong. My head slaps against the wet surface of the forest floor, and the sharp edge of a rock tears a slice through the skin by my eye.

'Here is better,' he says, settling me behind a thicker bush where the wind is quieter. 'But please,' he adds, wiping the blood with his dirty finger as it trails down my cheek. 'Don't try to get up again.' With a tissue he finds in his pocket, he wipes the blood from my face, then does the same to a wound on my lip that I didn't know was there. 'You got yourself into a bit of a state, I'm afraid. That's less than ideal.'

'You did it,' I say. 'Not me.'

'True. But I didn't want it to be this way. It could have all been different, Chloe. You must have known how I felt about you. We could have protected her memory together. But you never saw me in that way, did you? What did Iris have that I did not? Actually,' he says, a laugh then. 'Don't answer that. But surely it can't come as such a surprise that twins might fall for the same person. And don't try to tell me that you didn't feel something when I touched you. I remember the way you moaned. How you liked it.'

Using his hand, he cups my cheek, his thumb brushing the broken skin just underneath my eye.

'Goodness, you're right. You really don't deserve this. Not after what you did for Iris. When you lied for her like that it only made me care about you more. But you see, I was fighting a losing battle, because Baxter had seen the whole thing. I had no idea at first. That was my second mistake. If I'd have known at the time, I could have dealt with him there and then. I only discovered the truth when Francesca told me about how he was extorting her, because he knew she had hidden this thing,' he says, testing the weight of the clapper in his hand. 'God, you should have seen her when she told me. How scared she was. Nothing like the Francesca we knew. You would have enjoyed it, I think. He could have told her that he knew it was me, but he didn't. Didn't want to play every card he had. The idiot didn't dare try the same thing with me. But I thought if she just stayed quiet it would be okay. I told her, just pay the money. But she started talking about how she wanted to confess, that she needed peace or whatever it was she called it. That she was going to go to the police. She even had a lawyer, you know that? And it was like I was back at the start, still trying to find this bloody thing,' he says, holding up the clapper. 'I always thought it was in your room, but I never found it. I'm sorry about hurting you that day.'

My head throbs, and it's not easy to make sense of what he's telling me. Was it him who attacked me on the stairwell? My eyes fall to the clapper resting in his hands, and with a smile he heads to the edge of the cliff, just a couple of metres away. The wind blows his hair about, makes him unsteady on his feet as he launches it over the rocks. Lingering moonlight catches the metal, until it falls from view, towards the angry waters of the English Channel.

Stepping back, he dusts one hand against the other. 'That's almost everything dealt with now. Francesca is gone, Baxter too.' He crouches at my side, brushes his hand along my cheek, this time lingering over the wound. 'You are the only person left who knows the truth.' He lets his body rest closer to mine, rests his lips against my cheek. 'You are the last loose end, Chloe. It could have all been different. I used to think I loved you.' I go to speak, wondering if I might be able to sell him that lie. 'No please. Don't embarrass yourself. It's too late for that now.'

He drags my body down, slamming me onto my back. Movements too quick for me to keep up. I try to force him back, but my arms are weak, and when I try to look around for something to grab, to pull myself away, I can't quite focus on anything. The blow to my head still vibrates through me with every movement, but I open my eyes, try to stay present. He is dragging me towards the cliffs. I know what he will do. He will kill me. Another man, taking something from me that is not theirs to take. Edward Lyons. Simon Aides. And I realise now that I have never really escaped them. Part of me has remained trapped in the prisons they built for me all along. I have never learned how to escape. How to fight. But now, if I don't do both of those things, that will be it.

I will not lose myself to another man again.

I scour the rough ground for a weapon. Anything I can use to strike him. My fingers find a rock. The edge sharp. Sharp enough to cut him? To kill him? I have no idea, but I prise it from the cold hard ground as he pulls me along, and I drive it at the back of his knee. He goes down.

I land another strike, dodging his arm, and this time I catch him by the side of his eye. He reels backwards, and I find the strength to push myself up and stumble away. But there's no more than a metre between us, and even as I scramble towards the cliffs, I feel his hands reaching for my ankles. Fingers clawing at me. The whites of his eyes gleam bright as he turns me over as if I weigh nothing. Am nothing. The wind whips at my hair, and I realise just how close I am now to the edge. The top half of my body is already hanging over the side of the cliff. And I realise then that I find peace in that. Power in the knowledge of how close I sail to death. Iris stood here and took her life. And years before that, after Aides, I too sat here and contemplated the same. Then he stopped me, but he's not here to stop me now. And suddenly I can imagine myself falling, edging myself over like I did once before. Taking control of it. I would be the one to decide what happens to me. And besides, what would it even matter if I die? Who is left to miss me if I'm gone? What difference would it make? What's one more dead girl in this world?

The rocks beneath me are looser than they used to be. The weight of our bodies on top has loosened the soil, and I watch it cascade down the side of the cliff. And all I would need to do is push against them, and I too would sail to my death. But also, I realise, so would he. And that thought brings me a sense of calm. It would be over. Justice would, in some sense, be served. And with that, I take my decision. I reach towards the shifting earth, choose the rock that has already become loose.

I start to push.

His eyes widen then as he too feels the stillness of my body, the ground moving beneath us. And as the stone upon which his knee rests begins to shift, I feel his body peel away with it. Smaller rocks begin their tumble down the cliff, followed by the shift of the larger rock upon which we balance. His fingers wrangle against my body to save himself as he begins to fall, but my shirt rips away from me as he snatches at it, and he can't find anything else left to hold. And as he falls, his arms flailing and reaching, I feel my own body begin to slip away from the ground. The end dancing below like a whispered promise. But as he calls out the wind shifts, seems to push me up. And instead of falling behind him I snatch out, find the strong leaves of the foliage on the cliffside. I fight, finally, for my life. Decide, for the first time in years, as sirens blare in the distance, that it's time to save myself.

40

Weeks pass before I hear back from DS Lawrence, or Helen as I have come to know her since my night at High Hill Manor. A gentleness exists about her now, there since she found me clinging to the cliff tops, trying, half-naked, to pull myself up from a rock that was close to falling into the raging sea below. If it had, I have no idea whether the ferns I was holding onto would have held me up. But after tracking the cloned phone to High Hill, she came to my rescue. And it was only in that moment when I saw her running through the forest towards me that I realised just how much I wanted to live. For the fact she saved me when she did, I will always be grateful.

Within twelve hours of Stan falling over the cliff they were able to recover his body. The search for the clapper goes on. By that time they had already searched his house, found gloves, a balaclava. Notes and photographs of me. Others of Francesca, and Jimmy Baxter. Messages between him and Fisk, planning the attack on Aides. In the glovebox of his car they found a knife, ropes in the boot, and a bottle of the date rape drug GHB. A small boat tethered and waiting on the beach where we had first met. It was hard to accept how wrong I was about him. How many times had we dined together, shared a drink over the years? Mourned his sister. The time we nearly had sex has come into question now too, whether he had drugged me that night. Whether he planned to rape me even then, and if the reason he didn't was because he found a shred of conscience. But these are answers I will never know; I must learn to accept that I never really knew him at all.

In the days following Stan's death, I learned that what had happened between him and Emily was exactly as she had described it: an assault that occurred at one of the beach parties the previous academic year. Helen suspects he used GHB that he got from Baxter, on account of it being found in his car. His modus operandi. And on top of that, there have been two other women who had made similar complaints over the years, although neither had ever gone to trial. Not even an arrest. But this knowledge made it easier to accept any part I had played in his death. And understanding what had happened to Emily caused her mistreatment of me to pale in the monstrous shadow of the truth. She had confessed her assault to her mother, although would never tell her who. Feared reprisals even then. Stan was the headmaster's son. But also, she confesses, it was more than that. They feared the judgement of their daughter; there's always somebody asking what a girl might have done to encourage it. To deserve it. Always a man whose soul is searching for absolution and finds it in the sacrifice of a woman's. But everybody knows the truth about what Stan was now, and despite those who have died to make that possible, there is some peace in that.

Fisk has confirmed part of the story after they picked him up, and the toxicology results from Baxter's post-mortem show GHB in his system. Even his neighbour reported hearing a scuffle the night before he was found. Plus, he was missing a finger, which brought Baxter's presence at Francesca's death into question. Even though they had been in prison at the same time, the parts they played in our story weren't connected. But there wasn't a person involved in the historical crime who Stan hadn't intended to remove.

'As for your mother,' DS Lawrence says, sitting across from me in the café where we agreed to meet for what she said was the final time. Three coffees steam between us. 'I don't quite know how to tell you this, but when we looked into her finances, it seems that your uncle has been sending her money ever since your father died.'

'What?' I say, the suggestion not making any sense. 'But she had no contact with him. I had no idea who he was.'

'I appreciate that, but it doesn't seem that your mother had left that life behind quite as she would have liked you to believe. And in Fisk's place, there was...'

The pause, the hesitation. The look that tells me she wants no part in this. 'There was what?'

'We found correspondence from your mother to Fisk. She fed him the information needed to set the accounts up in your name. She helped make this happen, Chloe. That's why Stan killed her.'

And although I find it hard to believe, the world as I know it turned on its head, it makes sense now. The reason Stan wrote those words on the wall. It wasn't a confession that he couldn't help himself. He was telling me the truth.

A simple nod of her head. 'I don't suppose it matters anymore either way. But for what it's worth, we got the footage back from the Ring cameras in her street. He was in your mother's road the same morning she died. There's no doubt it was him. The CPS won't bring charges posthumously, but at least you know that it was Stan who took her life, and that you did, in some small way, get justice.'

I close my eyes, relive the horror on his face as he realised he was about to die. The wide eyes and gaping mouth; his expression will haunt me. But was it justice? I thought so at the time, but now I don't know. It's still possible to slip into a different recollection, a sliding-doors version of the past. It's not easy when the person who hurt you is also somebody you cared about. Who you did, in some way, love. Life becomes split down the middle, and I know I must learn to live in a world where two realities coexist; he is the person who helped me mourn, while also being the person who made it necessary.

'Same goes for your sister,' Helen says then, turning to Isobel. 'Aides will have his conviction overturned, and he will receive a full pardon. Besides your honesty,' she says to me, 'Francesca's confession clears his name. Not only for Emily's death, but also Iris. Francesca says that she agreed with Iris to plant that knife in Aides' home. She put the blood on his clothes and in the kitchen of his living quarters. It was done to frame him, Iris's attempt to take Aides down for what he did to you. One last act of vengeance, I guess, before she took her life.'

I'm grateful for the explanation, but I didn't need it. She promised me, after all, that he would never hurt me again. Sending him to prison was her way of ensuring that.

'And the blood on the rocks?' I ask.

'No mention. Part of the set-up, I guess. Make it look convincing. But I'm sorry, Isobel,' she says. 'Nobody will pay for Emily's death as they deserved to.'

Without a word, Isobel looks at me. I am at least in part responsible for that. 'No, they won't,' she says, and I can see it hurts. Without my lies it might have been different at the time. 'But Stan got what was coming to him,' she says with a nod. Then she stands up, signalling that her part in this meeting is over. 'That, at least, is one thing I can thank you for.'

We watch as she grabs her bag and leaves, weaving through the customers in the café. Helen drains her coffee and sets her mug back down.

'And me?' I ask.

'They are not bringing any charges. Aides still could, but like you said, I don't suspect he will. I'll be in touch if anything more comes up. I have to get going though. I volunteered to help him get his appeal in motion,' she says as she too stands up.

'That's good of you.'

'He deserves a chance at the truth, I reckon.'

And she is right. For too long he was forced to live a lie. He deserves to have that lie put right. But I also realise that so do I. For years I have carried what Edward Lyons did to me. The shame of it. The guilt. What he did to me was no doubt the catalyst for decisions I made after that. As it stands, I have no idea where he is, or what he is doing. Whether he is married or has kids. Knowing such things might make it harder to do what I need to do. But I have managed to give my statement, telling Helen everything about what he did to me at Clifton.

'Any news on Lyons?'

'We've located him,' she says, slipping her arms through her jacket sleeves. 'And I worked out the connection, how Emily knew what had happened to you. Lyons was her uncle, her mother's brother.' That at least goes some way in explaining Emily's hatred of me. 'It was as you reckoned though.'

'He denied it?'

'Afraid so. We're trying to trace the old staff members, if they are even still alive, but without a witness statement to corroborate your account, it'll be almost impossible to prove his guilt. Even then, he could try to claim it was consensual. It won't be easy to take it forward.'

Disappointing, but even if nothing comes of it, what matters is that I have told the truth. Something about doing that has fundamentally changed who I am. I can feel the shift within me like a fault line has opened up. Only this time instead of a fault, something has knitted back together.

'I still have the shorts. His DNA would be on that.'

'It proves contact but not guilt. I'll do whatever I can, and I'll let you know as soon as I have any progress. But Chloe,' she says, smiling for the first time. 'Take care of yourself, yeah? I think you deserve that. Too many people have died as a result of what he did that night.'

I try to stifle the question, but as I watch her ready herself to leave, I can't hold it in. 'And Iris?' I ask. 'Has anything come to light?'

With a sigh she shakes her head. 'I know you think there's a chance she is still alive, Chloe. Especially after Francesca's confession. But twenty years have passed since that night. She would have turned up somewhere.' I look down at my cold coffee, know deep down that she is right. But it feels so unjust, to think she died believing she was a murderer. I wish there was something I could do. Something to put things right. 'So, Chloe. Find some new people who care about you and rebuild your life. You have no other choice but to try to put the past behind you.'

—

The day we bury Mum is cold and wet. Only a few people attend the service, people I don't know, save her neighbour, Mr Baggins, who holds my hand and tells me I have been brave. Mr Payne takes no payment for his services. I don't organise a wake, and instead, after her ashes have been interred under a discreet stone next to my father's empty casket, I take the small amount that I asked to keep and leave for London. I travel by train, disembarking into the brick-lined passages of Baker Street station, follow them until I am on the platform where my father jumped all those years ago. Impossible now, to imagine when I look at it. To imagine who I was back then. All I see are dirty tracks still singing with the passage of the last train.

'She always wanted to be with you,' I tell him, talking to his ghost. 'She was never the same after you left.'

I pull the little wooden box from my pocket, no bigger than a walnut. A flyer comes with it, and at first I don't know what it is. Then I remember that I took it from the funeral director's office. I stare at the name of the therapist, the telephone number that I know I will call. Because I want to get past this. I want to live better than this. Think maybe, despite my own mistakes, that I deserve to. Want very much to discard the shackles that have kept me chained to this lesser existence. I must open the door to help.

I push the flyer back into my pocket then slide the top from the little wooden box. I stare at the small sample of what's left of my mother. Grey dust. For a moment I close my eyes and promise myself I will try to remember the good things. The way she used to brush my hair and put it in plaits, and the cakes we used to bake together on Saturday mornings. Jam tarts, and her singing along to eighties hits on the radio. Climbing in bed with me in the mornings for a quick snuggle, rather than turning on my light and pulling back the covers. Crouching down, I tip the ashes onto the tracks and watch as they settle. Then I wait for the next train and make my way home.

—

The police tape is still across my door when I arrive. I pull it away, then take my key from my pocket and let myself into my flat. The smell seems alien, as if it's not really mine. Footprints mark the wooden floor. For the last couple of weeks I have been staying in a hotel, haven't wanted to come here. Wasn't even allowed in the first days, when they were searching for evidence of Stan's presence. They found a print that is so far unidentified, a hair in the bathroom that could prove that he was the person who really attacked me. Proof I don't really need because I know in my bones it was him. But as I stand here, unsure what to do, I look across to the corridor that leads to my bedroom, the bathroom just to the side. My body trembles with the thought of him in there. It's as if he left part of himself in my flat, tainted it in some unavoidable, enduring way, and now I have no choice but to live with him.

Catching my breath, I close the door behind me, and head into the kitchen, pouring myself a glass of water. I stand at the counter, looking around at the bare space. At the way I have chosen to live for so long. No pictures of family, none of my life. I wonder if I should like to have some out now. Whether it might be easier to let people in now I have given myself a chance to stop hiding. I must have some: a picture of my father, who didn't know how to cope, or one of my mother, who struggled in grief. Their failings changed my life, but I don't want to hold their mistakes against them when I have made so many of my own. I lied in a police investigation. I sent Aides to jail for a crime he did not commit. There is nothing really either of us could do to make up for what we did to each other. *Nemo sine vitio est.* Accepting that I hurt him makes it possible to move forward from what he did. And in making the complaint against Edward Lyons I rediscovered my voice. One chapter is closing, another opening up. This is a beginning in many ways, not only an end.

I crouch down to the box by the door, things I have brought from my mother's home. I pull out the pictures I found of my family. Most of them are from a holiday in Bournemouth, us sitting on a picnic blanket on the beach. Mum leaning over a sandcastle we made, little flags sticking from the turrets. Not that one, I decide. Too much like High Hill. I flick through, find some of us with ice creams, standing in front of a lifeboat. A penny slot, a teddy grabbed in one of the machines. My father celebrating its retrieval. Good times, I think. A happy family. I pull a couple out, selecting them for display. A date on the bottom right corner, yellow digital numbers. The year I left Clifton. I was a child, I think, when I look at myself now. I can see it in every part of me. The clothes, the awkwardness, the smile over a teddy. But my parents are smiling too, and so maybe not everything was as bad as I remember it to be.

Then, at the back of the pack, I find some papers. Letters, I realise, in my own hand. Things I wrote to Aides. Thoughts I wanted to share. I go to crumple them up, but something at the last moment stops me. What did I write in those letters? Who was I then? Reading them might help me understand. I am not ready to see it now, but I set them aside for another day. But as I do I see the corner of the bottom one poking out. The envelope different. A crest in the corner, a cross with four golden lions, each with a front paw raised. *University of Cambridge* franked on the front. I open the envelope, pull the contents out just enough so that I can read the first line.

> Dear Miss Carter,
>
> We are delighted to offer you an unconditional offer for a place on the...

But I don't continue reading. Instead, let the letter fold in two, drop it back into the pocket from where I retrieved it. So much given away over the years. Lost. It's hard to know exactly why I didn't take the place. Guilt, for what I did. Grief, even, for my father. Shame, too, could also have been the reason. At the time I had too many doubts about everything, including myself, and I didn't have the strength to follow it through. I tried to forge something of a life in music at one point, until eventually that also fell apart on the cusp of success. But it was all such a long time ago. There is no point grieving for what might have been. Some lost things cannot be recovered, and all we can do is learn to live in the space those things leave behind.

The doorbell rings then, and I startle until I remember what I arranged. I cross the room, rest my hand against the chain.

'Who is it?'

'Jacob, from Tempo Installations.'

With a sigh of relief, I pull back the chain, open the door with some hesitation. I see his face peering through the gap.

'Hello,' he says with a smile. 'We've got the delivery for you.'

I stand back and watch as they wheel in the old wooden piano removed from my mother's house. They reposition it against the wall in the far corner, and I trace the golden letters with my finger and press a key for the first time.

'Not a bad sound for an old one,' Jacob says. 'You play at all?'

'Not for a long time,' I say. 'But I would like to start again.'

After they leave, I look at it for a while, as if there is a stranger in my house. But eventually I sit at the stool, find the position I haven't assumed for years, and press the first notes. Allow my fingers to run up and down a scale. I find a few simple chords, and then harmonise like I played only yesterday instead of years before. Maybe one version of me that got left behind is still sitting at this piano, has been ever since I lost her. I will try to find her again in the music. That was where the magic existed anyway. Not in the grand instruments or the bricks of High Hill Manor. But in me. Maybe it's been there all along.

The doorbell rings again, and when I look to the old desk, I realise that Jacob left his receipts book. I snatch it up, head to the door and open it. But it isn't Jacob standing there. It's my neighbour.

'You're back then,' he says with a smile. 'Nice to see you. I'm terribly sorry about what happened.'

'Oh, thanks,' I say, a little embarrassed.

'Hard to think somebody got in here, isn't it? None of us could believe it when the police told us. But while you've been away, we've all had a chat, and we thought it would be best to make the building a bit more secure. So, we've fitted some cameras.' He points to the top corner of the hall. 'Nobody's getting in here without being recorded now.'

'Oh,' I say, a little unsure whether to feel relieved or slightly alarmed about being filmed. 'That must have cost a fair bit.'

'Sure did.'

'So, what do I owe you?'

A quick shake of his head, his lips pursed. 'You've had enough to worry about. I didn't even know you were back until I heard the piano. Sounded great by the way. But I'd have let you know earlier if I'd realised.' He points to a box on the hallway table. 'You had a delivery a little while ago.'

I say goodbye, and then move across to the hallway table, where I find a box sitting on top, my name on the lid. I lift it up, see the word *Petals* written on the front. Mail-order flowers. I take it inside, close the door, and set it on the kitchen counter. Take a knife to slice the tape holding the lid in place. And inside I see a large bunch of blue iris flowers, the same as I received years ago. The same as I saw in Mrs Fairhurst's room only a few weeks before. Pulling them from the box, I draw in the scent. It smells of her. My trembling fingers fiddle at the card. I pull it out, but there is no writing on the back.

I think back to the flowers in Mrs Fairhurst's room, and how she never went to her daughter's funeral, and I get it. It makes sense in ways it never did before. They didn't go, because they knew she wasn't dead. Because they were pretending all along. Even from Stan. From Francesca. They hid her away to save her, and there could be no better hiding place than death.

I run to the door, open it and go to step outside. Because she's out here somewhere. Part of me even expects her to be waiting here, for our eyes to meet. Breaths catch like thorns in my chest. I look left and right, up and down my street. But she is not here. Or maybe she is, and I am just not supposed to see her. I don't know whether I would want to or not. But it doesn't matter what I want. This was never supposed to be a reunion. So I step back inside, and head to my apartment. Looking up, I see the camera. Maybe they caught her on film. Closing the door, I go to draw the chain across it, only to stop myself. Instead, I let it drop. I don't turn the key in the lock. Sometimes it's enough just for the door to be closed.

I take the flowers, put them in water. Set them on a table next to the piano. Picking up a pile of music, I root through the pages, looking for a piece to play. Third one in, I find it. *Clair de Lune*. It was always going to be that. I set it on the stand and the scent of Iris fills the room.

I rest my hands against the keys, but I don't need to look at the music. I know how to play this piece. Because some things I have not forgotten. They are part of who I am. I take them with me no matter where I go. Always have, no matter how long I pretended that I hadn't. But I also know now that there are some things I will leave behind. That I will shed like an old scaly skin. The shape of a person I once used to be. Because as I sit at these keys I realise that one life is over. That it's time for another to begin.

The keys are cold against my fingertips as I rest them against the notes. I take a breath before closing my eyes. And then, just like it was yesterday, I begin to play.

Acknowledgements

Writing the acknowledgements for a book always strikes me as strange. It's the point in time when I know I am all but finished. The book has been written, the structural edits are complete, and in this case the copy edits too. And yet as I write these thank yous, I know that we are still only approaching the very beginning of this story. Publication is yet to come. Knowing that this book is nearing that moment as I write this is a privilege I will never take for granted.

And so my first and foremost thanks must go to my agent, Joanna Swainson, who is responsible for this book coming to life. You have proven to be not only a kind and generous friend, but also a tenacious and staunch agent. Having somebody in my corner who works so hard on my behalf leaves me eternally grateful. I am so thankful I sent that email while your submissions were closed.

One thing I have learned in publishing over the last ten years is that everything is a team effort, and so thanks must also go to the wider team at Hardman and Swainson, Caroline Hardman, Hannah Ferguson, Hana Murrell and Lucy Malone. I am so honoured to be an author represented by your agency.

To my editor at Canelo, Louise Cullen, I will never forget that first moment of finding out you liked the sample of this novel and wanted to see more. I was sitting on a boat in the middle of the Ionian Sea, and all I wanted to do was get back to shore and start writing the rest. Your enthusiasm and support for me as an author has been such a humbling experience. Also, to Alicia Pountney, thank you for your insightful editorial input and guidance as we worked to bring this book into existence. I also want to acknowledge the much wider team behind the scenes, those whose names I do not know. I am grateful for the input of every person working to make this novel a reality. I cannot wait to meet you all and thank you in person.

Life as a writer is often solitary, but I am lucky to count so many writers as friends. There is always a chance of leaving somebody out, so perhaps it's best not to name anybody. But this time in particular, I would like to mention Darren O'Sullivan, Fionnuala Kearney, Anouska Knight, Abbie Greaves and C. L. Taylor, who each gave me their time, friendship, and sage advice when I really needed it. It did not go unnoticed, and I might never have written this book if it wasn't for their support.

I would also like to thank my family, Stasinos, Theodoros, Themis and Lelia. Each of you shape me into who I am, and that undoubtedly translates into my work. I am grateful every day to be part of our family.

The novel that I chose to write this time is ultimately about friendship, and so more than ever before, I must thank my friends. I am lucky to have had some of the very best over the years. Without them, I would not be where I am today. I would not be who I am today. I will not name them for the fear that somebody might assume they've helped me bury the bodies like the characters have in this book. But if you are reading these words and know that I count you as a friend, remember this: I don't open the door easily. If you got through, thank you. I cherish you more than I'll ever likely let on. If you ever need me to hide the weapon, just let me know.

And lastly, I'd like to thank you, the reader, for picking this up. Of all the people in the chain of publication, you are undoubtedly the hardest won. If you picked up this book, whether it be a paperback, an ebook, a library loan, or a second-hand volume, I want to thank you for taking a chance on my work. For giving me your time. I really hope you have enjoyed it. For every one of you, I am more grateful than you could ever imagine.

Do you love crime fiction and are always on the lookout for brilliant authors?

Canelo Crime is home to some of the most exciting novels around. Thousands of readers are already enjoying our compulsive stories. Are you ready to find your new favourite writer?

Find out more and sign up to our newsletter at canelocrime.com